Born in En... ...grew up
Hampshire. She is m... ...oag-Mon...
They live with their two children, Lily and Sasha, i...
Visit her at www.santamontefiore.com and si... ...er
newsletter.

Praise for Santa Montefiore:

'Santa Montefiore is the new Rosamunde Pilcher' *Daily Mail*

'A superb storyteller of love and death in romantic places in
fascinating times – her passionate novels are already bestsellers
across Europe and I can see why. Her plots are sensual, sensitive
and complex, her characters are unforgettable life forces, her
love stories are desperate yet uplifting – and one laughs as
much as one cries' Plum Sykes, *Vogue*

'A gripping romance ... it is as believable as the writing is
beautiful' *Daily Telegraph*

'Anyone who likes Joanne Harris or Mary Wesley will love
Montefiore' *Mail on Sunday*

'One of our personal favourites and bestselling authors,
sweeping stories of love and families spanning continents and
decades' *The Times*

'The novel displays all Montefiore's hallmarks: glamorous
scene-setting, memorable characters, and as always deliciously
large helpings of yearning love and surging passion' Wendy
Holden, *Sunday Express*

'Engaging and charming' Penny Vincenzi

Also by Santa Montefiore

The Summer House

The House By The Sea

The Affair

The Italian Matchmaker

The French Gardener

Sea of Lost Love

The Gypsy Madonna

Last Voyage of the Valentina

The Swallow and the Hummingbird

The Forget-Me-Not Sonata

The Butterfly Box

Meet Me Under the Ombu Tree

Santa Montefiore

Secrets of the Lighthouse

**SIMON &
SCHUSTER**

London · New York · Sydney · Toronto · New Delhi

A CBS COMPANY

First published in Great Britain by Simon & Schuster UK Ltd, 2013
This paperback edition first published 2014
A CBS COMPANY

3 5 7 9 10 8 6 4 2

Simon & Schuster UK Ltd
1st Floor
222 Gray's Inn Road
London WC1X 8HB

www.simonandschuster.co.uk

Simon & Schuster Australia, Sydney
Simon & Schuster India, New Delhi

A CIP catalogue record for this book is available
from the British Library

Paperback ISBN 978-1-47110-097-0
Ebook ISBN 978-1-47110-098-7

Typeset by M Rules
Printed and bound by CPI Group (UK) Ltd, Croydon, CR0 4YY

Dedicated to:

Miguel Pando and
Nathalie de Montalembert

Not gone, just out of sight,
and always in my heart

Prologue

It is autumn and yet it feels more like summer. The sun is bright and warm, the sky a translucent, flawless blue. Ringed plovers and little terns cavort on the sand and bees search for nectar in the purple bell heather, for the frosts are yet to come and the rays are still hot on their backs. Hares seek cover in the long grasses, and butterflies, hatched in the unseasonal weather, flutter about the gorse in search of food. Only the shadows are longer now and the nights close in early, damp and cold and dark.

I stand on the cliff and gaze out across the ocean to the end of the earth, where the water dissolves into the sky and eternity is veiled in a mysterious blue mist. The breeze is as soft as a whisper and there is something timeless about the way it blows, as if it is the very breath of God calling me home. I can see the sweeping Connemara coastline to my left and right. The deserted beaches, the soft velvet fields dotted with sheep, the rugged rocks where the land crumbles into the sea. I look ahead to Carnbrey Island, the small mound of earth and rock that sits about half a mile out, like an abandoned pirate ship from long ago. The old lighthouse is charred from the fire that gutted it, leaving a forlorn white shell where once it stood proud and strong, guiding sailors safely back to land. Only seagulls venture there these days to pick at the remains of unfortunate crabs and shrimps trapped in rock pools, and to perch on the fragile skeleton of burnt timber that creaks and moans eerily in the wind. To me it's romantic in its desolation and I remain transfixed, remembering wistfully the first time I rowed out to explore soon after we were married. It was a ruin even then, but just as I had hoped the lighthouse possessed a surprising warmth, like a children's playhouse that still resonates with the laughter of their games long after the children have packed up and gone. I remained captive in fantasy, oblivious as the wind picked up about me and the sea grew rough and perilous. When the skies darkened and I decided to row back to shore, I found myself stranded like a shipwrecked sailor. But shipwrecked sailors don't have heroic husbands to rescue them in gleaming speedboats, as I had. I remember Conor's furious face and the fear in his eyes. I still feel the frisson of excitement his concern gave me, even now. 'I told you never to row out here on your own,' he growled, but his voice had a break in it that pulled at my heart. I pressed my lips to his and tasted the sweet flavour of his love. The lighthouse never lost its allure and, to my cost, I never lost my fascination for that lonely and romantic place. It resonated with the lonely and romantic person that I was.

Now it beckons me across the waves with a light that only I can see and I'm almost sure that I can make out the figure of a child in white, running up the grass with outstretched arms; but then I've always had a fanciful imagination. It could just be a large seagull, swooping low.

I turn suddenly, my attention diverted by the people now arriving at the grey stone chapel behind me. It is a short walk up the hill from the car park and I watch with curiosity the mourners dressed in black, making their way up the path like a solemn line of moorhens. Our home is situated outside the village of Ballymaldoon, which boasts a much bigger church. But there is something special about this weather-worn little chapel, surrounded by ancient gravestones and shrouded in myth, which has always enthralled me. Legend says that it was built in the fourteenth century by a young sailor for his deceased wife, so that she could keep watch over him while he went to sea, but the headstones have all been eroded by the elements so that it's impossible to read what was once carved into them. I like to think that the gravestone at the far end, closest to the sea, is the one that contains the remains of the sailor's wife. Of course she's not in there and never was: just her bones, discarded along with the clothes she no longer needed. But it's a sweet story and I've often wondered what happened to the disconsolate sailor. He must have loved her very dearly to build an entire church in her memory. Will Conor build a church for me?

The chapel fills with people but I keep my distance. I see my mother, pinched and weary like a scrawny black hen, beneath a wide black hat embellished with ostrich feathers – much too ostentatious for this small funeral, but she has always tried to look grander than she is – and my father who walks beside her, tall and dignified in an appropriate black suit. He is only sixty-five but regret has turned his hair white and caused him to stoop slightly, making him look older. They have travelled up from Galway. The last time they made this journey was the year Conor and I married, but that time they were pleased to be getting rid of me. None of my six sisters have come. But I am not surprised: I was always the black sheep and it is too late now to make amends.

My parents disappear into the chapel to take their places among the congregation of locals and I wonder whether they feel shame in the glare of the people's love: for I am loved here. Even the one man I was sure would not attend is sitting quietly in his pew, hiding his secret behind a mask of stone. Tentatively, I step closer. The music draws me right up to the door as if it has arms that reach out and embrace me. It is an old Irish ballad I know well, for it is Conor's favourite: 'When Irish eyes are smiling'. And I smile sadly at the memory of those helicopter journeys from Dublin to Connemara when we'd all sing it loudly together over the rumble of the propellers, our two small children with their big earphones on their heads, trying to join in but unable to get their tongues around the words.

Just then, as I seek refuge in the past, I am wrenched back into the present where the tall, shaggy-haired figure of my husband is making his way up the path. Three-year-old Finbar and five-year-old Ida hold his hands tightly, their small feet stumbling occasionally as they struggle to keep up with his long strides. His dark eyes are fixed on the chapel, his long, handsome face set into a grimace as if he is already fighting the accusations muttered against him behind hands and pews. The children look bewildered. They don't understand. How could they?

Then Finbar notices a black-backed gull on the path ahead and suddenly drops his father's hand to chase it. The little boy flaps his arms and makes a whooshing noise to scare it away, but the bird just hops casually over the grass, careful to maintain a safe distance. Ida says something to her father, but Conor doesn't hear. He just keeps his eyes focused on the chapel in front. For a moment I think he sees me. He is looking directly at me. My heart gives a little leap. With every fibre of my being I want to run to him. I want him to enfold me in his arms like he always used to. I long for his touch as life longs for love. But his expression doesn't change and I retreat back into the shadows. He sees only bricks and stone and his own desolation.

The desire to gather my children against my breast propels me into hell and I realize then what hell is. Not a land of fire and torture in the centre of the planet, but a land of fire and torture in the centre of one's soul. My longing is constant and unbearable. I am unable to kiss their sweet brows and brush my lips against their skin and whisper my love into their ears. I am certain their little hearts would be lifted to know that I am close. And yet, I cannot. I am imprisoned here and can only watch helplessly as they walk on past me into the chapel, followed by the coffin and its six solemn bearers. The coffin, which contains within its oak walls the greatest lie.

I remain outside a while longer. Singing resounds from inside the chapel. The scent of lilies is carried on the breeze. I can hear the shrill voice of Conor's eccentric mother, Daphne, who sings louder than everyone else, but I don't feel a mocking sense of amusement as I usually would: only a rising fury, boiling up from the bottom of my belly because she is there to pick up the pieces and nurse her son's broken heart, not I. I think of Finbar and Ida and the coffin that rests in front of them, and wonder what they are feeling as they face death for the first time in their young lives.

I have to find a way to tell them. There must be *something* I can do to tell them the truth.

I gather my courage like a warrior gathering arms. I never dreamed this would be so hard. I thought, at this point, everything would be so much easier. But I have brought it upon myself so I will bear the pain bravely. It is my choice to be here, after all.

But now I am afraid. I step silently into the chapel. The

singing has stopped. Father Michael takes to the pulpit and speaks in a doleful monotone and I believe that he is truly sad and not just pretending. The congregation is still and attentive. I am distracted a moment by the enormous displays of tall-stemmed lilies on either side of the altar, like beautiful white trumpets lifting their muted lips to heaven. They vibrate with a higher energy that draws me to them and I have to muster all my will to resist their pull. I am like a thread of smoke being drawn to an open window. I focus on my intent and tread noiselessly over the stone floor towards the coffin. It is bathed in a pool of sunlight that streams in through the dusty windows, like spotlights on a stage. I was never the famous actress I once yearned to be. But my moment of glory has come at last. Everyone's eyes are upon me. I am where I have longed to be all my life. I should revel in their devotion but I feel nothing but frustration and despair – and regret, it is true: I feel a terrible regret. For it is too late.

I turn and face the congregation. Then I scream as loudly as I can. My voice reverberates around the chapel, bouncing off the ancient walls and ceiling, but only the birds outside hear my cry and take to the skies in panic. Conor's eyes rest steadily on the coffin, his face contorted with pain. Finbar and Ida sit between their father and Conor's mother, as still as wax-works, and I turn to the coffin wherein lies my death. My death, you understand, but not my life – for I am my life and I am eternal.

And yet no one knows the truth: that I stand before them as an actress who's taken her final bow and stepped off the stage. The cliché is true. My costume and mask lie in that coffin, mistaken for me, and my husband and children mourn me as if I have gone. How could they think I'd ever leave them? For all the riches of heaven I would never leave them.

My love keeps me here, for it is stronger than the strongest chain, and I realize now that love is everything – it is who we are; we just don't know it.

I approach my children and reach out my hand, but I'm made of a finer vibration, like light, and they feel nothing, not even the warmth of my love. I press my face against theirs, but they don't even sense that I am close, for I have no breath with which to brush their skin. They feel only their loss, and I cannot comfort them or wipe away their tears. As for *my* tears, they are shed inwardly, for I am a spirit, a ghost, a phantom, whatever you want to call me; I have no physical body, therefore I suffer my pain in my soul. In a rage I fling myself about the church, hoping for some reaction. I tear about like a maddened dog, but I am as a whisper and no one can hear me howl but the birds.

The strangest thing about dying is that it's not strange at all. One moment I was living, the next I was outside my body. It felt like the most natural thing in the world to be outside of myself, as if I had already done it a hundred times before, but forgotten. I was just surprised that it had happened so soon when I still had so much left to do. It didn't hurt nor did it frighten me. Not then, anyway. The pain was yet to come. What they say about the light and your loved ones who come down to escort you on is true. What they don't tell you is that you have a choice; and I chose to stay.

Father Michael clears his throat and sweeps his moist eyes over the grave faces of his congregation. 'Caitlin is with God now and at peace,' he says, and I attempt and fail to wrench the Bible from his hand and fling it to the floor. 'She leaves behind her husband Conor and their two young children Finbar and Ida, who she loved with a big and generous heart.' He looks directly at my children now and speaks with grand authority. 'Although she is gone to Jesus she leaves a little of herself with them. The love they will carry in their hearts throughout their lives.' But I am more than that, I want to shout. I'm not a memory; I'm more real than you are. My love is stronger than ever and it is all I have left.

The service finishes and they file out to bury me in the churchyard. I'd like to be buried near the sailor's wife, but instead I am laid to rest beside the stone wall a little further down the hill. It's farcical to watch the coffin lowered into the ground while I sit on the grass nearby, and it would be quite funny, were it not so desperately sad. Conor tosses a white lily into the trench and my children throw down pictures they have drawn, then step back into their father's shadow and cower against his legs, pale-faced and tearful. I am weary from trying to get their attention. A gull hops towards me but I shoo him away, just for the pleasure of watching him react.

Time does not exist where I am. In fact, I realize now that time does not exist where you are, either. There is only ever now. Of course, on earth there is psychological time, so you can plan tomorrow and remember yesterday, but that only exists as thought; the reality is always now. So days, weeks, years mean nothing to me. There is only an eternal present from where I watch the disintegration of everything I love.

It is as if, with my death, the life has gone out of Ballymaldoon Castle, too. It is as if we have died together. I watch the men in big vans motor up the drive, beneath the burr oaks that crowd in over the road to create a tunnel of orange and red, their gossamer leaves falling off the branches and fluttering on the wind like moths. On either side a low, grey stone wall once hemmed in sheep, but there haven't been sheep here since Conor bought the castle and surrounding land almost twenty years ago, so now the fields are wild. I like them that way. I watch the long grasses swaying in the breeze, and from a distance they look like waves on a strange green ocean. The lorries draw up in front of the castle where Cromwell's armies stood four hundred years ago to seize it for an officer, as a reward for his loyalty. Now the army of burly men is here to take the valuable paintings and furniture into storage, because Conor is boarding up the windows and bolting the doors and moving into a smaller house near the river. He has always been a solitary man; creative men often are, but now I watch him retreat even further into himself. He cannot live here without me because I breathed the life into this place and now I am dead.

I loved the castle from the very first moment I saw it, nestled here at the foot of the mountain like a smoky quartz. I imagined its imposing grey walls once scaled by princes come to rescue princesses imprisoned in the little tower rooms that rise above the turreted gables. I imagined how swans once glided across the lake and lovers lay on the banks in the evening sun to watch their courtship. I imagined the three Billy Goats Gruff trotting across the ancient stone bridge, unaware of the wicked troll lurking in the shadows beneath. I imagined the ghosts of knights and ladies haunting those long corridors carpeted in scarlet and never guessed that I would be one of them, imprisoned by the longing in my heart. I never dreamed I would die young.

I watch helplessly as most of the pieces I chose with such care are lifted and carried and piled high in the vans, supervised by our estate manager, Johnny Byrne, and his son Joe. It is as if they are dismembering me, piece by piece, and placing my limbs into coffins all over again; but this time I'm sure I can feel it. The George VI pollard-oak library table; the parcel-gilt mirror; the set of twenty George IV dining chairs

I bought at auction from Christie's. The marble busts, Chinese
lamps, my maple writing desk. The ebony chests, the
Victorian armchairs and sofas, the German jardinières; the
Regency daybed, the Indian rugs: they take them all, leaving
only the pieces of no worth. Then they lift down the paintings and prints, exposing pale squares on the denuded walls,
and I cringe at how ungallant they are, as if these brawny men
have robbed a lady of her clothes.

I fear they are about to remove the greatest prize of all: the
portrait of myself that Conor commissioned a little after we
were married, by the famous Irish painter, Darragh Kelly. It
takes pride of place above the grand fireplace in the hall. I am
wearing my favourite emerald-coloured evening dress, to
match my eyes, and my red hair falls in shiny waves over my
shoulders. I was beautiful, that is true. But beauty counts for
nothing when it lies rotting in a casket six feet beneath the
ground. I rest my eyes upon it, staring into the face that once
belonged to me, but which is now gone forever. I want to
weep for the woman I was, but I cannot. And there is no
point tearing about the place as I did in the chapel, for no one
will hear me but the other ghosts who surely lurk about this
shadowy limbo as I do. I'm certain of it although I have not
seen them yet. I would be glad of it, I think, because I am
alone and lonely.

Yet they do not take it down. It is the only painting left in
the castle. I cannot help but feel a surge of pride when the
doors are bolted at last and I am left in peace to contemplate
the earthly beauty I once was. It gives me comfort, that
painting, as if it is a costume I can slip on to feel myself once
more.

Conor and the children settle into Reedmace House, which
is built down by the river, near the stone bridge where the

goats and troll of my imagination dwell, and Conor's mother, Daphne, moves in to look after them. I should be pleased the children have a kind and gentle grandmother, but I cannot help but feel jealous and resentful. She embraces them and kisses them in my place. She bathes them and brushes their teeth as I used to do. She reads them bedtime stories. I used to mimic the voices and bring the stories to life. But she reads plainly, without my flair, and I see the children grow bored and know they wish that she were me. I know they wish that she were me because they cry silently in their beds and stare at my photograph that Conor has hung on the wall in their bedroom. They don't know that I am beside them all the time. They don't know that I will be with them always — for as long as their lives may be.

And time passes. I don't know how long. Seasons come and go. The children get taller. Conor spends time in Dublin but there are no films to produce because he no longer has the will or the hunger. The empty castle grows cold as the rocks on the hills, and is battered by the winds and rain. I remain constant as the plants and trees, with no one to talk to but the birds. And then one night, in the middle of winter, Finbar sees me.

He is asleep, dreaming fitfully. I am sitting on the end of his bed as I do every night, watching his breath cause his body to rise and fall in a gentle, rhythmic motion. But tonight he is restless. I know he is dreaming of me. 'It's all right, my love,' I say, as I have said so often, silently, from my other world. 'I'm here. I'm always here. Right beside you.' The little boy sits up and stares at me in amazement. He stares right at me. Not through me but at me. I'm certain of it because his eyes take in my hair, my nose, my lips, my body. Wide with astonishment they drink me in and I am as astonished as he.

'Mam?' he whispers.

'Darling boy,' I reply.

'Is it you?'

'It's me.'

'But you're not dead.'

I smile the smile of someone with a beautiful secret. 'No, Finbar. I'm not dead. There is no death. I promise you that.' And my heart lifts with the joy of seeing his face flush with happiness.

'Will you never leave me?'

'I'll never leave you, Finbar. You know I won't. I'll always be here. Always.'

The excitement begins to wake him and slowly he loses me. 'Mam . . . Mam . . . are you still here?'

'I'm still here,' I say, but he no longer sees me.

He rubs his eyes. 'Mam!' His cry wakes Daphne, who comes hurrying to his side in her nightdress. Finbar is still staring at me, searching me out in the darkness.

'Finbar!' I exclaim. 'Finbar. I'm still here!' But it is no good. He has lost me.

'It's only a dream, Finbar,' Daphne soothes, laying him down gently.

'It wasn't a dream, grandmam. It was real. Mam was on the end of my bed.'

'You go back to sleep now, darling.'

His voice rises and his glistening eyes blink in bewilderment. 'She was here. I know she was here.'

Daphne sighs and strokes his forehead. 'Perhaps she was. After all, she's an angel now, isn't she? I imagine she's always close, keeping an eye on you.' But I know she doesn't believe it. Her words satisfy Finbar, though.

'I think so,' he mumbles, then closes his eyes and drifts off to sleep. Daphne watches him a while. I can feel her sadness, it is heavy like damp. Then she turns and leaves the room and I am alone again. Only this time, hope has ignited in my heart. If he managed to see me once, he might see me again.

Chapter 1

Ellen Trawton arrived at Shannon airport with a single suitcase, fake-fur jacket, skinny jeans and a pair of fine leather
boots, which would soon prove highly unsuitable for the wild
and rugged countryside of Connemara. She had never been to
Ireland before and had no memory of her mother's sister, Peg,
with whom she had arranged to stay, under the pretext of
seeking peace and solitude in order to write a novel. As a
London girl, Ellen rather dreaded the countryside, considering it muddy and notoriously quiet, but her aunt's was the
only place she knew where her mother would not come looking for her – and the only place she could stay without having
to spend a great deal of money. Having quit her job in marketing for a small Chelsea jeweller, she was in no position to
be extravagant. She hoped Aunt Peg was rich and lived in a
big house in a civilized part of the country, near a thriving
town with shops and cafés. She didn't think she'd last if she
lived in the middle of nowhere with only sheep to talk to.

She stepped out into the Arrivals hall and scanned the eager
faces of the crowd for her aunt. Her mother was tall and still
beautiful at fifty-eight, with long, mahogany-coloured hair
and high cheekbones, so Ellen assumed Aunt Peg would be
similar. Her eyes settled at once on an elegant lady in a long

camel-hair coat, clutching a shiny designer handbag with well-manicured hands, and her heart swelled with relief, for a woman who lived in the middle of a bog would not be wearing such a stylish pair of court shoes and immaculate tweed trousers. She pulled her case across the floor. 'Aunt Peg!' she exclaimed, smiling broadly.

The woman turned and looked at her blankly. 'Excuse me?'

'Aunt Peg?' But even as she said it, Ellen could tell that she had made a mistake. 'I'm sorry,' she mumbled. 'I thought you were someone else.' For a second she felt lost in the unfamiliar airport and her resolve weakened. She rather wished she were back home in Eaton Court, in spite of having gone to such trouble to escape.

'Ellen!' a voice exclaimed from behind. She swung around to see a keen, shiny face beaming excitedly up at her. 'Just look at you! Aren't you a picture of glamour!' Ellen was surprised her aunt spoke with such a strong Irish accent when her mother spoke like the Queen. 'I knew it was you the minute I saw you coming through the door. So like your mother!' Aunt Peg looked like a smiling egg, with short, spiky grey hair and big blue eyes that sparkled irreverently. Ellen was relieved to see her and bent down to kiss her cheek. Peg held her in a firm grip and pressed her face to her niece's. The woman smelt of lily of the valley and wet dog. 'I hope you had a good flight, pet,' she continued breathlessly, releasing her. 'On time, which is a boon these days. Come, let's go to the car. Ballymaldoon is a couple of hours' drive, so if you need to use the lav, you'd better go now. Though of course we can stop at a petrol station on the way. Are you hungry? They probably didn't give you much to eat on the plane. I always take sandwiches from home. I can't bear the cheese they put in theirs. It tastes like rubber, don't you think?'

Ellen let her aunt drag her suitcase across the hall. She was quick to notice her sturdy lace-up boots and the thick brown trousers she had tucked into shooting socks. Aunt Peg lived in a bog after all, Ellen thought despondently. Judging by her coarse, weathered hands, she no doubt chopped her own firewood and did all her own gardening as well.

'You're not at all like Mum,' she blurted before she could stop herself.

'Well, I'm much older for a start and we've always been very different,' her aunt replied, without a hint of displeasure. The two women hadn't spoken in thirty-three years, but Aunt Peg did not look like the sort of person to hold a grudge. Ellen's mother, on the other hand, was the sort of woman for whom a grudge was a common complaint.

Lady Anthony Trawton was not a woman to be crossed. Ellen was well acquainted with the thinning of her lips, the upturning of her nose and the little disapproving sniff that always followed. It didn't take much to incite her disapproval, but being the 'wrong sort' of person was the *worst* sort of crime. Ellen had been a rebellious teenager, unlike her golden-haired sisters who were paragons of virtue at best and bland at worst. They hadn't needed moulding, because for some reason they had come out just as their mother had wished: obedient, pretty and gracious, with their father's weak chin, fair hair and slightly bulging eyes. Ellen, by contrast, had a wild and creative nature, exacerbated by her mother's unreasonable objection to her independence, as if striking out on her own would somehow turn her into the 'wrong sort' of person. With her raven-coloured hair and rebellious disposition, she was the quirk in what might otherwise have been a picture-perfect family. But Ellen was hard to mould; her mother had tried, pushing her every which way through the hole designed for proper aristocratic young ladies, and for a while Ellen had acquiesced and allowed herself to be pushed. It had been easier to surrender and give up the struggle – a relief, almost. But a woman can only go against her nature for a limited time before unhappiness overwhelms her and forces her into her own shape again. Ellen couldn't determine the exact moment when she had decided she had had enough, but her flight to Ireland was the result of a lifelong struggle for freedom.

Aunt Peg hadn't attended either of Ellen's sisters' weddings, even though Leonora had married an earl and Lavinia a baronet – anything less would have provoked a substantial snort from their mother – and her name was never mentioned. Ellen had picked up enough snippets of conversation over the years to know that there was some sort of estrangement. The Christmas cards and letters that arrived from Ballymaldoon every year were met with a disdainful sniff and promptly tossed into a bottom drawer in her mother's study. Unable to restrain her curiosity, Ellen had once or twice leafed through them and learned that her mother had a secret past, but she knew better than to ask her about it. The cards had always aroused her interest, and sometimes, when she caught her mother staring sadly into the half-distance, she wondered whether her wistfulness had anything to do with them. Perhaps, like the nostalgic smell of burning leaves in autumn, the letters gave off a fragrance that seeped through the drawer and pulled her back to her past. Now, when Ellen had needed somewhere to run, the letters had given her all the information she needed to find her aunt, thanks to the little address stickers stuck to the top of the page, which included her telephone number. Excited and a little afraid, she knew she was about to discover what her mother had hidden away all these years. She didn't dwell on the terrible consequences were she to be found out. She looked down at Peg's rough hands and thought of her mother's smooth white fingers and perfectly painted nails. Her mother had married well, Peg had not. Their lives were clearly very different. But why?

'You surprised the devil out of me when you telephoned,' said Peg. 'But it was a lovely surprise. It really was. Of all the people to call out of the blue, it was you! I'd never have believed it.'

'I hoped you wouldn't mind. I just needed to get out of London. It's far too busy and noisy there to think.'

'Not the right environment for a budding novelist, I agree. I can't wait to hear all about your writing. What a clever girl you are.'

Ellen had always loved words. Every time she looked out of the window she felt compelled to describe what she saw. She filled journals with poems and stories, but it wasn't until very recently that she had decided to change the course of her life, realizing that happiness only comes from doing what one really loves, and that if she didn't try to write a novel now, she never would. Her mother ridiculed her aspirations of becoming a 'scribbler', but Ellen's desire to express herself was stronger than her mother's desire to snuff out her creativity. Connemara would be the perfect place to be true to herself.

'I'm not just here to write, Aunt Peg. I'd like to get to know *you*. After all, you *are* family,' Ellen added kindly. The rate at which her aunt was talking gave her the impression that she wasn't used to company.

'That's very sweet of you, Ellen. I don't imagine you've told your mother you're here.'

'No.'

'I thought as much. So, where does she think you are, then?'

Ellen pictured the note she had left on the hall table, beneath the oval mirror where her mother arranged her hair and make-up every morning before going out to her ladies' lunches and charity meetings. She would have found it by now. No doubt it had aroused a monumental snort. She wondered what would have upset her more: the fact that Ellen had disappeared without telling her, or the fact that she had said she might not marry William Sackville after all. Her mother might have needed to sit down after reading *that* line in the note. Although William was neither baronet like Lavinia's husband, nor earl like Leonora's, his family was very well connected and owned a large grouse moor in Scotland. Her mother insisted that they were very distantly, but quite discernibly, related to the late Queen Mother. 'I told her I was going to stay with a friend in the country,' she lied.

'Ah, you're a bold little devil,' said Peg. 'Now let's see if I can remember where I parked the car.'

After scouring the rows of shiny vehicles, Peg cheerfully made for the dirtiest car in the building. It was an old Volvo, designed like a sturdy box. 'Excuse the mess, but it's usually just me and Mr Badger.'

'Mr Badger?'

'My sheepdog. I left him at home. You'll have the pleasure of his company later.'

'Oh, good,' Ellen replied, trying to sound enthusiastic. Her mother had a tiny Papillon called Waffle, which looked more like a toy than an animal, although its neurotic yap was only too real and very irritating. Leonora and Lavinia insisted on buying little dogs at Harrods, which they could carry around in their handbags, not because they liked dogs, Ellen thought, but because they were fashionable accessories like Smythson diaries and Asprey leather key rings. If they could have bought their babies at Harrods, she imagined they probably would have.

Peg climbed into the car and swept the newspapers off the passenger seat. Ellen noticed the dog hairs clinging to the leather. 'Where do you live?' she asked, all hope of a civilized town with elegant shops and restaurants now fading at the sight of the mud on the mat.

'Just outside Ballymaldoon, a delightful town near the sea. You'll find it very peaceful to write your book.'

'Is it *deep* countryside?'

'Oh, yes, very deep. I have lots of animals. I hope you like animals, Ellen. You might have noticed my country attire. It gets very cold there on the west coast, and damp. Did you bring any other boots, pet?'

'No, just these.'

'They're very elegant, Ellen, but you'll ruin them in a day. Luckily, I have a spare pair you can borrow.'

Ellen glanced at Peg's sensible leather ones and baulked. 'Thank you, but I'm fine. I probably won't go out that much.'

Peg frowned at her then laughed heartily. 'Now that's the funniest thing I've heard all week.' Ellen wondered whether her mother had fallen out with any other relations who might perhaps live in Dublin.

'So, how *is* Maddie?' Peg asked once they were on the road. Her voice was steady but Ellen noticed that she gripped the steering wheel tightly and kept her eyes on the way ahead.

'Maddie?'

'Your dear mother?'

Ellen had not heard her called by that name, ever. 'She's Madeline to her friends, you know, and Lady Trawton to everyone else ...'

'I bet she is. She always was rather grand. I suppose she still speaks like a duchess?'

Ellen was too impatient to hide her curiosity. 'Why did you two fall out?'

Peg squeezed her lips together. 'You'd better ask your mother,' she replied tightly.

Ellen realized she had to tread more carefully. 'I'm sorry, it must be painful to talk about it.'

'It's in the past.' Peg shrugged. 'Water under the bridge.'

Ellen thought of the letters and cards tossed thoughtlessly into her mother's bottom drawer and she felt sorry for her aunt. She had an air of loneliness. 'It must sadden you not to see your family.'

Peg flinched. 'Sadden *me* not to see *my* family? Jaysus, child, what's the woman been telling you? It should sadden *her* not to see *her* family, though I don't suppose it does. We haven't heard from her in over thirty years.'

Ellen was stunned. She had taken Peg for a spinster. 'Oh? I thought ...' She hesitated, not wanting to cause offence. 'Do you have children, Aunt Peg?'

Peg faltered a moment and her profile darkened, like a landscape when the sky clouds over. 'I have three boys, all in their thirties now, working. They're good boys and I'm very proud of them,' she replied softly. 'Maddie and I have four siblings. I don't suppose you know that?'

Ellen was astonished. 'Really? Four? Where are they?'

'Here in Connemara. We're a big family; a close family. You have loads of cousins.'

'Do I? I never imagined. I've only ever heard Mother

mention you and that's when I wasn't supposed to be listening! And you send Christmas cards every year.'

'Which I suppose get thrown in the bin!' Peg added bitterly.

'A bottom drawer.'

'Well, Maddie and I were once very close. We were two girls in a family dominated by boys, so we stuck together. But it was her decision to leave Ireland and break with her kin, not the other way around, and in so doing she broke our mother's heart. I don't feel it's wrong to tell you that. The boys never forgave her.'

'I never met my grandmother.'

'And sadly, you never will.'

'She's dead, is she?'

'Yes, she died ten years ago.'

'I don't suppose Mother made peace with her before she died.' Peg shook her head and drew her lips into a thin line. 'And my grandfather?' Ellen asked. 'Do I have a grandfather?'

'He died in a car crash when we were small. Mam took over the farm and raised us single-handed. Maddie hated getting her hands dirty, but I've always loved animals. When Mam died, Desmond, our oldest brother, took over the farm. I made a little farm for myself. It's the only thing I know how to do. Do you mind if I smoke?' She suddenly looked exhausted, as if the excitement of meeting Ellen had taken the energy out of her.

'You smoke?' Ellen asked, suddenly feeling more optimistic.

'I do, I'm afraid. I've tried to quit but I think I'm just too old to learn new tricks.'

'Smoking is a dirty word in our house. I have to sneak about and lean out of the bedroom window for a puff.'

'It's a dirty word everywhere nowadays. The world is a duller place for all the policing. The best parties are the ones on the pavements.'

'Oh, I so agree with you. I'm always standing freezing, puffing away, but in the very best company. Although I acknowledge I'd be an idiot not to try to quit. I just need a good reason to stop.'

'Have a look in my handbag and you'll find a packet of Rothmans. Help yourself and then light one for me, there's a good girl.'

'Don't tell me you still live at home, at your age!'

'I'm thirty-three.'

'Much too old to be living with your parents.'

'Well, I didn't always live with them. I went to Edinburgh University, then when I came back to London I lived with Lavinia before she got married. Mother persuaded me to return home when I got into financial trouble. It seemed silly to turn away the offer of free accommodation, especially when the house is so big and they were both rattling around like a couple of beans in a box. Mother's been trying to marry me off for years.' She thought of William and cringed. She had sent him a text but hadn't dared turn on her iPhone to see if he had replied. 'It seems rather outdated to mind so much about marriage.'

'Well, Prince William's gone so Maddie must be very disappointed. Though there's always Harry, of course.'

Ellen laughed. 'You're not wrong, Aunt Peg!' As she rummaged around in Peg's carpet bag she told her about her sisters' excellent marriages. 'In Mother's eyes, you're not a "proper person" until you've married well. Lavinia and Leonora are both extremely "proper" now.'

'Good heavens, Maddie must have been beside herself at that result!'

'I don't think she's too happy about me, though. I'm the

eldest, so, technically, I should have married first. Trouble is, I'm not sure I want to marry the sort of man my mother wants for me.'

'Follow your heart, pet, and you'll always be happy. Large estates and titles don't mean anything in the light of true love. In fact, I think they only bring trouble. A lot of hard work and responsibility. Life is better when it's simpler.'

Ellen lit a cigarette and handed it to Peg, then lit one for herself. She opened the window a crack and the smoke snaked its way out into the soggy February air.

'So, is there a Mr Peg?' she asked, inhaling deeply and feeling the tension in her shoulders melt away.

'There was a Mr Peg a long time ago, but we went our separate ways.'

'I'm sorry.'

'Oh, don't be. I have my youngest son and my brothers to look after me.'

'One can never tell whether or not a marriage is going to last. Mum and Dad seem happy enough, but there's no guarantee.'

'Well, you never know what life is going to throw at you and how you're going to react. Some things bring you closer while others set you apart.'

'Do you ever see your ex?'

'No, he emigrated to America. The boys go and visit him, of course. He married again, a much younger woman, and had a little . . .' She paused and took a long drag. 'A little girl,' she said softly, and her voice broke as if those words had caused her pain. 'Well, she won't be little now. Still, he's got no reason to come back.'

Ellen noticed the air change in the car. It grew suddenly heavy with sorrow as if the damp from outside had come in through the open window. Ellen felt sorry for her aunt, for she had obviously been very hurt when her husband married again and started another family. 'Tell me about your boys,' she said cheerfully, changing the subject.

Peg smiled and the atmosphere lifted. 'Well, they're good boys,' she began. 'Dermot, Declan and Ronan. Dermot and Declan are married with children and come and visit from time to time, but Ronan, well, he's still in Ballymaldoon and doesn't look likely to settle down any time soon.'

As they drove into the heart of Connemara, Ellen let her aunt rattle on about her sons. She watched the landscape change and the beauty of it took her by surprise. She found herself drawn to the wild, sweeping landscape of rocky mountains and wet valleys, where rivers trickled through the heather and ruined stone dwellings stood like skeletons on the hillsides, exposed to the wind and mists that rolled in from the sea. There was something melancholic about the sheer vastness of the wilderness, as if human beings had been defeated by its untameable nature and thrown up their hands in despair, abandoning their homes to seek a safer existence in the towns and cities. There were no pylons, few telephone masts, little but the long, straight road that cut through the bogs and long grasses, and the rugged hills that rose up into the sky, their peaks disappearing into cloud. Ellen had never seen anything quite like it and watched in fascination and fear as the civilized urban world with which she was familiar was replaced by this defiantly silent land.

At last they drove down the valley into the town of Ballymaldoon and Ellen caught sight of the ocean twinkling in the distance, as vast and untameable as the Connemara landscape. Aunt Peg would have driven around the town were it not for her niece, who she felt would enjoy a brief viewing.

'Not that there's much to see,' she remarked as they motored down a quiet street of pastel-coloured houses neatly positioned in a line behind stone walls and shrubbery. The town was dominated by a large Gothic church which sat regally on an incline, shielded by tall sycamore trees and rock. 'I don't go to church,' said Peg. 'Father Michael thinks I'm ungodly. He's wrong, of course; I feel God with me all the time, but that priest irritates the hell out of me, always has done. It's as simple as that. So you don't have to go if you don't want to. It's all the same to me.'

'Mother goes to Mass every morning in London, would you believe,' said Ellen.

'Oh, I would. But I don't think God has a great deal to do with it.' They both laughed.

'Ah, a pub, now things are looking up,' Ellen exclaimed as Peg slowed down alongside the Pot of Gold. 'Is it any good?'

'Full of locals and family. I prefer the quiet life, myself. But the boys will take you, if you like.'

'Your sons?'

'No, I mean my brother, Johnny, and his eldest son, Joe. Johnny is estate manager up at the castle and Joe works for him. I think Johnny and Joe can be found at the bar most evenings. Go with them. Joe will introduce you to everyone you need to know. Like I said, you have loads of cousins. They don't all live here in Ballymaldoon, of course, but there are plenty who do. You'll be amused by the Pot of Gold. I think you'll find a few characters for your novel in there.' She chuckled to herself, as if she already had a few in mind.

Peg drove down to the harbour, where fishing boats were tethered to the quay or tied to buoys, a little way out. Mounds of lobster pots were piled on the stones and one or two rugged-looking fishermen in thick jerseys and caps sat smoking and chatting as they mended their nets. A skinny mongrel lay on the cobbles, shivering in the cold. Ellen thought it wouldn't be long before the men set off to the Pot of Gold for a Guinness and the dog for a warm place beside the fire. Ballymaldoon was a pretty little town but there were obviously no decent shops to tempt her. Just as well, she thought, for she hadn't saved much money and she couldn't ask her parents after the note she had left them. She had certainly burnt her bridges in that respect. She wondered how long it would be before she suffocated down here in Nowhere and returned to London, gasping for excitement like a fish out of water, repentant and compliant. As pretty as it was, there was evidently not a lot going on.

Aunt Peg drove on through the town and out the other side. A mile or so further down the coast she took a turning onto a farm track and motored up the hill between grey stone walls and lush green pastures dotted with sheep, until they reached a pair of modest white farmhouses at the top. 'It's not much but it's home,' she said cheerfully, drawing up in front of the cottage on the left. Ellen was disappointed. She had rather assumed her aunt would have a bigger house. But it was quaint and picturesque with a high thatched roof into which little dormer windows had been cut and painted red to match the door. There were no trees to protect it from the elements, only the low stone wall, and Ellen imagined it had been built stout and sturdy in order to withstand the ferocious winter winds.

The house might have been a disappointment, but when she stepped out and turned around, the view took her breath away. There, twinkling through the evening mist, was the ocean, and right in the middle, looming out of the twilight like a phantom, were the charred remains of a ruined lighthouse. She stood a moment and watched it. The sun had sunk below the horizon and the sparkling lights of Ballymaldoon could be seen way off to the right, blending with the first stars that peeped through the cloud. Slowly, the lighthouse faded as the night and fog closed in around it, and then it was gone, as if it had never been there.

Ellen was drawn out of her gazing by the scampering sound of little paws. She turned to see Mr Badger, a black-and-white border collie, followed by a grunting ginger pig.

'I hope you like animals,' said Peg as she returned to the car to fetch Ellen's suitcase.

'Of course,' Ellen replied, not knowing whether to pat the pig or run away.

'Don't be alarmed by Bertie, he's a good boy and house-trained. See, he likes you,' she added as Bertie thrust his nose between Ellen's legs and grunted. Ellen jumped back in panic. 'Just stroke his ears, pet, he loves that.' But Ellen ignored her aunt's advice and hurried into the house.

Inside it was warm and cosy and smelt of damp dog. The hall was tiled with square grey stones, the walls painted a soft white, decorated with amateur watercolours of the sea. In the kitchen a dusty brown beanbag lay against the island for Mr Badger. A straw mat was placed in front of the yellow Stanley stove that was pushed into the chimney breast beside a neat pile of small logs. Ellen presumed that was Bertie's bed, if pigs had beds. The sideboards were cluttered with mugs and utensils, pots for teabags, coffee and pens. An old-fashioned-looking teapot sat on the Stanley, waiting to be boiled. Peg looked at the clock on the wall and smiled. 'I suppose it's too early for a wee drink. Would you like a cup of tea, pet? You must be hungry. I have ham and freshly made soda bread.' She opened the fridge. 'I made stew for your tea, but how about a snack now? There's nothing like a long journey to give you an appetite. Or would you prefer to see your room first and freshen up?'

'Yes, that would be nice, thank you,' Ellen replied, watching Bertie trot into the kitchen and take his position on the straw mat.

'Come on, then.' Peg hauled her suitcase up the stairs in spite of Ellen's protestations that she should carry it. 'I'm as strong as an ox. This is nothing compared to the sheep I've lifted.'

She opened the door into a floral-decorated bedroom with a low ceiling of old wooden beams, a big pine bed, wardrobe and chest of drawers. Striding across the carpet, she opened the window to let out a maddened fly that was buzzing against the glass. 'You have a view of the sea.'

Ellen's heart lifted. 'With the lighthouse,' she said.

'Yes,' Peg replied, her voice wary.

'It's a ruin. I love ruins.' She joined her aunt at the window.

'That's a very tragic one. A young mother died there five years back in a fire. Though what she was doing there at that time of night is nobody's business.'

Ellen stared through the darkness but saw nothing. 'How sad.'

'Joe will tell you all about it. He's full of it. The girl's husband, Conor Macausland, moved out of the castle after she died into a smaller house on the estate, but Johnny and Joe still work there, keeping the gardens nice. She was a very keen gardener.' She lowered her voice. 'There was talk that she was murdered.'

Ellen was horrified. 'By who?'

'Her husband.' Peg closed the window and drew the curtains. 'He was the prime suspect for a brief time. The guarda were all over the case like ants, but they found no evidence

whatsoever to prove that he did it. Some believe they found
no evidence to suggest that he *didn't*.'

'How awful! What do you think?'

Peg sighed. 'I think it was a tragic accident, but some
people won't be satisfied with that. They enjoy a bit of
mystery and murder.' She smiled wryly. 'You see, it can get a
bit boring down here and people like to embellish things for
entertainment. Personally, I like a quiet life.' Peg walked towards
the door. 'Your bathroom's down the corridor, second door
on the right. Don't go opening the first door, mind, because
Reilly's asleep in there.'

'Reilly?'

'A squirrel I rescued just before Christmas. I couldn't have
been given a nicer present.' She smiled fondly, as if speaking
about a small child. 'He's been hibernating in the laundry cupboard ever since. It's warm beside the boiler so I thought he'd
be cosy. He'll wake up in a month or two and then I'll try to
tame him. If you need clean sheets at all, ask me first because
I know which shelf he's on.'

Ellen smiled back casually, as if a squirrel in the laundry
cupboard was a perfectly normal occurrence. 'Sure,' she
replied. 'Any other animals I should be aware of?'

'Not inside. Only mice and bats in the attic, but they won't
be bothering you. Bertie won't come upstairs, but if you go
into the kitchen in the middle of the night he might fly at you
thinking you're an intruder. He rushed at Oswald when he
was a little piglet and managed to fracture his leg, so imagine
what he'd manage to break now!'

'Who's Oswald?'

'My dear friend. You'll love him. He rents my cottage next
door and comes in most evenings to play cards.'

'Does he help on the farm?'

Peg snorted a little like Bertie and laughed. 'No, if you knew Oswald, you'd appreciate how funny that sounds! Oswald is a retired English gentleman who paints in a three-piece tweed suit, no less. Those watercolours downstairs are his. They earn him enough to pay the rent but not much more. He does it for pleasure, I think. He's a dear friend. You'll like Oswald.' Her eyes sparkled as she said that and Ellen wondered whether she wasn't a bit in love with this English gentleman.

'I look forward to meeting him,' said Ellen.

'There's a nice little sitting room downstairs for you to write in. I'll light the fire and you can snuggle up in there while I'm out. Freshen yourself up now and come down when you're ready. I'll wet the tea.'

Ellen pulled her telephone out of her handbag and switched it on. After a few moments it rang with two messages and two texts. Two were missed calls from her mother but Ellen deleted the voicemails without listening to them. One text was from William: *Darling, what is this all about? I don't under-stand. Please call me so we can discuss.* His coolness didn't surprise her at all. William was the type of upper-class Englishman who was rarely rattled by anything. He'd enjoyed an education that gave him a strong sense of entitlement and the expecta-tion that everything would work out well in the end. After all, it always had, so there was no reason for him to believe that Ellen's sudden flight was any different. He was probably rolling his eyes and sighing, 'Women!' in the same way his father shrugged off his mother's foibles. The other text was from her best friend Emily: *OMG you've really gone and done it! Your mother has called twice but I'm too scared to answer. What shall I say? Please call.* Ellen switched the phone off and walked over to the window. She flung it open and breathed in the damp night air. A shiver rippled across her skin. She wasn't sure whether it was caused by the cold or the excitement at having run away. It didn't matter. She felt free from duty at last. She had pleased her parents for the first thirty-three years of her life; now, finally, she was at liberty to please herself.

Chapter 2

Downstairs, Peg was sitting at the kitchen table reading the newspapers over bread and cheese. Ellen noticed a menacing-looking bird perched on the back of her chair. It was as black as charcoal with eyes as pale as aventurine. 'I suppose he's another friend?' she said, pulling out the chair as far away from the bird as possible.

'Oh, yes, that's my little jackdaw,' Peg gushed. 'I raised him from the egg and he's lived with me ever since. I try to shoo him away but he always comes back. There's no getting rid of him.' She laughed and Ellen knew that Peg didn't really want him to fly away. 'Would you like a cup of tea now?'

'I'd love one, thank you.' The jackdaw watched her warily. 'What's he called?'

'Jack,' Peg replied, then laughed. 'Not a very inspiring name, but it suits him.' At the mention of his name, Jack flew onto the table to peck at the biscuit crumbs Peg had left for him. He was so big he dwarfed the biscuit tin.

'You have lots of animals.'

'I can't say no, that's the trouble, and everyone knows it. Any stray or hurt animal and they come knocking on my door.' Peg handed her a mug of tea. 'Milk is in the jug.

Oswald comes in at six for a glass of wine. He can't be doing with tea. I always keep a bottle of claret on the top of the fridge just for him, but if you'd like some, you're very welcome to share it. Tomorrow, I'll introduce you to Charlie the donkey, Larry the llama, my hens and sheep. I only have a dozen sheep. Snowdrop is my favourite; of course she's a big girl now, but I raised her after the fox got her mother. She kept me up all night with her demands. Worse than the boys when they were babies!'

Ellen sipped her tea and felt instantly restored. 'Besides the ghastly Waffle, Mother doesn't like animals.'

'Waffle's a dog, I suppose. With a name like that, I *hope* it's a dog.'

'Yes, a very small one.'

'Maddie was always worried about getting her clothes dirty, even as a little girl. I'm not sure people change all that much. She was like a swan among geese.'

'You're not a goose, Aunt Peg.' Ellen laughed.

'Compared to your mother, I most certainly am. She came out last but all the beauty was saved for her. Not that it matters. I'm old and wise now and know that beauty counts for nothing if a person's not beautiful on the inside.'

'I don't think Mother cares too much what's on the inside.'

'Well, she did once. Still, as long as she's happy.' She shrugged. 'Do you fancy another cigarette before Oswald gets here? He doesn't like smoking so I try to have one a little before he arrives so that the place doesn't smell.'

'Yes, please,' Ellen replied. It was true that Peg wasn't a beauty like her sister, but she had the wide, friendly face of a person always ready to see the good in others. 'I'm glad I've found you, Aunt Peg. To think, if I hadn't rummaged through Mother's letters, I might never have known you existed.'

Peg handed her niece the packet and Ellen placed a cigarette between her lips. 'It's never too late. All the rivers flow into the sea one way or another. She tried to keep us hidden but you've found us all on your own.'

They lit their cigarettes and sipped their tea in the cosy warmth of the kitchen. Peg chatted on about her family, her Irish accent curling around her words like pigs' tails, and Ellen was lulled by the gentle rise and fall of her intonation. Bertie lay grunting in his sleep on the mat, while Mr Badger was snuggled up on his beanbag. Jack returned to his perch on the back of Peg's chair but watched Ellen cautiously, still unsure of the stranger in their midst.

Ellen felt so comfortable in Peg's kitchen it might as well have had arms to embrace her. In London, her parents' kitchen was Mrs Leonard's domain. The family ate in the dining room and Mrs Leonard cooked and cleared away. Being old, Mrs Leonard was of the generation that had grown up with the green baize door, which, since the eighteenth century, had been a feature of every staffed house, and as a consequence she was perfectly at home in her domain behind it. Besides Mrs Leonard there was Mrs Roland, the housekeeper, who lived in the basement flat, and Janey, a sprightly girl straight out of university who was Madeline Trawton's personal assistant, though Ellen couldn't imagine what she had to do all day as her mother didn't have a job. Her father had a driver who spent most of his time chauffeuring her mother to boutiques in Bond Street and charity lunches. On reflection, her childhood had been dominated by Norland nannies in grey uniforms. She couldn't remember a time when the house hadn't been full of staff.

Ellen considered her home. It wasn't really a home at all, but a showpiece, decorated and regularly updated by the famous French designer, Jacques Le Paon – and the kitchen, which Mrs Leonard occupied like a territorial hen, was a functional and impersonal place rarely visited by the family. Not like Peg's. Ellen sat back in her chair and let the room absorb her. Peg's kitchen was the very heart of the home and Ellen soaked up the love appreciatively.

After a while, Peg got up to open a window and boil a saucepan of black coffee to disguise the smell of smoke. She glanced at the clock on the wall as the big hand made its way slowly up to the twelve. At five to six, Peg took two wine glasses down from the cupboard and fetched the half-full bottle of claret from the top of the fridge. She pulled out the cork and balanced it on the log pile beside the Stanley to warm it. Five minutes later the front door opened and in strode a reed-thin man of about sixty-five, in a three-piece tweed suit, cap and spectacles.

'Good Lord, is it that time already?' he exclaimed jovially as he strode into the kitchen. 'Ah, the lovely Ellen, all the way from the Big Smoke.'

'This is Oswald, pet,' said Peg, her smile almost swallowing her entire face.

Ellen stood up and extended her hand. 'It's very nice to meet you,' she said. 'I've heard a lot about you.'

Oswald's pale-grey eyes twinkled playfully as he shook her hand. 'We artists are going to get along like a pair of geese on a pond,' he announced. His English accent was as crisp as fine bone china. Ellen didn't think he looked anything like a painter. His hands were soft and clean, his tweed suit and shirt perfectly pressed.

Peg hurried to the table with the glasses then returned a

moment later with the bottle. Oswald sat down and let Peg pour him a large glass of claret.

'Well, isn't this nice.' He took a sip then raised his glass to Ellen. 'Welcome to the motherland.'

She laughed, liking Oswald already. 'Thank you.'

'This is the land of mermaids and magic. Don't think that all the stories you've heard of Ireland are folklore. No, they're absolutely true. If you look hard enough you'll see little green leprechauns hiding out in the heather and stealing coins to put in the pot of gold at the bottom of the rainbow.'

'Oh, really, Oswald. You're a rogue.' Peg laughed, handing Ellen a glass and sitting back in Jack's chair, with a small glass of Jameson and a jug of water for herself. 'Don't believe a word he says, pet. He's away with the fairies.'

'And there are fairies, too,' he added gravely, lowering his voice. Ellen wasn't sure whether he was joking just to tease her aunt. 'They hear everything,' he mouthed, glancing warily around the room. 'And they steal things, too, so you'd better watch out and keep your valuables locked away.'

'He's messing with you,' Peg interjected. 'And he's only had a sip.'

'It's true. Come on, Peg. You're constantly telling me how things have been mysteriously moved or vanished altogether.'

She shook her head. 'With the house full of animals it's hardly surprising. Bertie has a thing for shiny objects.'

'Have you caught him in the act?' Oswald demanded.

'No, but I know it's him.'

'There, you see, no proof. I told you, it's the fairies. Has she met Dylan yet?'

'Not yet. Tomorrow, I suspect,' Peg replied, a little uneasily, Ellen thought.

Oswald turned to Ellen to fill her in. 'Dylan knows where

all the leprechauns lie buried and he'll tell you if you buy him a whiskey — he's creative, like us, Ellen, and consequently a very sensitive soul, though sadly the drink has made him more eccentric than he once was. I'm not sure whether the leprechauns he claims to see aren't really swimming in the whiskey in that sodden head of his.' He grinned, revealing two crooked eye teeth that made him look like a wolf. 'But he still has a large dose of that famous Irish charm. One can't help liking Dylan.'

'All sounds good for my novel,' said Ellen.

'Oh, yes, you'll be very inspired down here,' Oswald agreed, raising his eyebrows. 'What's your book about?'

'Love, mystery . . . you know,' she replied vaguely. 'I'm not really sure yet, to be perfectly honest.'

'The less of an idea you have the better; that way you can soak up the atmosphere and let your imagination carry you to new and magical places. Leave your London stories behind, they have no place here in Connemara.'

Ellen felt uplifted by Oswald's advice. She was used to her mother squashing her enthusiasm. She was looking forward to exploring the place and finding inspiration among the ruined buildings and craggy hills. While she hid out in this remote part of Ireland she could work out what she was going to do, in her own time. Peg seemed happy to have her stay; and William, their impending wedding, and her controlling mother, seemed reassuringly far away.

Oswald took off his tweed cap and stayed for dinner, which Aunt Peg called 'tea'. Ellen presumed he always did. They ate stew, boiled cabbage and potatoes, which Peg called 'spuds' and put in the middle of the table to be individually peeled. For pudding she had baked a treacle tart, which was Oswald's favourite, not that one could tell from the size of him. He looked like a bullrush with a mop of curly grey hair on top.

After dinner, he stepped out into the hall and showed Ellen the paintings he had given Peg, explaining that if he ever fell short in paying his rent, he presented her with a picture. 'One day, they'll be worth a fortune and Peg will be very rich.'

'What good will that be to me?' said Peg from the kitchen.

'You don't know what's good for you.'

'Money only brings trouble. I've been very content without, thank you very much.'

'Money's got nothing to do with happiness, I agree, but it sure makes life more comfortable while you're looking for it!' he replied. Then he lowered his voice and pointed to a painting of the lighthouse, before the fire gutted it. 'There's your mystery,' he said, tapping it with his nail.

'Peg told me about the fire.'

'Dreadful business. Poor girl. She was only young, not that much older than you, and pretty, too. She had flowing red hair the colour of flame heather, green eyes, skin as white as cream and a wild yet fragile nature. There was something childlike about her. I suspect she was close to the fairies and leprechauns.' He chuckled and lowered his voice. 'But don't tell Peg. She doesn't like to admit that she believes in that sort of thing.'

'Peg told me that the husband . . .'

'Conor, yes, poor soul. If I was him I would have fled, with all the fingers pointing at me and murder unspoken on people's lips. But he has a house hidden away on the estate and no one ever sees him. He keeps himself to himself and spends most of the time in Dublin, I think. He was a very successful film producer, but I'm not sure he's managed to pull anything off since Caitlin died. The children go to school there now.'

'I gather they lived in a castle.'

'I've painted that, too. It's quite something. Johnny and Joe will take you up there and you can have a look around. For a novelist it's the perfect place to set a book.'

'I'm feeling inspired already,' she replied excitedly.

'No boyfriend?'

'No,' she lied, folding her arms across her chest.

'That's a very defensive gesture,' he observed thoughtfully.

'I had one, but it's over.'

'Ah, you've left some poor man back in London broken-hearted, have you?' He smiled kindly and peered at her over his spectacles. 'It's better to break his heart now than break both of your hearts further down the line.' Ellen imagined her mother's heart was breaking the most.

Ellen helped her aunt carry the tray of coffee into the sitting room. She had lit a fire and closed the curtains and the room smelt pleasantly of wood smoke. Mr Badger wandered in and climbed onto the sofa with the nonchalance of a dog simply carrying out his nightly routine. Peg and Oswald took their places at the card table set up in the bay of the window, while Ellen sat in the armchair beside the fire and watched as Jack flew in and positioned himself on the tallboy pushed against the far wall.

'Would you like to play?' Peg asked her niece.

'No, thank you. I don't play cards,' she replied, wondering where the television was and whether her aunt had Sky.

Peg read her mind. 'I'm afraid I don't have a television. I have a library of books in the little sitting room where you're going to write your book. What do you like reading?'

'Fiction mostly. Romance, mystery, beautiful places. Escapism, I suppose,' she replied, considering all the things she needed to escape from. 'And I love historical fiction, too, like Philippa Gregory. I've read all of hers.'

'And you must read the classics,' interjected Oswald; then he added wisely: '*In the long run, men hit only what they aim at. Therefore, they had better aim at something high*. There, that's a quote for you. Read Oscar Wilde, Dumas, Maupassant, Austen, Dickens. Read the Greats, Ellen, and you might end up writing like them.'

'Is that what you do with your paintings?' she asked with a grin.

'No, because I am old and I have reached my ceiling in terms of ability. You are young and have a long way to go.'

'I'm not sure I believe that, Oswald. I don't think one is ever too old to strive for greatness.'

'Now you're teasing *me*,' he chuckled.

'Don't you think you deserve a little of your own medicine?' said Peg, clicking her tongue and gazing at him lovingly.

'Deal the cards, Peg, old girl, and let's begin.'

Ellen realized that she would inevitably have to find a book to read, if they were going to play cards every evening and there was no television to entertain her. She wondered what Emily would think of that and smiled. She didn't think Emily would last five minutes in a house without a television. She wasn't sure *she* was going to last that long, either. But a house with two eccentric old people and no telly was certainly more desirable than home in London with a fiancé she didn't love and a pushy mother urging her up the aisle for all the wrong reasons.

She sank into the sofa and stared at the fire thoughtfully. She knew she owed William more than a text – and she should really have been clearer. 'I need to get away and have some time to think' was not synonymous with: 'I don't love you so I don't want to marry you.' The date of the wedding was set for June, almost five months away. The Church of the Immaculate Conception at Farm Street was booked for Saturday 22nd and the reception at Claridges afterwards gave her mother an excuse to lunch there weekly with Mr Smeaman, the oleaginous events manager. She had already made an appointment with Sarah Burton, who had designed the Duchess of Cambridge's wedding dress, because Madeline Trawton insisted she wanted a creation no less beautiful for her eldest daughter, although Ellen was quick to recognize that it had more to do with impressing her friends than pleasing her child. Leonora and Lavinia had both enjoyed lavish weddings, but when all was said and done, the brides had taken second place to their mother who had shone more radiantly than the two of them put together.

While Ellen ruminated on her predicament and Peg and Oswald played cards in the bay window, Jack began to squawk from the tallboy. 'Kak-Kak,' he went, frantically pacing the ledge where he perched. Then Mr Badger lifted his head and pricked his ears. He stiffened as if every one of his senses was alert to something only a dog can perceive. Ellen watched him absent-mindedly at first and then with growing interest. He began to wag his tail and follow some unseen thing with his eyes, as if it wandered about the room. Then he whined excitedly, his tail thumping on the cushions. It was all most curious, but neither Oswald nor Peg seemed to notice. Ellen pushed herself up from her seat and knelt on the carpet to stroke him. He glanced at her a moment, acknowledging her presence, but was immediately distracted again by the unseen entity.

'Aunt Peg, have a look at Jack and Mr Badger,' she said. 'They're behaving very strangely.'

Aunt Peg glanced over and grinned. 'They're a little eccentric, I'm afraid.'

'It's the fairies,' said Oswald, without taking his eyes off his hand of cards.

Peg shook her head. 'Don't you go scaring my niece, she's only just arrived. I won't have her fleeing back to London from the spooks.'

'If it's a spook, it's a friendly one,' said Ellen. Then, as Jack flew out of the room, she added, 'I can't vouch for your bird, but Mr Badger likes it. Look how he follows it with his eyes.'

'Dogs like fairies,' Oswald commented with an air of authority. 'But they're not so partial to leprechauns.'

'Are you going to make your move, Oswald, or are we going to sit here and talk rubbish?'

He dealt his card. 'There, old girl, that'll put you in your place.'

Ellen stroked Mr Badger's face and soon he calmed down and put his head between his paws. He closed his eyes and sighed heavily before drifting off to sleep beneath the rhythmic motion of her touch.

Ellen wondered what it was that had excited him so much. She didn't believe in fairies and leprechauns, but thought it quite natural that there should be ghosts. 'How old is this house?' she asked her aunt.

'Oh, it was built in the early eighteenth century,' Peg replied.

'So there might be ghosts?'

'I told you, my dear, there are fairies. Lots of fairies,' Oswald retorted before guffawing loudly. 'There, you see, *that* was a clever move of mine, wasn't it, Peg!'

'Anyone died in here that you know of?' Ellen persisted.

Neither Oswald nor Peg responded and she was too gripped by the idea of the house being haunted to notice Peg's fingers hover hesitantly over her cards. 'It's quite possible, isn't it, that you might have a resident ghost?'

'I don't believe in ghosts,' Peg replied sharply. Then she added in a quiet voice, 'People who see ghosts see them because they *want* to see them. It's that wanting that makes them see and hear things that aren't there. Tricks of the mind. Mr Badger goes off after a speck of dust glinting in the light or a fly so small you can't see it. Don't be fooled by Oswald's tales of fairies, Ireland's gone to his head. I don't want to hear such nonsense. Why don't you go and find a book to read, there are plenty in the library next door.'

Ellen realized she had touched a nerve and she was sorry. She got up and wandered out, leaving her aunt and Oswald at their card table. She heard them talking in low voices as she walked down the corridor, then all was quiet in the little library except for the ticking of an old grandfather clock.

It was a small room with two walls of bookshelves, a window at the far end with a desk positioned in front of it, and on the adjacent wall a big open fireplace that was dark and cold. Rugs were laid over the carpet and a coffee table was placed in the middle of the room covered in haphazard piles of magazines and books. It smelt of the remains of smoke embedded in the curtains and fabrics. The floor creaked as Ellen walked over to the bookcase in search of something inspiring. She hadn't imagined anyone lived in this day and age without a television. How did her aunt keep in touch with the world? She ran her eyes along the spines until she came across a title that appealed to her: *Castles of Ireland*. It wasn't a novel but it didn't matter. She flicked through it, reading the headings at the top of every page. It was a history of castles, some of them ruins, some intact, with beautiful glossy pictures. Her curiosity mounted. There was nothing she found more romantic than a ruin.

Chapter 3

The cockerel crowed at dawn, but Ellen was already awake. From her bedroom window she could see the lighthouse more clearly now. Part of its white outer shell remained, eerie in the feeble light of morning, but the blackened bones were exposed like the charred ribs of an old ship, exposed to the wind and gulls who dared venture there. She stood at the glass and stared at it for a long while. There was something compelling about the sight of neglect and it made her feel quite melancholy. It pulled at her in the same way ruined castles did, and she longed to know how the girl had died and why she had been there.

The sea was as smooth as satin, the rocks seemingly benign in the peace of the awakening earth. The silence was a novelty for Ellen, who was used to the noise of the city, but she felt it creeping over her, as soft as down, and for a moment she lost herself in the landscape. Her thoughts quietened, her head grew light, and she existed in the moment, sensing the infinite in the still, timeless panorama.

Then she heard the clatter of Peg in the kitchen downstairs, the scampering of paws and the grunting of the pig. The front door opened and Ellen watched her aunt leave the house with Bertie and Mr Badger, who sniffed the ground excitedly and cocked his leg against the fence. Peg strode across the field in a heavy brown coat and boots, a woolly hat pulled low over her forehead, a large black bucket in her gloved hand. She looked as if she could roll down the hill if she wanted to.

It was strange to think that Peg shared the same DNA as Ellen's mother, who was slender, immaculately dressed and polished. Madeline Trawton had her hair blow-dried at a chic Chelsea hairdresser three times a week, and regular manicures and facials. Ellen didn't imagine Aunt Peg had ever had a manicure, let alone a facial. She cut a solitary figure, slightly hunched, as round as a Christmas pudding, and Ellen was surprised to feel so fond of a woman she barely knew. She watched her counting sheep and then whistling loudly, her breath rising like smoke on the cold morning air. Ellen thought she was whistling for the dog, but a moment later a shaggy grey donkey trotted up over the lip of the hill. When he reached Peg, he thrust his nose into the bucket and let her stroke his head and ears affectionately. The sheep gathered around her too, until Mr Badger sprang into action, fending them away jealously. One sheep with a rather long neck resisted Mr Badger's shepherding and pushed his soft, woolly body closer to Peg. Ellen thought he looked very strange until she realized that he wasn't a sheep at all but a llama, and she smiled at the eccentricity of her aunt and wondered what her mother would make of her.

At the thought of her mother she moved away from the window and lifted her iPhone out of her handbag. She switched it on and waited for the messages to download. Her heart began to race and the anxiety she had felt in London returned to dispel the peace she had enjoyed only moments before. She began to sweat as the messages pinged in: texts, emails and onto the answering machine. News must have spread, she deduced. She glanced at them fearfully. William, her mother, her father who usually remained detached from domestic strife, Leonora and Lavinia, Emily and her large group of girlfriends, had all tried to get in touch with her one way or another. She felt a wave of panic. It was overwhelming. This is what she had escaped London to avoid: people, *countless* people, telling her how she should live her life. She wished they'd all go away.

With a rising sense of claustrophobia she hurriedly pulled on her jeans and sweater. She thrust her telephone into her back pocket and ran down the stairs, two steps at a time. Ignoring Peg's row of rubber boots, she wriggled her feet into her leather ones and threw on her fake-fur jacket. Once she was outside, the cold air hit her face and burned her lungs, bringing her to her senses with a jolt. Why hadn't she done this earlier, she asked herself crossly. She strode over the gravel and climbed the gate into the field where Peg was now talking to the llama.

'Good morning,' said her aunt when she saw her niece marching purposefully towards her. Then her face grew serious as she registered Ellen's troubled expression. 'Are you all right, pet?'

Ellen took a deep breath and shivered, ignoring the llama who studied her imperiously. 'I'm going down to the sea,' she stated, thrusting her hands into her pockets.

'Now? Before breakfast?'

'I feel like a bracing walk.'

Peg frowned. She knew fear when she saw it. 'Do you want me to come with you?'

'No, I'm fine.' Ellen smiled weakly.

'What would you like to eat when you get back: eggs and bacon, porridge?'

'I've never had porridge. I usually have fruit. Mother insists I don't eat too much in case I bulk up . . .' She was about to add, 'before my wedding', but stopped short. Peg frowned, as if she were speaking a foreign language.

'Jaysus, child, you need to eat! Look at you, there's nothing on your bones. Your mother's out of her mind. I'll make you porridge with honey and a little banana and you'll be a different person.'

Ellen swallowed back tears. She wanted so badly to be a different person.

Peg looked down at the girl's feet. 'Are you sure you want to ruin those good boots of yours?'

'I don't care.' Ellen turned away. 'Leather's hard-wearing, and frankly, I really couldn't give a monkey's. I'll be back shortly.' The sheep parted and she set off down the hill at a brisk pace. Peg stood a moment and watched her, hands on hips, a frown lining her brow beneath her hat.

The faster Ellen walked the better she felt. The air was bracing and her cheeks grew red and hot. She reached the lane and crossed it, taking a path that cut through the long grass down to the sea. An abandoned stone cottage stood forlornly beside the damaged remains of a fence. Shrubs and weeds flourished on its roof and seeded themselves in the gaps between the stones in the walls. In time it would return to the ground it came from and the waves would wash it away. One day everything would be gone, she thought philosophically, because nothing material lasts. *That's why I have to live the life I want to live, because one day I'll be gone, too.*

Right now, the tide was far out, leaving a wide beach of pale-yellow sand. Black rocks were scattered here and there, like sleeping seals, and white gulls hopped about the shallow pools in search of food. The wind swept through the abandoned lighthouse like ghosts playing among old bones, and she took a deep breath, right into the bottom of her lungs. As she exhaled she felt the tension slip away and her shoulders drop. The vision of endless sea and sky lifted the heaviness that weighed upon her chest and she felt a wonderful sense of relief. She walked over the sand, not caring that her expensive boots were getting wet, and marched on towards the ocean. As she neared the water the roar of the sea grew louder. It was a pleasant sound, nothing like the roar of traffic, and she inhaled the salty air hungrily. The wind whipped her hair and the damp curled it so that chestnut-coloured tendrils bounced down her back and across her face. Without a moment's regret, she pulled her iPhone out of her jeans' pocket and threw it as far out to sea as she could. It landed with a plop and disappeared.

With that she felt an immense sense of freedom. Gone were the harassing messages. Gone was all contact with London. It was as if she had thrown her mother and William, her sisters and friends – in fact, her entire life – into the water. They had all sunk with that telephone and there she was, standing alone on an empty beach, liberated at last from duty, responsibility and the dreadful mould that had imprisoned her. She had crossed a bridge and destroyed it in her wake. Now, she could be anyone she wanted to be. She smiled with satisfaction and let the wind take her past. Gazing out at the vast expanse of sea she realized the world was full of endless possibility.

She walked back up the beach with a bounce in her step, across the lane and up the hill where the sheep were quietly grazing and the donkey was standing alone, staring out to sea. When the house came into view she saw a few cars parked on the gravel next to Peg's dirty Volvo. They were as old and muddy as hers. She wondered who had come to visit so early in the morning.

As she opened the door, the smell of bacon hit her in a warm fug. Mr Badger came bounding into the hall. She patted him then took off her jacket and boots. The leather was stained on the toes where the water had soaked it but she didn't mind. The boots belonged to the life she was now sure she didn't want. Voices resounded from the kitchen, most notably deep, male voices. She wandered in shyly.

'Ah, there you are, pet. Come and meet your family.' Peg beamed at her happily. There, sitting around the table, hugging mugs of tea, were four men as old as Peg and one younger man, closer to her own age. Ellen stared at them in astonishment. 'These are your uncles: Johnny, Desmond, Ryan and Craic, and that's Joe, Johnny's boy.' None of them stood up to greet her, but they all took off their caps. The curiosity in their eyes was as ill-disguised as hunger in the eyes of wolves. 'I'm afraid when they heard you were coming they all wanted to be the first to get a good look at you,' Peg added.

This is my family, Ellen thought incredulously as she stood gazing at the gruff, hairy men as if they were another species. At first glance, they didn't look anything like her mother. Could they really share the same blood? She made a conscious effort to collect herself and extended her hand politely. Boarding school had trained her to hide her feelings. She could always find refuge in good manners when an unfamiliar situation threatened to unbalance her. 'So you're Mum's brothers?' she said. One by one they shook her hand, repeating their names, gazing up at her as if they, too, were struggling to find their own features reflected in hers.

'I'm Desmond and I'm the oldest Byrne,' the first said with

an air of importance. 'My wife, Alanna, wanted to come too but she had to get to work, so you'll meet her later.'

'I look forward to meeting her,' Ellen replied, finding Desmond's dark looks intimidating. He was the biggest of them all, with a large barrel chest, solid, muscular shoulders and a short, thick neck. His hair was black and wiry, speckled with grey, and a woolly black beard covered a wide and serious face. He looked like the sort of man capable of knocking a person down with a mere flick of his fingers.

'And I'm Johnny, and this is my boy, Joe,' interjected the smaller man beside him. Like Desmond, Johnny had deep-set blue eyes, but the expression in them was kinder and more sensitive than his brother's. He also wore a beard but the hair looked soft and covered less of his face, and unlike Desmond, who was blessed with a thatch of hair, Johnny was balding.

'Hi,' said Johnny's son, Joe. His hand was warm, his grip strong, and Ellen almost gasped when her bones crunched beneath his fingers. 'Sorry, I didn't mean to hurt you,' he said and grinned crookedly. He was very handsome when he smiled, she thought, and she imagined his father must have been handsome like him when he was young, for they were very similar, except for Joe's eyes, which were a rich moss green.

'Doesn't know his own strength, that boy,' said Ryan, shaking his auburn hair in mock disdain. 'I apologize for my nephew; he's all brawn and no brains!' He laughed and his teeth were yellowed and crooked. 'This is how it's done, boy,' he said to Joe, and he shook her hand gently. 'Pleased to meet you, Ellen. I'm Ryan.'

'Hello, Ryan.' She laughed, finding his hand warm and soft, like dough.

'And I'm Craic,' said the last, and there was a diffidence in his pale-grey eyes and a fairness in his colouring that he did not share with his brothers. Of all her uncles, he was the one who looked most like her mother, and Ellen smiled at him genially, reassured to discover something familiar in the unfamiliar faces staring back at her. But in spite of that similarity, they were worlds apart. The men's Irish accents were strong, their hands big and rough. Ellen thought of her father's soft skin and clean nails. His were the hands of a man who worked in a plush office in Mayfair and enjoyed long lunches with his friends at White's. Her uncles' hands reminded her of the builders who were constantly working on the house in Eaton Court, satisfying her mother's insatiable demands – or her need to avoid boredom at any cost.

'Come and take a seat, pet. I've got porridge for you, and tea.' Jack perched on the back of Ryan's chair at the head of the table. Her uncle didn't seem to notice him there, or he was so used to his sister's irregular residents that he ignored him as one would a chair or a teapot. Ellen took the empty seat at the foot of the table. Peg placed a bowl of porridge in front of her. She'd added a golden trail of honey in a spiral. It steamed seductively.

'So what are you all having?' Ellen asked, breaking the awkward silence. They were all staring at her as if she were an exotic animal Peg had rescued from a foreign country. 'Aunt Peg has cooked you up a feast!'

'Eggs and bacon for the boys,' said Peg, pouring tea into her mug. 'Tuck in, pet. We don't stand on ceremony here.'

'Do you get breakfast here every morning?' She directed her question at Joe because he was her age and the least scary.

He grinned and his dark eyes twinkled with mischief. 'Not likely. A cup of tea is usually all that's on the menu. Isn't that right, Peggine?'

She smacked him playfully on the head. He had thick, glossy black hair and a long, cheeky face. Ellen noticed the affection in his eyes when he looked at his aunt.

'Peg won't come to the boozer so we have to come here,' Johnny added with a grin.

'Why won't you go to the pub, Aunt Peg?' Ellen asked.

'Too many people,' she replied with a shrug.

'Peg's kitchen is a fine place to chinwag after a long day's work,' Johnny interjected kindly. 'She makes a strong cup of tea!'

'I'm the landlord of the pub,' interjected Craic. 'But I don't take it personally,' he added, winking at his sister.

'You own the Pot of Gold?' Ellen repeated, impressed. She had never met a publican before.

'I do, for my sins.'

Desmond raised his mug of tea and grinned lopsidedly. 'Practice makes perfect, there's many do think, but a man's not too perfect when he's practised at drink.'

'Who wrote that?' Ellen asked.

'I don't know, but he was Irish for sure!' They all laughed heartily. The awkwardness lifted and they all began to speak at once, their voices low and growly like bears. Peg fussed over them, making more toast and pouring more tea, and Ellen remembered the solitary figure she had been in the field, so far removed from the jovial hostess she was now, buzzing about her kitchen busily, her face aglow with pleasure.

Ellen had never known a big family. Her father, Anthony, came from an aristocratic Norfolk family who had owned the large and beautiful estate of Hardingham Hall for over four hundred years. When Anthony's father died, his elder brother, Robert, inherited the family seat and the title of Marquis of

Zelden. Robert's son George duly took up the earldom and Anthony, Ellen's father, was left as simply Lord Anthony Trawton. His sister, Anne, had married a Scotsman and had gone to live in Edinburgh, and Anthony, of course, had settled in London. Being a rather chilly family, they spent little time together beyond the traditional Christmas gathering up at Hardingham Hall, where they'd all put on a great show of family unity, parade at the local church and promise to make more effort to see each other the following year. They never did. Ellen sat in the midst of her newfound relations, trying to understand their cheerful banter, marvelling at the world her mother had chosen to hide away, and wishing she had always been part of it.

'I'd like to have a drink with you tonight in the Pot of Gold,' Ellen suggested, finishing the last spoonful of porridge with regret. 'I've never been in a proper Irish pub.'

'Well, you've missed out then, haven't you?' said Johnny.

'I'll come and get you,' Joe offered.

'You'll meet the lot of us, then,' Johnny added.

'But are you ready for the lot of us?' interjected Ryan, shaking his curly red head.

'I'm ready now, aren't I? And there are a lot of you here.' She laughed.

'You'll be just grand, pet,' Peg reassured her, patting her shoulder as she leaned down to take her empty porridge bowl away. 'You see, porridge was all you needed to put the colour back in your cheeks.'

'So how is Maddie?' Desmond asked, leaning back in his chair. The room fell silent and the awkwardness descended over them again like a heavy cloud. His brothers looked at one another uneasily but Desmond didn't flinch. He didn't look like the sort of man who cared too much about being tactful.

'She's very well,' Ellen replied casually.

'What does she make of you being here in the motherland with us?' Johnny asked, rubbing his beard nervously.

'She doesn't know she's here,' Peg answered for her. The men stared harder.

'She doesn't know you're here?' Ryan repeated. 'Where the hell does she think you are, then?'

'In the English countryside, somewhere, trying to write a novel.'

'You're a writer, are you?' said Joe. 'That's grand.'

'*Trying* to be a writer, would be more accurate,' Ellen said with a sniff, as if it really wasn't very important whether she became one or not.

'What do you write about?' Joe asked.

'Novels, you know, mystery, relationships, life,' she replied importantly. 'Oswald told me about the castle. That sounds like a good place to base a book.'

'You can come with me and Joe today, if you like. We work up there. I'm estate manager and Joe just smokes and watches,' said Johnny with a chuckle. 'The idle gobshite!'

'Yes, let's humour the old man,' Joe retorted, rolling his eyes. 'Let him think he's doing it all on his own.' He turned back to Ellen. 'There are plenty of ghosts up there for you to write about.'

'Don't listen to him, pet. The only ghosts are those two fooling about after a heavy night in the Pot of Gold,' Peg interjected.

'There's not a lot for them to do up there, I don't imagine,' Ryan added. 'The castle is locked up and Mr Macausland's in Dublin most of the time. If they sat having a picnic all day no one would know or care.'

'So, if your mam doesn't know you're here, how did you

find us?' Desmond brought the subject back to Ellen, his gaze steady and penetrating.

'From Aunt Peg's letters and Christmas cards that Mother keeps in a drawer. I thought Aunt Peg was her only sibling. I didn't know she had four brothers.'

'That'll be for sure,' Desmond muttered. 'And what'll you tell her?'

Ellen shrugged noncommittally. 'I'm not going to tell her anything. What the eye doesn't see the heart doesn't grieve for. She doesn't need to know I've found you.' She lowered her eyes because she sensed Aunt Peg saw through her facade. The older woman was watching her pensively from the Stanley. Her story was gaping with missing information that Ellen didn't feel ready to share, but a guilty blush warmed her cheeks because she knew Aunt Peg must suspect now that she had run away.

'I'd love to see the castle,' she said, longing to extricate herself. She didn't want to talk about her mother any more. She didn't like the feeling of being interrogated, especially when she was hiding so much.

'Well, there's no time like the present,' said Johnny, pushing out his chair. 'Thanks for breakfast, Peg.'

'Don't you all come to my door tomorrow expecting another fry-up, now will you?'

'Too late, Peggine.' Joe laughed. 'It's a grand way to start the day.'

'You're like a pack of dogs,' Peg retorted. 'Off with you all now. I've work to do.'

'How's that squirrel?' Craic asked.

'Hibernating. And he's called Reilly, by the way.'

'You're just grand, Peg,' said Desmond, patting her shoulder.

'Flattery will get you nowhere, Desmond Byrne. Now, out of my house, the lot of you.' She herded them out like a pack of sheep.

'You sure you won't come to the boozer?' Desmond asked, his gruff voice suddenly surprisingly soft and full of compassion.

'No,' she replied in the same tone, as if there was something unspeakable in the air between them of which they were both acutely aware but unwilling to articulate.

'OK, then we'll share a pint with our niece,' he conceded.

'Bring her back in one piece, won't you?'

'I'll keep an eye.'

Peg noticed Ellen shrugging on her fur jacket. It was the most inappropriate coat for the countryside. 'Take a pair of my boots, pet. You'll get very muddy up at the castle with the boys, and it might rain, so borrow an overcoat, too. Your furry thing looks very dear altogether, so you don't want to ruin it.'

Ellen decided to wear her own jacket but gave in to the boots. They weren't fashionable, but they were comfortable and fitted her perfectly. 'You and I have the same size feet,' she called to Peg.

'We must be related,' her aunt replied with a chuckle. 'I'll see you later. Don't be believing all Joe's stories, now, will you? He's full of rubbish.'

'I love ghost stories,' Ellen answered, following the men outside.

'So did I once,' Peg added, almost to herself. And when Ellen turned back, her aunt's face looked desperately sad, as if a fire had once burned through her heart, like the lighthouse.

Chapter 4

I am in a limbo, bound to the earth but not of it. The fact that I can be anywhere I want at will is little consolation. I have no body. I'm like a wisp of smoke that never dies, drifting from one place to another by the sheer force of my will. One minute I am in Dublin, the next in Connemara. How easy it would have been to have travelled like this in body! And yet the years have made me lonely. I have denied myself heaven but play no earthly part. I can only observe the lives of those I love as if in a dream. I have no need for sleep and I am never hungry. I don't feel the cold or the rain upon my skin, and yet I experience a deep and lasting pleasure in the beautiful Irish countryside, just as I always did; perhaps even more so now, because it is all I have.

The frustration I felt in the beginning has mellowed and I am resigned to this nonexistence. I am lonely, but not alone. Spirits pass through the corridors of the castle but take no notice of me. I could drive myself mad trying to chase them, searching the rooms for their company. They are like mist that disappears into the air like breath on a cold winter's morning. I imagine they were there when I was living, existing in this parallel dimension, as disinterested in me as they are now. I don't know where they go and why they won't communicate with me. It would be nice to have a friend.

I never liked Dublin. I'm a Galway girl born and bred, all right. I hated the noise and the concrete when I was alive and I still hate it now that I am dead. Yet I suffer it gladly to be near my children. I enjoy their good health and their happiness, for I have to admit that they are happy. They have buried their desolation like dogs who bury bones deep in the earth but always remember. One day they will dig me up and cry all over again for their loss, because that is the way grief works. It isn't so easy to erase such deep pain. A person can only cover it up and hope in time to forget. But inevitably, sooner or later, he will have to face it and overcome it because, just as the earth throws up all its buried bones in the end, so the human heart throws up its pain. I might not be able to wrap my arms around them when they need their mother's comfort, but I am right beside them like a shadow they cannot see, and I will be there when their loss rises up to challenge them.

And what of Conor? He has not buried his pain like Ida and Finbar. He carries it around like a burning coal in the heart of his heart. If I had known he loved me so much I would never have done what I did. Oh, Conor, my love, why didn't you love me like this when I was alive?

He now spends most of his time in Dublin, and yet the films he worked so hard and with such enthusiasm to produce have dried up like thirsty hydrangeas. He's drinking too much and partying too hard, in the hope that the noise of people and music will distract him from the pain in his heart and the nagging of his conscience. When he takes the children to Ballymaldoon he stays away from the castle. He rides out over the hills, his black hair like a mane in the wind behind him as his horse jumps the stone walls and ditches. He walks up the beaches, a dark and lonely figure against the white sand and wild sea. He doesn't know that I'm right beside him for I leave no footprints, and when I reach out to take his hand I am as cool and intangible as the wind itself.

He doesn't venture into town. The Pot of Gold is full of gossip and he cannot bear the condemning glances and the whispering. They were suspicious of him right at the start, when he bought the castle all those years ago. He was a townie from Dublin with an English mother and an Irish father, and as much as he thought of himself as Irish, the full-blooded Irish will always say that an Anglo-Irishman is Anglo first and Irish second. This simply isn't the case with Conor and never has been. He loves Ireland with all his heart and there's no space in there for England. But they resented the fact that he didn't socialize or throw lavish parties for the locals, and worse, that he didn't attend Mass. But Conor is not a religious man, although he is a deep thinker and I know he feels closer to God in nature than in a church. I wonder now whether he feels God has betrayed him – whether he doubts there is a God after all. I would like to say that I know, now that I am dead; but I have chosen to remain attached to the earth so I am as ignorant of God as he is. I only know that we don't die, for I am proof enough of that. But where we go after, I will have to wait and see. Right now, I have eyes only for those I love; I daren't raise them to heaven in case I'm tempted away.

When Conor married me, I was a dreamy Irish girl with aspirations to being an actress. We met on the set of a film he was producing in Galway. I had a small part and everyone said I caught his eye because I wanted to better my career. But the truth is we fell in love. I appealed to his romantic and creative nature and he to mine. He said I was the sort of girl who inspired poems and paintings and songs. But as much as I desired, I was not the sort of girl who could take the lead in a big film. So, I threw myself into Ballymaldoon Castle and into the nurturing of our two children and settled with the poems Conor wrote about me and the painting he commissioned to hang on the wall above the grand fireplace in the hall. Conor was everything I wanted and I knew that as long as I was with him, I would never desire anything more. I wouldn't lament the actor's life I had so readily given up and I wouldn't dream of fame and adulation because if I was the light in Conor's eyes I wouldn't need to shine in anyone else's. But love is a strange thing. Sometimes, however much love a person gets, it is somehow never enough.

When I can no longer bear the heaviness of Dublin, I fly about the tall trees and hills of Connemara and my heart sings with joy. I glide upon the surface of the lake where clouds are reflected on the water like scenes from my life that I view with detachment, as if they belong to somebody else. I stand on the clifftop, overlooking the ruined lighthouse where my life ended. I watch from afar as I cannot bear to go there. I linger in the places I love: the castle, the sailor's church, the beaches, cliffs and hills. But I cannot visit the lighthouse because my memories are too painful to relive. Regret is still the thorn in my heart and I suffer it every moment of my death.

And then, one cold morning in February, I am haunting the grounds of the castle when I see a stranger on my land: a beautiful, raven-haired stranger in the company of Johnny and Joe Byrne. While Conor is in Dublin, those men look after the estate. But besides Mrs Haggett, who comes weekly to clean and dust the shell that was my home, no woman has set foot there. Until now.

I am transfixed. It has been a long time since someone has ignited my interest. I move closer and see that she is indeed lovely. She has deep-set eyes, tawny-brown flawed by tiny flecks of gold. Her skin is young and plump, and she has full lips, which she has glistened with gloss. She has the air of a foreigner, that look of wonder and uncertainty when faced with an unfamiliar place, and is wearing the most ridiculous jacket I have ever seen, but I suppose fake fur is fashionable and that is why she wears it. Perhaps she is Joe's girlfriend, but they don't touch each other as lovers do and there is no frisson of attraction between them. They are as siblings, but I know Joe only has brothers.

They are wandering around the castle grounds. I can see that the girl is struck by the magnificence of my home. I'm not surprised. Today, the sky is as blue as the sea with foamy white clouds floating across it like boats. The sun is shining brightly and every now and then, when a cloud passes over it, the valley is plunged into shadow and the air turns damp and cold. Then the cloud sails on and light races down the hills like a bright wave, swallowing up the shade and breaking onto the castle in a dazzling burst of radiance. It is as if God has opened his treasure chest full of gold and it is that which lights up the sky. I am distracted a moment by the beauty of it, but then the mention of my name brings me back to the little group wandering around the lake.

'So, what was Caitlin Macausland like?' the girl asks Joe. Her accent is English and posh, like Conor's mother.

'She was off her nut,' Joe replies. 'Away with the fairies.'

'What, really mad?'

'No, not really mad, just eccentric, I suppose.'

'She was a stunner!' Johnny rejoins and there is admiration in his tone. 'There was something wild about her. She was an actress once, you know. She was born to be an actress, but she gave it up when she married Mr Macausland. I'd say that was a shame, because she would have made a good actress, I think.'

Joe laughs fondly at his father. Johnny looks short and stocky beside his tall son. 'Dad had a bit of a thing for her,' Joe says, grinning. 'Didn't you, Dad? Ah, go on, admit it to Ellen, she's one of us.' Ah, so she's family. An English cousin, perhaps. I wonder how that can be.

Johnny shrugs nonchalantly. He is used to his son's teasing. 'Sure, I felt sorry for her, rattling around in this big castle on her own while her husband was away all the time. She was a woman who needed a lot of looking after.'

'And you know all about that, do you, Da?' Joe smirks.

'You have a lot to learn about women, boy,' Johnny retorts. 'Especially beautiful women, and, aye, she was beautiful, all right.'

'Did she mix with the locals?' Ellen asks.

'When Mr Macausland was away, she was singing in the Pot of Gold with the best of us,' says Joe. 'She had a good, strong voice, altogether. Do you sing, Ellen?'

But before Ellen can answer, Johnny interrupts and his voice is heavy with wistfulness. 'She was mesmerizing. Ah, sure, you couldn't take your eyes off her,' he says.

'In what way was she mesmerizing?' Ellen probes.

'Well, she had these very green eyes, and when they looked at you, they looked right through you and you were a fish caught on the end of a hook, trapped there in her gaze. She was a beauty, all right. Flame-red hair and pale white skin. She was like a painting.'

'And she *was* painted,' Joe interrupts. 'There's a massive portrait of her hanging in the hall up at the castle. Mr Macausland told us to leave it where it is. He was very specific about it. We took out everything of value after she died, but not that painting.' He thrusts his hands into his trouser pockets and his breath mists on the damp air. 'Mr Macausland then moved down by the river and the castle was boarded up. It's like he's locked *her* up in there as well.'

'You mean, he couldn't bear to live there without her?'

'Not after what happened at the lighthouse.'

Johnny's face hardens. He doesn't look wistful any more, just angry. 'Jaysus, it was a terrible waste of a life!' he says hotly.

'Was she really murdered?' Ellen asks and the air stills around her.

'No, she wasn't murdered and Mr Macausland didn't kill her. Who told you that?' Johnny growls.

Ellen flinches at his tone. 'Aunt Peg said that people whisper it.'

'People whisper a lot, the fecking eejits! Doesn't mean it's true.'

Joe takes up the story. I have heard it all before, loads of times, but I'm interested in the girl and what she makes of it. She is bristling with curiosity. 'The night she died she was at the lighthouse with Mr Macausland. Apparently, they had a row and she ran up to the top of the lighthouse. Somehow it caught fire and she had to jump to save herself. But her body was found at the foot, broken on the rocks. That was about midnight, right? Well, Dylan Murphy was on the beach walking his dog about half an hour before that and he swears he saw a man rowing away.'

'Who was the man?' Ellen asks, intrigued.

'No one knows.' Johnny shrugs again.

'Or no one's telling,' Joe adds darkly. 'Mr Macausland insisted that he and Caitlin were the only people there that night.'

'Do you have a theory as to who that mystery person might have been?'

Johnny scratches his soft salt-and-pepper beard. 'Murphy's

imagination, if you ask me. He'd been down the boozer and was probably well langered.'

'So, how did the lighthouse catch fire? I thought it wasn't in use.'

'The guarda found loads of candles all the way up the stairs,' says Joe.

'Caitlin Macausland was a woman who liked a bit of drama,' Johnny adds. 'She would often row out to the lighthouse, but only when Mr Macausland was away. He knew it was dangerous and forbade her to row out even in the daytime. Of course, she rebelled. That was her nature. She was a wild one, all right. Many a time I'd be leaving Peg's late at night and see candlelight twinkling in the lighthouse windows. You wouldn't know what she was up to, but it was well known that it was her and no one thought anything of it, until the fire.'

'I wonder what she did in the lighthouse all night?' Ellen muses. 'It must have been frightfully cold. Didn't anyone ever ask her what she did?'

Joe laughs and his father laughs with him, sharing a private joke. 'Caitlin Macausland wasn't the sort of woman you asked things,' says Joe. 'And if you did, she'd answer in riddles. There was no getting anything out of her that she didn't want known.'

'I think she was afraid of Mr Macausland,' Johnny says darkly, nodding to himself as if that fear of my husband is the answer to everything. 'Because whenever he was down, she was never around. She wouldn't come to the pub any more and she wouldn't be seen in town either.'

'Those who saw her in the schoolyard said she became nervous and withdrawn when he was home. Nothing like the carefree girl she was when he was away.' Joe is pleased to have more gossip to relate.

'I wonder why that was?' Ellen murmurs.

'Ah, he's a demanding man, is Mr Macausland,' Johnny explains. 'I know that her heart was here in Connemara. She was a country girl, all right. She hated the city. She told me as much herself. She'd come and help with the gardening and grumble about having to go to Dublin when she'd rather be down here. They had some big fights. I think Mr Macausland wanted the children educated up there, but she insisted they live down here. She won that battle. I think she won most battles in the end. Mr Macausland gave in, probably for an easy life, and disappeared up to Dublin as often as he could. The marriage stank like sour milk.'

'As soon as she died, Mr Macausland took the children up to Dublin,' says Joe, in a tone that suggests this is of great significance. 'They don't come down much and when they do, Mr Macausland looks miserable.'

'He does indeed,' Johnny agrees. 'Like the life has been knocked out of him.'

'But he can't stay away, can he?' says Joe. 'I mean, he could sell the place, couldn't he? But he doesn't. Why's that, then?' Both men shrug and shake their heads.

They reach the front of the castle. Ellen takes in the towers and turrets and her face is full of wonder, as mine was when I saw it for the first time. The magnificence of the place takes your breath away, even on a cold February morning when the walls are damp and the trees are naked and twisted like arthritic old men.

Johnny pulls the key out of his pocket and pushes it into the lock. I follow them inside. I wish there was a fire in the hall grate, and furniture and rugs so that this stranger could know how lovely my castle used to be. But stripped of everything that gave her life, she is now left alone with her memories, sad and forlorn like me. It is almost colder inside than out and the air has the stale, musty quality of a cathedral. I want to open the windows but they are boarded up with wood. Ellen feels the sorrow there, I can tell, because she puts her hands in her pockets and barely speaks. She wanders over to my portrait, a splash of colour on the colourless walls, and gazes up. Her jaw slackens and she lets out a slow gasp.

I stare down at her through the eyes of the painting. We are gazing at each other. She is fixed on me and I am fixed on her, and she is seeing me. Yes, she is seeing me as if I am living. I hold her like a fish on a hook, and there is no getting away. Johnny and Joe come and stand quietly beside her, and look up at me as they have done so many times over the last five years, trying to make sense of my death. Johnny takes off his cap in reverence and Joe has no joke to crack. They all admire me in silence. Johnny's cheeks flush, for he loves me; Joe sees life in the portrait that he hasn't seen before; and Ellen, well, besides my beauty she is affected by my tragedy. A collective shiver ripples over them and I suddenly feel I am no longer alone. While I am in this painting, I can almost pretend I am alive.

At last the silence is broken. 'In that green dress she looks like an old-fashioned movie star,' Ellen whispers.

'She was an old-fashioned girl,' Johnny agrees sadly. 'She wasn't made for the modern world.'

'Her skin looks translucent, doesn't it? I mean, it's flawless. How old was she when she died?'

'Thirty-four,' Johnny says flatly. 'She was but a girl. Left two small children who'll grow up with barely a memory of their beautiful ma.'

'Don't you think it looks like she's staring back at us?' Joe says nervously.

'Yes, it does,' Ellen agrees. 'It looks like she's real.'

'It creeps me out altogether,' says Joe, moving away. 'I think this place is haunted. I'll see you both outside.' And he leaves.

I am triumphant. Joe knows I am still here. He can feel it in his bones. As for Ellen, this lovely stranger who I hold captive with my eyes, she senses it, too. I'm sure of it. She gazes at me for a long, long time, questions tottering on the end of her tongue. And as she gazes, I can read her mind as clearly as if she were speaking out loud. *Why did you die, Caitlin? Who was the person rowing away in the middle of the night? Why was he there? What were you doing on the island in the first place? What did you do there, Caitlin? Tell me, what were you doing all alone in a deserted lighthouse?*

'Where is she now, Johnny?' Ellen asks softly.

'What do you mean?'

'I mean, where is she? Do you think she's here?'

Johnny is a man who believes in life and death as two distinct states, as separate as night and day. 'I don't believe in ghosts, if that's what you mean. She's with the Lord now, Ellen,' he replies.

But Ellen stares boldly into my eyes and feels my presence beyond the oils and canvas. *I'm not so sure,* she thinks, and I know then that my hope of communication now rests with her.

Chapter 5

Ellen joined Joe outside. He was hunched in the cold, inhaling the last few drags of a cigarette. When he saw her he blew smoke out of the side of his mouth and shook his head. 'That portrait gives me the creeps,' he said. 'Want a smoke?' He pulled the packet out of his pocket.

She hesitated a moment, then relented. 'Just one.'

'What do you think?'

'I think she was very beautiful,' Ellen replied. She placed the cigarette between her lips and lit it with the glowing butt that Joe held out for her.

'She was a bit witchy, if you want to know what I really think. Dad won't hear a word against her, as you can see.'

'So what do you think *really* happened on the island that night?'

Joe lowered his voice and glanced uneasily at the door. 'I don't think Mr Macausland killed her, but he certainly drove her to her death one way or another.'

'How do you mean?'

'They were at each other's throats, as far as I could tell. She used to yell at him and he'd yell back. Mr Macausland has quite a temper on him.' He exhaled a cloud of smoke. 'Put it this way, if he hadn't been on the island that night, she'd still be alive today.'

They both fell silent as Johnny emerged from the castle and locked the door behind him. 'Besides the painting there's not much to look at inside,' he said, joining them on the gravel.

'I've seen enough,' said Ellen.

'Don't blame you. It's haunted in there.' Joe tossed his cigarette onto the ground and squashed it beneath his boot. 'Jaysus, it sends the shivers down me looking at that portrait.'

'Don't be a sap!' Johnny chuckled.

Joe turned to Ellen. 'She looked like she was about to step out of the fecking painting.' He laughed nervously.

'I agree with you, Joe. I've never seen a more realistic portrait in my life. She was looking right at me.'

'Let's go and have a jar,' Johnny suggested. 'Let's introduce Ellen to the Pot of Gold. We can have a good old blather out of the cold.'

The three of them climbed into the front seat of Johnny's red truck. 'It's a shame no one's living in the castle now,' Ellen mused as Johnny drove beneath the latticed arch of burr oaks.

'It was a grand place before we stripped it bare,' Johnny agreed.

'Will they ever move back?'

'Doubtful,' said Joe. 'Too many memories for Mr Macausland, I imagine.'

'You think he'll sell it in the end?'

'No, he'll pass it on to his boy, Finbar, when he's old enough to live there,' said Johnny.

'Poor children,' Ellen murmured. 'They lost their mother *and* their home.'

She gazed out at the wintry landscape that was now bathed in sunlight. Rugged fields stretched out to the left and right, divided by low stone walls, crumbling in parts from neglect. A flock of shiny black crows fought over the carcass of some unfortunate creature, their loud caws cutting into the air like shards of ice. There was something ominous about the sight of them, as if death pervaded the castle grounds. As the truck pulled out into the lane, Ellen was pleased to be leaving.

'So, do you think you got some inspiration for your book?' Joe asked, raising his eyebrows suggestively. 'You could write one hell of a good ghost story.'

'I'm not sure I'd want to go back to that castle to do the research,' she replied. 'How do you manage to work there every day?'

'I don't go inside,' Joe answered simply. 'But sometimes, when I'm in the garden, I feel as if I'm being watched.'

Johnny rolled his eyes. 'Jaysus! Will you listen to the two of you?'

'I swear that place is haunted,' Joe retorted firmly. 'Maybe that's why Mr Macausland never sets foot across the threshold; he's afraid she'll get her revenge!'

'Don't be a gobshite, Joe,' Johnny growled into his beard. 'He doesn't set foot across the threshold because his fecking heart is bleeding and that's the truth.' With that, Joe was silenced. They drove up the lanes into Ballymaldoon without saying another word.

The Pot of Gold was positioned on the main street, painted as red as bull's blood with the name emblazoned in heavy gold lettering along the top. Johnny parked his truck in the car park behind and they walked round together. 'Welcome to my second home,' said Johnny. The thought of a pint and a hearty meal had transformed his face into a wide smile.

'*Second* home, Dad?' quipped Joe.

'Quit codding about, lad,' his father shot back, but his eyes twinkled with merry anticipation as he pushed open the door.

Ellen followed them inside, where it was warm and stuffy. The smell of old cigarettes was ingrained in the carpets and upholstery from before smoking in public places was banned. There was a pleasant fire at one end and the walls were covered with prints, cartoons and other paraphernalia. She recognized Johnny's brother Craic at once. He stood behind the bar, grinning at them. There was something in his smile that reminded her of her mother. Ellen felt a momentary stab of guilt, but it was gone before she was able to brood over it.

'You're a bit early,' Craic said to his brother. 'Suppose you're using Ellen as the excuse not to work.'

'I'm too old and knackered to need an excuse,' Johnny replied, leaning on the bar like a big liner docking into its habitual berth. 'What's your poison, Ellen?'

'I suppose I'd better have a Guinness.'

Johnny was pleased. 'She's a Byrne, all right.' He chuckled. Craic put a fat-bellied glass beneath the tap and began to fill it with stout. Ellen tried not to grimace. She'd have rather asked for a Coke, but she was a little frightened of Johnny and thought he'd like her more if she ordered a Guinness. Craic placed it on the bar in front of her. The creamy head looked appealing, at least. She wanted to scoop a bit up with her finger and taste it first, but Johnny and Craic were watching her enthusiastically. She was left no alternative but to put it to her lips. It was strong and bitter and more disgusting than anything she had ever drunk in her life. She swallowed with feigned relish. Her performance was convincing enough. Craic filled a couple more glasses for Johnny and Joe and then began to talk about things of which she knew nothing. She wondered whether she'd give herself away by asking for a glass of water. The stout was burning her throat.

They took their drinks and sat at a table in the corner so that Ellen had a clear view of the locals coming into the pub. She realized pretty swiftly that they had a clear view of her, too. Everyone who entered came straight up to talk to Johnny, as if he were hosting some sort of private party, but they never took their inquisitive eyes off *her*.

'Word has got out that Maddie's daughter is in town,' Joe whispered to Ellen. 'I'm afraid they're all coming in to have a look at you.'

'If I'd known, I would have made more of an effort with my appearance,' she replied, feeling painfully conspicuous. 'I'm like an animal in a zoo.'

'We don't get many newcomers here, but you're more than a curiosity, I'm afraid. Your mother was notorious.'

'So, tell me, what happened? Why hasn't she spoken to her family for so long?'

Joe shrugged. 'You'll have to ask Peg. I'm not good at family history.' He took a swig of Guinness, leaving a line of cream on his upper lip. 'I only knew of your existence this morning.'

'That doesn't surprise me at all. I asked Peg and she told me to ask my mother. But Mum's never spoken about it, ever. I thought her only sibling was Peg. I never knew she had four brothers as well. I never knew I had cousins. It's like none of you existed.'

He shook his head mournfully. 'That must have broken Grandmam's heart.'

'What was she like, our grandmother?'

Joe beamed a devilishly handsome smile. 'She was a right character, God bless her. She was only tiny and yet she raised

six children all on her own. It can't have been easy as the farm
didn't make much money, but she had a strong faith and
somehow she managed. Father Michael's her first cousin and
he came for lunch every Sunday come rain or shine. You
know, she wore black for my grandfather until the day she
died. As long as I knew her I never saw her wearing anything
else. It made her look hard, but she had a soft centre, all right.
She could knock back a pint with the best of us and box your
ears for being an eejit, but if you were in trouble or unhappy
or anything, she would sort you out. She'd kill anyone who
threatened her family. Family was everything to her. That's
why it must have broken her heart when your mam left and
never came back. She never spoke of it, though. She wasn't a
complainer.'

'What did Mum do?' Ellen bit her lip, trying to think of a
good enough reason for her mother to abandon her family.
'Do you think she did something really bad?' Ellen lowered
her voice. 'Something so bad that no one's willing to talk
about it, not even her?'

At that moment their attention was diverted by the door,
which opened with a sudden thrust, giving way to a cold gust
of wind and the dark presence of a man. He strode into the
pub in a black beanie hat pulled low over his forehead and a
heavy black coat, and swept his eyes over the room, settling
them on Ellen like a missile locking onto its target. Ellen
flinched. His eyes had a touch of madness in them.

'God, who's that?' she hissed to Joe.

'*That's* Dylan Murphy,' he replied, in a tone that suggested
notoriety. 'And he's coming over to meet *you*.'

'Does he bite?' She glanced at Johnny, who began to scratch
his beard nervously.

Joe laughed. 'No, he's just off his nut. Hello, Dylan!'

Dylan took the chair opposite Ellen without waiting to be invited. He shrugged off his coat and sat down, greeting Johnny and Joe as if he had seen them only minutes before. 'So, you're Maddie's girl, are you?' he asked, gazing at her across the table with brown eyes the colour of Connemara peat.

'Yes, Ellen, how do you do?'

He stared at her more intensely. 'You know that's a name out of a novel, don't you?' he said.

Ellen laughed nervously. 'Well, I know it means "bright light" in Greek.'

'It's a beautiful character from the novel *The Age of Innocence*, by an American author called Edith Wharton. Ellen Olenska, the infamous Countess Olenska.' He inhaled through his nose, savouring the sound of it, then repeated it with a swing in his voice as if the name were notes rising and falling. 'Countess Olenska.'

'Are you joining us for dinner?' Johnny asked. For a moment, Ellen assumed they were talking about the evening meal, until it became apparent by the context that 'dinner' meant lunch. The three men discussed food for a few minutes. The pub had filled up with fishermen in heavy jerseys and Ellen recognized the dog she had seen the day before. He wandered over to the fire as if it had been lit especially for him.

'I'll go and put in our orders,' Joe suggested. 'What do you want, *Ellen Olenska*?' he asked, with emphasis on her new nickname.

She ignored the mischievous curl to his lips. 'I'll have lamb stew. Will you get me a glass of water as well?'

'You're not a Guinness girl, really, are you?'

'Oh . . . I . . .'

'Doesn't matter, Ellen. If water's your poison, fair play to you.' She shifted her gaze to Johnny, but he wasn't listening. He was leaning towards Dylan, with an angry look on his face, speaking in a hushed voice so she couldn't hear. She stared into her Guinness, uncomfortable beneath the weight of the many pairs of eyes watching her from all corners of the pub.

'So, how do you like Ballymaldoon?' Dylan asked, and the change in his tone suggested that Johnny had told him off for being rude.

'I haven't seen much of it yet, but what I have seen is lovely.'

'Good.' There followed an awkward pause. The fighting spirit with which he had entered was now snuffed out, leaving him strangely deflated. He gazed at her with troubled eyes, as if searching her features for the answer to some unspoken question.

'We've just been up to the castle,' she said, desperate to fill the silence, and wishing he'd take those crazy eyes off her. 'It's a sad place now there's nothing in it.'

'I showed her the portrait,' Johnny interjected. 'You should have heard the two of them carrying on about ghosts!'

Dylan seemed relieved to have something to talk about, and his gaze softened on her face. 'Johnny's an old cynic,' he said, and his mouth twitched at the corners. 'He only believes in what he can see.'

'I'm not saying there aren't ghosts; I'm just saying that Caitlin Macausland isn't one. If you ask Joe, he'll tell you she's in the garden making sure he's not pulling out the good stuff. What a load of rubbish!'

Dylan shook his head and grinned at Ellen. As he did so, something in his face gave way and his character shone through, handsome, humorous and bold. 'And what about you, Ellen Olenska, do you think Joe's talking rubbish?'

She was surprised to find she liked the man, who was now grinning at her raffishly. 'Ask me again in a week. This is my second day and I've only just met Joe so I couldn't tell you whether or not I think he's talking like a gobshite.'

'I like the way you said that.' Dylan chuckled. 'Gobshite, said in the poshest London accent.'

'She's very posh, my niece,' said Johnny. 'A posh London bird!'

Joe returned to the table with a glass of water for Ellen. She took it gratefully. 'Bet you were surprised to find your family has working-class roots,' he said, sitting down.

'*Honest* working-class roots,' Johnny added. 'There's nothing wrong with those!'

'Aunt Peg said that Mother was always grand. Is that true?'

Johnny's eyes slid to Dylan then back to Ellen. He took a swig of Guinness. 'Aye, she was grand, in her dreams,' he replied cagily.

'I know nothing of her childhood,' Ellen said, casting a line and hoping to catch a large fish full of information. She didn't miss the sly looks that passed between her uncle and Dylan. Perhaps she wasn't the only person keeping secrets after all. 'It's as if her past doesn't exist. I mean, I felt sorry for Aunt Peg, missing out on knowing all of us, when it's the other way around. We're missing out on knowing all of you! I didn't even know Mum had brothers, let alone four of them! It's crazy.'

'Do you have brothers or sisters, Ellen Olenska?' Dylan asked, rubbing his bristly chin nervously.

'Two younger sisters.'

He raised his eyebrows. 'Really?'

'They're both married.'

'Are they now?'

She shrugged. 'I'm the last to marry, if I marry at all.' She

was about to add that her mother was doing all she could to
marry her off, but she didn't. Something inside warned her
against giving too much away.

'You don't want to be marrying too young,' said Joe. 'Life
is long.'

Dylan stared at her across the table, saying nothing. The
touch of madness in his eyes was now replaced by a solemn
curiosity and he devoured her features as if he'd starved himself for years.

'So, what was my mother like as a girl?' Ellen asked, steering the conversation away from marriage and wishing Dylan
wouldn't look at her like that. He made her feel very uncomfortable.

'Wild as a snake,' said Johnny, draining his glass of stout.

'Really, Mum? Are you sure?'

'Sure as I'm sitting here now. Peg was always sensible but
Maddie, well, what can I say?' He shook his head. 'She was
headstrong. It was only a matter of time before she did something really stupid.'

Ellen frowned. 'So, what *did* she do?'

At that moment the waitress appeared with a couple of
dishes. She leaned over the table. 'Bangers and mash for you,
Johnny?' she said, smiling at him warmly. 'Same for you,
Dylan?'

'Another round of Guinness,' Johnny replied, taking the hot
plate from her. 'And another . . .' He peered into Ellen's glass.

'Water,' said Joe with a regretful shrug.

Johnny shook his head. 'Another water. Jaysus, let's not
waste a good pint!' And he picked up her glass of stout and
took a long swig.

The waitress returned with the rest of the food and they all
tucked in hungrily. Ellen asked the question again. 'So, what

did she do? Someone must know?' She looked at Dylan, but he avoided her eyes and said nothing.

'She ran away,' said Johnny simply.

'Just like that?'

'Just like that,' he replied, chewing on a large mouthful of sausage. 'She met your dad, fell in love and was never seen again.'

'But that doesn't make sense,' Ellen complained.

'It didn't make sense to any of us, either.'

'So, she eloped?'

'I suppose you could call it that. Like I said, she was a wild card. She was always going to go and do something stupid.'

'Did your mother disapprove or something? People don't run away for no reason.'

'Mam wanted her to marry a good Irish Catholic. She chose a good English Protestant. That's all there is to it.'

Ellen was silenced. Madeline Byrne might have married a Protestant but she was a Catholic to the marrow of her bones. Ellen and her sisters had been brought up Catholic and both Leonora and Lavinia had married Catholics. It was as clear as crystal that her mother had never doubted her faith.

'So, that's why she never came home, because your mother thought she'd turned her back on her faith? That's ridiculous. She's a devout Catholic. You know she goes to Mass every morning!'

'Your mother wanted a different life, Ellen,' said Johnny softly. 'No one turned her away and no one would have shunned her had she come home. It was her choice.'

'So, did you come here looking for something?' Dylan asked, gazing at her steadily. His eyes no longer had the look of madness, but of something sadder, the worn-out remnants of hope.

My freedom would be the honest answer, she thought, but

she replied: 'No, I came here by chance, actually. I never expected to stumble upon my long-lost family.' She dropped her gaze to her food. 'I don't suppose my mother ever expected me to want to find it.'

'So, she doesn't know you're here?' Dylan asked, but he nodded to himself as if something had just clicked into place. He grinned, eyes now flashing with renewed optimism. 'Sometimes fate lends a hand when people grow stubborn.'

Ellen frowned at him. 'You think I'm *meant* to find my family?' she asked.

'Aye, that's exactly what I mean.' He grinned at her and once again the warmth in his face took her by surprise. 'There's no such thing as coincidence, Ellen Olenska. Everything always happens for a reason.'

'She's a writer,' Johnny interrupted. 'She's come here to write about the castle and its ghosts.'

'A writer, eh? Fancy that,' Dylan murmured, the corners of his mouth beginning to twitch. 'So, you chose to come here to write your book when you could have gone anywhere in the world.' He nodded to himself again and stabbed at the last piece of sausage. 'Fancy that, eh?'

'Fate,' said Joe, winking at Ellen. 'Dylan *knows*.'

'Oswald says you know where all the leprechauns lie buried,' Ellen said to Dylan. 'Do you?'

'Oswald is crazy,' said Johnny. 'But he makes Peg happy.'

'He's a rotten painter,' Dylan added.

'But he's a demon at cards,' interjected Joe.

'He's a character,' Ellen said, picking up her glass of water. 'Wonderful characters are rare and must be treasured. So many people are regular, like bread sauce without any salt. I can't bear ordinary and bland. Oswald is made of primary colours. He's fabulously unique.'

'You *are* a writer, aren't you?' Dylan mused.

Ellen felt a terrible fraud and blushed. 'I'm afraid I'm not, really. I've had nothing published and I probably won't.'

'Yet,' said Dylan. 'You haven't had anything published *yet*.'

'Thank you for your encouragement.'

'He's a fortune-teller as well,' Johnny joked, now flushed with stout. 'Go on, Dylan. Tell her what's in her future.'

'You have writer's eyes,' Dylan continued, ignoring Johnny. 'Deep and enquiring.' She laughed, embarrassed. 'And you have a beautiful smile,' he added wistfully. 'Just like your mother.'

Chapter 6

Johnny dropped Ellen back at Peg's after lunch. She noticed that her aunt's car wasn't in front of the house and presumed she must be out, shopping for groceries perhaps. If Ellen were a proper writer she would now relish the opportunity of having some quiet time in the little sitting room in front of her laptop. As it was, she rather dreaded the idea of starting a novel, having never attempted to write one before. She lingered outside the front door, wondering what to do. With Peg gone she could call Emily in London from the house telephone and find out the news, but she wasn't sure she wanted to know that her mother was going crazy trying to track her down or that William was beside himself with anguish. She hadn't tossed her iPhone into the sea for nothing. She thrust her hands into her coat pockets and hunched her shoulders. The sky had clouded over, turning the air misty and damp. She could see the light-house looming out of the fog like a ghostly galleon. It looked lonely and cold out there. She wondered what on earth had possessed Caitlin Macausland to row out so often, and at night. She shuddered at the thought of being alone in the middle of the sea with only the gulls to talk to.

She decided to take a walk rather than face the empty house and her laptop, and set off into the field where Peg's woolly llama and weathered donkey munched the grass alongside her sheep. It was strange to be out of communication with her London life. She was so used to having access to her friends at the press of a button. Texts and emails had punctuated her days as often as commas and full stops on the page of a book. But now she had no means of getting in touch other than Aunt Peg's landline.

Connemara was so quiet. She could hear the cries of gulls, feel the wind on her face and the drizzle on her skin. She could hear the roar of the ocean and smell the salt and ozone that saturated the air. And as she did so she became aware of a stillness inside that she hadn't noticed before. In London, she was constantly on the run: running to get to work on time, running to a meeting, running to get ready to go out – always running, against a backdrop of constant noise. There was never any time to just *be*. Even when she was staying with friends in the countryside she was never alone like this: never alone and alert to the quiet stillness that is at the heart of every rock, flower and tree.

Here in Connemara, there was no reason to run anywhere. She had no alternative other than to 'be', and it was this surrender to the moment that made her realize just how hollow her life had previously been. She wondered now, as she strode down the hill towards the sea, whether she had been deliberately running into a future of promise with William to release her from an unsatisfactory present at home. And what *was* her present? *Why* was it so unsatisfactory? The stillness enabled her to see her situation more clearly, as if the answer had always been there, unnoticed, a small voice fighting to be heard against the racket of her running. It was unsatisfactory because it hadn't belonged to her. She had been living the life her parents wanted for her, but it wasn't the life she wished for herself. She was tired of the constant struggle to conform to their expectations, the relentless effort of pretending to be something she was not, as if she had been wearing an ill-fitting suit and had now, at last, burst out of it.

She realized, as she walked past the abandoned house on the beach, that she was also running from herself. She didn't like the person she had become or the person she would grow into were she to follow her sisters' carefully prepared path into a materially comfortable but soulless existence as Mrs William Sackville. There was something dreadfully empty about the routine of her daily life in London: the parties, the air-kissing, the fair-weather friends, the shopping and lunching. There was no depth to it. It gave her no sense of fulfilment. She braced herself against the wind and walked up the sand just out of reach of the waves. Leonora and Lavinia would laugh at her if she told them she was sick of holidays in St Barts, sick of reading glossy magazines by the pool that promised happiness with a new a lipstick or handbag, sick of skiing in St Moritz, sick of the people – the endless shallow people who live for invitations and for moving in the right circles; the heaving mass of superficial, socially upwardly mobile *people*. She chuckled bitterly, astonished by the sudden clarity of her vision and the fact that she was talking out loud like a woman possessed. Her mother would take her to visit her therapist, her father would stare at her in bewilderment, shaking his head once again at the child he had never understood. But the truth was, none of it made her happy. Oh, there were moments of happiness, many of them, but they were as fleeting as bursts of sunshine; deep down in her soul she was restless – and unhappy.

She had always had a strong desire to create something. Whether a book, a poem, a song or a garden – she didn't know quite what yet; she just knew that she wanted to express herself somehow. As a teenager she had taught herself the guitar, but when she had requested lessons at school her mother had screwed up her nose and replied that she didn't want her daughter joining a band 'or anything silly like that' and signed her up for extra French lessons instead, because apparently, according to her mother, every young lady should speak French. So she had formed a band to spite her and written pop songs with her friends, performing at school concerts her parents weren't invited to. She had dabbled at writing stories, been very good at art and had sung in the choir. But she had fallen in with a gaggle of rebellious girls and spent most of her teens behind hedges smoking cigarettes and bitching about authority, rather than doing the things that would have made her spirit grow. She regretted all that wasted time now. She regretted having let the creative part of herself wither. But it was never too late to let the sunshine in. There was still time to write the book, compose the song, plant the garden. Right now, life seemed to be opening up for her like a surprise door onto a vast new horizon.

She took a deep breath and her shoulders dropped. Here in this beautiful place she felt peace – the peace that comes only from being in harmony with nature. The feeling of joy was so strong she began to cry. It was so surprising that she began to laugh at the same time. She had never laughed and cried together, and with such abandon. It was the most wonderful feeling she had ever had. The clouds grew grey and heavy and it began to rain. Her faux-fur jacket, which was so inappropriate on that beach, quickly became sodden and clung to her like the soggy hair of a dog. If it hadn't been so cold she would have taken it off and tossed it into the sea, to die a watery death with her iPhone.

The trouble was, she didn't know what or who she wanted to be. She just knew that she didn't like the person she was. One thing she was sure about, however, was that she wasn't going to go back to London until she had achieved a sense of who she *really* was, beneath her parents' conditioning. Until then, she was going to stay in Connemara. She began to walk back up the beach in the direction of Peg's house. The rain was falling heavily now and she was wet to the bone. She quickened her pace and shivered as a drop of water rolled down her back. If she was going to stay with Peg, she'd better pay rent, she thought. It was obvious that Peg didn't have a lot of money and it wouldn't be fair to sponge off her, however convenient that might be. If she stayed more than a week it would only be right to contribute something.

When she reached the hill she almost ran. The thought of a hot bath and a cup of tea spurred her on. She stumbled up the sodden grass, past nonchalant sheep who were perfectly dry beneath their woolly coats, and the poor old donkey, who looked rather bedraggled and miserable in the rain even though there was a shed for him at the bottom of the hill so he could shelter out of the wind. The house came into view and she wasn't surprised to see more than one vehicle parked outside. It was becoming clear that Peg's large family ensured that she was never lonely.

She burst in, sending Mr Badger leaping into the hall with excitement. Bertie the pig remained in front of the Stanley, snoring loudly. Peg jumped up from her chair where she was having a cup of tea with a young man. 'Jaysus, child, will you look at you? Where have you been? Did Johnny leave you up at the castle? Take that jacket off at once and I'll hang it up to dry.'

'I went for a walk,' Ellen explained, peeling off her jacket like a skin.

'In this weather? Are you off your head?'

'Throw the jacket away. I've ruined it.'

'Animals are meant to get wet,' interjected the young man dryly.

'Not fake ones,' Ellen retorted.

Peg gestured to the man. 'This is my son, Ronan.' The young man, who appeared to be about the same age as Ellen, looked up from beneath a thick blond fringe but didn't smile.

'I would shake your hand,' said Ellen apologetically. 'But I'll only get it wet.'

'I'll shake it when you're dry, then,' Ronan replied.

'I think I'd better go up and have a bath.'

'I think you'd better, pet. Really, you Londoners know nothing about the countryside, do you?' Peg turned to her son. 'You should see the boots she came in . . .'

As Ellen made her way upstairs, she reflected on the members of her family she had met that day. They were all very handsome, with intense eyes and strong characters. It was almost as if she had walked through C. S. Lewis's wardrobe into an enchanting new world that had always been there beyond the fur coats. For a moment she felt a wave of anger that her mother had hidden them all away: after all, they were Ellen's family too! And what about Lavinia and Leonora? How could their mother have simply erased them from their lives as well? What could she have done that was so dreadful as to make her return impossible? Didn't the memories of her childhood count for anything? Didn't they keep her awake at night? Did she miss her family?

Ellen bathed in hot water, steaming up the windows as the rain pelted against the glass like pebbles. When she went back downstairs in a pair of jeans and sweater, her aunt was still at the kitchen table with Ronan. 'Come and have a nice cup of tea, pet,' she said, getting up to fetch the kettle from the stove where it was keeping warm. 'You look better now. What have you done with your wet clothes?'

'They're in the bathroom,' Ellen replied, sitting down opposite Ronan.

'Well, they're not going to get dry in there, are they? Bring them down here later and we'll hang them over the Stanley.'

'Ah, cake,' Ellen exclaimed hungrily, glancing at Jack who was perched on his usual chair. 'I'm surprised that bird hasn't scoffed the lot,' she said to Ronan.

'He knows he'll be shooed away,' Ronan replied. 'It's good. Have a slice.'

Ellen cut herself some cake and Peg set about making a fresh pot of tea.

'So, I suppose those boys took you to the pub for lunch?' said Peg, sitting down again with the pot and a mug for her niece.

'Yes, I met Dylan Murphy,' she replied, watching her aunt carefully.

'Oh, Dylan. He's a character,' Peg replied, giving nothing away.

Ellen decided to come straight to the point. 'He loved Mum, didn't he?' Peg paused the flow of tea. For a moment she seemed lost for words. 'I could tell. He was staring at me with these big, sad eyes.'

'Trying to find your mother in your face, no doubt,' said Peg, pouring again.

'So, what's his story?'

'Dylan? I suppose there's nothing wrong with telling you the truth. It was a long time ago now. This will be new to you, too, Ronan.' She poured milk into her cup and stirred it thoughtfully. 'Dylan grew up with all of us, but he always loved Maddie the most. She loved him for a time, too. But then she met your father and, well, the rest is history, isn't it?'

'It's a history I'd like to know,' Ellen persisted. Peg sighed and helped herself to another slice of cake. Ellen thought she did so out of nervousness. 'Please, Aunt Peg. I think I have a right to know, now I'm here. If you don't tell me, someone else will, eventually.'

'Very well. The truth is that she was engaged to Dylan when she met your father.'

Ellen was astonished. 'She was going to marry Dylan?'

Ronan looked as surprised as his cousin. 'Get a load of that!' he exclaimed, his serious face breaking into a smirk. 'Old Dylan Murphy, the dark horse.'

'He was very handsome when he was younger, you know.' Peg smiled at her niece. 'A lot of women think he's even more handsome now. He's never married, probably because he still holds a candle for your mam. Poor old Martha has the patience of Jove and she's a good woman. He'd do well to marry her, but I'm not sure he'll ever let your mother go.'

'No wonder he looked at me like he did.'

'We all assumed she'd walk up the aisle with Dylan. They were so well suited, like a pea and a pod. They were both bohemian and creative. But then she met your father.'

'How? What was he doing over here?'

'He was spending the summer with the Martins, who used to own the castle.'

'He was staying up at the castle? The same castle I visited today?'

'The very same. Conor Macausland bought it off Peter Martin. It nearly killed the poor man, having to sell it. The Martins had owned it for generations, you know. But Peter had a building business that hit some trouble and he ran out of money. They moved to Australia, of all places. I suppose to put as much distance between them and Ballymaldoon Castle as they possibly could.'

'How weird! To think that my parents met here and I never knew.'

'Where did you think they met?' Ronan asked.

It was at that moment that Ellen realized her parents had lied to her. 'Scotland,' she replied quietly. 'Mum said they met at a shooting party in Scotland.'

'As if your mother would have been at a shooting party,' Peg scoffed, nearly spilling her tea. 'Really, I know she always had aspirations of grandeur, but to suggest she was living that kind of life is ridiculous, to say the least. She'd never set a foot out of Ireland!'

'Did you even know she was Irish?' Ronan asked.

Ellen felt herself bristle. Ronan was looking at her with an incredulous expression on his face, as if he thought her a simpleton for having been so gullible. 'Of course I knew she was Irish, but she's never really talked about Ireland. She only ever mentioned you, Peg, and never when she thought we were listening. If I asked about the past, she'd purse her lips and change the subject. We knew not to probe and to be honest, we weren't really very interested. Was it really considered so terrible to run off with an English Protestant, Aunt Peg?'

Peg toyed with her teacup thoughtfully. 'I don't think it was the fact that your father was an English Protestant that was the problem,' she began slowly. 'It was the fact that she was meant to be walking down the aisle with Dylan. One day she was planning her wedding, the next she was packing her bag and leaving in haste.'

'So she really did elope?'

'I'm afraid she did.' She hesitated, as if she knew something she wasn't willing to divulge, and then added quietly: 'She was carrying on with your father behind Dylan's back. It wasn't kind, considering how devoted he was to her. That's why she didn't come back. Because she felt guilty,' she said firmly.

'But to feel guilty for over thirty years is a little dramatic.'

Peg seemed keen to close the subject. 'She chose a different life, pet. She married a rich man, started a new life and didn't want to have anything to do with her old one, and that's all there is to it.'

Ellen was mortified. 'Was she ashamed of you?'

'I think so,' Peg replied softly. 'I don't think we were good enough for her. She had aspirations, did Maddie. She was always going to be a princess, one way or another. She didn't want the life Dylan offered her. She wanted something better and the minute the opportunity arose, she grabbed it, regardless of breaking poor Dylan's heart. Don't forget she was very beautiful and beguiling, Ellen. She had only to click her fingers and the men would be down on one knee, offering her the world if they could get it.' Peg bit off a piece of cake. 'I suppose she got the world.'

'But to not include you all in *our* lives is so selfish.'

'I'm afraid Maddie was always rather a selfish girl.'

'It's so unfair,' said Ellen passionately. 'I wish I had known you my whole life.'

Peg's face softened. 'That's very sweet of you, pet. But don't get emotional. Your mother did what she felt was best, and you and your sisters have done all right, haven't you? But now you've found us, you've really gone and put the cat among the pigeons. Lord knows what she'll do when she finds out.' Peg looked anxious. 'Don't you be letting on to her that I've gone and told you the whole story!'

'Of course not. You have my word. But it makes me so cross. I don't ever want to go back.'

Peg gave her a stern look. 'Then you'll be just as bad as your mother.' Ellen realized that, in fleeing from her own wedding, she already was.

'Poor Dylan,' she said sadly. She took a sip of tea. She'd been talking so much it was almost cold.

'Let me give you another cup,' Peg suggested, getting up. 'You know, people are the sum of their experiences. It's easy to see why Dylan took to the booze when you consider his past. He was a very happy boy growing up, but Maddie broke his heart. He never recovered. He was desperately hurt. He's had a sadness about him ever since. I think his life has been a big disappointment.'

Ronan's face crumpled into a frown. 'I never knew that, Mam. Poor sod! It's a brutal thing to love and lose like that.'

'What does he do?' Ellen asked.

'He's a songwriter. He's very talented. Such a shame he turned to the bottle because I think he could have really made something out of his life. He used to have a band, you know. It was quite successful once, in Ireland at least.' Peg laughed. 'Hard to imagine now, isn't it? He plays the guitar and sings.' Ellen wondered whether her mother's decision not to give her guitar lessons had had anything to do with Dylan.

'And now he props up the bar,' interjected Ronan sadly. 'Poor sod!' he repeated. 'I always thought he was a bit of a joke. What an eejit!'

'Don't be hard on yourself, Ronan. You weren't to know.' She turned to Ellen. 'He wrote for himself in the beginning, but then he stopped performing, so he wrote for other bands,' she continued. 'You'd be amazed if you knew some of the big stars who sing his songs. He had great success with one or two ballads. If you give me a moment, I'm sure I could hum them.'

'What do *you* do, Ronan?' Ellen asked, noticing that he was very quiet and wanting to bring him into the conversation.

'I'm a carpenter,' he replied defensively, challenging her with a look.

'Don't be defensive, Ronan,' chided his mother. 'There's nothing wrong with being a carpenter. You're a very good carpenter. He can do anything with wood, anything at all. You look at all those fancy pictures of kitchens in magazines and Ronan can copy any one of them. You'd never know the difference. He's very talented.'

'She would say that, wouldn't she?' He rolled his eyes, looking uncomfortable.

'He did a lot of work for Caitlin Macausland up at the castle.'

At the mention of Caitlin's name Ronan's face grew dark and sulky. 'Yes, well, that was a long time ago. I've done plenty of stuff since.'

'Ronan doesn't like to be tied down,' Peg continued, to her son's embarrassment. 'He likes to work for himself, when it suits him.'

'Being self-employed is a real privilege,' said Ellen, wanting Ronan to smile again. 'I'm trying to be a writer. I've just spent the last six years of my life working in the marketing department of a jewellery company in London and I hate being chained to an office from nine to five. I try so hard to be on time but I'm late every morning. I'd do anything to be my own boss like you.'

'So, what have you written?' he asked.

'Nothing very good yet, but I'm hoping to be inspired down here.'

'She can base a story around the castle and the lighthouse,' Peg suggested.

'Why?' he asked.

'Because they're surrounded by mystery,' his mother answered.

'Do you want to write a *murder* mystery?' he asked Ellen.

'Now that's enough, Ronan!' Peg exclaimed crossly. 'I don't want to hear any of your nonsense on that subject. I wish I hadn't brought it up.'

'Because there's one hell of a story for you here.'

Ellen interrupted. 'Oh, I'm not going to write *their* story. Goodness, I know nothing about it. I simply find the ruined lighthouse and castle romantic.'

'Not a lot of romance there, I don't think,' he said, chuckling cynically. 'The two of them were at each other's throats like a pair of rats.'

'Now why speak of them like that, Ronan? You were once full of admiration for her,' said Peg.

'I saw her portrait today. She was very beautiful, wasn't she?' Ellen commented.

Ronan cut himself a slice of cake. 'But that counts for nothing now she's dead,' he said.

Ellen put down her mug. 'Tell me, why did he take everything out of the castle and leave only that painting? Why would he do that? Wouldn't he want to take the painting with him?'

Ronan sighed impatiently. 'Perhaps it's too big to put up in his house? I don't know. What does it matter?'

'I'm curious. I mean, why not pack it away? But to leave it in the house is spooky, isn't it? It's like she's still there.'

'I don't know, Ellen, and I don't care,' he replied gruffly.

Peg smiled at her son indulgently. 'Don't mind Ronan, Ellen, he's just tired of it all.'

'Spend a little more time here and you'll tire of it all, too, I promise you,' said Ronan. 'It's all anyone can talk about, still!' He bit into the cake and chewed vigorously.

Now Peg nodded in agreement. 'Well, you're right about that, Ronan. Five years on and they're still talking about it. Mind you, it's hard not to when the lighthouse is sitting in front of their noses as a constant reminder.'

'Is that why you don't go to the pub, Aunt Peg?' Ellen asked. 'Because you're sick of the gossip?'

'No, I don't go to the pub because I like to keep myself to myself,' she replied tightly. 'Why don't you take Ellen, Ronan? Joe said he would, but I'll tell him you've already gone. You can introduce her to the rest of the family.'

He looked at his cousin quizzically, raising an eyebrow. 'Do you think you're ready for an overdose of Byrnes?'

'I don't know. I might be happier staying here playing cards with Oswald and Aunt Peg.'

'You said you don't play cards, pet, and there's no television. So, you might as well go with Ronan. He'll look after you, won't you, Ronan?'

'You'll be just grand,' he said, but he still hadn't given her a smile. Ellen hoped she could coax one out of him in the Pot of Gold. 'I have to drop my tools off at home first,' he said, getting up. 'If you don't mind stopping by at mine then I'll take you.'

'I don't mind at all,' said Ellen, compensating for his sulkiness by being overenthusiastic. 'I'd love to see where you work.'

'Oh, Ronan's workshop is a treasure trove,' Peg gushed.

'Yes, Mam, like Michelangelo's!' he retorted, but when he looked at her his face softened and one corner of his lips grinned reluctantly.

Chapter 7

It didn't take long to drive to Ronan's cottage. Positioned between his mother's and Ballymaldoon, it had the same spell-binding view of the sea. He pulled up his van in front of the house and hauled his heavy toolbox out of the back. 'You can come and have a look if you want,' he said to Ellen. 'My workshop is round the back.' She followed him along a path that cut through the long grasses and weeds to the end of a very unkempt garden. The light was fading now, the early stars twinkling in the darkening sky like distant boats approaching through mist. The air was damp and chilly and a sharp wind blew in off the sea. Ellen pulled the coat she had borrowed from her aunt tightly across her body and shivered.

Ronan's workshop was a large wooden shed, built up against a high grassy bank. It looked unremarkable from the outside, yet when he opened the door and switched on the lights, Ellen realized that this was indeed a treasure trove as Peg had said. Rows of tools hung in neat racks on the walls, planks of wood lay in tidy piles, strange machines rose out of mounds of wood shavings and a sturdy workbench was positioned in the middle of the room with various tools slotted into ingenious, tailor-made slots. That in itself was like a work of art. She ran her fingers along the surface, marvelling at the cleverness

of design. 'You invented this, didn't you?' she said and he must
have detected the admiration in her voice, for he put down his
toolbox and began to show her around.

'Necessity is the mother of invention,' he told her. 'So, I've
made things along the way for my own use, as I've needed
them, to make my work more efficient.'

'Your mother is right, you really can fashion anything out
of wood.'

'Oh, this is nothing. This is just my workplace,' he replied.
'Would you like to see my portfolio?'

'I'd love to,' she replied, watching the pride turn his cheeks
pink as he pulled out a large black book of photographs from
behind his desk and brushed the dust off with his fingers. 'I
don't show it very often, as everyone knows me here and most
of my jobs come by word of mouth. But I keep a record of
everything I've made, for my sake more than anything else.
I'm fond of them, I suppose.' At that, he finally smiled. Ellen
felt her spirits rise on it, like a glider on a thermal. They sat
at the workbench and Ronan showed her all his commissions.
There were complete kitchens and bathrooms, a child's
Wendy house, dressers, tables and chairs.

'How did you learn to do this?' she asked, taking a closer
look at the intricate heart carvings in the shutters of the playhouse.

'Well, my uncle Ryan has a building company and his carpenter, Lee, is a wizard with wood. He taught me everything.'

'You were apprenticed?'

'For eight years. Then Lee retired and I worked for Ryan,
then set up on my own. I had made a name for myself by
then.'

Ellen turned the page and instantly recognized a bench by
the castle lake. 'Ah, this must have been for Caitlin Macausland.'

She felt him stiffen beside her. 'It's a lovely bench,' she added, hastily. She soon realized, as she turned the pages, that Ronan had made her more than just a bench. There was a seat that encircled a tree, a pentagon-shaped summer house, a swing chair, a garden gate and cold frames in the vegetable garden. 'Goodness, you're prolific. I bet you didn't have time to work for anyone else when you were working for her.'

He nodded. 'That's true. She gave me the chance to make things most carpenters only dream about.'

'You must have known her very well,' she murmured without thinking. Then, remembering his earlier reaction to the subject, she added, 'I'm sorry. I know how sick you are of the whole business.'

'I'm sick of the lies, Ellen,' he replied, to her surprise, then took a deep breath. 'Everybody claims to know something, but they know nothing. There are only two people who know what really happened that night at the lighthouse. One won't talk and the other can't.'

'So, if you don't know anything either, how come you're so sure he killed her?' she asked, smiling to make light of her comment. 'Aren't you just as bad as everyone else?'

He inhaled through dilated nostrils. 'I knew her and I know that she was frightened of him. He has one hell of a temper on him. I think he'd be capable of anything, in a fit of anger.'

'So, we're not talking about murder then?'

'Well, if you're going to nit-pick, call it manslaughter. But he killed her one way or another.'

'But you don't really know.'

'No, I don't,' he agreed, grudgingly. Then, without being able to find anything more substantial on which to base his opinion, he closed the book. 'But he's to blame, all right. I'd bet my life on it,' he added resolutely, and Ellen deduced from the hardening of his profile that he *wanted* to believe it. She wondered whether there was a man in Ballymaldoon who wasn't a little in love with Caitlin. 'I don't know about you, but I need a drink,' he said, getting up. He replaced the portfolio behind his desk and switched off the lights.

When Ellen and Ronan arrived at the Pot of Gold it was full of locals. The air was misty with body heat and smoke from the open fireplace, and it was very noisy. The clamour of voices hushed a little, however, when Ellen walked in, and she could see unfamiliar faces craning their necks to get a better look at her. She was relieved to see Johnny and Joe at a table against the wall and hurried over to join them.

'You're like a film star,' Johnny commented when she reached him. 'They'll be asking for your autograph next.'

'And I'll be charging a pound a turn,' Joe added, rubbing his hands together. Ellen recognized Desmond, who introduced her to his wife Alanna, a fair-skinned, fine-boned woman with strawberry-blonde hair falling in curls over her narrow shoulders. She smiled and patted the bench beside her.

'Come and sit next to me, love. I've heard nothing all day except how beautiful you are. Joe, go and get her something to drink. What would you like? I'm having a vodka tonic.'

'I know what she *won't* be having, right, Ellen?' He grinned playfully and winked at her.

She smiled back, his teasing giving her a pleasant sense of belonging. 'I wanted to impress you,' she retorted.

'Well, you might have fooled Dad but you didn't fool me.' He threw his head back and laughed.

Alanna was confused. 'What's all this about?'

'You should have seen the look on her face when she tried to drink a Guinness this afternoon. Priceless, it was!'

'Oh, quit codding about, Joe!' Alanna jumped to Ellen's defence. 'Don't listen to him, he's always acting the maggot and no one takes any notice!'

'Don't think I won't get my own back, Joe Byrne!' Ellen answered.

'I wait with bated breath. So, what'll it be, then?'

'The same as Alanna, please.'

'Good, I'd be ashamed to ask for water!' Joe disappeared into the crowd.

'Now who else don't you know here?' Alanna wondered, narrowing her eyes and looking about the room.

Ellen noticed Dylan's dark presence at the bar. He was deep in conversation with Ronan, drinking a glass of Guinness. Occasionally, he looked up beneath his wild black fringe and his piercing black eyes watched her like a buzzard watching his prey. She tried to ignore him. After all, there was nothing she could do about his hopeless love for her mother. She wondered whether, if he met her now, he'd regret having wasted so many years in pining.

Ellen concentrated on meeting her uncles' wives and grown-up children. She couldn't imagine ever remembering all their names. She had more cousins than she could have dreamed of. Her family life in London seemed sterile and dull by comparison with this jolly clan of Byrnes. They certainly made a lot of noise. It wasn't long before a sea-weathered fisherman called Eddie began to play the accordion and the pub burst into raucous singing.

Ellen thought of Caitlin Macausland, singing along with the best of them, as Joe had put it. She could imagine her in the midst of all these people, shining brighter and more beautiful than an angel, among them but tantalizingly out of reach. No wonder her death still shocked and saddened people. Ellen suspected she had grown more intriguing in death than she had been in life. That was always the way.

'So, how are you enjoying staying with Peg?' Alanna asked when the singing had died down and people started to leave.

'I love Aunt Peg already,' Ellen replied truthfully. 'She's such a sweet lady.'

'She must love having you around the house.'

'I hope I'm not going to be a burden.'

'Not at all. I'm sure she'll be very happy with the company.'

'She has Ronan.'

'Yes, he looks out for his mam. He's a good boy, complicated though, I warn you.'

'He's serious, not like Joe.'

She laughed. 'Oh, we have the craic all right with Joe!'

'I really like Johnny and Joe. I don't ever want to go back to London.'

'Of course you don't. You've only just arrived.'

'I feel at home already.'

'Connemara does that to people.' She laughed lightly. 'Look, I was born here, as were all the Byrnes, and we're all still here. Is there any reason why you have to go back?'

Ellen sighed. She longed to be honest and tell her new family that she had left a fiancé in London but she cared too much about what they thought of her. 'Well, I haven't told my mother that I'm here,' she said, which was true, at least.

'Yes, Desmond told me.'

'So, I'll have to let her know at some stage, won't I?'

'Just let her know you're safe. That's all mothers worry about. Then she'll leave you in peace.'

'I'm not so sure. I think she'll be furious with me for digging up her past.'

'Do you have to tell her?'

'Well, I'm not letting on at the moment. I'm going to stay with Aunt Peg for a while and write my novel . . .'

'What's it about?'

'I'm not sure. I'm hoping to be inspired here.'

'Oh, you'll definitely be inspired,' she laughed.

'I could write about Aunt Peg and all her animals. That alone would make an amusing read.'

'I know, she fills the place with them, doesn't she? And animals aren't stupid; if there's a wounded one, or perhaps one who just wants a warm night's sleep, he'll find his way to Peg's.'

'It's a shame she doesn't come to the pub.'

Alanna's face grew serious. 'She doesn't feel comfortable with all the gossip.'

'That's what she said.'

'There's *always* gossip in a small town like Ballymaldoon.'

'Astonishing still to be gossiping about Caitlin and Conor Macausland after all these years.'

'Oh, it's not that kind of gossip that stops her coming to the pub. It's gossip about *her.*'

'But why would they gossip about Peg?'

Alanna put down her glass and lowered her voice. 'You know that your aunt lost a little girl, don't you?'

Ellen stared at her in horror. 'No, I didn't know. When?'

'Many years ago now. She had her boys and then she had a little girl called Ciara.'

'What happened to her?'

'She died when she was seven, bless her. It was a terrible tragedy.'

'How did she die?'

'She drowned in the sea. It was an accident, of course. But Peg has never got over it. I don't think a mother ever gets over losing a child, she just learns to live with it.'

'God, that's awful,' Ellen gasped. She envisaged Peg's lonely figure striding out across the field to see to her sheep and knew now why she had an air of sorrow about her. 'Did they find her?'

'Yes, they'd only taken their eyes off her for a moment and there she was face down in the water. They'd been arguing about something, so, naturally, they blamed themselves. The marriage was a difficult one before that, but afterwards it became intolerable.'

'Oh, poor Peg. That's terrible. What a burden to carry around.'

'Her brothers look after her. They're very protective. And she has Ronan just down the road. No one talks about it, but we're all aware. It's impossible to move beyond something like that.'

'So, that's why her husband went to live in America.'

'A tragedy like that either binds you tighter together, or pulls you apart. In their case, it pulled them apart. It was no one's fault, but they blamed each other and themselves and when Bill said he wanted to leave, Peg dug her heels in. She wanted to stay to be close to Ciara. She's buried in the church here.'

Ellen's heart went out to Peg. She realized now why she had looked so sad when she had spoken in the car about her ex-husband and his daughter.

'Is that why she still calls herself Peg *Byrne*?'

'She's always been Peg Byrne in spite of her married name. It never stuck.' Alanna patted her arm and gave her a mean-ingful stare. 'You won't mention this, will you?'

'No, of course I won't.'

'I probably shouldn't have told you, but if you're going to be living with her, it's important that you understand why she is the way she is.'

'I don't imagine my mother knows.'

'No, she wouldn't do. When your mother left, I think Ronan hadn't yet been born.'

'I'm sure she'd be devastated that she wasn't there to comfort her own sister when she lost a child.'

'Don't tell her. It's for Peg to tell her, should she ever want to.'

'I won't, I promise.'

Ellen left the pub feeling low. Johnny, his wife, Emer, and Joe dropped her back at Peg's on their way home, too merry to notice the change in her mood. She remained a moment outside as their tail lights disappeared down the hill and into the lane. The lighthouse was silhouetted against the sky, which was now clear and starry. She thought of Ciara drowning in that sea and wondered how Peg could bear to look at it every morning when she opened her curtains. Perhaps it gave her comfort to think of her child's spirit out there, not too far away. Maybe her proximity to the place where her daughter drowned made her feel close to her child.

She stood there in the damp, gazing out at the vast horizon and wide sea. A crescent moon shone brightly, like the wind filled sail of a little boat, dribbling a pale ribbon of silver onto the water as it slowly climbed the sky. Ellen felt fonder of Peg now that she knew the sad undercurrent of her life. Oswald must know too, she thought, for he was her close companion and probably her confidant. She remembered the breakfast scene that morning and the cheerful banter between Peg and her brothers. There was consolation in a big family. She thought of hers back in London. There was little consolation in that.

Later, she lay in bed and listened to the roar of the sea and the moaning of the wind as it blew around the corners of the house. It was a soothing lullaby. There were no wailing sirens, buzzing motorbikes or cars. No voices of drunken revellers staggering up the street after a heavy night out and no noisy neighbours playing loud music. The sounds of the countryside were soft and mysterious, and the darkness deep and impenetrable. It wasn't long before Ellen drifted off to sleep.

In the morning, she awoke to the cry of a lapwing and Mr Badger's barking as he chased sheep around the field with Peg. She lay a moment, savouring the novelty of not having to get up to go to work. The day spread out before her like the blank pages of her novel. She could make it up as she went along.

'So, how was the pub last night?' Peg asked, as Ellen tucked into her bowl of porridge.

'Very noisy,' she replied. 'I met so many relations. You seem to dominate this town.'

'I think we do. Though there are a few other big families besides us.' Peg hand-fed Jack a small lump of bread. He grabbed it greedily in his beak. 'So, what are you going to do today? Are you going to start writing?'

'I think I'll go for a long walk and maybe try and work out a plot in the afternoon.'

'That's a good idea, pet. There are plenty of nice places to walk around here.'

Ellen took a sip of tea and wondered why it tasted better in Peg's kitchen than her own. 'Can I get you anything in town?'

'What do you mean?'

'Food?'

'Oh, that. No, I went out to get the messages yesterday.'

Ellen assumed messages meant groceries. She was beginning

to get used to their Irish accents and slang. 'I'd like to contribute, Aunt Peg.'

Peg's face flowered into a smile. 'So, you like it here, do
you?'

'Yes.'

'Good.' Ellen looked baffled. 'Well, if you want to contribute that means you're intending to stay a while. No one
offers to contribute if they're only staying a few days.'

Ellen smiled back, a little embarrassed. 'If that's all right?'

'Of course it's all right, pet. You can stay as long as you
want. There's no one angling for your bedroom.'

'Then I shall claim it for now.'

'That's grand. Now don't be silly. If I need you to contribute, I'll ask you. I call a spade a spade, so you'll know.'

'OK, deal.'

'Now, it's a beautiful day, so you'll have a nice time exploring. You can take my car if you like. I'm not going anywhere
today.'

'Do you think Johnny and Joe will mind if I wander around
up at the castle?'

'I suspect they'll be delighted. Any excuse to stop working.'
She clicked her tongue. 'I can't imagine those two getting
anything done up there. When Mrs Macausland was alive they
were always planting and planning new things to do to the
gardens. My Ronan built a bench around a tree so she could
sit and enjoy the lake, and he built a tree house, too, for the
children. She was full of ideas. I think she must have been
bored.'

'I got the impression that Ronan really liked her.'

'That he did. He made a lot of money out of her commissions.' She chuckled fondly at the mention of her son. 'Ronan
was a little star-struck, I think. He became very angry when

she died. He ranted on about how Mr Macausland had killed her and really, we all got quite fed up with him. The police never arrested anyone and there was no proof whatsoever that there was any foul play, but Ronan was adamant. The truth is that no one knows what happened there that night, not Ronan, not anybody but Mr Macausland. Ronan can think what he likes. Now he doesn't like to talk about her – or for anyone else to, for that matter.'

'I can understand that. He was one of the only people here who really knew her.'

'Well, she didn't belong to him, but she had a talent for making everyone who met her feel special. Ronan thought he was special, but so did Johnny and Joe, too. She was as captivating as an enchantress and they all fell for her charms. So, it's understandable that he was affected by her death. Death is so final. It's hard to come to terms with it.' Ellen looked away. Now that she knew about the tragedy of Peg's little girl she felt uncomfortable looking at her when she talked about death, as if to watch her face would somehow be intrusive.

A while later, Ellen drove beneath the burr oaks to Ballymaldoon Castle. Having initially found the place frightening, she was now drawn by its beauty. The sun shone through the branches, projecting crisscross patterns that quivered on the drive as the wind gently blew them. In the dazzling light of day the castle itself looked benign, its towers and turrets the stuff of fairy tales. Johnny's red truck was parked in front of the castle beside another little car that probably belonged to a cleaner or caretaker. As much as she wanted to look around the castle interior, she knew that might be considered prying were she to be caught. So she contented herself with the grounds instead.

She wandered about looking for Johnny and Joe, but the estate was so big and full of walled gardens, arboretums and orchards that she gave up after a while and set off she knew not where. Every now and then the sun disappeared behind a cloud, plunging her into shade, only to re-emerge a minute later, chasing the shadows down the hills and across the valley. It was a dramatic sight. She felt her spirits lift and her chest expand with happiness as she marched alone over the wild terrain. She climbed steep slopes and jumped over little streams, clambered up rocky crags and scaled meandering stone walls. The sound of birdsong filled the air and the breeze was rich with the smell of fertile soil and pink Irish heather that grew up from the rocks, giving the stark landscape a surprising flourish of colour. She lost herself in nature, letting her curiosity take her further into the wilderness.

She walked for a long time. She didn't know how long because she hadn't remembered to put on her watch that morning. Her stomach told her that it must be near lunchtime and she cursed herself for not having brought a biscuit at the very least. Trying to remember which way she'd come, she began to retrace her steps. The trouble was, every hill and vale looked the same to her inexperienced eye. Just when she thought she was on the right track, another horizon rose up to contradict her.

At first, she didn't panic. She was sure she'd hit a path eventually, or spot the castle towers or even the sea. She grew thirsty and her legs got heavier with each step but the splendour of the landscape distracted her from discomfort and her spirits remained optimistic. She walked for about half an hour before deciding to climb the hill to the top. Surely from up there she would see the castle and be able to navigate her way back. Hastily she set off, her throat tightening with anxiety. But as she neared the crest she became aware that behind it was simply another peak to climb. She was nowhere near the top; she was well and truly lost. At that point she panicked. What if she never found her way home? Would she die out there from exposure? It was mid February, after all. Would anybody know where to look for her? If she screamed would anyone but the birds hear her?

Just when her courage was about to slump, she heard the sound of whistling followed by a man's voice shouting for his dog. Her heart leapt at the prospect of being rescued and she ran as fast as her tired legs could carry her in the direction of the voice. She scrambled over rocks and stumbled down the slope until she almost skidded straight into a big chestnut horse and his rider, walking over the brow of the mountain towards her.

The horse tossed back his head in surprise and lifted his front legs off the ground. The man steadied his steed with an experienced hand and glared down at Ellen in fury. 'What the devil do you think you're doing?'

But Ellen didn't hear him, so great was her relief. 'Thank God!' she panted, staggering out of the way. She was gasping for breath and flushed from running, and the desire to cry was almost overwhelming. She didn't notice the man's irritation, which quickly gave way to a grudging concern when he saw how frightened she was.

'Are you all right?' he asked brusquely. His Irish accent was mild compared with the Byrnes'. She nodded vigorously, catching her breath. 'Magnum!' he bellowed. A moment later an enormous pale-brown mastiff appeared over the lip of a knoll and came trotting towards them.

'That's a very big dog,' she said as the muscles in her legs suddenly began to shake from fatigue.

'Don't worry, he won't eat you. You're too small.' He

appraised her curiously, after which his tone softened. 'You're not from here, are you?'

'No, I'm from London.'

'You've come a long way.' The corners of his mouth curled into the beginnings of a smile.

His joke inspired a weak smile in return. 'I mean, *originally* from London. I'm staying with my aunt.'

'Who is?'

'Peg Byrne.'

He nodded in acknowledgement. 'Another family member, eh?' He looked her up and down.

'Yes, there are an awful lot of us, aren't there?'

'What's your name, then?'

'Ellen.'

'And what are you doing out here?'

The commanding tone in his voice made her heart give a sudden thump. She stared up at his face, partly obscured by a brown fedora hat and a soft black beard, and recognized his features from the mental picture she had drawn during her conversations with Johnny and Joe. He was handsome, with dark skin and the brightest cornflower-blue eyes she had ever seen, deep set and framed by thick black lashes. His hair reached his shoulders and looked like it hadn't been brushed in a very long time. He stared down at her imperiously, waiting for her response, and she guessed at once who he was. It couldn't be anyone else. He had the air of a man who owned every inch of those mountains.

'I'm afraid I'm trespassing,' she said, forgetting her exhaustion now that she knew who she was talking to.

He nodded. 'I'm afraid you are.' But his smile reassured her that he wasn't angry. 'Conor Macausland. This is my land and I'd hazard a guess that you're lost.'

'Yes, I was so happy walking I didn't imagine I'd be unable to find my way back. I didn't intend to stray so far.'

'Where did you come from?'

'Your castle. I was with Johnny and Joe,' she added hastily, keen to justify her presence at his castle. 'I was helping out, you know . . .'

'So, you want to go back?'

'Yes, please. Just point the way. I'm sure I'll manage.' She was embarrassed to have been so foolish.

He laughed and shook his head. 'I like your spirit, but I couldn't let you walk all the way back to the castle, it's further than you think and you look worn out. My house is just around the corner. If you come with me, I'll drive you back.'

Her heart began to pound. The thought of accompanying Conor Macausland to his house was surprisingly alarming. But she shrugged off her doubts and the little voice inside her head that told her not to go anywhere with a stranger, let alone a man who might have killed his wife, and followed him back over the lip of the hill and down into the valley.

Chapter 8

I know that look well. The way Conor's lips curl up at the corners and his eyes grow intense and warm. They can be such a cold, icy blue. But there's nothing like the presence of a beautiful woman to thaw them into a softer, cerulean hue. He used to look at me with those gentle eyes, and when he did my resentment would melt away and I'd sink into a blissful state of amnesia. I'd forget the rows and the accusations. I'd forget my loneliness and the gnawing hunger for love that was constantly craving. When he looked at me like that I was satisfied.

Now his curiosity is aroused by this strange girl who is trespassing upon his land. She can barely keep up for the trembling in her legs. She's afraid of him, but she doesn't let it show. Johnny and Joe Byrne have put the fear of God into her with their idle talk. She's anxious about Magnum, too, who is more like a lion than a dog, and her allergy to horse dust is already making her eyes water and her skin itch. Her beauty is masked by the flush on her cheeks and around her nose where she has been exposed to the cold, but I suppose Conor can see through that. Like his hound who can smell a bitch a mile off, Conor can sense an attractive female, even when her hair has frizzed and her sensual body is hidden beneath a big coat.

He talks to her, asking her questions about herself. She answers cautiously, giving him little. The house comes into view and I can feel her relief as she sets eyes on it. I think she is much wearier than she lets on. Reedmace House is a simple grey manor with white sash windows and an ordinary slate roof, and yet it has a certain charm. In summer the front is adorned with white wisteria, and the garden is planted with apple trees. In spring the blossom is carried on the breeze like snow. When we lived in the castle Conor renovated it with the intention of giving it to his parents. But his father died and his mother decided to stay in Dublin rather than live alone in a big, isolated house, miles from anywhere. So, it remained empty, like a lovely girl, all dressed up with nowhere to go.

I love the stream that twists and turns down the valley, and I love the grey stone bridge, which is now partly overgrown with ivy. It was once used as a road when people used to travel by horse and carriage. When cars became too heavy for it, they re-routed the way and the old dirt track was left to the mercy of trees and heather and the bridge to the trolls and goats of my imagination. There's something magical about it, as if it is part of a lost world you happen to stumble upon, quite by chance, and you almost feel as if you are stealing upon it, as if you shouldn't really be there. I am free now to linger as long as I want. Sometimes I see dancing lights, like little fairies, but they could just be the mischievous play of sunshine.

When they reach the house, Conor takes his horse round to the seventeenth-century stable behind. It is a weathered building with a generous-faced clock positioned above the archway which opens like an embrace to welcome you. The clock hasn't worked for years, centuries perhaps. It is stuck at a quarter to five and will probably always be. I like to think that something magical happened at a quarter to five, a hundred ·

years ago, which stopped the clock forever: something romantic and sad, like the death of a lover.

Ellen sits on the old stone steps built against the wall to make a mounting block, and smokes a cigarette. I can see that her hands are trembling. I am delighted that she smokes because Conor detests the habit. While she inhales poison, Conor takes the horse inside and gives him to the son of the couple who look after the place while Conor is in Dublin. They are not from Ballymaldoon. Conor was careful to find people who knew nothing of the scandal that surrounded my death. Meg and Robert are discreet; if they know anything they do not let on. Meg cleans and cooks while Robert tends to the stables and the gardens. Their son, Ewan, is an eager boy of about nineteen, who readily plays with Finbar and Ida when they are down from the city for the school holidays. It is half term and they have been building a camp out of rocks and wood. They are planning to make a fire and cook their own tea. If I were alive I would weave tales of enchantment and we'd sit beneath blankets under the stars until it was time for bed. Finbar and Ida used to love my stories. Now they are older they would appreciate them all the more. But they have Daphne still and her reading has not improved with the years. I must be grateful; they are loved.

'You look cold and tired, Ellen,' says Conor, standing over her with his hands on his hips. I noticed his hips when I first met him, the way his jeans hung low, accentuated by the buckle of his belt. He is a tall man, with broad shoulders and long legs. He's well made and athletic, and clothes hang well on him. Even now, when his unhappiness has led him to drink excessively, he has not lost his form. He likes the look of this girl. But he has liked the look of many girls, and taken them to his bed, only to discard them in the morning like the bottles of wine which alleviated his pain only temporarily.

Now he smiles down at her. His face transforms when he smiles. His mouth is generous and sensual, and the way it turns up at the corners makes him look devilishly handsome. When I was alive he didn't have a beard, but he has developed a certain laziness about his appearance now and cannot be bothered to cut his hair or shave. It is an outward reflection of his deep unhappiness, as if there is little point to life now that I am gone.

He turns his warm blue eyes on her and she cannot resist. She smiles back, her reservations dissolving in the bright light of his charisma. I know how she feels; I have been there, too. But she mustn't think it will last. Many have been attracted to him, like little ladybirds to sunshine, and they have all felt the chill of disappointment when he turns away and they are plunged into shade. Only I was constant; when he turned away from me he always came back. *Always*. Even though I am dead, I bask in the eternal sunshine of his love.

'Come inside and I'll make you some tea to warm you up,' he says.

'Are you sure? I don't want to be any trouble.' She stubs out her cigarette and gets to her feet.

He grins, as if she couldn't possibly be trouble to anyone. 'It's no trouble, really. To be honest, I could do with one myself.' They walk to the house and enter through the back door. The children are in the kitchen with Daphne. They have just finished their tea. When they see Magnum they jump down from the table and rush over to cuddle him. Ellen looks amazed that anyone would dare put their arms around such a large beast. But Magnum is very gentle. The children miss him when they are in the city and I don't doubt that Magnum misses them as well, but he is too big to take with them.

'Mother, meet Ellen, Peg Byrne's niece,' says Conor. 'And those two meerkats are my children, Finbar and Ida.'

'How do you do, Ellen,' says Daphne, and she frowns, wondering where Conor picked up this unfamiliar girl with the well-to-do English accent. 'You can call me Daphne,' she adds as Ellen stifles a sneeze. The girl's eyes are now puffy and watering incessantly. Finbar whispers something to his sister and they both giggle behind their hands.

'My dear, you look like you're allergic to something,' says Daphne kindly.

'Horses,' Ellen replies.

'Let me get you an antihistamine. Finbar gets hay fever in the summer so we'll have some in the medicine cupboard.'

'I'm sorry. I don't usually have such an adverse effect on women,' Conor jokes. Ellen laughs and sneezes again. A moment later Daphne returns with a pill.

'I'll make you both a cup of tea. You look freezing, the two of you.'

'I found Ellen on the hill,' says Conor, sitting down at the kitchen table.

'I got lost,' the girl explains.

'No wonder you're cold. Why don't you take off your boots and coat and come and sit down? Are you hungry? Have you had anything to eat?'

'I'm fine, really.'

'Well, I'll put some food on the table and you can make yourself a sandwich, should you wish.'

Daphne is happy to have company. She is keen for her son to move on. I would tell her not to waste her energy. Conor is never going to move on. It's been five years. Still, she is ever hopeful. She puts food on the table and cups of tea. Ellen puts her pink hands around the mug and hunches over it like a street beggar over a cup of coins. She said she wasn't hungry, but she soon makes herself a ham sandwich and bites into it ravenously. Conor is always hungry. Men seem never to be satisfied. He cuts himself some cheese and a large wedge of bread and tucks into them as if he hasn't eaten for weeks. The food recharges them both. They share their meal while Finbar and Ida play with the dog and interrupt their father with questions, and Daphne makes herself a cup of tea while Meg appears and discreetly clears away the children's dinner.

'You know, I would never take you for a Byrne,' says Conor, narrowing his eyes and looking her over. She has taken off her coat and his gaze rests a moment on the swell of her bosom beneath her sweater.

'Probably because I've spent all my life in London,' she replies.

'That would account for your English accent. You don't sound anything like them.'

'That's what *they* say. My father's English and my mother lost her Irish accent.'

He arches an eyebrow. 'Your mother married an Englishman. The family must have loved that.' He glances at his mother, because she is an Englishwoman who married an Irishman, though at least she was Catholic.

'I don't think it went down very well at all. My father's Protestant but I was brought up Catholic, of course.'

'So, how long are you staying?' Daphne asks. My mother-in-law is a sculptor, and eccentric as artists usually are. She is wearing wide khaki trousers, purple trainers and a bright floral scarf hanging over her thick jersey. She has artist's hands — rough and encrusted with old clay.

Ellen likes Daphne, I can tell. I liked her too, at first, before she interfered.

'I don't know right now,' Ellen replies. 'I have no plans. I came to write a novel, so I suppose I'll stay a while. Besides, I really like it here. I feel at home already even though this is only my third day.'

'That's Connemara for you,' says Daphne with a big smile. She fell in love with it, too.

Ellen smiles back. 'That's what everyone says.'

'They're right,' Conor agrees. 'I came here once on location and ended up buying the castle.' He laughs as if he now thinks his impulsiveness absurd.

'Are you working on any films at the moment?' Ellen asks. I could tell her that he hasn't the will. That since my death he hasn't produced a single film, but Conor shrugs.

'There are things in the pipeline,' he lies and his mother buries her face in her teacup. She knows the truth. He's in the pub in Dublin when he should be in the office, and he's whacking balls against the walls of the squash court to vent his frustration. His restlessness is rootless, like sycamore seeds on the wind with nowhere to settle.

'I suppose the film business is hard with the recession and everything,' says Ellen.

He cuts another chunk of bread. 'A good story is always a good story but they're like precious stones, very hard to find. There's a lot of rubbish out there.'

'I came here for inspiration,' says Ellen and her eyes light up. 'I have to tell you, I'm *incredibly* inspired. It's the beauty, it does something to a person.' She thumps her chest where her heart is. 'Right here.'

'That's very true, Ellen. Beauty is the most inspiring thing on earth,' Daphne concurs. She brings her mug of tea and joins them at the table. 'When Conor's father was alive we spent every spring in France. The bougainvillea was spectacular and

those darling town squares with their little park benches and
fountains were so delightful. I was never short of inspiration.
But nowhere is as inspiring as Connemara. I think my best
work has been done down here. Perhaps yours will be, too.'

Conor doesn't speak. I know he would like to tell them that
Connemara reminds him of me and that since my death the
place gives him no pleasure. If it wasn't for the children, who
love it so much, he probably wouldn't be here at all. But for
some reason he hasn't sold the castle or the estate. Perhaps he
keeps them to remain connected to me, so that he and our
children have something of me that they can touch. If only
they knew the truth: that I am here in the breeze that blows
about the castle walls and the troll's bridge, in the sunshine that
warms their faces as they search for firewood to build their
fires and stones to construct their camps. I am on the beach
and in the hills. I am with them, always. If only they knew
that.

Ellen doesn't tell them that she has seen my portrait hanging in the castle hall. Conor is a formidable man and although
he smiles with charm and appraises her with interest, she must
discern that he is quick to anger. He has a darkness in his eyes
in spite of the humour in his smile. I've always loved that
about him. He's the kind of man who is impossible to tame.
I did my best, but I didn't succeed. I admit that now; it is my
greatest failing, besides my death

As they talk, Ida comes over and sits on her father's knee.
He wraps his arms around her waist and pulls her closer, nuz-
zling his head into the crook of her shoulder. His expression
softens and he lets out a long, contented sigh. Ellen watches
him and I can tell that she is moved by the obvious affection
he feels for our children.

'How old are you, Ida?' she asks.

'I'm ten,' Ida replies, shyly.

'That's a big number, ten. You're in double digits now. Very grown up.' Ida smiles proudly. 'When's your birthday?'

'July the eighth.'

'A summer birthday.'

'Last year we were in Spain for my birthday and Manuela painted my nails pink with little flowers and glitter on them.'

'How pretty!' Ellen exclaims. She lowers her voice, pretending to speak to Ida in confidence. 'You know, I can do that. I'm very good at nail art. I have nieces in London who like to have their toenails painted and decorated with jewels.'

Ida's eyes widen. She's a child who loves anything that shines and the thought of jewels on her toenails is more than she can resist. 'Are they *real* jewels?' she asks. The grown-ups laugh at her innocence.

'No, they're not real, otherwise we'd have to carry you into the bank and put you in a safe. I don't think you'd like it in a safe.' Ida screws up her nose and shakes her head.

'I can see that you have imagination,' says Daphne. 'I've never thought of putting a child in a safe!'

Finbar hears the fun they are having and wanders over to the table. He wants to sit with his father, too, but there is no room. Daphne puts out her hand and he takes it. My heart suffers a little stab of jealousy. She pulls him against her and plants a kiss on his soft cheek. I yearn to feel the texture of his skin, where it meets the hairline just above his ear. I can remember what it feels like. I can remember what he smells like. I leave them and linger in the garden where the apple trees are just beginning to bud. Ida has hung a birdfeeder on one of the branches. I approach and my presence disturbs the blue tits, who fly off into the bushes in fright.

After a while, Conor and Ellen leave in Conor's Range

Rover. Out of curiosity, I follow. They are now chatting away together like old friends. There's nothing like sharing a meal to make two people feel comfortable together. It is a short drive to the castle but a long walk over the hills. Ellen's aunt's car is parked outside and Conor pulls up beside it. They remain talking a while before he gets out in order to open the door for her. He is an old-fashioned gentleman in that respect. I would wait for him in my seat, but Ellen has already opened the door herself and is climbing out.

'Thank you so much,' she gushes and they are suddenly awkward with each other, as if they don't really know how to say goodbye. I watch in amusement because I know they will probably never meet again. Conor doesn't go into town and he certainly won't be going up to Peg's to pay her a visit.

'I'm glad I rescued you off the mountain,' he says and he gives her one of his most charming smiles.

'Me too, although I feel rather embarrassed to have taken up so much of your time – as well as eating you out of house and home.'

'All that walking made you hungry. I'm constantly ravenous down here.'

'Well, thank you again.'

'Drive carefully.' I can tell that Conor would like to prolong the conversation.

'I will.'

'And good luck with the book.'

'Oh, yes, thank you. I shall start tonight. If I leave it any longer it'll never happen.'

He laughs – I think he'd laugh at anything she said – and watches her climb into her aunt's car and turn on the ignition. His eyes stray to the castle door a moment and his face suddenly darkens. Ellen waves as she drives past him. He is distracted and waves back. He watches her car disappear beneath the burr oaks then turns his gaze back to the castle door. I know he is fighting the impulse to go inside and look at my portrait. He remains a long while just staring at it, but he doesn't move towards it. Eventually, he thinks better of the idea and returns to his car.

My interest in this English girl is now aroused further, for she is possibly my only means of communication. She has sensed me once; she will sense me again, I am sure of it. I don't know how, but I feel I will let Conor and my children know I live on, through *her*.

I know Peg's home well from the days when Ronan used to live there, but I haven't been back since my death. I know the sheep and the obnoxious llama, the gentle donkey and that pig. Mr Badger used to bark at me from the hill when I was at the lighthouse, as if he knew of the danger I was in and wanted to warn me. I stand on the hill and gaze over the sea at my death. The water is black now that the sky has clouded over. The waves rise and fall and crash against the rocks, breaking into froth and foam. Darkness falls early in February and the lighthouse is already silhouetted against the indigo sky. I remember the times we made love there on the grass in summer. The times he held me and whispered into my ear that I was everything to him. I remember nights beneath the stars, gazing up at the moon, knowing that he'd do anything for me. Anything at all. Oh, what a feeling to be so loved. And now? The lighthouse was mine. My very own secret island. The one place I truly felt safe – the one place I wasn't safe at all.

And now, as I stand on the hill waiting for Ellen to arrive, I see a little girl in front of Peg's house. She is dressed in white and has a radiance about her that does not belong to the living. Her hair is long and black and yet it has a shine to it that earthly hair does not have. She is staring at me with big, bold eyes and her smile is shy but serene. I know then that she is a spirit, but unlike me she has an other-worldly glow. I am of this world, but she? No, she is not. She is finer, as if she is made of soft beams of light. I smile back.

The door opens and Peg strides out with Mr Badger. She does not see the little girl, but that is no surprise to me. I have been in this limbo long enough to know that only very rarely do the living see the dead. And when they do see us, there are plenty of people to call them crazy, deluded or liars. If only I knew then what I know now. But it is no good to wish for something one cannot have, I know that too. I watch Peg and I watch the child and I suddenly realize that the little spirit is the daughter Peg lost to the sea. I don't know how I know, I just do.

Peg is going to check on her sheep. She marches off into the field. Mr Badger walks up to the little girl and then the most extraordinary thing happens. I cannot believe it. The little girl puts out her hand and strokes the dog's head. She touches him with her fingers *and he feels her touch*. I notice the hair flatten beneath her hand and yet I know that she is not solid. This spirit child is a beam of light, but somehow she can affect the material world in a way that I cannot.

Peg turns and sees that Mr Badger is distracted. She shakes her head fondly, because she believes her dog to be simply eccentric. She whistles and he pricks his ears. The little girl withdraws her hand and Mr Badger runs off into the field. Then she follows, skipping happily after him. I look up at the sky, certain that the moon has come out and is now shining upon us. But no, the clouds are thick and grey and the air is now damp with drizzle. There is no moon, but the little girl has a light of her own, and as she stands beside Peg, the old woman is bathed in its radiance. I wonder whether, on some subconscious level, she can feel it.

Chapter 9

Ellen stopped the car in a lay-by and took a deep breath. For the first time since she had been in Ireland she wanted to call Emily and share her excitement. *Oh my God, he's the most handsome man I have ever seen,* she said to herself. *Conor Macausland! I have just had lunch with the notorious Conor Macausland.* She closed her eyes then opened them again to make sure she wasn't dreaming, and gripped the steering wheel to stop her hands from trembling.

She knew she shouldn't feel excited by a man many blamed for his wife's death. He was obviously dangerous: the sort of man mothers warn their daughters about. But the darkness that muddied his name served only to enhance his allure and strengthen the power of his charisma. The fact that he might be dangerous simply made him more attractive.

How suddenly this one small meeting had shifted the subterranean plates of her life. Her perspective, having been so concentrated on London, now focused in on this tiny Irish county of Connemara. More specifically, to the wild and beautiful Ballymaldoon Castle and the compelling man who owned it. Her parents, William and her London friends faded into the blurred backdrop behind her new focal point, leaving her aware only of Conor Macausland and the desire that had taken her so much by surprise.

She pictured his raffish smile and the indigo eyes that shone the brightest blue by contrast with his brown, weathered skin and long black lashes. The tragedy in them only served to endear him to her all the more. She had never fallen for a man with a beard before, but there was something wild and exciting about the hair on his face, as if he were a storybook hero or a knight of old, and it looked incredibly soft. She imagined what it would feel like against her skin and the thought made her shiver with a sense of the forbidden. She remained in the car until it was too cold to sit there any longer without heating. Her hands were stiff with cold but her body was warm inside Aunt Peg's heavy coat. By the time she started the engine she had projected all her desires onto this man who seemed so capable of embodying them, and she wondered how she could contrive to see him again.

She arrived at Peg's in a jolly mood and found her aunt in the kitchen with Ronan and Oswald. When he saw her, Bertie trotted up and nuzzled her with his wet snout. Because she was so happy she bent down and stroked his spiky head. It was softer than she expected. 'Well, would you look at you!' Peg exclaimed, folding her arms across her woolly jumper. 'We were about to send out a search party.' For three people about to send out a search party they looked very settled and comfortable, Ellen thought.

'Where the devil have you been?' Oswald asked. 'Your cheeks are very flushed. Have you been up to no good?'

Peg stood up. 'I'll pour you a cup of tea. You look cold to the bone! Have you eaten, pet?'

Ellen pulled off her boots. 'I had lunch with Conor Macausland,' she replied nonchalantly, relishing the effect that piece of news was bound to produce. Peg stopped in her tracks, halfway to the Stanley, and Oswald stared at her loose-jawed, while Ronan's face darkened with fury.

'You had lunch with Mr Macausland?' Peg repeated. 'Did I just hear right, or are you messing with me, girl?'

'Why would you go and do that?' exclaimed Ronan hotly.

Ellen shrugged out of Peg's coat and hung it over the door. 'I got lost and he rescued me,' she said, unable to turn down the light in her eyes.

'A knight in shining armour,' said Oswald with a sigh.

'Yeah, right!' Ronan added sarcastically.

'What were you doing getting lost?' Peg asked.

Ellen wandered in on socked feet and pulled out the chair next to Oswald, opposite Ronan. 'I went for a walk over the hills. It was so beautiful. The sun was out, the place smelled so delicious. I was inspired.'

'Ah, the glory of Connemara.' Oswald sighed again.

'So, then what happened?' Peg persisted.

'I walked and walked until I thought I'd better be getting back. But I got lost. Every hill looked the same. I think I was walking in circles. I was scared, actually. I didn't know where I was. That's when Conor came round the hill on his horse and rescued me.'

'Did he brandish a sword and smite your enemies?' Oswald teased.

Ellen tutted and rolled her eyes. 'He invited me back to his house and I had lunch with his mother, Daphne, and his two children, who are adorable. His dog is pretty terrifying, though.'

Peg looked appalled. 'I should think that Mr Macausland is pretty terrifying, too.'

'I'd say your brothers look terrifying, Aunt Peg, but when you get to know them you realize how nice they are. Conor is like that. At first sight, with his dark beard and shaggy hair, he looked quite alarming. But he was charming, actually.'

Ronan leaned forward and put his elbows on the table. 'Don't be an eejit, Ellen. There's nothing charming about Conor Macausland. Don't be blinded by his handsome face.' But he couldn't contain his curiosity. 'So, what did you talk about?' he asked.

'Oh, I don't know,' she replied vaguely. 'Lots of things. He asked me about myself. I told him I was your niece, Peg, and he made a joke about the size of our family.'

'Well, he knows Johnny and Joe well, doesn't he, so you weren't really a stranger.' She put the kettle on the stove.

'Daphne's an artist like you, Oswald,' Ellen added.

'Ireland is full of artists,' Oswald replied, unimpressed.

'What's he doing down here, then?' Ronan asked.

'It's the children's half-term,' Ellen answered, feeling impor-tant now that *she* had information to share with *them*.

'I suppose he'll fly back to Dublin in his fancy chopper the moment it's over,' said Ronan.

Ellen was disappointed. 'Do you think?'

'He's rarely here, isn't that right, Mam? I wouldn't want to show my face around here either if I was him,' he added.

Peg nodded. 'It was a dreadful business, dreadful. I'm not surprised he doesn't come here more often. Every corner of the estate must remind him of his beautiful wife.'

Ronan drained his mug of tea. Ellen noticed the furious shadow that darkened his face.

'I had so many questions I wanted to ask,' she continued.

'I don't think you'd have found him so charming had you asked them,' said Ronan sulkily.

'I'm not a fool,' Ellen retorted. 'I wouldn't have dreamed of prying. The poor man has suffered horribly.'

Ronan's dark eyes flashed. 'But he's alive, isn't he?' He took a sharp breath, as if preventing himself from saying any more. Jack flew off his perch and settled on the curtain pole above the kitchen window. It was pitch black outside and the wind had picked up. It moaned around the house like a ghost. 'He only has himself to blame,' Ronan added quietly. 'They *both* have themselves to blame.'

'Ah, the gossip and speculation,' said Oswald. 'Twenty years from now the people of Ballymaldoon will still be talking about it.'

'And no one will be any the wiser,' Peg added, taking the kettle off the stove and pouring boiling water into the teapot. 'Now, let's all have another cup of tea and talk about something else for a change.'

A little later, Ronan drove off to the pub and Peg settled Ellen into the small sitting room and lit the fire. It crackled comfortingly in the grate. 'Does Ronan have a girlfriend?' Ellen asked her aunt as she plugged her laptop into the socket in the wall behind the desk.

'Chance would be a fine thing,' Peg replied. 'He's a very difficult young man, as you can see.' She sighed heavily. 'Probably my fault. Children never come out of a divorce unscathed.'

'He's very handsome, though, isn't he?'

'Ah, yes, he's a good-looking boy, all right. The Byrne men are all very handsome.' Peg closed the curtains. 'It's a gusty night. I'm glad you're not going out.'

'Lovely staying in here. It's a very sweet room.'

'It's yours for as long as you want it.'

'Aunt Peg, I'm very conscious of being a burden to you.'

Peg turned round and smiled at her niece. 'You're no

burden, Ellen. I'd tell you if you were. It's nice to have a girl about the house. I only ever had big boys. Since Ronan moved out it's been so quiet. I have Oswald.' Her smile broadened. 'He's a lovely rogue, but it is nice to have a girl to look after.' She hesitated a moment, considering Ellen's concern. 'You know, if you want, you can help me with the messages. I don't need your money. I have enough for our needs. I'm not extravagant, as you can see. But if you want to help I'd appreciate you going into Ballymaldoon for me. This damp weather is bad for my bones.'

Ellen was pleased there was something she could do, although she suspected Peg was just being kind. The damp didn't stop her from spending all day outside with her animals. 'I'd love to. Just give me your lists and I'll do the shopping for you, and anything else you require. I'll even help with the animals. Consider me your Girl Friday.'

'It's a deal, then.' Peg glanced at her watch. 'Now, I'd better go and look after Oswald, he's very demanding. He wants me to help choose paintings for an exhibition in the town hall. Mr Badger might come and lie in front of the fire. He loves fires. So, don't be alarmed. He won't bother you. I'll just be across the way with Oswald, if you need me.'

'Thank you, Aunt Peg. I really appreciate that you're happy to have me here. It feels like home already.'

Peg smiled. 'I'm happy to hear it, pet. Now get some writing done, will you?'

'I will.'

Peg departed, leaving the door a little ajar. The fire began to rustle and crunch as it devoured the kindling and set upon the logs with orange tongues. Ellen switched on her computer and waited dreamily for it to start up. She rested her chin in her hands and let her mind revisit the moment Conor had appeared over the knoll on his horse. She wasn't aware of the small smile that crept across her face as she pictured him in his felt fedora with his wild hair and troubled eyes. The screen lit up in front of her but she was unaware of that too, until Mr Badger wandered in and settled in front of the fire with a contented sigh, alerting her to his presence and drawing her out of her head.

She almost clicked onto her emails before she remembered that Peg didn't have email access in her house. It was probably for the best that she didn't begin communicating with the very people she had travelled to Ireland to avoid. Instead, she opened a blank page and wrote NOVEL UNTITLED in looped writing, adding her name beneath. She spent at least twenty minutes playing around with the fonts. When she scrolled down to the next page, she found she had nothing to write. The clean white of it made her shrink back in defeat. Until she had a plot there was no point even beginning. But she had her hero all right, and she put her head in her hands and thought of him again.

It was eleven o'clock when Johnny and Joe banged on the door of Peg's house. Ellen was in bed, reading a Daphne du Maurier novel from Peg's bookcase. She put the book down and cocked her ear. She could hear Peg in the hall, berating them for waking her up, but in truth she had only just finished her card game with Oswald and had retired barely ten minutes before. Ellen threw a sweater over her T-shirt and striped pyjama bottoms and hurried downstairs to see what the commotion was about.

'Just the person we came to see,' said Joe when he saw his cousin in the doorway. He looked her up and down in amusement, taking in the boyish pyjamas and her dishevelled hair. 'Sorry we got you out of bed,' he added wryly.

'Did they wake you up, pet?' Peg asked.

'No, I was reading,' Ellen replied. 'What's going on?'

Johnny sat at the table and looked at her gravely. 'Mr Macausland came into the pub, asking after *you*.'

Ellen's heart gave a little skip. 'Really?'

'He came into the pub,' Joe repeated. 'Can you believe it? He hasn't set foot in that place since the fire.'

'What did he say?' Ellen asked, trying not to look too interested, but failing abysmally.

'He walked in and the whole place went quiet. You could have heard a mouse fart,' Joe continued.

'Craic poured him a pint and they chatted a while,' said Johnny gravely. 'It takes a lot of courage to come into a hostile place like the Pot of Gold.'

'Fair play to him,' Peg added, putting the kettle on the stove.

Joe sat down beside his father. Ellen was so distracted she took Jack's chair, forgetting that the bird was perched on the back until she felt him peck at her hair.

'Good God!' she exclaimed, getting up and moving to the other end of the table. 'That bird is the limit!'

'It took him a while to get the conversation around to you,' said Joe with a mischievous grin. 'He talked about the estate first. Then he said he found you lost on the hills and gave you lunch.'

'Which is true,' said Ellen excitedly.

'He said his little girl wants you to paint her nails.'

Ellen smiled. 'I told her how good I am at bejewelling them.'

Peg observed quietly from the Stanley, a thoughtful expression on her face.

'He wants you to go and give her a manicure, or whatever

you call it,' said Joe. He raised his eyebrows. 'I think he's got the hots for you.'

Ellen blushed. 'Don't be silly. I'm good with children, that's all.'

'He must have the hots for you if he took the trouble to come into the pub. He must have thought you'd be there.'

'Why didn't he just call you?' Peg asked. 'I might not have Internet or a TV, but I do have a telephone!'

'That would be too obvious. He was being subtle,' said Joe, winking at Ellen.

'There's nothing subtle about Mr Macausland walking into the Pot of Gold,' Johnny retorted. 'You can say you're busy writing. I'll make sure he gets the message.'

'You think I shouldn't go?' Ellen asked in surprise.

'Of course you shouldn't go,' said Peg from the stove. 'I won't have you getting involved in all of that.'

'I'd only go and paint the girl's nails.'

Peg narrowed her eyes. 'You'll be stepping into the wolf's lair, pet. He'll be gone in a week.'

Ellen felt a sudden sense of urgency. Her mind scurried like a mouse trying to find a way out of a maze. 'Why don't you come with me, Peg?' she suggested. Peg looked appalled. 'I think it would be unfair not to paint Ida's nails. I mean, she doesn't have a mother to do it for her, does she? Poor little thing. She looked so excited when I told her I could stick jewels on them.'

'But where would you buy such things?' Peg asked.

Ellen shrugged. 'There must be a gift shop in town?'

'Yes, Alanna has a little boutique, but it doesn't sell jewels for nails, I'm quite sure of that.'

'It'll sell something I can use. Something I can cut up and stick on with polish.'

'The chemist will have polish.'

'Good, that's all I need. I'll go into town tomorrow and have a look.' She turned to Johnny triumphantly. 'You can tell Mr Macausland that Aunt Peg and I will come for tea to paint Ida's nails. You'll see him tomorrow at the castle, won't you?'

Johnny frowned at his sister. 'Aye, we will. But are you sure you want to go, Peg? What will Desmond say? He won't like it one little bit.'

'Of course I don't want to go,' Peg answered. 'But I don't want Ellen to go on her own, so I have no choice.'

'You're right, she mustn't go alone, if she has to go at all,' Johnny agreed gravely.

Ellen laughed. 'I feel like I'm straight out of Jane Austen, having to take a chaperone.'

But Peg didn't laugh with her. 'You don't know what you're getting yourself into. I do, and as you're staying with me, you're my responsibility. I think your mother would have a heart attack if she thought you were going anywhere near a man like Conor Macausland. He's trouble, believe me.'

'Easy now, Peggine,' said Joe. 'She's only going to paint the girl's nails.'

Peg threw him a stern look. 'No, she's not. She's going to tea with Mr Macausland. Painting Ida's nails is just an excuse. Really, Joe, do you think I came down in yesterday's snow-storm?' She took the boiling kettle off the stove. 'Now, seeing as you're here, we might as well have a cup of tea.'

Ellen was unable to sleep for excitement. Conor Macausland had braved the pub for *her,* and they had only met once. But once had been enough to ignite *her* interest, so why not *his*? But then in the darkness of her bedroom she began to doubt her appeal. Perhaps he had braved the pub for Ida: after all, the little girl was motherless and he clearly loved her very dearly. Maybe it really *was* all about the nails and nothing to do with him *fancying* her.

She tossed in her bed, unable to find a comfortable position. Her heartbeat galloped, preventing her from sleeping. She wondered about Caitlin and why she had been at the lighthouse that night, and she wondered about the fire and whether Conor had really been responsible for her death. Had the man in the boat, rowing away as the lighthouse burned, been Conor, rowing away from her murder? And why had he left her portrait hanging in the house? Was it so that he could still look upon her? Or because he wanted to lock her away with the rest of his memories in the castle that was now a tomb?

Was she as mad as a moth fluttering about the flame? If she got too close, would it consume her? Or was Conor unfairly maligned?

And then she thought of William and how safe he seemed compared with Conor. She wondered whether he was trying to contact her and cringed at the memory of the text she had sent him. He deserved better. But then, wasn't she just sitting on the fence, hedging her bets, not wanting to burn the bridge in case she got the sudden urge to run back across it, into a secure, albeit dull, future?

She hadn't even been away a week and yet these few days in Ireland felt like months. She had travelled extensively in her life. Holidays in South Africa and Switzerland, Thailand and India, shopping trips to New York and Milan, weekends in Italy and France, and yet none of those places had ever given her a sense of belonging. She had always been a tourist, a guest, just passing through. Connemara, on the other hand, had a sense of permanence about it: more than simply a destination, like a wandering tree reunited with its roots. With this comforting thought, she finally drifted off to sleep.

Chapter 10

The following morning she awoke early, having slept a shallow, fitful sleep. Dawn was breaking behind the house, casting the lighthouse in a soft pink light. She stood at the window and watched the sea swell around it, frothing as the waves hit the rocks. Large white gulls perched on the blackened wood and squabbled over urchins left stranded by the tide. A while later, Peg left the house with Mr Badger and strode across the field to count sheep and talk to the donkey and llama. Ellen watched her in her brown trousers and big coat, a woolly hat pulled over her short grey hair, and felt her heart expand with compassion. There was something very poignant about the slight stoop in her shoulders, as if the weight of her grief had, over the years, crushed her. Was it possible ever to get over the death of one's child? Ellen watched Peg stroke the llama behind the ears. She looked very solitary out there in the field, against the backdrop of the sea. Of course it wasn't possible, she knew, her aunt had just learned to live with it.

After a hearty breakfast of porridge and tea, Ellen took Peg's car into town to buy polish and sparkly things for Ida's nails. She parked down by the harbour, which was busy with fishermen attending to their boats and their early catch, and set off in search of Alanna's gift shop. She wandered up the narrow streets, past pretty pastel-coloured houses and boutiques designed to entice the summer tourists with fishermen's sweaters, pottery, sheepskin and crystal. Alanna's was easy to find, nestled between a café and the chemist. She had painted the shopfront a bright fuchsia pink.

A bell tinkled as she opened the door. Alanna looked up from her desk at the back of the shop and her face registered recognition and delight. 'Well, look at you, Ellen! You have the bearing of a local now.'

'So this is your shop. It's lovely.' She swept her eyes over the cluttered shelves of shiny ornaments, pretty stationery, painted crockery, embroidered linen, old-fashioned-looking soaps and scented candles. It was a fragrant treasure trove of indulgences one didn't need. The sort of place Ellen loved.

'Business is slow at the moment,' Alanna lamented. 'It'll pick up in the summer when the tourists come, and right now I'm on my own. Mary, who helps me, has had to go to Waterford to visit her sick mother, so I suppose it's just as well.'

'*I'm* a customer,' Ellen announced.

Alanna raised her eyebrows. 'So, not just a social call, then?'

'That too, of course. But I need something sparkly like glitter to decorate nails with.'

'Oh, yes, Desmond told me. You're going to have tea with Conor Macausland.' Her eyes widened with fascination. 'Be careful, won't you, Ellen? He's a fine-looking man but I fear he's trouble.'

'I know, but I can't help being curious. It would be mad not to go, don't you think? As a writer it's my compulsion to seek inspiration wherever I can find it.'

Alanna laughed and pushed herself up from her chair. 'I suppose it's hard to resist the allure of a handsome rogue. Now let me see what I can find for you. I have sequins.' She walked over to a stand at the back hanging with all sorts of packets. 'These are pretty.'

'Yes, they'll do. Fantastic. Thank you.' Ellen continued to browse. 'It's such a pretty town.'

'Oh, yes. It's pretty all right and the people are good, hard-working folk. I couldn't live in a place like London. Too much noise, crime and rushing about. The few times I've been there I've come home exhausted. I like a quieter life.'

'I didn't realize how much I needed to be in the country-side until I left the city. What you haven't had you haven't missed, I suppose. But now I know what it feels like to be alone on the hills, I don't think I'll ever be able to do with-out that space again.'

'I gather you got lost up there?'

'Yes, I did. Very silly of me to lose my way like that but I'm not born to the country.' Ellen turned away to hide her blushes.

'Be careful,' Alanna repeated. 'I'm sure you're a sensible girl, but don't forget who he is when you're painting his little girl's nails and he's looking at you with those deep eyes of his. He's nothing but trouble.'

'He didn't look like the sort of man who could murder his wife,' Ellen retorted defensively.

'Oh, I don't think he murdered her, not for a minute. I know Ronan does, but he would, wouldn't he. In his eyes she was the princess in the tower and Conor was the ogre keep-ing her prisoner.' She laughed. 'Poor Ronan, he took her death very hard.'

'So, what do you think happened?' Ellen asked.

'Her death was suspicious, and people do like their con-spiracy theories, but I don't think Conor's bad like that. He's just selfish and spoilt, I imagine, and very arrogant. He never came to the pub or got involved with the community. He just kept himself secluded up there in his castle as if he was too good to mix with the common folk. Caitlin, on the other hand, would come down to the Pot of Gold when he was away in Dublin and lean on the bar for a good chinwag with Craic. She'd knock back her glass of Murphy's and join in all the singing. I think she loved those times best of all, when she could come down from her gilded tower and be herself. She was very beautiful but desperately unhappy. You could see it in her eyes. I don't think it was easy being married to him, in spite of all the money. She deserved better, poor girl.'

'Did you get to know her?'

'Not really, she was a man's woman. But I did get to know Molly, her nanny.'

Ellen's interest was roused by this new angle. 'Really?'

'She was bored, I suppose, and used to come in for a chat when the children were at school. She was a lovely girl, very sweet and gentle. She worshipped her mistress, had stars in her eyes when she spoke about her. I think she was a little frightened of Conor. She saw too much, I imagine. Anyway, after the tragedy, she told me that Caitlin knew Conor was coming back the evening she rowed out to the lighthouse, but she went anyway. Molly thought that was odd, given that he had forbidden her to go there. It was dangerous, you see, and he worried about her in that little boat. But she was headstrong and determined to go. Well, that night, she had an air of intent about her, Molly said, like she wanted him to go and find her. When it emerged that the lighthouse was full of little candles, Molly thought that she had made it all romantic in order to seduce him. Their marriage was really bad; perhaps it was an attempt to win him back.'

'But why the lighthouse, if he hated her to go there?'

Alanna shrugged. 'I don't know, but Molly said that all the

other times she went, she made sure he was away so she didn't get caught. This was the only time she had ever gone knowing he would find out. She wanted him to go and find her. Why? I don't know, and Molly didn't know either. We couldn't work it out. She was interviewed by the guarda but they didn't seem to think that was relevant.'

Ellen stared at Alanna and her heart began to race. 'You don't think that she lured him there to murder *him*, do you, and it all went wrong?'

Alanna's eyes widened. 'Jaysus, Ellen, I never thought of that!'

'I watch too much crime TV.' Ellen laughed, dismissing the idea.

'Well, don't you go giving the boys any more fodder with that suggestion, will you?'

'I think Peg would round on me if she heard me talking like that.'

'She certainly would. You and Ronan with your dark theories.'

'And I'm stepping into the very heart of the mystery,' Ellen said with relish.

'Well, you take care now,' Alanna warned. 'Men like him prey on pretty young girls, then toss them aside when they've had their fill. I'd steer well clear of him. If you want a nice Irishman, there are plenty of decent boys on offer.'

'But they're all related to me!'

'Well, that's true, of course. Don't you go falling in love with one of your cousins. That wouldn't do at all!'

'Joe's handsome. Why doesn't he have a girlfriend?'

'Because he's too busy playing the field. Why settle with one when ten will do?'

*

Ellen found pink nail polish in the chemist next door and bought a couple of things that were on her aunt's list. Just as she was on the point of leaving, Dylan Murphy appeared in the doorway and hooked her with his mad eyes as if he had been doing nothing with his time but fishing for her. 'Well, hello there, Ellen Olenska,' he said and grinned. He looked surprisingly dapper in a jacket and tie, but she wasn't sure she wanted to contend with him on her own.

'Hello, Dylan. How are you?'

'Not too bad,' he replied, thrusting his hands into his coat pockets. He smelt strongly of tobacco. 'How's that book of yours coming along?'

'I haven't written a word yet.'

'You will. You're a talented girl, I can tell.'

His compliment disarmed her, as did the fleeting sweetness in his smile. It was gone as quickly has it had come, as if he were embarrassed to have revealed a softer centre. 'I hear that you and Peg are going to tea with Macausland.'

'Really, nothing is secret in this town, is it?'

'If you want to keep a secret, you tell only the fish.'

'He asked me to paint his daughter's nails.'

'I don't suppose that's on a father's list of duties, is it?'

'Nor a grandmother's,' Ellen added. 'Still, I'm happy to do it.'

'You watch out now . . .'

'Not you as well. Everyone's warning me to take care, as if Conor's some sort of demon. He was very nice to me.'

'Well, of course he was, you're a beautiful girl and he's a red-blooded man like any other.'

Ellen was embarrassed by the way he emphasized the word *beautiful*. He almost sang it. 'Aunt Peg's coming with me, you know,' she told him, then wondered why she felt the need to explain.

'Yes, that will be interesting.'

She didn't know what he meant by that comment. 'Well, I'd better be going.'

His face suddenly darkened with disappointment. 'Off to do the messages, are you?'

She pulled Peg's list out of her coat pocket. 'I've got to go to the butcher's and then to the grocer's.'

'Let me show you where they are, then.'

'No, really, I don't want to trouble you. I'm sure I can find them. It's a very small town.'

But Dylan was already opening the door.

Ellen smiled to herself when, five doors down, they arrived in front of the butcher's. 'I'm glad you came with me,' she quipped. 'Otherwise, I might not have found it.'

Dylan grinned bashfully. 'Sometimes it's not so easy to notice what's right under your nose,' he said, and opened the door for her. She stepped inside. 'So, how long are you planning to stay?'

'I don't know.' She walked up to the counter and appraised the meat behind the glass. 'Right now I've got no intention of going back to London.' She sighed. 'But I suppose I'll have to go back sometime.'

'What have you got to get back for?'

The very thing I'm running from, she thought, but said instead, 'My life.'

'That's a load of rubbish, Ellen Olenska. *You* are your life so your life is wherever you are.'

Ellen was surprised by the wisdom in his words and pulled her gaze off the counter. 'I've never thought of it like that.'

'Well, it's true. Your life isn't something you can leave behind or run away from, because *you* are *it*. People, on the other hand, are another matter altogether. You can run away from them, all right.'

She looked at him steadily. He seemed suddenly smaller and she wanted to put her arms around him because of the callous way her mother had broken his heart. But they were in the shop and the butcher was now ready for her. She pulled out her list.

A few moments later, they were walking down the pavement towards the grocery shop. The sky was as grey as porridge, but every once in a while the clouds parted and the sun shone through, surprisingly warm for February.

'You look like your mother,' he said softly, keeping his eyes on the way ahead as if looking at her at that moment would cause him pain.

'I'm sorry about what happened,' she found herself saying. 'Aunt Peg told me the two of you were engaged once.'

'That we were. A long time ago.' Ellen read the words that hung between them, unspoken: *but yesterday in my heart*. They continued a minute or so in silence before Ellen felt the need to fill it.

'I didn't realize how much I'd dig up by coming to Ireland. I never knew she had such a big family and I never knew she had run away from them, or from you. She completely reinvented herself. What's she going to say when she finds out that I'm here and that I know the truth?'

'That it's none of your business?'

'Yes, that's probably true. But it *is* my business: well, the family stuff at least.'

At that moment he turned his heavy eyes on her. She felt the weight of them, as if he were about to divulge something important. She looked back at him anxiously. But he thought better of it and said nothing, settling his eyes back onto the pavement again.

'Perhaps I shouldn't tell her,' Ellen added to smooth over the awkward moment.

'You'll have to tell her eventually, Ellen Olenska. You can't open Pandora's box then pretend you never did.'

'I'm scared.' But without telling him the whole truth he couldn't imagine what she was scared *of*. He touched her arm and she was taken aback by the natural affection with which he gently squeezed it.

'The Maddie I knew had a big and generous heart. She might have been wilful and a little wild, but she had a great capacity for love. She'll forgive you.'

'Maybe I can convince her to come over and make it up with her family. I can be the catalyst that brings everyone together.'

He chuckled cynically. 'I think you'll find it's a great deal more complicated than you imagine.'

'No, it isn't. What's done is done. It's all in the past. Blood is thicker than water.'

'You're very young, Ellen Olenska, and I admire you for being bold, but I'd let sleeping dogs lie. You might wake them up and get bitten.'

They reached the grocery shop. Dylan helped her find the bottle of Jameson and the Barry's tea that were on Peg's list. Then he pulled a bottle of sloe gin off the shelf and showed it to her with a mischievous grin. 'Father Michael's own brew!'

'You can't be serious? Your priest makes gin?'

'That's Ireland for you. It's powerful stuff, too.' He laughed. 'He only sells it locally and he's getting on a bit now, but he justifies the business by putting all the money into the church. I think it was the gin that repaired the church spire.'

'What an entrepreneur! And all for a good cause.' She remembered Alanna telling her that Peg and the priest had fallen out. 'So, what's he like, Father Michael?'

'He's a good man altogether, a little overbearing perhaps. Likes the sound of his own voice, but don't they all? I've never met a reticent priest!' He chuckled.

'Do you still write music, Dylan?' she asked.

He looked surprised. 'So, Peg's told you all about me, has she?'

'She can even hum your tunes.'

He chuckled. 'Anything else you need to buy, Ellen Olenska?'

'I don't think Peg will want any sloe gin.'

'Not this brew, anyhow.'

'Do you still write?'

He gazed at her and narrowed his eyes. 'A little here and there.'

'I bet it's good.'

He shrugged. 'I'm a bad judge of my own work.'

'I'd like to hear it,' she said, following him up to the counter. 'But I wouldn't presume to judge it.'

He smiled, and once again she was surprised by the sweetness in it. 'You're a good girl, Ellen Olenska,' he said, but he didn't offer to share his music. 'Right, let's go and pay and I'll get me some tobacco.'

Ellen drove back to Peg's with a warm feeling towards Dylan, where before she had simply felt uneasy. They had parted down by the harbour and he had waved as she drove off. She wondered what her mother would make of him now. He was still handsome. In fact, the more she got to know him the handsomer he became. He had a profound intelligence in his eyes, and when he smiled they lost their madness and his whole face softened quite unexpectedly. She could almost imagine what he had been like as a young man, in love with her mother. He would have been leaner and less hairy, of course, and his exuberance wouldn't have been soured by disappointment or his joy dampened by sorrow. He would have been mischievous and outspoken, she imagined, rather like Joe. She really could envisage him singing in a band and writing poetry because he was clearly a deep-thinking, sensitive man. He had mentioned love in a way that her father had never been able to do, being so English and emotionally repressed. Dylan and her father were as different as a bear and a trout; her mother had traded passion for security, of that she had no doubt.

When she arrived back at Peg's, her aunt was in the garden behind the house, cutting back shrubs with a large pair of secateurs. When she saw her niece she smiled warmly. 'Did you get what you need for the nails, pet?' she asked.

'I got everything and I bumped into Dylan.'

Peg resumed her cutting. 'Weaving his way down the pavement, no doubt.'

'Actually, he was perfectly sober.'

'Well, that's a first.'

'He was in a suit and tie.'

'Jaysus, on a weekday? What's got into him all of a sudden?'

'He looked rather dapper.'

Peg laughed throatily. 'That's a word I'd never use in the same sentence with Dylan Murphy!'

'Everyone knows we're going to see Conor.'

'Of course they do. Everyone always knows everything around here. If you want to keep a secret . . .'

'Tell it to the fish,' Ellen finished her sentence for her.

'Exactly.' Peg crossed the lawn. 'Are you hungry? Shall we have something to eat? What do you fancy?'

Ellen was almost too nervous about seeing Conor again to eat but she followed her aunt into the house and helped her prepare lunch. Potatoes seemed to be at the heart of all Peg's meals, boiled with their skins on and always on a plate in the centre of the table with butter. Ellen laid the table, watched by Jack whose beady eyes followed her around the kitchen. Bertie lay in front of the stove, stretched out in blissful slumber, while Mr Badger kept coming in and out through the kitchen door, as if he wasn't sure where he wanted to settle.

'Dylan told me I look like Mother,' said Ellen, pouring them both a cup of tea.

'So, he's finally mentioned her, has he?'

'Yes, I think he wants to talk about her.'

Peg drained the spuds and put them on the table. 'He should have moved on years ago, married and raised a family, not pined for Maddie.'

'I feel sorry for him.'

'Aye, there's a lot to feel sorry about, all right,' Peg agreed. 'Life's current takes most of us downstream, but some, like Dylan, are left behind among the weeds.'

'I wonder what Mum would think if she saw him now.'

Peg inhaled deeply through her nostrils. 'I don't suppose we'll ever know.' She changed the subject quite deliberately. 'Did you get anything written yesterday?'

'Not really,' Ellen replied, then added hastily, 'I was mulling around a few ideas. I have to work out a really good plot before I begin to write.'

'I see.' They sat down and began to eat. 'Don't you think you should call your mother to let her know that you're all right?'

'I threw my iPhone into the sea.'

'Well, that was a silly thing to do. I imagine those telephones are very dear.' She scrutinized her niece through narrowed eyes. 'Do you want to use my telephone?'

'Mum won't be worrying,' Ellen replied, but even as she said it she knew she didn't sound convincing.

'You know, it doesn't matter how old you are, or how independent, you're still your mother's daughter and she'll be worrying about you, especially if you've gone and told her a whole pack of lies.'

Ellen put down her knife and fork and cupped her mug of tea. 'OK, you're right about the lies. I came here because I wanted to get away from her and I knew this was the one place she wouldn't come looking for me.'

Peg smiled kindly. 'I thought so. Still, you could get a message to her through a friend or one of your sisters if you don't want to speak to her directly. Whatever your differences, she's still your mam and you ought to let her know you're OK from time to time. That's the deal, all right? You can stay here as long as you want, but you mustn't leave her to worry.'

'OK, I'll call Emily. She's the only person who knows where I am.'

'Good girl. I knew you'd see sense.'

Peg helped herself to another spud and began to peel it in silence. She didn't ask why Ellen wanted to run away from her mother: she didn't have to, for no sooner had her niece revealed that she didn't want her mother to find her, than all her grievances came pouring out in a rush of accusation and complaint – all except William. Ellen was too ashamed to mention that she was engaged to be married not five months from today.

When Ellen had finished, Peg touched her hand gently and

said only a few wise words: 'Don't go repeating the mistakes your mother made, pet. Life is precious and short.' Then she stood up and cleared away the plates. Ellen felt better for having shared her thoughts and although her aunt didn't get involved in a lengthy discussion, she knew she was a sympathetic ear.

Peg washed the dishes while Ellen dried, then she fed Mr Badger and Bertie from the various sacks kept out in the larder. She had a habit of running her hand down the pig's spine a few times every day. When Ellen asked why, she explained that if she could feel the bones clearly he was too thin and if she couldn't feel them at all, he was too fat. 'We don't want an overweight or underweight Bertie, do we now?' Peg laughed, tickling him behind the ears and making him squeal with delight. Mr Badger trotted over jealously and thrust his nose beneath her armpit, demanding his share of attention. Peg had to pat them both at once and found herself pulled onto the beanbag until she was lying on her back with both animals on top of her.

'Be a good girl, Ellen, and go up to my bedroom and open the bottom drawer of the chest against the right-hand wall. You'll find an old bound book in there. Be a love and bring it down.'

'What is it?'

'Pictures of your mother as a little girl.'

Ellen's face brightened. 'I'd love to see those.' And she hurried from the kitchen, bounding up the stairs two steps at a time.

Peg's room smelt of talcum powder and violets. It was simply decorated with pink rose wallpaper and curtains, and very tidy. The window looked out onto the ocean where the lighthouse stood defiantly against the wind and rain, stubbornly refusing to be ignored, as if daring Ellen to uncover its secrets.

Her eyes wandered to the bedside table where a silver-framed photograph of a little girl in a pretty white dress with long black hair and a wide, carefree smile was placed beside a flickering votive candle and a statue of the Madonna. Ellen crept over to take a closer look. She knelt down and saw two patches of worn carpet beneath her knees where Peg must so often kneel in prayer. A lump formed in her throat as she stared into the face of the child Peg had lost to the sea. As she did so a small gust of wind blew in from somewhere and snuffed out the flame quite suddenly. Ellen sat up with a start. Had she blown it out with her breath? Surely not – she wasn't close enough, and a flame like that would require a more determined blow. She looked about in panic. Where were the matches so she could light it again? Aware that Peg might start to wonder what she was doing in her bedroom, she hurried over to the chest of drawers and pulled out the album. Before leaving she turned back to look at the candle once more, baffled by the strange extinguishing of so hearty a flame. A thread of smoke rose from the wick before dispersing into the air. She glanced at the window. It was closed.

Chapter 11

I am no longer alone. Although the little girl does not talk to me, I know that she is aware of my presence. I think she must be an angel because she is bright and golden as if she is made of sunbeams, while I am dark like a shadow and bound to the earth. But she smiles at me when I catch her eye and I smile back. I wonder whether she sees the desperation in my gaze. I try not to let it show.

I know now that the child I saw on the island was not a gull swooping low, but this little ray of light who seems to enjoy playing with the birds and in the ruin as if she were a normal child, propelled by curiosity. She is full of joy; in fact, I would say that light and joy are synonymous, for that is what she is made of, while I am as flawed as I was when I was living, only more unhappy in my solitude.

Yet my existence is suddenly getting more interesting now that Conor has set his sights on this girl from London. She is pretty with lustrous dark hair and chocolate-brown eyes. Her skin is smooth and radiant and her nose is scattered with small freckles, but she is nothing special. Conor has always been attracted to women who stand out. I would not say that Ellen stands out, though I concede that there is a sweetness in her heart-shaped face, which is charming. Were I alive I most certainly wouldn't feel threatened by her, but now that I am dead I am jealous of any woman who steps into Conor's path, even though most have not lasted more than a night.

Conor is a widower of forty-four, and she is a fresh young woman of about thirty, so I am certain that my fears are unfounded, but still, I saw the interest in his eyes when he encountered her on the hill and I watched him go looking for her in the Pot of Gold. He must be very keen to have ventured in there, where he knew he would not be welcome. I saw the locals stunned into silence by his appearance and I heard the whispers as he made his way to the bar and ordered a pint. Craic pretended the sight of him at the bar was a normal occurrence and shared a bit of banter as he filled his glass with stout. I noticed Conor scanning the room for the girl, rubbing his beard anxiously as he searched the curious faces for hers, and I couldn't fail to see the disappointment when he didn't find her. With no friends to talk to, he sought refuge with Joe and Johnny, and I saw his face light up when they spoke about Ellen and agreed to pass on an invitation to paint Ida's nails. I was not at all happy that he should use his own daughter as an excuse to invite the girl back to his house. I'm sure she will smile at the flimsy pretext, but she will go. Of course she will go – Conor has a strong allure. I know that better than anyone. To think I invested hope in her. I'm disappointed that she is not worthy of it. I'm disappointed that she has set her lustful eyes on my husband and will be of no use to me, after all.

But I don't want her coming to paint Ida's nails. I don't want her stepping into my house again. I wish she'd disappear back to London and leave my family alone. But no, she comes with her aunt Peg and there is nothing I can do to stop her. She has applied make-up, for her lashes are thick and black and her lips are shiny with gloss. I can tell that she is nervous, for her fingers tremble as she lights a cigarette in the car and blows smoke out through the open window. I smile triumphantly at the thought of Conor smelling it on her when he greets her. He used to smoke many years ago, but I made him quit. How can a person savour the scents of the garden if their nostrils are full of tobacco? Now he finds the habit unbearable.

Ida is beside herself with excitement. She has put on a pink party dress and Daphne has tied up her hair with a ribbon. She misses the castle because she used to pretend she was a princess in the tower and now she is only a princess in a house. Today, she looks every inch a princess, but how I wish it were me painting her nails and not some upstart from London.

They arrive and Peg parks the car in front of the house. Ellen steps out first and when she sees Conor in the doorway her face breaks into a wide grin. I can see now why he is attracted to her. It is very simple. He is dark and she is light and like all dark creatures he is attracted to the light. Her smile is uninhibited and confident and the way she kisses him is very 'London'. She has an air of sophistication that the rest of her family do not have. If Conor likes women who stand out, I suppose it is fair to say that Ellen stands out because she is not Irish, and she is not melancholy, and she is not old enough to be embittered by tragedy or disappointment. She is exuberant and it is infectious.

Ida is standing in the hall behind her father. She has suddenly grown shy. But Ellen crouches down and shows her what is in her bag. My daughter's eyes grow wide when she sees the sparkly things Ellen is going to stick onto her nails. She gasps with delight and Conor looks on, admiring the natural way Ellen interacts with children. Oh, cynical I may be, but really, it is not hard to buy a child's affection for a while.

Ida would love a witch, if she smiled and offered to paint her nails.

Peg is anxious but Daphne is in the hall to welcome her. The two women have met before. In the old days, Ronan didn't have a car and Peg used to drive him up to the castle when he was working for me. But they are not friends. Peg is very different from my mother-in-law, but they do have one thing in common. They are both eccentric in their own way and it is not long before they are sipping cups of tea in front of the drawing-room fire and chatting away like old friends. The Irish are very good at talking and although Daphne has no Irish blood in her veins, she is as loquacious as an Irishwoman born and bred and she and Peg do not draw breath.

I suppose Peg has come to chaperone Ellen. I imagine from the cool way she greeted him that she does not think much of Conor. Her niece, however, does not share her reservations. She spreads the polish and glitter and shiny little baubles on the card table at the other end of the drawing room while Conor sits with Ida and watches Ellen with admiration. Ellen's cheeks are flushed and every now and then she raises her eyes and looks into his intently, as if she is fascinated by everything he has to say. They are like teenagers, excited by one another but unable to be alone and this sense of the forbidden makes their encounter all the more thrilling.

I watch them closely and feel the power of their attraction in warm waves that quiver between them like electricity. They talk in low voices but every so often their conversation is punctuated by loud bursts of laughter from Conor and husky giggles from Ellen. Peg glances over anxiously, but Daphne quietly tells her that she hasn't heard Conor laugh with such abandon in many years. Peg looks over again, but this time she is no longer anxious, but compassionate, as if she is seeing him in quite a different light. As if she is for the first time seeing him as a man who has lost his wife and not a two-dimensional character from a Shakespearean tragedy.

Daphne likes Peg, I can tell. She has been looking after her son and his children for five years now and every time she comes down to Connemara she has no one but her family to talk to. She is grateful now for the company, but more than that, she feels she can confide in Peg. I could tell her that she is right to unburden her heart to this woman who has suffered too. Peg might not be of the same social class as Daphne and is certainly much less worldly, but Daphne is not a person to judge by such superficial things. I might have found her interfering in life, but in death I can appreciate that she is above all a decent human being with a kind heart. Peg no longer looks over at her niece and as far as Ellen and Conor are concerned, they might just as well be on their own for all the flirting and banter.

Ida is delighted by her sparkly nails. Ellen is certainly creative. She has cut the little pieces of glittery paper into tiny hearts and stars and placed them on Ida's small nails, painting over them with pale-pink polish. The effect is magical and Ida skips off to show her grandmother. Daphne and Peg admire her fingers with much oohing and aahing, like a pair of pigeons, then Ida runs off to show her brother, who is watching television and will certainly not care.

This time, when Conor asks Ellen about herself he is genuinely interested, as if everything she says is fascinating, and he gazes deeply into her eyes in that intense way of his that few women can resist. Ellen gazes back, her cheeks pink with pleasure, and I know that she is basking in his attention just like I basked when he first set his sights on me. They finish their cups of tea and Conor announces that he is going to take Magnum out and show Ellen the gardens, as if there is anything to see in February but bare trees and empty flower beds! Peg and Daphne remain by the fire, anxious not to be interrupted.

Ellen is still wary of the big dog and watches uneasily as Conor fetches him from the kitchen. Excited to be out, Magnum cocks his leg on the yew hedge before bounding off onto the lawn. They amble over the grass and Ellen admires the bird feeder where finches and robins and flurries of blue tits squabble for seed. The light sound of courting birds fills the air and on the ground snowdrops gather in clusters like patches of snow yet to be burnt away by the sun. Fresh buds are beginning to emerge through the hardened bark and little green shoots can be seen pushing their way up through the soil. The air vibrates with the promise of spring and this seems to invigorate Conor and Ellen as they wander happily through the apple trees, yet to blossom.

After a while they stray from the garden, away from Daphne, Peg and the children. They stroll into the wild so that they can be totally alone. Conor takes her to the Billy Goats' bridge and they lean on the stone balustrade and watch the stream trickle beneath it. My fury rises. I feel as if they are trespassing on my territory. That forgotten place is a small slice of heaven set mistakenly on the earth. It is a between place where I can go and contemplate what is surely to come when I am able to move on at last. I feel strongly that they shouldn't be here, not together, not with their attraction building around them in waves of mounting energy. It is an affront to my memory.

I rage and thrash about in my silent world. The injustice of his behaviour drives me mad. Doesn't he know that I chose him and the children over heaven? Doesn't he realize what I sacrificed so that I could remain close to him? They talk for a long time, in this magical place among the dancing orbs of sunlight that look like fairies. The stream trickles beneath them and how I wish there was a troll down there to swallow them whole.

Chapter 12

Ellen leaned on the bridge and turned her face to Conor's. His eyes were heavy, the look in them intense, and she knew then that he was going to kiss her. She didn't have time to think, but even if she had she wouldn't have moved, or broken the moment with weak excuses. The reckless part of her *wanted* him to kiss her, while the more cautious part was silenced by desire.

Conor needed no invitation. He wound his hand beneath her hair and pressed his lips to hers. She closed her eyes and let him kiss her deeply. His beard was soft against her skin, his mouth warm and passionate, and for that long while she existed in the moment, aware only of the ripples of pleasure coursing through her body.

'You're very adorable, Ellen,' he whispered, pulling away and slowly curling a tendril of hair behind her ear.

She felt her face flush. 'This is all very sudden, I don't usually—'

But he cut her off. 'You don't usually let strange men kiss you on bridges?'

'Not really, no.'

'Well, I'm glad to hear it. If it makes you feel better, I still respect you.' There was a twinkle in his eye and Ellen realized he was teasing her. She laughed, feeling foolish. But how could she explain that everyone had warned her against him? That they'd told her to be careful? What did they think he was going to do?

He traced his fingers down her cheek, his blue eyes taking in her face as if seeing it in a different light. He didn't look like the kind of man who could kill his wife. 'I'm glad you got lost on the hills and found your way to me,' he said quietly.

'So am I,' she replied, as her stomach responded to the tenderness in his tone with a little flip. He grinned and, lifting her chin, kissed her again, this time more ardently, and she felt as if his very presence was wrapping itself around her and lifting her off the ground.

They set off up the river hand in hand, trudging over the damp heather and long grasses to the sonorous sound of trickling water. They talked and laughed and every now and then Conor swung her around and caught her in a bear hug, to kiss her again. 'I don't want this moment to end,' he said, pressing his lips to hers so that she was unable to reply. But he knew from the way she wound her arms around his waist that she didn't want it to end, either. Soon, however, the light began to fade and the air grew cold and they reluctantly headed for home.

Peg and Daphne were still in the drawing room when they arrived back at the house. They had barely noticed how long Conor and Ellen had been away. Daphne was telling Peg about her life and had another forty years to go. Ida and Finbar were in the playroom. Finbar was now engrossed in a football game on his iPad, while Ida had taken Ellen's nail polish and was busy painting the hand of a doll she had tossed into the back of the toy cupboard years before.

Conor stole another kiss in the porch before coming in to

make tea. 'Your cheeks are cold,' he whispered, gently rubbing them with his thumbs.

'Your beard would warm them up,' she grinned, eyes sparkling with the excitement of a schoolgirl flouting the rules.

'Give me time and I'd warm you up all over.'

'We'd better go in. What if your mother or Aunt Peg sees us like this?'

'Now that would be entertaining. I don't know who'd be more shocked, your aunt or my mother?'

They took off their coats in the hall and wandered into the kitchen. Conor called for Meg, but the kitchen was quiet except for Magnum's loud lapping at his water bowl. Ellen leaned against the sideboard and looked out of the window at the darkening garden. She sensed the afternoon draining away and was suddenly gripped by the hopeless desire to stop the sand running out of the hourglass. How long before he bolted back to Dublin? Conor switched on the kettle. When he looked up he caught her troubled profile. 'What are you doing tomorrow?' he asked.

'Oh, I'm very booked up,' she replied, turning away from the dusk. 'I have a date with a donkey and a llama.'

'And then?'

She sighed melodramatically. 'Chickens and a pig.'

He reached across her to unhook a couple of mugs. 'And then?' His face was so close that her heart began to accelerate at the danger of being caught.

'And then, I might find time for you,' she whispered, edging away.

He smiled, pleased, and walked back to the kettle. 'So, let's spend the day together. What do you think? We'll take a drive and I'll show you more of Ireland. I know a nice pub where we can have lunch, without the eyes of your family upon us.'

'It's hard to get away from my family in Ballymaldoon.'

'Where there's a will there's a way.' He grinned at her mischievously and she smiled back. 'So, tell me, what do you like to do?'

She shrugged. 'Oh, lots of things.'

'Tell me.'

'I love to walk on deserted beaches. I love to explore ruined castles.'

'Ireland has plenty of those.'

'I love to be outside, in nature.'

He looked at her for a long moment. 'So do I. That's why I bought Ballymaldoon Castle in the first place. I wanted to be in the hills, surrounded by beauty and tranquillity. I work in the city but the countryside draws me and every time I come I realize how much I've missed it.'

'I like a simple life, Conor. If you'd asked me a couple of weeks ago my answer would have been very different.'

'What changed?'

'Coming here and standing back. I gained perspective. I don't want the life I had before.'

He poured boiling water into the teapot. At that moment, Ida and Finbar came running into the kitchen. 'Will you paint my toes?' Ida asked Ellen.

Ellen laughed at the child's enthusiasm. 'If you're allowed to have sparkly toenails as well, of course I will.'

'Can I, Daddy?' she pleaded, clamping her hands together as if in prayer.

'I don't see why not. But another time, sweetheart. Ellen's enjoying grown-up time now.'

'Can I have a snack?' Finbar asked.

Conor looked at the clock on the wall. It was nearly six o'clock. 'Go and ask Grandma,' he said, but Finbar didn't listen and lifted the biscuit jar down from the island in the middle of the room and pulled off the lid. He thrust his hand in and extracted a chocolate Hobnob, then grinned triumphantly at Ellen.

They made their way to the drawing room, where Daphne was still talking to Peg, settled into the armchair and sofa by the fire. Ida skipped ahead and asked her grandmother to make her something to eat. Peg glanced at her watch. 'Well, would you look at the time? The afternoon has flown by. Ellen and I must be going.' She pushed herself up from the sofa, suddenly flustered with embarrassment. 'I hope we haven't outstayed our welcome.'

'Not at all,' said Daphne truthfully. She had never had such a rapt audience for her stories. 'You must come again. We have few local friends. It would be nice to have adult company from time to time. When we're down here I'm always with the children. You've been a breath of fresh air, Peg.'

'Oh, you've made a fresh pot of tea,' said Peg, noticing Conor standing in the doorway with the tray.

'It would be a shame to waste it, don't you think?' said Daphne. 'Why don't you stay a little longer? Then I'll make the children their supper. They can last another fifteen minutes or so.'

Peg raised her eyebrows at her niece, then, noticing the girl's flushed cheeks, she narrowed her eyes suspiciously. 'Well, what do you think, Ellen? We don't want to take up any more of their time.'

'We've got nothing else to do,' said Conor and he placed the tray on the coffee table, putting an end to the debate.

Ellen sat on the sofa and Peg flopped back down too. Conor

tossed a log onto the fire, then took the other armchair and languidly stretched out his long legs. Daphne sank back into the cushions already flattened to her shape and they all drank more tea. Peg helped herself to a couple of the biscuits that Conor had put on a plate and it wasn't long before Finbar had stolen a few of those, too. He then lay on the floor to eat them with Magnum, who was now spread out on the carpet like a lazy lion. Ida played with the sparkly shapes and baubles Ellen had left on the card table, humming softly to herself.

It was a cosy scene, bathed in the golden light of the lamps. The air was warm and smelt of wood smoke from the fire that crackled merrily in the grate. Daphne had closed the curtains, which were a pale-yellow colour to match the walls, and lit a scented candle, so that the room seemed to shimmer with an other-worldly glow. They chatted like old family friends and only Conor and Ellen felt the current of attraction that ran between them, building all the time. They exchanged knowing glances and their secret made an island out of them, drawing them ever closer in their isolation.

Chapter 13

'Well, that was a very pleasant afternoon,' said Peg as she drove the car back down the narrow lanes towards home. 'I have to tell you, I wasn't at all happy about going, considering what I know about Mr Macausland, I mean Conor, but he was very charming and so was his mother.'

Ellen gazed out of the window. She could still feel his beard against her face. She ran her fingers across her lips dreamily. 'I don't want to say I told you so, but . . .'

Peg laughed. 'Light me a cigarette, will you, pet? I noticed there weren't any ashtrays in the house. I don't suppose they smoke, do you?'

Ellen rummaged around in Peg's bag and took out her packet of Rothmans. 'I think you're right. Well, it *is* a nasty habit. I'm going to give up right now,' she declared.

'I'll quit one day, but not now.' Ellen lit one for her aunt with the car lighter. 'So, you're really going to stop? Just like that?' Peg asked, surprised. 'I thought you said you had to have a very good reason to give up.'

'I do have a good reason – the fresh country air. I want to taste it.' Ellen turned to face the window. It was now dark and all she could see was her own reflection, staring back at her abstractedly, and the stars in her eyes.

'Daphne told me the most interesting things,' said Peg.

'Was she very indiscreet?'

'Oh, yes, terribly.'

'So, what did she say?'

Peg rolled down her window to let out the smoke. 'Well, you know ever since Caitlin died Conor hasn't made a single film. He's uninspired, that's the problem. She said that they had a tumultuous relationship right from the beginning and that Caitlin let him down. She didn't say how, but she raised her eyebrows suggesting that Caitlin did something very wrong. I couldn't ask what it was, but it obviously knocked the wind out of Conor. She said that people are wrong about him and that because Caitlin was so beautiful people always assumed she was an angel, but she wasn't. Daphne said she was a very needy and possessive woman, not an angel at all. Men don't like neediness, or perhaps they like it at the beginning when they are in love, but it loses its charm after a while and becomes irritating. She was jealous of Daphne's closeness to her son and jealous of his friends; she even tried to make him get rid of his dog. Can you imagine being that insecure?'

'Gosh, Daphne didn't hold back, did she?'

'I think she was longing to get it all off her chest and I'm not one of her circle so it doesn't really matter, does it?'

'I'm sure Conor would have hated to hear her being so indiscreet.'

'I'm sure he would, but there was no stopping her. I barely got a word in. I think she's fed up of the whole business. She must know what people are saying. She probably relished the opportunity to defend her son.'

'She knows you'll go back and tell everyone.'

'Well, she's not wrong. Though, it would take a lot more

than Daphne's word to convince Johnny, Joe and Ronan that Caitlin was no angel.'

'What's her story?' Ellen asked.

'She came from a middle-class family in Galway. But she was never a city girl. She had dreams of being an actress, but Daphne said she'd never have made it past Dublin because she was timid and insecure and afraid of the big wide world. You know, in all the time they were married, she never went abroad. Isn't that a funny thing in this day and age? With all that money, because Conor is very successful, she could have gone anywhere she wanted and yet she chose to stay here in Connemara. I bet Conor fell in love with her and married her very quickly, then discovered what she was really like. Daphne didn't say as much, but reading between the lines, I suspect that's what happened. She said Conor tried very hard to make her happy. He really loved her but it wasn't enough. She was insatiable, apparently. Daphne said she always had a faraway look in her eyes, as if she wasn't the full shilling, if you know what I mean. She was vague and whimsical. I must say Conor looks like he's been through hell, doesn't he? He looks terrible.'

Ellen was quick to defend him. 'Oh, I thought he looked handsome.'

'If you like your men wild and rugged.'

Ellen smiled and turned to the window to hide her scarlet cheeks. 'He's romantic-looking.'

'What did you two get up to on your walk?'

'He showed me the most beautiful place. There was a stream and an old stone bridge. Once, there was a track going through it, but now it's all grown over and only the bridge remains. It's very romantic.'

'Don't you go falling in love, now, will you? He's very

handsome altogether, but he's a complicated man with a complicated history. I'd leave it all well alone if I were you.'

Ellen didn't have the heart to lie to Peg. She felt her aunt deserved better than that. So she said nothing. Instead, they talked about the children and how pretty the house was and they both wondered why Conor had closed down the castle and left only Caitlin's portrait hanging in the hall. 'Maybe he'll put it away one day when he's at last able to move on,' Peg suggested. 'Or perhaps he'll never move on. I imagine, deep down he still loves her and feels desperately guilty that he didn't do more for her. I think he chooses to stay in Ballymaldoon because he wants to remain close to her and maybe he keeps the picture up there on the wall for the same reason. I don't think there's a mystery at all. It's very simple; he wants to remain close to her. I understand that.'

Ellen felt her aunt was speaking more about herself than about Conor. She wanted to ask her about her little girl, but Peg's profile looked so rigid she feared her questions would be unwelcome. She wondered whether her aunt would notice that the votive candle had gone out on her bedside table. She would like to have told her, but she didn't want to admit that she had been snooping. Instead, she knitted her fingers on her lap and watched the road ahead, illuminated by the headlamps.

When they arrived back at the house, Johnny's truck was parked outside, next to Desmond's. 'Well, would you look at that? We've got an audience,' said Peg, pulling up beside them.

'They want to know how it went.'

'They most certainly do.' Peg switched off the engine and climbed out with a groan. She never complained about her aching bones, but Ellen noticed she walked with a slight limp, and getting up and out of chairs seemed uncomfortable. 'Well, they've let themselves in so I suppose we have no choice but to join the party. Really, they do take liberties!' But it was clear from the small smile creeping across her face that she was pleased they had come.

Ellen wished she could go directly to her bedroom and shut the door so that she could lie on her bed and replay the moment Conor had kissed her. She still had butterflies in her stomach. The gentle tugging on her conscience went unnoticed, however, because right now Conor had eclipsed William like a big, beautiful moon.

As soon as they heard the kitchen door open the room fell silent. Peg strode in to find Joe and Johnny, Desmond and Alanna sitting at the table with Oswald. She bent down to pat Mr Badger, keeping them all in suspense for a long moment. 'Hello there, old friend,' she said as the dog wagged his tail and nuzzled her with his wet nose.

'So, are you going to tell us or not?' Desmond growled. Ellen stepped in behind her aunt and grinned at Joe, who raised his eyebrows suggestively.

'I might. But first, I need a wee Jameson.' She went to the sideboard and reached for a glass in the cupboard above. 'I hope you helped yourself to wine,' she said to Oswald.

'Oh, yes, Peg, it's perfectly warmed, straight from the Stanley,' he replied with a smile.

'So, you're all making yourselves at home, I see,' she said, glancing at the table and the cups of tea and plates of biscuits and cake.

'We thought we'd come and surprise you, Peggine,' said Joe.

'No, you didn't,' Peg retorted, pouring the whiskey into the glass. 'You came to hear the gossip. I know you. And it isn't at all surprising!'

'Dad and I brought cake,' Joe added.

'Jack likes cake,' said Peg.

'Was the little girl happy with her nails?' Alanna asked Ellen.

'She was thrilled,' Ellen replied, standing awkwardly by the door.

'Well, don't stand in the doorway. Come and sit down and tell us all about it,' said Joe, patting the bench beside him. 'We won't bite you.'

'It's not your bite I'm concerned about, Joe,' Ellen answered back. 'It's your irresistible charm!'

Joe laughed. Johnny shook his head. 'Irresistible charm!' he scoffed. 'The boy's pleased enough with himself already.' Ellen climbed in behind the table to sit next to Joe.

'So, what's the house like?' Alanna asked.

'Jaysus, woman, we don't want to know what the house is like!' said Desmond. 'Peg, bring your drink over here and put us out of our misery.'

Peg brought her glass and a little jug of water to the table and sat down on Jack's chair. The bird didn't move and no one took any notice of him. Peg sighed and took a sip of whiskey. 'I'm to the brim with tea,' she said. 'Ah, this is nice.'

'So, Conor's got the hots for Ellen, eh?' said Joe, smirking at her. 'Bet he was surprised when you turned up with Peggine!'

'I suppose he might have been,' Peg replied, lifting her chin self-importantly. 'Although he shouldn't have been. What sort of aunt would I be to let my niece go to a strange man's house on her own?'

'Did he moon at you across the table?' Joe asked provocatively.

'No, Joe, he didn't moon at all,' Ellen retorted.

'Did you sit between them, Peg, like our Aunt Sheila who used to come between us at dances to make sure our bodies weren't getting too close?' Johnny asked.

'I certainly didn't. I sat and talked with Conor's mother, Daphne.'

'Oh, so it's Conor now, is it?' Joe teased.

'I suppose it is,' Peg replied, unable to suppress the small smile that alighted on her face. Peg was a woman who was quick to laugh at herself. 'I can't very well call him Mr Macausland if I call his mother Daphne.'

'What's Daphne like?' Alanna asked.

Peg smiled. 'Ah, she's a guinea a minute. Full of gossip, she is. We had the craik, all right.'

'So, what did you and Mr Macausland talk about when Peg was busy with his mother?' Desmond asked Ellen. Unlike his brother and nephew, Desmond didn't find the situation at all amusing.

Ellen shrugged. 'I don't know, this and that. I was painting his daughter's nails.'

'And he was mooning at you across the table,' Joe repeated.

'Quit codding about, Joe,' said his father. 'Does he want to see you again? That's what I want to know.'

'Oh, do be careful, Ellen,' Alanna warned, her face crinkling with concern. 'He's nothing but trouble.'

'Aye, don't you go running about the countryside with him. He's not to be trusted,' said Desmond, and the forbidding way he looked at Ellen was almost enough to make her crumble into submission.

'He's not one of us,' said Alanna.

'How do you mean, not one of us?' Ellen asked.

'He's not Irish,' Desmond replied firmly.

'Neither am I,' Ellen pointed out. 'My father's English, don't forget.'

'And there's no shame in that,' Peg added fiercely. 'If Ellen wants to go running around the countryside with Conor, that's her business. She's old enough to look after herself.' Ellen was grateful for her aunt's support, albeit a little surprised. Peg had warned her against him just like the others.

Oswald piped up from the other end of the table where he had been listening to their banter with delight. 'If you forbid someone to do something it'll only make them want it more.'

Desmond scowled into his tea. 'It's only right that she should know how we feel,' he said.

'Sometimes it's better not to know anything at all and make up one's own mind,' Oswald added wisely. 'Knowing can be very cumbersome.'

'So, what did Daphne tell you?' Alanna asked Peg, drumming her fingers on the table with impatience.

Peg gave a sigh, but she told them anyway. 'People thought she was an angel, but she wasn't,' she said finally.

Johnny reacted as Peg expected. 'What rubbish! Of course she's going to say that, she's his mother.'

'Our mam would have done the same. Why, she'd have defended us even if we'd committed murder,' said Desmond.

'Conor didn't murder anyone,' said Peg wearily. 'It was an accident and that's all there is to it.'

'But who was rowing away?' Joc asked, his voice heavy with insinuation.

'The leprechauns in Dylan's mind,' Peg replied smartly. 'Really, you can't believe anything he tells you!'

'Did you get a load of him today, in a suit!' Joe laughed.

'I don't know what's got into him,' Alanna agreed. 'He came into my shop and I hardly recognized him. He had his hair all brushed back.'

'What the devil was he doing in your shop? Did he buy anything?' Desmond asked.

'No, he was just looking around.'

'He was probably langered, got lost and thought you were the pub.' Joe chuckled.

Alanna shook her head. 'No, he wasn't drunk. He looked good. You know, I'd even go as far as to say he looked handsome.'

'That's nice to hear,' said Peg. 'He was always handsome in the old days.'

'Maybe he's going to finally make an honest woman of Martha,' Desmond suggested.

'Poor Martha.' Alanna sighed. 'She's devoted to him. I'd tell her she's wasting her time if I could. I don't think Dylan will ever settle down, do you?'

'Maybe she's not wanting to get married, Alanna,' said Peg. 'Perhaps she's just happy to be near him.'

'You can go to the pub for that.' Desmond chortled.

'People are better when they're married, at least *I* think so,' said Alanna. 'I don't think human beings are designed to be on their own.' They sank into silence for a moment. Ellen wondered what Oswald and Peg thought of that. Then, Alanna tapped her fingers on the table again. 'Hey, Ellen. Will you come for Sunday dinner after Mass? Father Michael is very keen to meet you.' Ellen hesitated. 'You *do* go to Mass, don't you?' Alanna added and Ellen knew instinctively that the answer had to be yes.

'Of course. I'd love to come. By dinner, you mean lunch, right?'

'She's such a posh bird!' Joe chuckled.

'Give it up, Joe,' chided his father. 'She can call it what the devil she likes.'

Alanna beamed happily. 'That's grand. It'll be a right family get-together.'

They chattered on. Peg and Alanna rustled up some cold meat and potatoes and everyone stayed for supper. It was late when

Peg finally got rid of them all. Oswald shuffled back to his cottage next door, having drunk a little more wine than usual, and Peg took Bertie and Mr Badger outside for a quick walk around the house before putting them to bed.

Ellen finished clearing away the remains of supper. As she gathered up the salt and pepper and put them back in the cupboard, she felt a warm sense of belonging. She knew Peg's kitchen intimately now. It felt like home. She had been part of the family gathering around the table, and this time she had no longer felt such an outsider. It had given her pleasure to see how anxious they all were about her now that Conor Macausland had shown interest. It gave her a comforting feeling to think of Desmond, Joe and Johnny rallying round to protect her. They were like three grizzly bears and it was hard not to feel safe in their presence. However, she was determined to see Conor, whether they liked it or not. She'd have to be careful, though, to keep her encounters to herself.

Peg put Mr Badger and Bertie in the kitchen and shut the door. They climbed the stairs, reflecting on the evening like two old companions, and Ellen couldn't fail to notice her easy relationship with her aunt. It was as if they had always been together.

'Well, you get a good night's sleep, now, Ellen.'

'I will, Aunt Peg. It's been a lovely day.'

'What do you fancy doing tomorrow?'

'I think I'll go and explore.'

'I think that's a very good idea. Borrow my car and see a bit of Ireland.' She lingered on the landing a moment. 'You won't be lonely on your own, now, will you?'

'Not at all. I'm very good on my own. I like the peace.'

'That's because you're a writer. You need time to be alone with your thoughts. Well, see you tomorrow then. Sleep well.'

Ellen watched Peg wander down the corridor to her bedroom and thought of her kneeling beside the picture of her
child and praying. It brought a lump to her throat to think of
her grieving in solitude, without her husband to share it with.
She wondered again whether she'd notice the votive candle.

Ellen lay in bed and struggled to control her thoughts. She
didn't want to think of William, but he kept surfacing like a
stubborn cork in the choppy ocean of her mind. There he
was, in his beautifully cut Savile Row suit, with his blond hair
pushed off his forehead, and his brown eyes questioning and
indignant. He was young and fresh with skin that barely
needed shaving and hands that were naturally soft and manicured because he had never done anything other than work in
the City. His laughter was light and carefree because he had
never had a single worry besides the odd invitation that hadn't
arrived or an important item of clothing that had gone missing at the dry-cleaner's. He was pampered and privileged and
in contrast to Conor, his good looks seemed shallow and too
easily won.

It was easy to see why she had been attracted to William.
He was charming and nice, but she had also subconsciously
known he was 'right' for her in the eyes of her parents and
friends. They were a natural match, like a pair of well-bred
dogs, designed to mate. The life predicted for them ran along
the same tracks as the one she had lived so far: comfortable,
safe and unsurprising, like the first-class carriage of a well-
oiled train. But Ellen didn't want that any more; she just didn't
know how to tell William. Running away had seemed much
easier than facing her change of heart. And yet, what if this
small mutiny was a phase, as her mother would no doubt say?
Pre-wedding nerves? What if her attraction to Conor was

simply because he was the opposite to William? What if this adventure would run its course and in the end she'd return to London and that well-oiled train, full of repentance and regret? What if William found someone else in her absence and she was left to spend the rest of her days like Dylan, pining for her lost love?

But in the morning, when the pale light of dawn tumbled in through the gaps in the curtains, she felt nothing but excitement for the coming day. She stood by the window and watched the lighthouse rise up out of the mist like a new shoot emerging through the wintry earth. William had sunk to the bottom of her thoughts and all she had room for was Conor.

Chapter 14

Ellen drove beneath the avenue of ancient oaks on her way to Reedmace House, praying that Johnny and Joe wouldn't see her car. There was every chance that they were there, and as far as she knew, the only way to Conor's house was through the park. So it was with some trepidation that she motored past the castle, where Johnny's truck was parked in its usual place. There was no chance of the two of them slacking off work while their boss was in residence, and as luck would have it they were nowhere to be seen and Ellen was able to drive around without being spotted.

The mist had dissolved, leaving a pale-blue sky and radiant sunshine. She rolled down the window to hear the merry twittering of birds and the sporadic hooting of a woodpecker in the trees. Clusters of snowdrops glistened on the banks and the grass shone a vibrant green. Soon the blossom would be out and the estate would burst into wondrous colour. She inhaled deeply and smelt the earthy scent of spring.

As she pulled up outside the house, she rather regretted having ruined her coat and boots, for Peg's attire was not very appealing. At least her well-cut jeans and blue V-neck sweater were her own. She snatched a final glance in the rear-view mirror before stepping out onto the gravel. Her heart began to thump wildly as she approached the door. William had never sent her nerves into such a state of excitement. She didn't have time to knock and gather herself because it opened at once and Conor appeared with Magnum at his side.

'Well, good morning,' he said, and his smile was full of affection.

'Good morning,' she replied shyly, trying without success to suppress her nervousness. He stepped forward, put an arm around her waist and kissed her on the lips, thus defusing any awkwardness. She laughed through her nose. 'That's better,' he said. 'Now, do you want something to drink before we go?'

'No, I've just had breakfast.'

'Right. Let's head off, then.' He let Magnum out then closed the door behind him. She followed him round to the stable block at the back of the house where he opened the boot of his Range Rover and let the dog in. 'Magnum hates to be left behind,' he told her. 'And he doesn't mind being a gooseberry. He's also incredibly discreet.'

'I'm pleased to hear it. I'm afraid I have the entire Byrne family on my case at the moment.'

'That's no surprise.' He opened the door for her and she climbed in. 'You're lucky you have so many people who care about you.'

They set off, but this time Conor turned left out of the driveway and drove down a mile or so of farm track, joining the country lane via an inconspicuous entrance at the bottom of the hill. 'Just to be on the safe side,' he said with a grin. 'I don't want to ruin your reputation.'

'I'm not sure I have one yet.'

'All the more reason, then.' He accelerated down the lane. 'So, was your aunt suspicious?'

'I think she had such a nice time chatting to your mother that she didn't notice us.'

'That's good. Mother is very short on company down here. She loved letting her hair down with Peg.'

'I have to tell you, Conor, that this is the first time I have met my mother's family.'

He didn't seem very surprised. 'Well, I hadn't ever heard your name mentioned before and I know most people in Ballymaldoon.'

'The truth is that my mother, Peg's sister, ran away with my father and never came back. I'm hiding out here because I know it's the one place my mother won't look for me.'

He raised his eyebrows. 'Ah, so you've run away from home, have you?'

'Well, I'm too old to run away, but I haven't told anyone where I've gone. If you knew my mother, you'd understand why. I just need time without my family bearing down on me. You know my parents met in your castle, before you bought it. Of course, Mother never told me. Peg did. I think Mum's embarrassed by her working-class roots; she's a terrible snob.'

'They're nothing to be ashamed of. The Byrne family are good people.'

'I know. I feel rather let down, actually. All this time, I've had a wonderful family over here that I never knew existed.'

'She must have had good reason to cut ties.'

'Is marrying an English Protestant a good enough reason, do you think?'

'If her mother was a very devout Catholic, perhaps.'

Ellen crinkled her nose. 'It just seems a bit drastic to me, to run away from your mother and siblings and never return, all because you fell in love with the wrong man.'

'I'd say that you only know the half of it. Nothing is ever

simple.' He smiled at her. 'So, tell me, what's your family in England like?'

Ellen told him about Leonora and Lavinia, and her descriptions of their superficial lives and her ruthless imitations made him roar with laughter. 'They're like my father,' she said. 'Fair with flawless skin, big blue eyes and long legs. They're so similar it's hard to tell them apart, although there are two years between them. I'm the black sheep of the family. Dark and troubled – the more I learn about my mother the more I realize that I am probably something like her. And that's not an easy admission. I find my mother intolerable!'

'You'll feel happier when you break the mould and start being yourself. It sounds to me as if you're struggling against your mother's ambitions. She should relax and let you make your own way.'

'She wants me to marry a duke at the very least.'

'She sounds like Mrs Bennet.'

'I know, that sort of attitude seems so old-fashioned, doesn't it?'

'Oh, it's alive and kicking all right. There'll always be aspirational people climbing up the social ladder, leaping to the top with a good marriage. I don't suppose she's thought for a minute what sort of man *you* want. What does your father think about it?'

'I'm sure he'd be happy with whoever I married as long as I'm happy, but deep down, he'd prefer me to marry a man like him, of course: Eton-educated, good at sport, rich and well-connected.' She paused a moment, reflecting on her parents' marriage. It was a miracle that it had worked, considering the very different worlds they came from. 'You know, I think my mother has tried so hard for so long to fit into Dad's world that she has lost sight of the important things in life. As I was growing up, all she cared about was appearances. That I looked right and said the right things and was invited to the right parties. She forced me to attend the debutante balls even though the debutante thing was way out of date and no longer glamorous. She was desperate to find me a suitable husband – but all the boys were chinless and gauche, especially the aristocratic ones! All interbred, I'm afraid.' She sighed and shook her head in mock despair. 'I mean, really, what was she thinking? I shouldn't laugh, though, she hasn't given up yet!' She began to imitate her mother ruthlessly. She had always been an excellent mimic.

'You're a funny girl, Ellen,' he said, wiping a tear from his eye. 'You should have been an actress.'

'I bet you say that to all the girls,' she retorted dryly.

'I don't, actually. But I wouldn't recommend it, even to someone as talented as you. You're better off behind the camera, writing stories.'

'I have never wanted to be an actress.'

'Always a writer?'

'I like words and I like to express myself that way. But I'm not sure I'm very good at it. I'm feeling my way, just trying to find how best to channel my creativity.' She laughed. 'I hope I'm not deluding myself, and that I do have *some* creativity!'

'Of course you do, otherwise you wouldn't even be considering it. So, if you weren't a writer, what would you be?'

'I don't know. At the risk of sounding like a self-help book, I'm very confused about *who* I want to be right now.' She gazed out of the window at the green velvet fields and grey stone walls and said the first thing that came into her head. 'A gardener, perhaps.'

'A gardener?' He was surprised.

'Yes, my mother would *hate* me to be a gardener! She'd like me to be a grand lady who lunches and sits on charity committees like her. But I think I'd like to plant things and watch them grow. I know nothing about gardening, and didn't realize until I arrived here that I liked nature so much. But yes, I think gardening would make me very happy.' She turned to him and smiled. 'Do you think there's something magical about Connemara?'

'Yes,' he replied, smiling back. 'But only if you're willing to be enchanted.'

After a short drive, Conor parked in a lay-by on the crest of a hill. 'Right, now for some serious castle-creeping,' he announced, switching off the engine.

'I'm surprised you like castle-creeping when you have a castle of your own.'

'It's not the same, you'll see. This one's a total ruin. You're going to love it.' They both climbed out and Conor walked round to the boot to let Magnum out. The dog bounded down in a rush of excitement and cocked his leg against the wheel of the car. Conor opened the gate then took her by the hand and led her down the field.

There, on the cliff overlooking the ocean, were the stony remains of a once magnificent castle. Hollow towers and crumbling walls were all that was left of a mighty fortress, protecting the land from invasion by sea. The wind whipped through the empty windows and whistled around the redundant ramparts where once soldiers had kept watch for the enemy and ladies in rich velvet dresses had looked out for trade ships bringing silks and spices from foreign lands.

'Ireland is full of ruins,' said Conor, as they approached.

Ellen wanted to bring up the ruin that fascinated her the most every morning on waking, but she knew instinctively that Caitlin was unmentionable. 'Ireland's a very romantic country,' she said instead.

He smiled down at her and gripped her hand tighter. 'I like you, Ellen Byrne.'

'I'm Ellen *Trawton.*'

'So you are. Well, I like you whatever you're called. You're like a ray of sunshine.'

Ellen smiled at him quizzically. 'You know my name means "bright light" in Greek?'

'No, I didn't,' he replied. 'Greek was never my strong subject at school. But did you ever see the movie *The Age of Innocence* with Daniel Day-Lewis and Michelle Pfeiffer?'

'The infamous Ellen Olenska,' she said, repeating what Dylan had already told her.

'That was a tremendous film.'

'I'm ashamed to admit that I haven't seen it. Nor have I read the book.'

He looked pleased. 'Then I'll get the DVD and we'll watch it together. I think you'll like the Countess, your namesake. She's a wonderful character – very mysterious, rather manipulative, I think, but utterly compelling. It's a beautiful and sad love story.'

They reached the ruins and began to wander around. Magnum sniffed the ground, following the scent of fox. There was no one else there besides them and the dog. The castle was hidden from the road and those who knew of it didn't bother to look at a pile of old stones. Ellen's stomach began to tingle with nerves as she anticipated him kissing her again. 'I think this would have been the sitting room,' she announced, letting go of his hand and jumping playfully over a knee-high wall into a large, grassy square where the remains of a chimney could be seen against the outside wall.

'You think?' he questioned, following her.

'Oh, yes, I can imagine them all sitting around drinking wine, can't you?'

He laughed. 'Or it could have been the kitchen. Can't you just see a big, fat cook roasting a pig on a spit?'

'No, it's much too elegant to have been a kitchen.' She hopped over another wall into a smaller room where a big arched window looked out over the sea. 'This might have been a library. What do you think?'

He put his hands on his hips and frowned. 'Or a study.'

'Yes, it might have been a study. Perhaps it was a smaller sitting room. You know how grand houses always have so many sitting rooms?' She looked out of the hole where the window used to be. 'I wonder who gazed out of here. A young maiden in love with a sailor, perhaps, waiting for him to return across the sea?' When she turned around, Conor was standing right behind her.

'Are you playing hard to get, Ellen Trawton?' he asked, pressing her against the wall. She caught her breath. 'Well, you've caught me, all right, Conor Macausland,' she replied, mimicking a strong Irish accent.

'Not bad for a posh English bird!' he exclaimed, his gaze heavy with intent.

She laughed. 'You sound just like my uncle Johnny.'

He swept a lock of hair behind her ear. 'You don't have to be nervous. I'm not going to eat you.'

'I think it's the beard. You make me feel like Little Red Riding Hood.'

He laughed and pressed his lips to hers. 'Let's hope it's the woodcutter's day off, then.'

He kissed her passionately and for a moment she was quite overcome by the force of it. She could feel the heat through his clothes and the sexual energy that escalated between them. He smelt of lemon and spice, and the very masculine strength of his physique made her go weak with desire. She forgot herself and her inhibitions, aware only of the sensual pleasure now creeping over her. He buried his face in her neck and kissed the curve of her shoulder and the feeling of his tongue against her skin made her gasp out loud and long for a bed they could both tumble into.

At last, he pulled away, breathless. 'You drive me wild, Ellen!' he whispered, kissing her lips again, this time with more tenderness.

'What's the name of Ellen Olenska's lover?' she asked, attempting to quieten the noisy pounding of her heart.

'Newland Archer.'

'Do they have a happy ending?'

'I'm not going to tell you.'

'That's unfair!' she protested.

'If I tell you, I'll ruin it for you.'

'I want to know whether the name Ellen is lucky or unlucky.'

He looked at her for a long moment as he considered her question. The frown that lined his brow suggested that it wasn't an easy question to answer. 'I can't tell you that without giving away the end of the story. But I can tell you that *you* are lucky, whatever you're called.'

Later, they walked along the clifftop, hand in hand, while Magnum ran on ahead, invigorated by the wind. Gulls cried mournfully from the skies and birds twittered in the gorse bushes. The ocean roared below them, breaking onto the rocks in small eruptions of foam, and the sun peeped out every now and then from blue holes in the cloud to sprinkle them with optimism.

'I suppose your Aunt Peg has told you about my wife,' he said softly, holding her hand tightly as if he thought she might run away at the mention of his marriage.

'A little. I'm sorry, for you *and* the children. It must have been dreadful.'

He glanced at her and smiled sadly. 'It was.' They walked on for a while in silence. Ellen wondered whether he was going to talk more about Caitlin, or whether he was just making sure that she knew his past, as she had done earlier by telling him about her mother. 'You don't want to believe everything they tell you, all right?' he added, giving her hand a gentle squeeze. She wasn't sure how to respond, for she didn't want to let on how much she had already heard. 'My wife died in an accident and that's the truth.'

'That's what I've heard,' she replied, eager to dispel the tortured expression in his profile.

'Your Aunt Peg is a good woman,' he conceded. 'Others aren't so well intentioned. There's a lot of small-town gossip in a place like Ballymaldoon. There always was and there always will be. But until something else dramatic happens there, I shall be their favourite subject. That's why I don't venture into town much.'

'You came to the pub.'

He grinned across at her and pulled her a little closer. 'That's because I wanted to find *you*.'

'You could have spoken to Johnny or Joe at work.'

'They had already left.'

'Then you could have dropped by Peg's.'

He shook his head. 'No, I couldn't, not after . . .' He hesitated a moment, then rejected the thought with another toss of his head. 'I knew I'd find you or a Byrne or ten in the Pot of Gold.'

'You must have given them all one hell of a shock, just turning up like that, out of the blue.'

'Oh, I'm sure I did.' He chuckled to himself. 'I must admit, it did give me a certain pleasure to see the look on their faces.'

They reached an old-fashioned little fishing village, nestled in a sheltered cove out of the wind. Conor knew the pub. It was smaller than the Pot of Gold and much quieter. Only a couple of old men in caps sat at the bar, drinking Guinness, while a group of four women played cards at a table beside one of the windows.

The publican greeted them with typical Irish warmth and poured Conor a pint. Ellen asked for a Coke and told Conor about the time she had tried Guinness to impress Johnny and had nearly thrown up all over the bar.

'Oh, that was brave of you!' he teased, taking their glasses and choosing a table at the other end of the pub to the card players. 'I could have told you you're not a Guinness girl just by looking at you.'

'I think Johnny could, too. He must have thought I was mad, asking for a pint.'

'I bet he was impressed by your spirit, though,' he said kindly.

She took a sip of Coke. 'This is much better.'

'I bet the whole town is talking about you, almost as much as they're talking about me.'

'Do you think?'

'Absolutely. They're probably still talking about your mother running off with her Englishman all those years ago.'

'The morning after I arrived, Johnny, Joe, Craic, Desmond and Ryan all turned up for breakfast at Peg's.'

Conor laughed. 'I bet they did. Imagine, they hadn't seen your mother for, what, thirty years?'

'Thirty-four, to be precise.'

He stared at her quizzically. 'And you are?'

'I'm thirty-three.'

'So, what's your mother doing trying to marry you off then? You're young!'

'Not in her eyes. She married my father at twenty-five and had me the same year.'

He narrowed his eyes and looked at her steadily. 'Then you know why she ran off, don't you?'

'Well, like I said—'

'She ran off because she was pregnant with you. I mean, getting pregnant out of wedlock would have been enough to have sent your grandmother to an early grave.'

Ellen's eyes widened. She looked incredulous. 'No! Not my mother!' But then she frowned. It did add up, after all. 'You think?' She was about to protest, but stumbled on the words.

'Of course. Good Catholics don't have sex before marriage and we're talking over thirty years ago. Ireland thirty years ago was still in the Dark Ages and your grandmother was a different generation altogether.'

'Oh, my God! I mean, my mother is so Catholic and so quick to criticize others for misdemeanours far less serious than that!' She swallowed a gulp of Coke. 'Do you think my grandmother knew that she was pregnant?'

'I doubt it very much. Your mother would have known what a sin her mother would consider it to be. You know, girls who got pregnant out of wedlock were put in nunneries and their babies were given away. Your mother would have kept her pregnancy very secret, I can assure you.'

'So my grandmother must have wondered why her daughter never came back.'

'Perhaps.' He rubbed his beard thoughtfully. 'Though I imagine one person would have known everything.'

'Who?'

'Father Michael. If your mother was a good Catholic—'

'She still *is* a good Catholic. Or rather, she likes people to think she's a good Catholic.'

'She most likely confessed to the priest. I'll bet he knows the whole story.'

'Would he tell *me*?'

Conor shook his head. 'Not likely.'

'Might he have told my grandmother? They were cousins, you know, and Joe told me that Father Michael had lunch with her every Sunday without fail. How indiscreet do you think he is?' She grinned mischievously. 'I mean, he manufactures his own sloe gin.'

'And it's quality gin, too! Perhaps he's not entirely discreet under the influence. But I'm afraid I don't really know Father Michael well enough to answer that question.'

Ellen took another sip of her drink. 'So, the plot thickens. Johnny did say that my mother was wild and bound to do something really stupid – getting pregnant then would have been really stupid.'

Conor's eyes twinkled at her fondly. 'She fell in love. There's nothing stupid about that, Ellen. When you fall for someone you want to make love to them. There's nothing stupid about that, either.' He took her hand across the table. 'I want to make love to you,' he said, lowering his voice.

Ellen felt a blush flower on her cheeks. 'You're very direct, Conor,' she replied. But her smile was enough to tell him how much she wanted him to.

They ordered food and ate it slowly as they shared stories. Ellen didn't mention William, and Conor didn't mention

Caitlin. At that point it didn't seem to matter that they both harboured secrets. At that point it didn't look as if those secrets would have any impact on their budding relationship. Falling in love forced them into the present and neither the past nor the future really seemed to matter at all.

Chapter 15

I watch their flirtation with a mixture of curiosity and rage. Ellen gazes into Conor's eyes believing she sees love in them, and I smile because it is all too easy to mistake lust for love. Conor is not a man so easily won. He is wild and independent, selfish and strong. Many beautiful women before me tried and failed to capture his heart, and there will be many more after Ellen who will break themselves against him like waves against rock.

He wants to bed her and she believes his longing is a physical reflection of his growing affection: If I could I would tell her to run right now and never look back, because he will surely crush her dreams and tear her heart to shreds. But I cannot and I admit there is some pleasure in watching the story unfold before me. After all, I have been in this limbo for so long, don't I deserve a little entertainment?

The fact remains that no woman will ever match up to me. Conor loves only me and always will. All the Ellens in the world will never replace the only woman he has ever loved. I know that we argued and fought and that I went to terrible lengths to force him to prove how much he cared, but beneath the tempest that was our life together, we needed each other. We truly did, as the flower needs the bee and the bee needs the flower.

It is getting dark when they return to Reedmace House. Daphne took the children to the beach where they built castles and flew their kites with Ewan, but she is back now, baking potatoes for their tea. She notices their rosy cheeks and sparkling eyes when they walk into the kitchen.

'Did you have a good day?' she asks, and I know she is eager for details. She watches her son closely for anything that might give more away than he is willing to share.

'We had a great day,' he replies, switching on the kettle.

She turns to Ellen, hoping for more. 'Why, you look so well, dear. I love your hair all wild like that. You must have been blown about by the wind.'

Ellen catches Conor's eye and he suppresses a smile. 'It was so windy,' says Ellen. 'We went to a beautiful ruined castle on top of a cliff, then walked for miles and had lunch in a pub. The more I see of Ireland the more I fall in love.' She bends down and pats Magnum as he wanders past like a lion that has been out hunting all day and is now tired and docile. I notice how Ellen has lost her fear of dogs. I notice too that she hasn't smoked. It is interesting what women do for love – but no one has gone as far as me, although Conor would argue that what I did was so terrible it couldn't possibly have been motivated by love. Oh, Conor, how wrong you are. How very wrong. Everything I did was propelled by my love for you: even that.

Ellen has taken off her coat and boots and is standing in her socks, leaning against the kitchen counter. Conor gives her a cup of tea and they both warm up as Daphne bustles about the kitchen, searching for signs to corroborate her suspicions that her son has at last fallen in love. She listens to their banter, for now they are as intimate and close as two people who have known each other years, not days, and the excitement between them is as tangible as heat.

The children come in for tea and Ida shows Ellen her nails. She has already chipped a few burrowing in the sand as she built her castle this afternoon. Ellen promises to repaint them. Another excuse for her to come to the house – not that she needs one because Conor is keen to see more of her. In fact, he is drunk with lust. I can see it in his eyes. It is a long time since he was so excited by a woman. The darkness he has carried around for the last five years like a shroud of misery has suddenly begun to disintegrate and light is shining through the holes, making him dizzy with happiness. He cannot believe that this woman has walked into his life and so quickly transformed it. The children seem to notice and are infected by his good mood. They laugh and joke at the kitchen table, sharing the adventures they had today with Ewan and Daphne, and Conor laughs too, delighted by their tales.

Conor does not want Ellen to go, but it is late and she worries that Peg will wonder where she is. 'Can't I call you?' he asks as they stand in the hall and Ellen shrugs on Peg's coat. She explains that she threw her telephone into the sea. 'Now why would you go and do something like that?' he asks.

'Because I don't want to speak to my mother.'

'You could have just ignored her calls.'

'No, I couldn't.'

He sighs, frustrated. 'I'll get you another one.'

She laughs. 'You don't have to do that.'

'I have to fly back to Dublin tomorrow night. The children go back to school on Monday. I'll get you one there and send it to you.'

She pales. 'But you'll come back?'

He pushes her into the boot room and closes the door behind them. 'As long as you're here, I'll come back, Ellen,' he murmurs, and kisses her. I can see that he frightens her a little. Conor is a passionate man. She obviously isn't used to men like him; men who aren't afraid to be men. 'I want to see you tomorrow.'

'I have to go to Mass and lunch with Desmond and Alanna.'

'Then I'll come to Mass, too.'

'But you'll have to face all the gossiping locals again.'

'I'll do it for *you*.' He grins at her with such fondness that his face softens quite dramatically. I haven't seen his face do that except when he looks at the children. I am gripped by a cold and furious jealousy. 'I want to be alone with you, Ellen. I want to kiss you all over,' he says, and the urgency in his voice leaves her breathless. I can almost feel her heartbeat accelerating beneath her coat. He kisses her again, deeply and ardently, and her body sags beneath the weight of his desire. She is like a rag doll being mauled by a wolf. But she likes it. I liked it, too. For a minute, I feel as if it is me standing there against the coats. I am alive again and Conor is loving me like he used to, before . . . he is loving me like he did when we first met and I was all he ever wanted. Oh, Ellen, Ellen, you think you're all he wants, but you're not. I was there first and my imprint is still indented on his heart.

He sees her to her car and watches her drive away. He remains standing for a while, watching her headlights disappear up the track. She has chosen to drive past the castle because she is unsure of the other way. But she needn't fear being seen by Johnny and Joe. They are probably in the pub by now, enjoying a pint with their friends and family, as they do every evening. I used to enjoy the pub. Life was lonely up at the castle on my own when Conor was away. I loved the throng of people, the noise of their chatter, the stuffiness of the room with the fire lit and all the windows closed. I relished the attention. I was aware that everyone was staring at me, as if I were a rare bird among chickens. Now they are more curious about me than ever. But tomorrow they will see Conor at Mass, which will set their tongues wagging even more than when he walked into the pub, because the last time Conor set foot in a church was at my funeral.

Ellen drives back to Peg's. Her aunt is at the card table with Oswald. The fire is lit. Mr Badger is curled up on the sofa, while Bertie is in the kitchen by the stove. Jack is perched on the tallboy in the sitting room, watching the card game from his lofty post. When Peg hears the car she pricks her ears and raises her eyes from her hand of cards.

'That must be Ellen,' she says to Oswald. 'She's been out all day.'

Oswald takes a sip of wine. 'What's she up to, do you think?'

'She's in love, I'm afraid.'

'With Conor Macausland?'

'Of course. It was written all over her face.' Peg shrugs helplessly. 'There's nothing I can do about it.'

'Do you think she'll own up?'

'I don't think she'll lie. She's already confessed to running away from home. Although I'd guessed as much. But I won't be telling the boys. Desmond won't have it, and you know him, he can be very fierce when he wants to be.'

'Ellen's a grown woman. Surely it's up to her who she dates?'

'Not when her date is Conor Macausland. Not that I have anything against the man. In fact, he has my pity, poor fellow. To lose a wife is bad enough, but to be suspected of her murder is beyond the pale.'

Oswald looks at her with such tenderness, I am quite astonished. She doesn't notice because her eyes are now lowered to her cards – not that she's looking at them. So she doesn't see the way he's gazing at her. His face is soft and full of compassion and I know that he is thinking of her little girl. She is thinking of her, too. And there, right beside her, *is* her little girl. It is incredible that she is bathed in the loving aura of her child and she doesn't even know it.

The door opens and Ellen strides in, all pink-cheeked and shiny-eyed. 'Hello!' she calls out. 'Aunt Peg?'

'We're in here,' her aunt calls back. Mr Badger lifts his ears but he doesn't bother to get down from his warm sofa. Jack now knows Ellen well enough not to be alarmed. He simply moves his head from side to side in that jerky manner as if he's listening intently. Bertie is so fast asleep, he doesn't hear the door open and close or feel the cold wind as it breezes into the kitchen.

'Hi,' she says, striding into the sitting room. She brings the outdoors with her and Peg shivers. Ellen smiles, unable to hide her excitement.

'Well, look at you. Aren't you the cat that got the cream!' says Peg.

'What have you been up to?' Oswald asks, peering at her over his spectacles like a schoolmaster.

Ellen flops into the armchair with a contented sigh. She closes her eyes a second and I know that she is struggling with the thought of lying to them. She wrestles with her conscience for a moment, but honesty prevails. 'Oh, Peg, I'm crazy about him!' she declares, and she grins at her aunt with such charm that the old woman is immediately won over.

'Oh, dear, you wouldn't be speaking about Conor Macausland, now would you?' She sighs, unable to share the girl's enthusiasm.

'I know you warned me against him. Everyone has. But I can't help it.' Ellen puts her hands up in defeat. 'I cannot resist him.'

'Well, don't you go telling the boys, now, will you? Desmond won't have it.'

Ellen laughs. She cannot believe that her uncle has any power over who she chooses to fall in love with. 'But really, Aunt Peg, that's absurd.'

'To you it might be, but we do things differently over here.' She inhales deeply and her large bosom expands even further onto the table. 'I'm afraid it won't do to have a Byrne stepping out with that man.'

'But you know he's not a murderer!' Ellen cries.

'Well, of course he isn't, pet.'

'It's the gossip,' interjects Oswald calmly. 'No one wants their family name dragged through the mud.'

'I'm a Trawton, too,' Ellen retorts sulkily.

'Not over here, you're not. You're a Byrne through and through,' Peg corrects her. Then she softens and puts down her cards. 'So, where did you go?'

'To a ruined castle and a pub for lunch. It was all very innocent, you know.'

'I'm sure it was.' Peg smiles at her niece. 'Whatever anyone says about him, no one can deny that Conor Macausland is a gentleman.'

At that moment, the little girl wanders over to the sofa and kneels beside Mr Badger. The dog opens his eyes and twitches his ears. She puts her nose so close to his that they are almost touching. Mr Badger thumps his tail on the cushion. 'What's got into him?' Ellen asks, but neither Peg nor Oswald is particularly surprised.

'A fairy,' says Oswald.

Peg smiles and shakes her head fondly. 'Are we going to continue our game or are you going to lower the conversation into the realm of peasant superstition and fantasy?'

'You're a hard woman, Peg Byrne,' he replies, shaking his head. They resume their game.

'I'm going to get something to eat. Can I get either of you anything?' Ellen asks, getting up.

'Don't forget to call London,' Peg reminds her. 'That's the deal, remember?'

'I'll do it now,' Ellen replies. She pats the dog as she walks past him, but he has eyes only for the little girl.

I have been into Peg's bedroom and watched her kneel in prayer beside the votive candle and the photograph of her child. I have watched that same child kneel beside her like a guardian angel, filling the room with a light that Peg cannot see. I remain close to my children, but not in the same way as this happy spirit. I am anxious and tormented, frustrated and sad. She is serene and at peace, unaffected by her mother's grief. It is as if she has a deep understanding that reaches far beyond the human senses, as if she can see the bigger picture that I cannot see nor begin to comprehend. Grief, sorrow, happiness, delight: they are all but ripples on a vast lake that come and go according to how the wind blows, but beneath is something else, a deep and contented knowing. I wish I knew what it was and had access to it.

Ellen helps herself to food from the fridge then sits beside the telephone, staring at it for a long while, lost in thought. She eats and chews and stares. At last, she picks up the receiver and dials a number. It rings a few times before it is answered.

'Emily?'

'God, is that you, Ellie?'

'Yes, it is.'

'I've been trying to get hold of you for a week.'

'Sorry.'

'So, how's it going over there in deepest, darkest Ireland?'

'It's fabulous. I'm loving it!'

'Well, I'm glad *you're* having a great time, because you've left *me* on the front line over here, fighting all your enemies.'

'I'm so sorry. Is Mum being a pain?'

'Not just your mother, but yes, she's called about a hundred times. Aren't you getting any of your messages?'

'I threw my phone into the sea.'

'Well, that explains it, then. I've had Leonora and Lavinia on the phone as well, wanting to know where you are, but more importantly, your mother wants to know what's going on with William.'

'Ah, William.'

'Your fiancé, remember?' Ellen hesitates. The word 'fiancé' appalls her. 'From the way he's behaving I presume you haven't called it off,' Emily continues.

'I just told him I need space.'

'Oh, Ellie, that's pathetic!'

'I know. I just couldn't bring myself to end it. He's a nice guy. I don't want to hurt his feelings.' She inhales deeply, then lowers her voice. 'I can't be sure I won't bolt back to London and still want to marry him.'

Her friend's voice changes now. She is more sympathetic. 'So what's it like there?'

'Beautiful.'

'Are you actually writing anything?'

'No.'

'I thought not. So, what are you doing with your time, then? Besides throwing your mobile into the sea!'

'I'm hanging out in the pub with the locals.'

'God, Ellie . . .'

Ellen laughs. 'It's called the Pot of Gold.'

'I bet it is. How quaint. Do they all say "top of the morning" and sing ballads?'

'That's just silly!'

'Aren't you missing civilization?'

'It's very civilized here.'

'You surprise me. I didn't think you could live outside a mile radius of Harvey Nichols!'

'Neither did I. But Emily, I've fallen in love ... with Connemara. Right now I have no intention of coming back.'

'You know you're the talk of the town. London is buzzing with gossip. Why did you leave your job? Where have you gone? Has anyone spoken to you? Have you had a row with William? Is it off? Is it on? What does your mother say?'

'Where do they think I've gone?'

'Thailand.'

Ellen laughs. 'To do what, exactly?'

'People are saying that you've gone to a retreat in preparation for your wedding.'

'Oh, really!'

'I know. Aren't they all shallow!' Emily gives a smoky laugh. 'So, what do you want me to tell William?'

'How is he?'

'Confused and worried. He came round last night for a drink.'

'Does he look dreadful?'

'Not at all. Tragedy suits him, actually.'

'What did he say?'

'That if you need time you can have all the time you want. But he's put out that you didn't tell him to his face and that you haven't told him where you are.'

Ellen cringes. 'I know, I've been horrid.'

'He's quite cross.'

'Well, he has every right to be, I suppose.'

'And he doesn't like the fact that everyone is talking about it. I think it's dented his pride. Why you couldn't have taken a week's holiday instead of *quitting* your job, I can't imagine. Why did you have to be so dramatic and make such a scene? The whole of London is gossiping about you and you haven't even been away a week. It's ridiculous.'

'I just snapped, all right. I wasn't thinking. I just had to go. Anyway, isn't he worried about *me*?'

'He thinks it's pre-wedding nerves, Ellie, which a lot of brides suffer. I'm sure he's worried about you, too.'

'Doesn't sound like it.'

'Shall I tell him that I've spoken to you and that you're fine? Would it hurt if I tell him where you are?'

Ellen is horrified at the thought. 'Don't you dare tell him where I am! Don't tell anyone where I am. I mean it, Emily. I don't want to be found right now. I haven't even been away a week. You can tell Mum that you've spoken to me and that I'm OK. For God's sake, don't let on that I'm in Ireland.'

'OK, OK, don't lose your rag. I'll keep my mouth shut, but you owe me, big time! I'm fighting a war over here while you sing "Danny Boy" in the Pot of Gold! It isn't easy fending them all off. It would have been easier to have told them you were going away on a short break to some faraway place which has no mobile reception. That way, no one would have worried – and no one would be calling me up to find out where you are!'

They talk on but their conversation no longer interests me. Finally, after promising to call again, Ellen hangs up. She remains a while, thinking about what Emily has said. I don't know what is in her mind, but she frowns and her face has lost its earlier cheerfulness.

So, Ellen is engaged to be married and has run away. I am delighted by this important piece of information. Although I am not with Conor and Ellen all the time, I am pretty sure she hasn't told him. That would be enough to send him into a violent rage. He won't be able to trust her any longer and *that* will be my greatest weapon. If Conor has a chink in his armour it is trust. I let him down, but only because he drove me to it, so desperate and deep was my love, but he won't cope with it a second time. It will be Ellen's undoing.

She washes her plate and puts it away, then wanders into the library. She carefully searches all the spines until she seizes upon the one she wants. I am not at all surprised that she is after *The Age of Innocence*, by Edith Wharton. Ellen pulls it out and looks it over, the joy returning to her features. I know why she wants to read it, because she is desperate to know whether it has a happy ending. I could tell her that it does not.

Chapter 16

The following morning, Ellen awoke to the sound of rain rattling against her bedroom windows. She lay a moment in the semi-darkness, listening to the wind while still warm beneath the covers. A shiver of excitement rippled over her skin as she remembered the feeling of being enveloped in Conor's arms. She stretched her limbs and writhed with wanton pleasure at the thought of his hands caressing her body.

She ran a bath and hummed as she brushed her teeth and pulled a pair of navy corduroy trousers out of the cupboard. It had been years since she had gone to Mass. Her mother had dragged her to church every Sunday as a child, but since she had left home and gone to university she hadn't attended much except for weddings, christenings and the annual religious festivals. She had nothing against church, it was simply that it had ceased to play a big part in her life. As for God, she didn't doubt the existence of a higher power; she just didn't spend very much time thinking about it. The fact that she was going to church today had nothing to do with religion at all. She was going to please her family. And she was going to see Conor.

Peg came in from feeding her animals and they breakfasted together. 'Well, don't you look smart for Mass! I suppose you'd better wear that silly fur thing of yours. It dried very nicely.'

'I thought I'd ruined it.'

'Sadly not. Still, it's better than an anorak and I'm sure you'll think my best coat too old for you.' She sat down on Jack's chair and hand-fed him a piece of bread. 'So, did you telephone London last night?'

'Yes, I called my friend Emily. Mother is fine. She's not worrying at all.' She winced at her lie and dropped her eyes to her porridge.

'Good. You see, it wasn't so difficult, was it? It wouldn't do to worry your mother when a simple phone call can put her mind at rest.'

'I'm meeting Conor at the church,' Ellen added, trying to sound casual.

Peg was astonished. 'Conor's going to Mass?' She frowned so that her whole face crumpled like a walnut.

'Yes. Is that odd?'

'Odd? It's unbelievable. Why would he want to put himself through that again?'

'Through what?'

'The last time he went to Mass was for Caitlin's funeral. It wasn't at the big church in town where you're going today, but a small, derelict chapel up on the hill. Still, most of the locals went and they all whispered goodness knows what accusations that he left without talking to anyone. It was a dreadful occasion. I didn't go, but Johnny and Joe did, and they said it was devastating to watch.'

'Surely it won't be that bad five years later?'

'I wouldn't be so sure. I don't know whether he's brave or foolish. Why is he going, anyway?'

'I don't know. Perhaps he wants to go with his children. The man's entitled to go to Mass.'

'Of course he is, but I think he's going to see you.'

'He doesn't need to go to Mass to see me. He only has to ask me over.'

'Then I don't know why he's going. But you be careful, now. Don't go making a holy show of yourself, will you? The boys won't like it at all. Be discreet, Ellen.' Peg gave her a long, hard stare as Ellen stared back defiantly. 'Jaysus, sometimes you have such a look of your mother it alarms me.'

'It alarms me, too,' Ellen replied with a laugh. She didn't want to be like her mother, but the photos she had seen of her as a child resembled her much more than she had realized. 'I'll be careful, Aunt Peg. I promise.'

At a quarter to ten, Joe drove up in his father's truck. He looked quite different in a pair of clean trousers and a jacket, with his hair brushed off his face. 'You scrub up well, Joe,' she said, climbing in out of the rain.

'So do you, Ellen,' he replied, starting the engine. 'Which is lucky, because everyone's going to be looking at you.'

'Don't say that!'

'Why not? It's the truth. The entire Byrne clan will be there, except for Peg, of course. Everyone'll want to get a good look at you.'

A shadow of anxiety passed over her happiness. She didn't want attention drawn to herself and Conor. 'They'll get over me very quickly,' she added hopefully.

'That's what you think. But they're talking about nothing else at the moment.'

'You're such a tease!'

He glanced at her seriously. 'I'm not teasing you, Ellen. The entire town's having a good old chinwag.'

'I can't believe you all have nothing else to talk about.'

'Oh, we have plenty to talk about. The trouble is we talk so much we need twice as much fodder as anyone else.' He laughed. 'Don't look so freaked out. I'll look after you.'

She rolled her eyes and replied with sarcasm. 'Oh, that makes me feel so much better, Joe. Thank you!'

Joe drove down the drive and out into the lane. It was still raining hard. The windscreen wipers moved rhythmically and loudly across the glass, struggling to keep it clear. The landscape looked bleak beneath the low cloud, the sea grey and tempestuous, pounding the island where the lighthouse stood defiant against the elements like the last soldier standing.

They drove into town, where the locals were making their way to Mass beneath wide umbrellas. They were all elegantly dressed in their Sunday best and Ellen was pleased she'd brought a pair of smart trousers and shoes, although she felt a little ridiculous in her fake-fur coat. She was reminded of her mother, who always dressed up for church as if she were going to a wedding, in an immaculately tailored suit, an appropriately sober hat and always high heels to give her stature, for she was not a tall woman. Her attire made her feel important, Ellen thought, and reinforced her position in the highest echelons of London society. Who would guess that she came from this small town in deepest Connemara? And if they knew, would they mind? To Ellen it seemed absurd to think that anyone would care.

Ellen and Joe dashed up the path and into the church because Joe didn't have an umbrella. By the time they were under cover it was too late. They were wet almost to the skin. Had it not been for Ellen's fur jacket she would most certainly have been wet right through. She walked down the aisle and scanned the faces for Conor's, as much as she could without being too conspicuous. The pews were full of chattering people and there was an air of expectancy and excitement in the atmosphere that mingled with the damp smell of hot bodies. She felt the weight of their curious stares but bore them bravely, encouraged by the thought that Conor was somewhere in the church. She noticed Dylan in a black hat and suit. He was even wearing a tie. She smiled at him and his whole face glowed with affection. But where was Conor?

The Byrnes were all seated on the left of the aisle. They took up at least six pews with their wives and children. Ellen squeezed in on the end beside Alanna, whispering brief hellos to her uncles. There was a great deal of turning round and hissing introductions before the priest stepped into the nave and a hush fell over the congregation.

Father Michael was old and bristly like a fat badger. His thinning hair was black at the whiskers but the rest, what little he had, was grey. He parted it at the side to cover his baldness, but it often got caught in the wind and stood up like a lid to reveal a shiny pink crown, sprinkled with freckles. He wore purple robes which draped over the large expanse of his belly and fell to the ground in thick folds.

As he welcomed his congregation, Ellen glanced across the aisle and was surprised to see the profile of a fine-boned man in a black fedora hat and heavy black coat, seated in the middle of the pew. He was arrestingly handsome, with a strong nose, smooth skin and a boldly defined jaw. It was only when her eyes slid along to the two children and Daphne, who sat beside him, that she realized who he was, and the colour rushed to her cheeks in a hot lava of surprise. Conor had shaved off his beard and cut his hair.

At that moment he turned, as if the intensity of her stare was as physical as a tap on the shoulder. He might have looked different without his beard, but his eyes were the same sapphire blue. When he saw her his lips curled only very slightly, but his eyes softened and twinkled with mischief, acknowledging her reaction to the unexpected change in his appearance with undisguised pleasure.

She turned back to her prayer book, hoping that the racing of her heart and the heat of her blushes didn't draw unwelcome attention. She tried hard not to look at him again but the desire to do so was overwhelming, and once or twice, she slid her eyes across the aisle only to retract them a moment's later as if the sight of him had scalded her. She was surprised to see that he looked much younger and no longer tormented, as if his anger had fallen away with his hair. If she had thought him attractive before, she now thought him devastatingly so. She grew hot beneath her coat and unbuttoned it for relief. How many 'Hail Mary's would she have to recite to make up for the lascivious thoughts that now evoked ungodly images in her mind?

When the congregation stood to queue for Holy Communion, Ellen found herself facing Conor across the aisle. She glanced up at him in alarm, not knowing how to respond when so many people were staring at them. But Conor smiled coolly and gestured for her to go first. She stepped out into the aisle and found herself standing almost directly in front of him, with Alanna sandwiched between them like a piece of wood between a pair of attracting magnets. Ellen couldn't turn around, but she could feel his eyes upon her back and chewed her thumbnail nervously. When at last they knelt before the altar, Alanna took the place on Ellen's right, leaving her left open for Conor. He took it and knelt, waiting for the approach. They didn't look at each other, for they both sensed that they, and not Father Michael, were the focus of everyone's attention. But their arms were so close, almost touching, and

Ellen could see him out of the corner of her eye. His face remained impassive like the calm surface of a lake, but she could sense the pull of attraction, like an undercurrent, in the small space between them.

Father Michael reached them much too soon and offered them the blood and body of Christ. Once she had sipped from the cup and put the Holy Bread on her tongue, she managed to glance at Conor before standing up and returning to her pew. His new face was compelling. She wondered what it would feel like to kiss him now that his skin was smooth, and ran a finger absent-mindedly over her lips. He glanced back at her, giving her just enough time to see the humorous gleam in his eyes, as if he was relishing her astonishment and trying hard to conceal his pleasure.

As Conor walked back up the aisle, Ellen noticed how everyone's attention was drawn to him. A low murmur, like the hum of bees, vibrated through the congregation. A couple of old ladies in black mantillas whispered behind gloved hands, their mouths pursing into tight O shapes. If Conor noticed their ill-disguised curiosity, he didn't let it show. He held his chin up and kept his gaze above their heads, a facade which could easily be mistaken for arrogance. He didn't even look at Ellen, and after a hasty glance, she didn't look at him either. How ridiculous, she thought, for grown people to behave in such a childish way. It was as if they were schoolchildren, defying their parents.

When Mass ended, the congregation spilled out into the churchyard. The rain had stopped and a brief burst of sunshine broke through the cloudy canopy above them, catching the drops on the budding branches of the sycamore trees and causing them to sparkle. Ellen was gathered up by her family. She felt like a small fish besieged by a large shoal of bigger fish, barely able to see beyond them. Alanna began introducing her to those she hadn't yet met, and while she shook hands and smiled, she felt a rising sense of urgency and the need to get away. She looked over the heads to see Conor and Daphne speaking to Johnny, while the children were walking down the path towards their car, parked below on the grassy verge. Every time she raised her eyes she was pulled back into the throng, well and truly caught in the net, unable to wriggle out.

'I'm so pleased you're coming to lunch,' Alanna said. 'Johnny and Emer are coming with Joe. It'll be a good opportunity for you to get to know more of your family. Joe's not the only one of your age, you know.' Ellen half listened as others joined in and fired questions at her without giving her time to answer; they were all very excited to meet the daughter of the notorious Maddie Byrne.

Ellen raised her eyes as a drowning woman raises her lips to the air, and spotted Dylan a short distance away, staring at her with dark, brooding eyes. His wasn't the stare of the curious crowd of locals. It was the stare of a man filled with longing. Ellen turned away, for his pining alarmed her; she might *look* like her mother in the days when he knew her, but she *wasn't* her – and if he met Maddie now he'd realize that *she* wasn't her, either.

At last, Alanna was distracted for a moment and Ellen seized her opportunity. 'Back in a minute,' she mumbled, pushing through the crowd. She hurried down the path to where Ida and Finbar were now playing on the steps that led down to the road. When Ida saw Ellen, her face lit up. 'Hello, Ida,' Ellen said, smiling back. 'I want to paint your nails before you return to Dublin. You can't go back with chipped nail polish!'

'Grandmam says I'm not allowed to have nail polish at school.'

'Really? When do you go back?'

'Tomorrow.'

Ellen tried not to show her disappointment. 'But you'll be coming back soon, right?'

'Maybe. I don't know.' The little girl shrugged. 'You'll have to ask Daddy.' Ida lifted her eyes and Ellen knew from the affectionate look on the child's face that Conor was approaching and her stomach gave a nervous little lurch.

She turned to face him. His smile was now unguarded, raffish and bold. He rubbed his chin. 'So, what do you think?'

She grinned back. 'I didn't recognize you!'

'I thought so. Do you like it?'

'I love it. You look younger.'

He winked at his daughter. 'Doesn't she say all the right things, Ida! Are you hungry, Finbar?'

'Yes, can we go home now?' The little boy pulled a sulky face.

Conor put his hands into his coat pockets and glanced back at the throng. 'I think we've set the town talking,' he said, not at all worried about it.

'I think it's the loss of your beard.'

'If only! I spent the first half of Mass without anyone knowing who I was.'

'Does it feel different?'

His eyes twinkled at her and he rubbed his chin again. '*You*'ll have to tell *me*,' he replied quietly so that the children couldn't hear.

She coloured, but the suggestive tone in his voice made her smile. 'I'll be happy to.' She folded her arms in front of her chest because the desire to reach out to him was almost unbearable.

'Shame you have to join your family for lunch. Meg is cooking a roast.'

'Father Michael is coming.'

'And you have lots of unanswered questions for him, I know. I'm not sure lunch will be the right time to ask them, though.'

'I might be able to take him off into a corner.'

'I'm sure you will. After a few glasses of wine, he might be more garrulous.'

Daphne now joined them and the formality of their conversation was torturous. Aware that the eyes of the locals were still upon them, questioning their acquaintance, they remained a polite distance apart, Conor's hands deep in his coat pockets, Ellen's still folded across her chest. The children began to get impatient.

'All right, sweetie,' said Daphne, taking Ida's hand. 'We'd better go. It's nice to see you, Ellen. Send my regards to Peg, won't you?'

'I will, thank you,' Ellen replied, as Daphne and Ida walked away.

Conor hung back a moment. 'It's killing me that I can't kiss you, Ellen,' he said in a low voice, his gaze unwavering.

'I think my newfound family would send me straight back to London.' She laughed, but inside she felt suddenly desperate. Conor was leaving and she didn't know when she'd see him again. If it hadn't been for the throng of spectators who stood like a herd of cattle outside the church, she'd have thrown herself against him and begged him not to go. 'I'll just have to wait to experience the feel of your new face,' she said instead, trying to steady her voice so she didn't come across as needy.

'The woodcutter won the day,' he grinned.

She smiled back at the shared memory. 'Yes, he well and truly slew the wolf!'

'We'll make up our own fairy tale, Ellen,' he said, looking serious for a moment. 'Come on, Finbar, let's get you home.' He took the child's hand, then turned to Ellen and gave her a meaningful nod. 'I'll be back.'

She watched him walk down the steps to the Range Rover where Daphne and Ida waited for him. The boy looked very small beside the tall figure of his father. Ellen wished she were climbing in with them, but she had committed to lunch with Alanna and Desmond. There was nothing she could do but watch them drive away. No doubt her family would all be asking her about Conor. She resolved to keep her cards very close to her chest. She didn't want to raise Desmond's suspicions any higher than she already had.

Lunch was a jolly affair. Joe's sister, Ashley, was there with her husband and two young children, and Alanna's brother Patrick had come with his wife, Clare. Father Michael said grace, then they all sat down at the long dining-room table and tucked into a hearty Sunday lunch. Ellen had been deliberately placed next to Father Michael, but it wasn't until the end of the meal, when people began to disperse into the sitting room, that her mother's name was mentioned.

'Don't you look like your mother, Ellen?' he said quietly, as if it was a secret.

'I don't know. Perhaps,' Ellen replied. In London no one ever mentioned that she resembled her. It was becoming clear that Maddie Byrne had shed a skin when she left Ireland all those years ago, and emerged an entirely different person.

'Well, I'd say that you do,' the priest continued in his melodious Irish drawl. 'She had the same-shaped face as you, the same chin and the same smile. She had a very sweet smile, you know. And your eyes, I wouldn't say they're the same colour or shape; no, yours are bigger and hers were blue, but there's something of her in the expression. One can't be sure what you're going to do next.' He chuckled tipsily, pleased with his analysis. Ellen wondered whether, by the way he was speaking about her mother in the past tense, he thought she was dead.

'I think you'd find her very different now,' Ellen said to remind him that she was alive.

'Well, people grow up, don't they, and your mother was very young when she lived here.' He toyed with his empty gin and tonic glass, rolling it onto its edges like a boat in danger of capsizing.

Ellen lowered her voice too, hoping to lure Father Michael into revealing things by pretending to confide in him. 'You know, I didn't even know Mother had a family over here. It came as a complete shock when I discovered she had brothers. I knew about Peg, but I knew nothing of the others.'

His eyebrows crawled together like fluffy white caterpillars. 'So I heard. What a brutal thing not to have known your grandmother.'

'I wish I had known her,' said Ellen, sadly.

'Aye, she was a fine woman, Ellen. A fine woman indeed.'

'I'm sure she was. A strong woman, to have brought up six children and run a farm on her own?'

'Oh, she was never on her own, Ellen. She was a community-spirited woman and everyone rallied around her, although it would have hurt her pride to have acknowledged that she was helped. She was a very proud woman, altogether.'

'It must have hurt her when my mother ran off.'

Father Michael dug his chin into his neck as he contemplated how best to answer. The round balls of his cheeks shone with the whiskey he had had before Mass and the two gin and tonics since. He inhaled through hairy nostrils. 'It rocked the whole community,' he said softly. 'Your grandmother was a strong woman but Maddie floored her.' He shook his head at the memory.

Ellen decided to take a gamble. 'Was that because ... because of me?'

She almost held her breath as he turned his rheumy eyes to her in astonishment. After a hasty glance into the sitting room, he leaned closer and spoke so softly Ellen could only just hear. 'So, you *know*?'

'I *know*,' she replied with equal emphasis.

'Did Maddie tell you?'

'No, I worked it out.'

He nodded gravely. 'Of course you did. You're a clever girl.' He patted her hand unsteadily.

'I assume no one else knows, though?'

'Only your grandmother knew, because Peg told her.' Ellen clamped her teeth together to stop her jaw swinging open. Her mind was racing, trying work out how her mother might have discovered her sister's betrayal. But as she had told Father Michael she *knew*, she had to mask her shock and curtail her questions. He was too tipsy to notice and pursed his lips with the residue of bitterness. 'And Maddie knew the consequences of bearing a child out of wedlock. But she was a bold girl, was Maddie Byrne. She was always a bold girl.' He heaved a sigh. 'She saw an opportunity and she took it.'

'I suppose it was the only option.'

'It was the only option for *her*. A terrible choice to make for any young woman, but brutal for Maddie because she had to leave so much behind. Poor Dylan Murphy is still living with the consequences to this day. I don't know whether he's forgiven her. I have tried to gently lead him in that direction, but it's a mighty thing to ask of a man. As for your grandmother, she wrestled with her faith but I'm afraid she died without making peace with Maddie. One day, they will meet again and I hope then they will be able to forgive each other.'

Ellen frowned at Father Michael. 'What did my *mother* have to forgive?'

Father Michael frowned at Ellen, as if surprised that she didn't know. 'Well, a great deal, Ellen. A very great deal.'

Chapter 17

Conor has shaved off his beard and his mother has cut his hair. Something dramatic is going on and I don't like it at all. I watched the hair fall in feathers onto the bathroom floor and felt that *I* was being cut with those scissors and swept away with the dustpan and brush. He emerged looking young again and happy, as if he had shed his grief along with his hair. I can feel he is now fired up with inspiration and energy and I know it has nothing to do with me. I follow him around the house and listen to him humming contentedly, knowing that it is another woman and not I who has infected him with joy.

What does he see in Ellen? She is nothing compared to me. I was passionate and hot-blooded as well as beautiful. I was a firefly, bright, compelling and unpredictable. Conor loved my eccentricities. He loved my romantic nature. There is nothing eccentric about Ellen. She is not beautiful and she is not exciting. She is ordinary.

I followed him to Mass. He wore a suit and tie beneath his smart black coat and fedora hat. He looked so handsome and dignified, like an old-fashioned gentleman, but I could tell that he was nervous, for his fingers fidgeted at his sides. Ida and Finbar found the transformation astonishing because neither can remember a time when their father didn't have hair on his face. They couldn't take their eyes off him and grew suddenly shy as if he had become someone else entirely. Daphne lifted her chin with pride as she walked up the aisle, because the last time she accompanied her son to church was at my funeral in the little chapel, when Conor had looked like Edmond Dantès after a few years in the Château d'If. I know she feels that she has got her son back. I am no longer around to keep him away from her, so perhaps she is right.

It was only when Ellen and Conor caught eyes across the aisle that I realized how strongly they feel for one other. They held that stare for a long while and somehow their eyes communicated more than words ever could. Conor's eyes were full of tenderness. His whole face was aglow with a brighter light than lust alone and I was consumed with jealousy. I raged about the church, like I did at my funeral, but affected nothing. Not even a flicker of candle flame or a rustle of prayer book. Nothing. I am lighter than air but I feel heavy with earthly emotions. Why is it that Peg's little girl can blow out flames and stroke dogs when all I can do is frighten the birds?

Outside in the churchyard he smiled at her like he had once smiled at me. Conor has a smile that is so irresistible it can melt the stoniest of hearts. He doesn't realize how powerful it is. If only he smiled on the locals of Ballymaldoon like that, he would win their love and their trust. But he won't. Conor is a man who doesn't care what other people think of him. He is his own man and won't be held to ransom by anyone. I even think he took pleasure in their curiosity.

Ellen has inflated his confidence and lifted him out of the quagmire that was his grief. But while he was in that quagmire he was mine. Unhappy though he was, he belonged only to me. I was his present as he is mine. But now I am his past. I have died all over again. But I will not have it. I will find a way to stop it before it flowers. I will nip it in the bud and Conor will belong to me once again. I thought Ellen would be my saviour, but she is my curse.

And so Conor returns to Dublin a different man. He walks with a bounce in his step and smiles at everyone he encounters. The heavy atmosphere in his office evaporates like summer fog burnt away by the sun. It is as if his happiness is sunshine that infuses the place with joy. He takes trouble with his appearance and even opens the bottle of cologne that has been sitting in his bathroom unopened for years. Everyone in his office is astonished by the extraordinary transformation and the scent of verbena that he leaves in his wake. His secretary loses the years that stress has engraved on her skin, although she cannot quite trust that it will last, so traumatized is she by his constant anger that has smouldered and sparked during the last five years like a fire which feeds on itself. He has not treated her well and is determined to make it up to her. He wants to make it up to everyone. To his partner, Robert, and their team of twenty capable and creative men and women who have suffered from his long inferno. He wants them to know that it is over and he is now back.

He sends his secretary out to buy a new phone for Ellen. He wants to call her but is reluctant to dial Peg's number. I understand his reluctance; after all, he is only human and there is only so much a man can forgive. But his desire is stronger than his reservation and he eventually calls her. He sits in his office, overlooking the river that runs through the city, and dials Peg's number. It is on his system because her son Ronan used to work for us when I was alive, transforming my ideas into reality with pine and oak. He used to live with his mother in those days. I liked having him around because he worshipped me with the unquestioning love of a puppy. He'd do anything for me. Anything at all.

'Hello, Peg, it's Conor,' he says when Peg answers the phone.

'Oh, hello, Conor,' she replies, surprised. 'You'll be wanting Ellen, I expect.'

'Please.'

'Hang on a minute, I'll go and get her.'

He sits back in his chair and runs a hand through his hair. It is still thick and glossy, like the hair of a young man, although it is now greying at the temples, close to the crow's feet which fan out in deep lines across his skin. But his ageing only serves to make him more handsome.

Ellen comes to the phone breathless with excitement. 'Hello,' she says.

'Are you missing me?' he asks. He has an appealing voice, deep and grainy like sand. If she could see him down the line she would know that his smile is wide and his eyes are full of laughter.

'A little,' she teases.

'So, you haven't forgotten me, then?'

'Not yet.'

'Then I better not leave it too long.'

'Oh, I wouldn't if I were you. With all the other handsome young men here in Ballymaldoon . . .' She laughs. They both know that none of them can hold a candle to Conor.

'I have a few things to sort out up here. Then I'm coming down on Thursday. Wild horses wouldn't keep me from you. I'm leaving the children here with my mother.'

'That's good,' she replies, which is an understatement, but I suppose she is trying to play it cool.

'I'm going to have you all to myself,' he says, lowering his voice. He picks up a pen and flicks it between his fingers. 'I've thought of little else since I got back to Dublin.'

She inhales deeply. 'I hope you're managing to get some work done, too.'

'I'm good at multitasking. Julia, my secretary, has gone out to buy you a phone.'

'What's wrong with the landline?'

'I want to be able to call you whenever I like without having to go through your chaperone.'

'Ah, yes, well . . .'

'Will I have to ride beneath your bedroom window in the middle of the night to steal you away?'

'Not if you want me looking my best when you get me home.'

'Oh, yes, your allergy. I forgot. I'll have to use the car instead. Not as romantic, though, nor as quiet.'

'You don't have to tiptoe around Peg. She knows. I've been very honest with her. It's the others I have to watch out for. Desmond in particular.'

He chuckles, for he couldn't care less about Desmond Byrne. 'I don't think you have to watch out for anyone, Ellen. You owe them nothing.'

'I know, but I have to be sensitive.'

'How was Father Michael?' he asks, changing the subject.

She lowers her voice. 'You were right. Mum left Ireland because she was pregnant with me.'

'So, you got him into the corner, then?'

'Metaphorically speaking, yes. He was longing to talk about it.'

'He's only human and it's a gripping story.'

'You know, Mum must have confided in Peg, because Father Michael told me that it was Peg who told their mother.

Can you imagine? I don't know how Mother found out, but that could be the reason they haven't spoken in over thirty years.'

'Now, why would Peg sneak to her mother?'

'She must have had good reason. She's not a malicious person. But it's a terrible thing to do, considering her mother's strong religious beliefs. She must have known how she'd react.'

'She would have been appalled that her daughter got pregnant out of wedlock. That's an unforgivable sin.'

'It seems so small-minded now, doesn't it?'

'There are still lots of small-minded people around, believe me. You come from London where things are very different. People are more tolerant. You can be anything you want to be in London, but not in Ireland. Certainly not in a small town like Ballymaldoon. They're very old-fashioned and set in their ways. It's no surprise that your mother hasn't come back. Perhaps she never will.'

'Time is a great healer,' Ellen says wisely.

Conor sighs and smiles philosophically. 'Yes, it is,' he replies and I know that he's thinking of me.

They chat on in the senseless way lovers do. They flirt and tease and neither wants the conversation to end. They both wish it was Thursday. But the conversation must end eventually. 'So, I'll come and pick you up on Thursday afternoon?' he says.

'I can't wait,' she replies, no longer playing it cool.

'I don't think I can stand the anticipation.'

She laughs. 'Oh, I think you can, Conor Macausland. You're a patient man.'

'That's what I thought. You behave yourself now.'

'I'm trying to write.'

'Give me a story I can make into a film.'

'No pressure, then!'

'You said you were inspired down there.'

'I am.'

'Write about the ruined castle we went to see.'

'You just want me to write about you.'

'Surely it goes without saying that I'm your hero!'

'Of course.'

'Until Thursday, then.'

'Until Thursday, Conor.'

'I kiss you all over,' he murmurs. She does not reply, but he can hear her gentle laughter like a whisper down the line.

He smiles and cuts off. He stares out of the window for a while, at the river that flows directly below his building, and contemplates the woman who stumbled so unexpectedly into his life that day on the hill and transformed it. He is marvelling at the extent of the transformation in so little time. I could tell him that time is irrelevant. On the earth plane, time is measured in minutes, hours, days and weeks – from where I stand I can see that there is only one eternal present. It matters not that they have known each other little more than a few days, for love is not of the earth, but of the eternal present that cannot be measured. It is timeless. If their love is true, they might as well have known each other forever.

I should be pleased that Conor has at last found someone who makes him happy, but I am not. Jealousy eats away at my soul like a parasite. It feeds off me and grows strong. I feel powerless where I am, unable to influence events or make people notice my presence. Only the birds respond, but I am determined to learn how to extend my power. After all, it seems that all creatures can see Peg's little girl as if she were alive. If she can do it, surely I can too. So I go to Connemara with that intention in mind, and look for her.

I find the little girl without any trouble, for she seems to hang around her mother most of the time. So far, I haven't spoken to her. I am so used to existing alone in this strange limbo that is neither heaven nor earth, that I am afraid to approach her. She looks like an angel, and as I near her, the brightness that surrounds her causes me pain. I don't have eyes as I once did, so it is not the usual pain that comes from looking at sunlight after hours of sitting in darkness. It is hard to describe the discomfort to those who have never been out of their bodies. All I can say is that the light she is made of is too intense for me to bear.

But she smiles and as she does so her glow expands towards me. I want to bathe in it, but I can't. I am too dark and fragile. I feel it would consume me like a moth in flame.

'Caitlin,' she says.

'You know my name?' I reply, astonished.

'My name is Ciara.'

'You're an angel.'

She laughs. 'No, I'm not. A human soul can never become an angel.'

'Then what are you?'

'A soul like you.'

How can she be a soul like me, when she shines so intensely? Why don't I shine like that? 'But why are you so bright?' I ask.

She shrugs. 'I don't know. I just am.'

Perhaps she really is an angel and doesn't know it. 'Why do you stay here?' I probe.

'Because my mother is not ready for me to leave her yet.'

'Does she know you're always with her?' I ask, hoping that if Peg knows, then perhaps Ciara can tell me how to pass a message on to my own children.

'No,' she replies without sadness. 'But I can help her from where I am in other ways besides her knowing.'

'How?'

'With love.' As she says the word *love* her light expands again. 'We are all made of love, it's only a shame that when we're down here we forget. We forget who we really are.'

'Are you lonely?' I ask, although I know it's a silly question, because she is clearly not.

She frowns. 'Lonely?'

'Yes, I'm lonely. I'm very lonely.' The words tumble out in a desperate rush.

She gazes at me with compassion. 'But you're not alone,' she replies, and she looks surprised that I could think myself alone. Her gaze sweeps around me as if she is contemplating other beings that I can't see.

'Oh, but I am,' I groan, and saying it out loud makes me feel more isolated than ever. 'I saw you stroke the dog,' I venture. 'How did you do that? Only the birds seem aware of *me*.'

'All creatures are aware of you. It is only human beings who have lost the sensitivity to intuit what they can't see with their eyes.'

'But when you touched the dog, I saw his hair flatten. You actually touched him as if you had real hands. How did you do that?'

She laughs. 'You can do it, too. You have to concentrate. Your mind is much stronger than your hands ever were. Your hands were so limited and clumsy. It is amazing what you can do with your mind if you concentrate.'

'Where did you learn all of this?' I ask, for she doesn't speak like a child at all.

'When you decide to move on, you'll go there, too, and

when you do you'll realize that home was never here, on earth. Home is where you come from.'

'But I'm frightened to leave my family.'

'You never leave them, Caitlin.'

'I wouldn't know the way to this home now, even if I wanted to go there.'

'Yes, you would. It's love, Caitlin. That's all it is. Love.'

I leave her at Peg's house and think myself into the field of sheep. Ciara is right about the mind; it is amazing that without the encumbrance of the physical body, my mind will take me wherever I want to go. The thought is the deed and here I am among sheep. I stand with them and watch to see if they notice my presence. Of course, they wander right through me because I am as immaterial as light. At first, I am frustrated. But I remember Ciara's words and concentrate. I place my hand on their woolly backs and feel nothing. They graze away, unaware of me. And then it occurs to me that perhaps it is not that they are unaware of me, but that I am like the wind and rain, and they accept me as part of nature. Could it be that? I ask myself.

I concentrate fully on the back of a sheep. I try to imagine the texture of her wool. I try very hard to focus. I kneel down and look her straight in the eye, rubbing my fingers up and down her long nose. I practise without pause for I don't know how long. I have no concept of time. Then suddenly, without warning, the sheep notices me and tosses her head. I am shocked. It has been so long since I have been noticed. With a tremor of excitement I try again. At first, it doesn't work; I have to concentrate as before, and practise. But then I master it. Mind over matter, it is really very simple.

If I can stroke the sheep, surely I can stroke my children? If I can affect the living then I can put a stop to the flowering romance between Conor and Ellen. With the force of my will I can drive them apart. But there must be limits, for surely if it were so easy to influence lives from where I am, then jealous, angry, resentful spirits bent on revenge would wreak havoc. They would maim and murder without restraint. No, there must be limits to my power, but I will go as far as I am able. I'm not asking for much. I just want what is mine.

Chapter 18

Ellen sat in front of her blank computer screen, chin in hand, dreaming about Conor. So far she hadn't written a word. She was much too excited to concentrate. She pictured his generous features and his wide, infectious smile, and found herself grinning as she recalled their telephone conversation line by line. She didn't know how she was going to last until Thursday.

Frustrated at the lack of inspiration, she went to find her aunt. Peg was moving the sheep into the next-door field, with the help of Mr Badger. 'I thought you were meant to be writing?' Peg said when her niece approached.

'I can't think of my plot,' Ellen replied.

'Your head is full of other things,' Peg said with a knowing smile. 'Why don't you go for a walk and clear your head of Mr Macausland?'

Ellen smiled. 'I can't, Peg.'

'Well, sitting in front of your computer won't do you any good either. At least you'll get some fresh air.'

'I'm afraid I'll get lost again.'

'And your knight in shining armour isn't around to rescue you. I tell you what. If you walk along the coast you won't get lost.'

'That's a good idea.'

'Keep to the path with the sea in your sights and you'll always know where you are.'

'I'll do that,' Ellen replied happily. 'I'll see you later.'

'If you don't, I'll send Oswald out to find you. And be sure to wear a coat, pet, that wall of cloud is coming this way.'

Ellen set off up the hill behind Peg's house and joined a well-trodden path that cut through the grass like an old scar. It was a damp day. Light drizzle floated on the breeze and every now and then a hole was burned through the cloud and the sun shone through, flooding the sea with soft pools of light. She listened to the birdsong and watched the slow wheeling of gulls and allowed her mind to still in the quiet serenity of her solitude. The more time she spent in the countryside, the lighter her spirit grew. Her chest filled with a fizzy kind of joy she had never experienced before in the concrete wilderness of London. Out here on the hills, she truly felt that anything was possible, even her novel, her burgeoning relationship with Conor, her newfound independence, happiness. Somehow she sensed that everything would sort itself out.

After a while she turned a corner to see a pretty little chapel on the horizon. It looked old and abandoned from where she stood. There were gravestones dotted about and a surrounding stone wall that protected them from the winds that blew in off the sea. A path led down the slope to a little wooden gate that had swung open. Curiosity propelled her forward and she hurried along the path.

As she walked through the gate, a few blackbirds hopped about stones half buried in the long grasses. The sun shone a spotlight onto the chapel and Ellen noticed that the front door had been carelessly left ajar. She took in the magnificent view of the ocean, which stretched out vast and wide to the end of

the earth where it was swallowed up by cloud. It was a beautiful, tranquil spot and she thought it a shame that the chapel
appeared to have been neglected, like so many castles and
houses that lay scattered on the hills like old bones.

Just then, a flash of scarlet caught the corner of her eye. The
vibrant colour stood out brightly amidst the green grass and
yellow heather. She took in the jar of red roses, surprised that
anyone had been laid to rest here in this forgotten corner of
Ireland. They were placed against a gravestone near the wall
and were clearly a few days old, for their petals had opened
wide and one or two had already wept like tears onto the
ground. She wandered down to get a better look and was even
more surprised when she read the name *CAITLIN MACAUSLAND*
engraved on the headstone. She bent over and read the epi-
taph. So, this was the little chapel where Caitlin's funeral took
place, and where Conor was shunned by the locals.

Suddenly a familiar voice broke the silence and almost
made her jump out of her skin. 'That's the grave of Caitlin
Macausland.' It was Dylan, striding down the slope towards
her.

Ellen stood up. 'Oh, hello, Dylan,' she replied, hand on
heart. 'You gave me a fright.'

'Sorry, I didn't mean to creep up on you.'

'What are you doing here?'

He put his hands in his coat pockets and swept his eyes over
the sea. 'I like the peace. No one bothers me in this chapel.
I find it inspiring.' Then he gazed at her, his brown eyes smiling warmly. 'I've always loved the romance of ruins.'

'Me too,' she replied. 'I just stumbled upon this one.'

'Caitlin Macausland loved it, too. I used to bump into her
from time to time, just sitting up here in a pew, contemplating life.'

'Is that what *you* do, too?'

'I suppose I do. I write, as well. Some of my best poetry was written right here, with this view. I think you'd find it inspiring, too.'

'I know I would. No one uses it now, I don't suppose.'

'No, the last time it was used was at Caitlin's funeral, and that was five years ago. I don't think it had been used for a hundred years before that.'

'Sad.'

'All ruins are sad. They're like shells, hinting at the life they once housed, but giving little away. They arouse our curiosity. We want to know more.' He pulled out a packet of cigarettes and popped one in his mouth. Shielding it from the wind, he flicked his lighter and lit it. 'Want one?'

'No thanks, I'm trying to give up.'

'Good on you.' He blew a puff of smoke into the damp air.

'So, why is she buried here and not in Ballymaldoon?' Ellen asked.

'Because she belongs in a romantic place like this. She wouldn't have wanted to be buried in town. It was I who told her the story of the heartbroken sailor who built this little chapel for his young wife who tragically died soon after they were wed. Caitlin loved the romance of it, even if it's a load of old rubbish.' He shrugged and gave a jaunty grin. 'I don't know. It's a good story and she was the sort of woman who loved stories. Conor knew that better than anyone. The sailor's wife is buried up at the top there.' He pointed. 'The sailor wanted her to keep watch over him when he was out at sea.'

'Lovely idea.'

'That's what Caitlin thought, too.'

'You knew her quite well, then?'

'I don't think you could ever *know* Caitlin Macausland well.

I'm not sure that even her husband knew her well. There was something unfathomable about her. But she was lonely in that castle when Conor was away, and would come up here from time to time and find me. She was grateful for someone to talk to.'

'He obviously loved her. He's still leaving her flowers five years later.' Ellen tried to hide her disappointment. She had a strange feeling that Dylan had the ability to read her thoughts just by looking into her eyes so she dropped her gaze.

'Perhaps,' Dylan replied. 'The funny thing is that there are always roses up here.'

'What's funny about that?'

'Well, Conor's in Dublin most of the time, isn't he?'

'Perhaps he arranges for someone to put them here for him when he's away.'

'That's a possibility. I happen to think it's more mysterious than that.'

She smiled in response to the mischievous glint in his eye. 'Are you a conspiracy theorist, Dylan?'

'Just an old romantic.'

'You think someone else loved her?'

'Yes, I do.'

'Who?'

He shook his head and took a long drag before blowing out the smoke like an old dragon. 'I don't want to go setting the cat among the pigeons,' he answered finally.

Ellen recalled that he had seen someone rowing back to shore from the lighthouse the night Caitlin died and wished he'd tell her who he thought it was, but she knew it wouldn't be right as a newcomer to look too interested. 'The plot thickens,' was all she said, which closed the subject.

'Come, do you want to see what I've been up to?' He trod

his cigarette butt into the grass then began to walk back towards the chapel.

'OK,' she replied, although she wasn't in the least curious. She followed him inside. It was a classic chapel with a stone floor, wooden pews, glass windows cut into thick walls, a carved wooden pulpit and a religious painting designed around the arch window behind the altar. The air was stale and cold as it always is in churches.

Dylan picked up his guitar from the front pew. 'I've been composing,' he said proudly.

'So, you *have* been inspired.'

'Very.' He grinned broadly, as if he was guarding a wonderful secret.

'Are you going to play me something?'

'If you like.' He sat down and put the guitar over his knee. Ellen sat in the opposite aisle and watched him strum a few chords and adjust the tuning pegs. The sound echoed around the church. 'I'll play you one of my old ones,' he suggested.

'Why not the one you've been composing?'

'Because it's not ready.'

'OK. Play me one of your old tunes then.'

'It's called "Lost to Me".'

Ellen frowned. 'I'm sad already and you haven't even sung a note.'

For some reason she was surprised when he began to play beautifully. She had expected to feel a little embarrassed and to have to feign admiration. It wasn't that she had doubted his ability to play the guitar, but the way people laughed at him had given her the impression that he was rather useless. She hadn't expected him to play *well*, even though Peg had told her he had been quite successful in his day and had one or two hits in Ireland. He sang with confidence, as if he were used to an audience, and his voice was unexpectedly rich, with a sad, plaintive tone that Ellen knew could break a heart.

He sang of his lost love and Ellen understood immediately that the poem was about her mother. The imagery was so beautiful as to have been inspired by only the very deepest sorrow. She listened, without moving, to every word. Whatever anyone thought of Dylan, he was an extremely gifted and talented man.

As he sang, Ellen grew serious. She now looked with fresh eyes at the man everyone mocked as the local drunk, the local *joke*. He wasn't mad at all; he was broken.

Dylan played the final chord and Ellen waited until the last sound had echoed off the walls and died before she picked up her hands and clapped. 'That was beyond lovely, Dylan. It was heavenly.' And she smiled with pleasure because she really meant it.

'Thank you,' he said softly, then lowered his eyes as if he were suddenly ashamed to have exposed himself.

She gazed at him with a new fondness. 'You wrote that for my mother, didn't you?'

'The greatest work is often born out of the greatest sadness.'

'You still love her, don't you?'

He was pensive a moment, staring at the flagstone at his feet. Then he trained his big eyes on hers and said, 'I think when you love like that, you never stop.'

'Even though she's not the same woman now?'

'She'll always be the same Maddie, inside.' He said this hopefully, Ellen thought, as if he couldn't bear to imagine her being any different.

'Life can be dreadfully disappointing, can't it?' she said, longing to show that she understood.

But his face brightened and he grinned. 'And then something happens to restore your faith. Just when you think you have lost everything, an unexpected gift is placed on your doorstep to show that all was not lost. Sometimes it takes a lifetime, but you have to be patient and know that even your cloud, however dark, will eventually be lined with silver.'

Ellen wasn't quite sure what he was talking about, whether he was referring to himself or to 'one' generally. 'I hope you're right,' she said impartially. 'You know I taught myself the guitar when I was at school,' she told him.

'Do you want to have a go?' He lifted the instrument off his knee.

'I don't think I'd remember much now.'

'Try.'

'Mum didn't want me to learn guitar. She was terrified I'd play in a band and bring the family into disrepute.'

'So you taught yourself?'

'And formed a band.' She grinned triumphantly. 'Not that we were very good. But I loved it.'

'Who wrote the songs?'

'I tried.' She laughed and crinkled her nose. 'I'm not sure I'd remember them now. It was so long ago.'

'Have a strum. See if it still feels familiar.'

She took the guitar and put it on her knee. Then she placed her fingers over the strings and strummed a rather nervous G chord. Then she went from G to D to F, her confidence rising as it all began to come back to her.

'There, you see, your fingers remember.'

'Let's see if I can remember any of *my* old tunes.'

She couldn't remember the words but she could hum the tune to one of the songs she had played in her band at school. Dylan was quick to catch on and hummed too, until they were both jamming together. Dylan started to put words to the tune and to sing in harmony. It wasn't long before they had composed a catchy chorus together. They sang it over and over, Dylan drumming his hands on the pew in front and moving his body to the rhythm. They grinned at each other in mutual admiration as their music filled the chapel and bounced off the walls in a satisfying echo.

They were enjoying themselves so much that neither noticed the time pass. It was only when Dylan's stomach began to contribute, too, that they decided it was time to go and eat. 'Let me treat you to dinner at the pub,' Dylan suggested. 'You've earned it by humouring an old man!'

'You're not old, Dylan!' Ellen laughed, handing him back his guitar. 'And you're extremely good.'

'So could you be, if you'd let me teach you.'

'Do you think? I'm not sure I could compose like you do.'

'Of course you could, and you have a beautiful voice.'

'Maybe I have to wait until I'm sad. Maybe you can only create beautiful things when inspired by some deep sadness.'

'There are many ways to compose and not all songs are sad. It just happens that most of mine were inspired by your mother. If we play together, I might be inspired by happiness instead.'

They put on their coats and walked out into the drizzle. The clouds had moved inland off the sea and now hung low and heavy over the coast. 'You're going to get wet,' said Dylan. 'Do you want to borrow my hat?'

'No, you wear it. I don't mind the rain. In fact, I like it when it's in the countryside. I feel the water is clean and good for me.'

'Oh, it's clean all right and there's plenty of it.' They set off down the path at a brisk pace, past the jar of roses and Caitlin

Macausland's grave and on through the little wooden gate. 'How is your novel coming along?' Dylan asked.

Ellen sighed. 'I haven't written a word.'

'Why's that?'

'I don't know. I'm inspired by the countryside, but I haven't figured out a plot yet.'

'Why don't you put on some music, light a candle, inject a bit of atmosphere into the room, then empty your mind and see what comes.'

'Do people write like that, or just *you*? I thought it was preferable to work out a framework first.'

He grinned. 'Everyone works differently, but I guess that you'd work well like that. To let inspiration come you have to empty your thoughts and wait for it to run *through* you.'

'So, you're saying not to intellectualize too much?'

'That's exactly what I'm saying. You're thinking too hard.' He chewed on a thought for a moment. 'You have to let the music take you somewhere.'

'OK, I'll ask Peg for some inspiring music.'

'Do you have an iPod?'

'Yes.'

'Give it to me and I'll put together a playlist for you.'

'You'd do that for me?' she asked in surprise.

'And why wouldn't I?'

'I don't know. It's such a lot of work.'

'Not for me. I love music, I've got it all downloaded onto my computer already. It's nothing, really.'

'Well, that would be fantastic, thank you.'

'So, you let inspiration come from the deepest part of you, not the shallow machinations of your brain. If you feel your brain churning and groaning, you're not letting the ideas flow *through* you, do you see?'

'I think so.'

'Try it and see what happens.'

'I shall. I'll give you my iPod tonight in the pub.'

'That'll be grand.'

'Thank you, Dylan. You're very kind.'

He chuckled. 'I don't think that word has been used in the same sentence as my name for a very long time. But it feels good to be kind, Ellen Olenska.'

When they reached the Pot of Gold, Ellen's hair was sodden and her coat as wet as Peg's poor bedraggled donkey. It was only a matter of time before she'd have to splash out on a new coat, but she couldn't imagine where she'd find a nice one in Ballymaldoon.

Inside, it was warm. The fire crackled in the grate and a few locals sat having lunch and a pint at the tables and on stools around the bar. Craic looked surprised to see Ellen come in with Dylan. He broke off his conversation a moment and watched them in astonishment. Ellen registered his reaction but pretended she hadn't noticed. 'Hi, Craic,' she said breezily, finding a space at the bar.

'You look like a pair of drowned rats,' he said.

'We've been up on the hills,' she replied, as if it was perfectly normal for her and Dylan to take off together.

'What were you doing up there?'

She caught Dylan's eye and smiled secretively. 'Walking.'

'All right then, what'll you have?'

'A Coke for Ellen and something non-alcoholic for me,' interjected Dylan, leaning on the bar, hat in hand. 'And we'll have something to eat, too. What'll you have, Ellen Olenska?'

The way he said that name made her feel warm inside.

'Something hot,' she replied. 'You choose.' She grabbed her glass of Coke and made for a free table against the wall.

It wasn't long before Dylan was telling Ellen about her mother. Whatever reservations Ellen had had about Dylan had evaporated in the beautiful music she had heard up in the chapel, and if Dylan had been careful not to reveal too much about his past, he now felt sure enough of Ellen to take her into his confidence. Their music had bonded them; now their shared interest in Madeline Byrne drew them even closer. 'I always had a soft spot for your mother,' he said, chewing on his sausage. 'She was different from everyone else. She had the poise of a duchess.'

'Even then?' Ellen chuckled.

'Even then. Her mother spoiled her.'

'I didn't think she had money.'

'She didn't, but what little she had usually went on Maddie. Poor old Peg had to accept second-hand clothes, but those weren't good enough for Maddie. She proves the saying: *The baby who cries the loudest gets fed*. Maddie was the sort of girl everyone bent over backwards to please.'

'You too?'

'Dead right. I'd have done anything for her.'

'But she was rebellious, too?'

'She wasn't one for playing it by the rules. For Maddie, rules were there to be broken, whether it was playing truant, passing notes in church, running off and not helping her mother – Maddie was unconventional.' He looked at her with big, sad eyes. 'That's why I called her Ellen Olenska.'

Ellen stared back at him, aghast. 'You called her Ellen Olenska?'

'Aye, I did. I'd read the book and gave it to her to read. We both loved it.'

'And she called *me* Ellen, after the book, because that had been your special name for her?' He nodded. Ellen felt the blood drain from her face. She took a swig of Coke. 'My God, she still loved you, Dylan.'

'I guess she did.'

'You didn't know?'

He was quick to answer. 'How could I have known? She disappeared with your father and that was the last I ever heard of her.'

Ellen felt a wave of emotion unbalance her. 'She called me Ellen because of you. God, that's incredible.' She couldn't imagine her mother being romantic.

Dylan put his rough hand on hers. It was brown against her white skin. 'She got into trouble, Ellen. Your father got her out of it. I forgive her, but I've never got over her.' His eyes were big and glassy, and the pain in them almost too naked for Ellen to bear, but she was drawn into them as a person on the top of a cliff is drawn into the danger of looking down. Dylan lowered his voice. 'She ruined love for me because after her I could never love anyone else.'

They remained staring at each other for what felt like a long moment. Dylan didn't remove his hand and after a while Ellen put her other hand on top of it and squeezed it compassion-ately. 'You can't let a love affair that happened long ago ruin your life, Dylan. Surely, you have to find a way to move through it. For your sanity?'

He seemed to return from some faraway place and blinked. 'I channel it into my poetry and music.'

'But you have a girlfriend, don't you?'

'That makes me sound like a teenager. I have a lover, Ellen. She's a widow. Lost her husband a while back. She's a good woman, but she's not Maddie.' He withdrew his hand and began to eat the remains of his lunch.

'Maddie is not Maddie. You have your memories, but they are not real *now*, and you can't ever get them back.'

His grin was surprising; it had a knowing air. 'No? I'm not so sure. I might get them back, but not in the way I expected.' Ellen frowned, but Dylan didn't elaborate. 'Fancy another drink?'

'No, thank you. I'm fine,' she replied, wondering whether Dylan did, in fact, have a small touch of madness after all.

'I don't suppose Dad had a clue why she chose the name Ellen. The names Leonora and Lavinia couldn't be more different, could they? I mean, Ellen isn't very English, is it?' Dylan didn't reply. 'How ironic that I'm the child who most resembles her. Leonora and Lavinia look just like Dad.' She grinned. 'They have his weak chin, so I should be grateful!'

'You have a bold face, Ellen . . . and . . .' He smiled to himself, as if he had suddenly decided, against his natural inclination, not to reveal any more. 'And your smile reminds me of her, too. But you're yourself. You're not a carbon copy. You're grand just the way you are.'

Chapter 19

That evening, Ellen brought her iPod to the pub and gave it to Dylan. He remained at the bar with Ronan, who greeted her without smiling, his eyes dark and resentful. He was evidently unhappy about her escalating friendship with Conor, so she went and sat with Alanna, Desmond, Joe and Johnny at a table against the wall, and watched the comings and goings of locals. People were still curious about her, she could tell by the furtive way they looked away when she caught their eyes and the way their lowered their chins and voices when they spoke. But she felt safe in the bosom of her new family. No one would mess with Johnny and Desmond. She imagined they could be as fierce as bears if provoked. It wasn't long before Ryan arrived with more Byrnes and her family took over the pub with their noisy, cheerful banter.

'So, what did you make of Mr Macausland shaving off his beard?' Alanna asked Ellen. 'I'd forgotten how handsome he is. Like a movie star, don't you think?'

Ellen blushed. 'I didn't recognize him at first.'

'I don't think anyone did. He sat through half the service before anyone cottoned on.'

'He looks better like that.'

'You're not wrong. I like a beard, but if a man has a face like his it's a crime to hide it.'

'What does Desmond look like without his beard?'

Alanna laughed and gazed tenderly at her husband who was talking to Johnny at the other end of the table. 'He's not a looker like Mr Macausland, but he's handsome in his own way. I think he'd look younger without it, but I'm so used to it I think I'd miss it. It's part of who he is now.'

'The men here have a real beard thing going on, don't they?'

Alanna swept her eyes over the faces, now flushed with alcohol and heat. 'I suppose you're right. I've never really thought about it. Don't men have beards in London?'

'Not so many. Or perhaps it appears that more men have beards here because all the bearded ones are collected together in this pub. Do Irishwomen like beards so much?'

Alanna giggled. 'They're ticklish,' she said, then knocked back her vodka.

Ellen laughed, recalling with a frisson of excitement the sensation of Conor's beard against her face and neck. 'Quite nice, I imagine,' she said.

'*Very* nice,' Alanna agreed. 'I think I'd be very disappointed if Desmond shaved it all off!'

Suddenly Ellen heard the sound of an accordion breaking through the rumble of voices. One by one the locals hushed and listened. Alanna gave Ellen a sharp nudge. 'Jaysus, it's Dylan!' she hissed. 'I think he's going to sing!' Ellen craned her neck to see Dylan perched on a stool with the accordion resting on his knee. A raffish smile spread across his face and his wild eyes sprang from face to face in a silent challenge. He looked as if he was relishing their surprise. He looked a little mad, too, Ellen thought. For a moment they all stood in silence like a herd of stunned cattle. Then the chords changed from minor to major and burst into a song they all knew. Dylan started singing but before he finished the first line the pub erupted into song as if slotting into an old and familiar pattern of behaviour.

> Swinging to the left, swinging to the right
> The excise men will dance all night,
> Drinkin' up the tay till the broad daylight
> In the hills of Connemara.

Ellen was smiling so broadly her face began to ache. She felt so proud of Dylan and began to clap her hands with happiness. She clapped them until her palms stung. When the song changed, Ellen could no longer remain seated. She leapt to her feet, followed by Alanna, and although she didn't know the words, she sang anyway. Looking around, she could see that only the very old remained in their chairs. All the rest were standing, stamping their feet, raising their glasses of stout and singing at the top of their lungs.

It was late when they all left the Pot of Gold, patting Dylan on the back as if he had returned from a long journey. 'How are you getting home?' he asked Ellen when she came up to say goodbye.

'Johnny's dropping me off,' she replied, her eyes twinkling at him with affection. 'You were amazing tonight. You got everyone singing.'

'Just like I used to do,' he replied with ill-concealed pride.

'It was tremendous. I didn't know you played the accordion.'

'I can play anything. When you know one you know them all.'

She touched his arm. 'I really loved hanging out with you today, Dylan. Thank you for lunch.'

He looked pleased, like a little boy who had at last found a friend to play with. 'We had fun, didn't we, Ellen Olenska?'

'You know, I've borrowed that book from Peg: *The Age of Innocence*. I'm going to start reading it.'

'You'll love it. Your mother did.'

'I think she should read it again,' she said, giving him a meaningful look. It was time her mother remembered her roots.

The following morning the mobile telephone arrived from Conor with a note to call him as soon as she received it. 'What have you got there, pet?' Peg asked, surprised that a parcel had arrived at her house for Ellen.

'It's a telephone from Conor.'

'Can no one survive nowadays without one of those nasty things stuck to their ears? I wonder how we all got along in the old days.'

'I won't give anyone else the number. I didn't chuck mine into the sea for nothing.'

Peg bent down to run her fingers over Bertie's spine. 'So when is he coming back?'

'Tomorrow.'

'I see.' If Peg had reservations she was wise enough not to voice them.

Ellen retreated into the little sitting room. She lit the fire and settled into the armchair with Edith Wharton's *The Age of Innocence* resting seductively on her knee. But first, she would call Conor. She smiled as she rang the number because he had already programmed it into the phone. 'So you got it,' he said when he came on the line. His voice was soft and languid and she sensed him settling into his chair, too.

'I didn't even need to dial,' she replied.

'I like to provide a good service,' he said provocatively, and Ellen felt her body stir with arousal. 'So, are you still missing me?'

She laughed. 'Maybe.'

'I think you are.'

'A little bit, perhaps.'

'Your reserve is very British. I'll have to do something about that.'

'You think you can crack it?'

'With a good dose of Irish charm.'

'From what I've seen of your Irish charm, I think you've got a pretty good chance.'

'And that was *with* the beard,' he replied. The thought of kissing him *without* his beard made the hairs stand up on her skin. 'What are you thinking?' he asked and she could hear that his mouth was very close to the receiver.

'Of kissing you.'

'*Only* kissing?'

'If I think of anything else this phone will become too hot to handle.'

'I want to kiss you all over.'

She looked to the door, hoping that Peg wasn't listening. 'Mmmm, that sounds nice. Shame we have to wait until tomorrow.'

'I've got meetings today. I've been a bit distracted recently, so I've got a lot of ground to make up.'

'Absence makes the heart grow fonder,' she said positively.

'And makes a man grow hornier. Jaysus, woman, I don't know what you're doing to me, but it's a hell of a ride.' Ellen laughed, thrilled. 'I want to be beside you,' he whispered.

'Me too,' she replied with a longing that belied her British reserve.

He chuckled. 'I'll make an Irishwoman of you yet.'

They talked for almost an hour, during which time Ellen grew restless and began to pace the room. One moment she was sitting, the next standing gazing out of the window, the next sitting again. She was unable to remain still because Conor whipped up feelings in her that she didn't know quite how to manage. Finally, they said goodbye, although they both knew that they would speak again that evening, before going to sleep. She rang off and sat gazing at the telephone for a long while, a smile hovering on her lips, the resonance of his voice still clear in her memory.

At last, she opened her book and turned the first page. There, written in ink, was an inscription. Ellen felt the tears sting the backs of her eyes as she read it. *To my own Ellen Olenska, May you always be wild and curious, your spirit free. May your heart for ever belong to me. Dylan. July 1977.*

She was astonished that the book in her hand was the very one Dylan had given her mother all those years ago. Now it held more than her curiosity, it held her reverence. She wondered whether Peg was aware of its significance. Dylan obviously didn't know it was there. He hadn't imagined, when she said she was going to start reading it, that the book in Peg's library was the very one he had given to her mother. She resolved to give it back to him once she had finished reading it.

She turned the pages and was immediately swallowed up in Old New York of the late nineteenth century, and what a pleasure it was, so beautifully and lyrically written with a wry, intelligent sense of humour. She only remembered her mother and Dylan when the mysterious Countess Olenska appeared in the box at the opera at the end of the first chapter. She smiled to think of her mother reading it. Then her smile was replaced by a frown as she wondered what her mother would think if she knew that her daughter was sitting in her sister's house reading the book Dylan had lent her, the year before she ran away.

She spent all morning in the armchair, reading *The Age of Innocence*. She paused for lunch, which she ate in the kitchen with Peg and Oswald, who invited himself to join them because he was 'bored to death' of his own company. In the afternoon, Peg insisted she help her nurse the donkey, who had somehow got a nasty scratch just beneath his left eye. Ellen suspected her aunt just wanted to get her out of the house and into the fresh air. She was of the generation of earthy women who thought it was unnatural to stay inside all day. So Ellen helped her tether the donkey to the fence and bathe his eye with cotton wool soaked in disinfectant. She stroked his neck while her aunt soothed him in dulcet tones: 'You're a good boy, aren't you? There, you see, it's not so bad, is it? You're going to get better. Peg's going to put you right. See if I don't.' It amused Ellen to hear her talk to the animals as if they were humans. She spoke in the same way to Mr Badger and Bertie, and even Jack.

'I hear you spent the day with Dylan yesterday,' said Peg, as she dabbed the donkey's eye with a dry cloth. 'Johnny and Joe dropped by this morning on the way to work. You were asleep so I didn't bother to wake you. You must have found him on your walk because Craic said you both stumbled into the pub as wet as dogs.'

Ellen marvelled at the efficiency of the Ballymaldoon grapevine. 'Yes, I found him in the little chapel on the hill. You know the one?'

'I most certainly do. Caitlin Macausland is buried there.'

'He was playing the guitar. You know, he's amazing. He's really good.'

Peg laughed, but not in the way the others laughed. Her laugh was full of affection. 'So, he sang to you, did he?'

'Yes. I guessed it was a song he composed for Mother.'

'I don't doubt it.'

'He's going to teach me to play the guitar like him. You know he played the accordion last night and got everyone singing.'

'So I hear. I'm glad he's coming out of himself. I think it's the drink, or lack of. Craic says he's sobered up.'

'Well, he certainly wasn't drunk when we were in the chapel and he didn't drink at lunch.'

'That's good. There, donkey's better now.' She rubbed him under his chin until he stuck out his top lip with pleasure. 'You'll be all right, won't you? Yes, you'll live.'

'He's taken my iPod away to input a new playlist to help me write my book.'

'You still haven't started?'

'Not yet.'

'Really, Ellen, are you ever going to write a word?'

'I'm a little distracted.'

'You'll never write if you don't sit at that desk. Write anything, it doesn't matter, but for goodness sake make a start, or you'll be an old woman before you finish it.'

Ellen grinned. 'There's too much going on.'

'Well, I think it's grand that you and Dylan are getting along. I'm not sure what your mother would think of it, but *I* think it's grand. He's a good man, Dylan, with a big heart, and he's certainly got a soft spot for you.'

'I think he likes to be with me because I'm a link to his Maddie.'

'Oh, I'm sure you're right. You make him very happy. Craic said that the *old* Dylan came back last night. He was playing tunes and everyone was singing just like in the old days.'

'Before Mum ran away.'

'Yes. Everything changed after that.' Peg untied the donkey and led him back into the field where she let him go, with a carrot.

'Aunt Peg, can I ask you something?'

'Of course.' Peg picked up the bowl of antiseptic water and waited expectantly.

'Dylan used to call Mum Ellen Olenska.'

Peg looked at her blankly. 'Ellen Olenska, why?'

'She's the heroine in the novel I'm reading. Edith Wharton's *The Age of Innocence.*'

'Oh.' Peg had clearly never heard of the book.

'Mum called *me* Ellen.'

Peg looked surprised. 'Oh.'

'It's rather romantic, don't you think? I was named after Dylan's special nickname for her.'

'Well, it's a bit surprising, isn't it?' said Peg, a little bewildered.

'Mum was still thinking of Dylan when I was born. She might have run away, but her heart was obviously still here in Connemara.'

'I dare say it was.' Peg lifted her chin. 'Well, she could always have come back,' she added defiantly.

'Could she?'

'As a married woman, she most certainly could.' Peg carried the bowl inside.

Ellen followed her. 'Maybe she didn't trust herself,' she went on.

'What do you mean?' Peg poured out the water and placed the empty bowl in the sink to be washed up.

'She didn't trust herself to see Dylan again. Perhaps she was frightened she'd want him back.'

'Oh, that's nonsense. She knew what she was doing when she ran off with her English lord.'

'But what if she later regretted it?'

'You can't say that about your own father, Ellen,' Peg retorted firmly.

'I'm not suggesting that they're not happy *now*. I'm just wondering whether Mum ran off because she was pregnant with me, but then had a moment of regret when I was born. Otherwise she would have called me something else. *Anything* else but Ellen. Don't you see? She must have held a candle for Dylan.'

'She probably just liked the name.' Peg shrugged uneasily.

'No, I think it's more than that. One day, I'm going to ask her.'

Peg shook her head. 'Rather you than me, pet. I think you might have to take this whole episode of your life to the grave.' But both women knew that that simply wasn't possible. Ellen was in too deep ever to extricate herself completely.

'I feel Irish, Aunt Peg,' she insisted. 'My mother can't hide what's in my genes.'

'No, I don't suppose she can. Now, why don't I wet the kettle and make us some tea.'

That night, Ellen lay in bed chatting to Conor. He sounded so close that if she closed her eyes she could imagine him lying next to her. Their conversation was so full of nonsense that when she hung up she couldn't remember what they had talked about – only the sweet feeling of having been caressed by his softly spoken words remained warm upon her skin.

When she switched off the light she lay watching the sliver of silver that sliced through the gap in the curtains, and thought about her mother. She would have heard the same roar of the sea, the same moaning of the wind, the same nocturnal rustlings as Ellen heard now. How much she must have changed since her youth here in Connemara. How dramatically her life must have been transformed when she married Anthony Trawton and moved into No. 12 Eaton Court. Had she thrown herself into her metamorphosis with such determination and grit that she had somehow lost herself in the process? Was the wild and playful Maddie Byrne still in there somewhere, or had she suffocated her on purpose by denying her air?

Chapter 20

It is one thing communicating with sheep, but quite another communicating with humans when they cannot even sense that I am there. I realize that all creatures have a sixth sense, but humans have become so distracted by the concerns of the material world that they have lost their psychic ability. It is all about focus. If you concentrate hard on your left arm, you quickly become unaware of your right, or indeed of any other part of you. In fact, you can focus so intently that you *become* your arm. Humans are so focused on their physical form that they have forgotten who they really are. I'm not sure how I know these things; I just do. Possibly because my strange situation has given me perspective. I realize now how fragile and transient the human body is and how our intelligence survives beyond it. I wonder whether animals know it, too, instinctively.

And so I am determined to let Ida and Finbar know that I am here, watching them grow up, celebrating their triumphs and wrapping them in love when things do not work out as they would like. I am here, always, as a mother should be. I have practised on the sheep; now I will see if I can get my children's attention. I don't care how long it takes; it is not like I have anything else to do.

I know that I could be capable of rattling doorknobs and blowing out candles; after all, other spirits manage it so why should I be any different? But as hard as I try I am unable to affect material things, even when I focus with all my energy. I tire quickly, but I am sure with practice I will grow stronger. I stroked the sheep, didn't I?

I watch little Ida as she sleeps. Her face is white in the moonlight, her skin as translucent as the petals of a lily. She breathes softly and her eyelashes flutter as she dreams. I run my fingers down her cheek as I did with the sheep, although I feel nothing. I will her to wake and see me in the semi darkness as Finbar once did, but she does not stir. I try Finbar; after all, he has already seen me once, so I know he is capable of seeing me again. But he doesn't stir, either. The two of them sleep so soundly. If only one of them would open their eyes, I'm sure I could communicate with them.

I don't give up. I am sure that with practice I will manage to make them aware of my presence. I stare into their faces, I tell them over and over that I am with them and always will be. I am their mother; they are a part of me. My love binds me to them and it is indestructible.

By morning, I am overwhelmed with frustration and despair. Now I am sure that I have the possibility of communicating with them, my failure to do so is all the more heartbreaking. I feel wretched and helpless.

And then, to my astonishment, Finbar announces at breakfast that he dreamed of me last night. Conor has already left for Connemara so it is just Daphne and the children who are at the town house in Dublin. 'Was it a nice dream?' Daphne asks.

'She was by my bed, telling me that she is with me and always will be,' he says and I feel a shift in my consciousness, as if I have suddenly been infused with light. I feel weightless and dizzy with joy.

'That is a nice dream,' Daphne agrees. 'I'm sure she is with you, sweetheart.'

'I'd like to have a dream like that,' says Ida, her face long and sad.

'Once, when you were a little boy, you woke up and said that you saw your mother sitting on the end of your bed. Do you remember?' Daphne says to Finbar. He shakes his head and pops a piece of toast and jam in his mouth. 'I think your mother is an angel watching over you both.'

'I think she is, too,' Ida agrees.

Finbar isn't so sure. 'No, she's not an angel, she's still Mam,' he says firmly and I love him all the more for knowing what I am.

My whole being vibrates with happiness. I dance about the kitchen and it doesn't matter that they can't see me, because I know now that I can break into my son's dreams. With perseverance perhaps I'll break into Ida's, too. I wonder whether Conor is so distracted by Ellen that he will be deaf to my subtle attempts to communicate with him.

With that thought I turn my attention to Ellen and I find myself at Peg's house. Dawn has flooded the hills with a pale, liquid light and gulls are collecting in droves upon the island where I died, for the tide is out and there is food trapped in the little pools and on the rocks. The lighthouse looms eerily out of the morning mist like a ship limping home after a battle at sea and I remember the moment I climbed her mast and threw myself onto her deck as if it wasn't me but someone else, demented with jealousy and drunk on love.

Today, of course, is the day that Conor is coming down to see Ellen, so it is no wonder that the girl is excited. My happiness drains away as I face the young woman who has set out to steal my husband's heart away from me. If she thinks she can win him, she is wrong. I will not let it happen. I will do everything in my power to prevent it. Whatever it takes.

As my thoughts turn black so I lose the bright, fizzy feeling in my soul. How quickly my vibration changes from fast to slow and with the slowing down I feel the world around me sink into shadow. But all I can think of is Conor and my children and how I long for things to go back to the way they were before I died. I could be different, I know I could. With the knowledge that I have now I know that I could change. I wouldn't make the mistakes I made. If only I had a second chance. If only I could tell him that I haven't left him, that although he cannot see me I am still here, loving him from another dimension. He doesn't need anyone else but me.

And so I trail Ellen like a dark and heavy shadow. As happiness makes her step lighter, my vengeful heart makes me as dense as fog. She sits in the sitting room, beside the fire, reading a novel while Bertie snoozes on the rug at her feet, grunting in his sleep. I wander around Peg's house and nearly scare the jackdaw out of his feathers, so that he flies out of the window and doesn't return. I am full of jealousy and resentment. I focus on the doorknob, trying with all my might to rattle it, but nothing happens besides the energy I lose in that futile and frustrating activity.

I expect to see Ciara, but she is not here. I assume she is with Peg. It is a relief because I would be ashamed for that sweet and loving spirit to see me as I am now, so full of hate.

When Conor's car motors up the drive Ellen is at the kitchen window. She has been waiting here for over an hour. The hour before that was spent in her bedroom trying on all her clothes. Not that she has brought many from London. She has chosen a knee-length, hippy-style floral dress, which she has unbuttoned to her breasts, and a teal-coloured little cashmere cardigan. She has long, slim legs with elegant ankles which she now shows off to their best advantage, although she is wearing black tights and purple velvet ballet pumps, which I would have advised her against, had I her best interests at heart. Her hair is long and shiny and falls in waves over her shoulders. Conor likes women with lots of hair. He used to love *my* hair. He loved the colour, red like a fox, and the silky way it slipped through his fingers. I doubt he's going to think of that now, when he's running his fingers through Ellen's.

I watch with distaste as she opens the door and stands there a moment, waiting for the car to stop and Conor to climb out. She is smiling broadly, but I can see that her body is trembling, like a racehorse in the starting block. The adrenalin makes her cheeks burn and she takes a deep breath in an attempt to calm her nerves. I see Conor's white teeth through the car window. He is smiling, too. After having not smiled for five years, he seems to be doing a very good job making up for it. He opens the door and steps out. Encouraged by his grin, Ellen runs to him and throws herself into his arms. He hugs her tightly and lifts her off the ground so that her feet in those dainty purple shoes are kicking the air. They are like the wagging tail of a happy dog. He buries his head in her neck and swings her round. Then her feet touch the ground and they kiss. A long and passionate kiss, and this time, Ellen isn't overwhelmed by his ardour. She presses her body against his and winds her arms around his waist, beneath his jacket, absorbing his passion with eagerness and responding in kind.

'So, you *did* miss me,' he laughs, cupping her face in his hands and gazing at her lovingly.

'Yes, I did,' she replies.

'I'm glad. I missed you, too. These last few days have been so long, I thought today would never come. Now, get in the car because I don't want to waste another minute.'

They drive to Reedmace House, holding hands all the way across the gearbox. He can barely take his eyes off her and she keeps telling him to watch the road. The air between them is charged, as if it is made of threads of electricity, pulled very tight. They laugh and talk at the same time then laugh again. Flushed with desire and impatient, they are scarcely able to control themselves. When they reach the house, Conor leaps out and unlocks the door. He takes her hand and leads her upstairs at a run. She hurries after him, laughing at his enthusiasm. But soon she isn't laughing. His mouth is on hers and he's peeling away her clothes like the petals of a flower.

I cannot watch any more. It is beneath my dignity to witness their intimacy. I retreat to the garden where I pace up and down beneath the apple trees, waving my arms at the birds to shoo them away. I wish I could wave my arms and scare Ellen away.

Chapter 21

The feeling of Conor's bristly face against her neck was quite different from the feeling his beard had given her. She shivered and let out a sigh of pleasure as a warm wave rippled over her skin, from her head to her belly. Closing her eyes and lifting her chin she nuzzled her cheek against his hair and let him devour her neck like a friendly lion, his gentle mauling leaving her legs weak and trembling. 'Your skin tastes so good,' he breathed, pulling away. 'I want to taste every inch of you.' He grinned down at her, anticipating the feast to come, and peeled away her cardigan, dropping it to the floor. Then he slowly unbuttoned her dress and slipped it over her shoulders so that it hung loosely from her hips, revealing her naked stomach and pretty lace bra. He smiled appreciatively, tracing his eyes and his thumbs over the generous swell of her bosom, lingering in the valley just above the lace where her skin was warm and damp. Her chest expanded and her breathing grew hoarse. Dazed from the sensual pleasure of his touch and more agitated than she had ever been, she could only follow her instincts because experience hadn't prepared her for this.

He pressed his lips to the sensitive place just below her ear, running his fingers over her collarbone and shoulders and around to her back, where he unclipped her brassiere, exposing her breasts to his touch. She let out a gasp and closed her eyes. She could hear his breathing, shallow and heavy beneath her ear, and her own thumping heart, sending the blood pulsating into her temples. Then he hooked his thumbs over the waistline of her dress and panties and with one deft movement removed the last of her clothes. She stood naked and unashamed, her desire having burned away all that remained of her reserve.

'Now you are all mine,' he laughed, lifting her into his arms and carrying her over to the bed.

She laughed, too. 'With pleasure, Rhett Butler,' she replied, hoping she wasn't heavy.

'The pleasure is all mine, Scarlett.' He placed her on the bed and knelt over her, unbuttoning his shirt to reveal the toned body of an athlete. Conor might have spent the last five years letting his hair and beard grow long and unkempt, but he hadn't neglected his body. He tossed his shirt onto the carpet and unbelted his jeans.

'You're a fine-looking man, Conor Macausland,' she said, running her eyes over his muscular stomach.

'Not bad for a forty-two-year-old,' he replied.

'Not bad at all. Come here and let me get a closer look.'

He made to fall on top of her, but stopped in a press-up just before crushing her. 'No, let me get a closer look at *you*,' he said, and before she could reply he was kissing her again, deeply and passionately, in the way that had at first alarmed her.

He began to devour her, inch by inch, agonizingly slowly, until she was crying out with impatience. 'Why rush? We've got all afternoon!' he murmured as he ran his lips across her belly, just beneath her tummy button.

'Because I can't stand the suspense,' she gasped, her belly giving a sudden shudder.

'But I've only just started,' he replied. His breath was hot against her skin as he parted her legs and ran his tongue up the inside of her thigh. As he reached the top she threw her arms above her head and lifted her chin, abandoning herself with the greatest delight to the most sensual of rides.

A long while later, they lay entwined, worn out and dazed but deeply satisfied, as if their lovemaking had righted every wrong in their world. Nothing else existed but the two of them, alone in the house in the middle of the wild hills of Connemara; they might as well have been on a cloud, far above the cares and concerns of daily life, for everything but their desire for each other seemed so unimportant now. They softly ran their fingers over skin still tingling with the rever-berations of their pleasure, greedily taken, and murmured the sweet nothings of lovers drunk on love.

Ellen had never before experienced the practised hand of a man, for William was just a boy in comparison to Conor. Everything about this Irishman was intensely masculine, from his weathered skin to his powerful physique, and there was something dark and unfathomable in his eyes which drew her to him like the curious hand of a child to fire, because as much as she knew he could love her, she knew he would never belong to her, nor would she ever tame him. He was too old to change and had been too long in the wild.

She knew she should tell him about William, but she quickly convinced herself that owning up to her engagement would give it an importance it no longer had. From the moment she met Conor, she had known in her heart that, even if nothing ever came of it, she could never go back to William. Not after he had been so diminished by the com-parison. She realized now that there was an unconventional side to her that William would never understand, and for which, one day, he would most likely end up resenting her. It was in her attraction to Conor that she recognized that part of herself, because it was reflected in him. Conor had not only peeled away her clothes but he had peeled away her pretences. She knew now who she was and what she wanted.

Ellen resolved to deal with William kindly but swiftly. The ramifications would be tremendous, but she'd have Conor and the Byrnes and she'd be strong enough to cope. She lifted herself onto her elbow and ran a finger down Conor's face. He turned and frowned up at her. 'What are you thinking about, Socrates?'

She sank into his deep blue gaze and smiled softly. 'You.'

'What about me?'

'How I found you up there on the hills.'

'Correction, *I* found *you*, and if I hadn't you'd still be up there.'

She laughed. 'But *I* stumbled upon *you*.'

'And nearly threw me from my horse.'

'You're far too accomplished to allow that.'

He caressed her cheek and sighed. 'I knew you were special, even though you looked a sight.'

'No, you didn't.'

'If I hadn't, I'd have pointed the way and left you to your own devices.'

'I don't believe that for a second. Beneath your rugged exterior, you're an old-fashioned gentleman.'

His gaze grew tender. 'But your eyes were welling with tears and your face was all red and you looked so lost and frightened. I sensed you'd stumbled into my path for a reason.'

'And what reason might that be, do you think?'

'As a ray of light into my dark world.'

She raised her eyebrows. 'That's dramatic.'

'But true.'

'You're very sweet, Conor, but I'm no angel.'

'Angels come in many guises.' He grinned wickedly and the lascivious glint had returned to his eyes. 'But I'm doing my best to bring you down to my level.'

It was dark when he drove her back to Peg's. They had feasted on the cottage pie Meg had left in the fridge and Conor had opened a bottle of wine. Later, Conor had gone over to the stable block to fetch Magnum, whom Robert had taken out for a long walk over the hills, and the dog had lain on the floor at the end of the bed while his master and his new girlfriend fooled around beneath the sheets. Conor had asked her to stay the night and Ellen had wanted to, very much, but she knew Peg would disapprove and she didn't want her uncles appearing in the morning for an impromptu breakfast to find that she wasn't there.

So, they drove down the lanes, holding hands over the gearstick. 'I'll be lonely in my bed tonight,' he said, dimming the lights as a car appeared around the corner ahead of them. He turned to her, his eyes twinkling momentarily in the glare, and Ellen thought how incredibly handsome he was and how lucky she was to have found him.

'I'd like to stop you feeling lonely,' she replied softly. 'And I'd like to wake up with you in the morning.'

'The invitation stands. I could turn the car around now and we could go back.'

'No, I can't do that to Peg. It's just not right.'

He chuckled. 'You're not a girl any more, Ellen.'

'I *am* in my aunt's house.'

'All right. I won't try to persuade you. But I'll come and get you tomorrow and we can spend the day together.'

'I'd like that.'

'Did you finish *The Age of Innocence*?'

'Not yet.'

'Then I'll wait until you have before we watch the movie together.'

'It's a beautiful book. It sweeps me into another world. A fascinating world.' She squeezed his hand. 'You know, the novel belonged to my mother. It's inscribed by Dylan. It reads: *To my own Ellen Olenska, May you always be wild and curious, your spirit free. May your heart for ever belong to me. Dylan. July 1977.*'

Conor raised an eyebrow. 'So he called her Ellen Olenska. That's interesting.'

'I know we . . .' She was about to tell him of her walk to the little chapel but stopped herself in time, remembering that Conor's wife was buried there. 'We met in the pub and had lunch together. He told me that he gave her the book. I never expected to find it in Peg's library. I was astonished when he told me that she named me after his nickname for her.'

Conor stared at her pensively before turning his eyes back to the road. 'What does that tell you?'

'That she still loved him when I was born.'

He nodded. 'Yes, but don't you think . . .'

Ellen cut him off with her own train of thought. 'I wonder whether she regretted running off with my father? Whether she still held a candle for Dylan?'

'If she didn't, you'd be called Elizabeth or Alexandra.'

'Then maybe she ran off against her will, like it was her only choice. God, perhaps she has always loved him and that's why she kept her childhood in Ireland quiet, because she couldn't bear to go back here, in conversation or anything else. It was too painful.'

Conor smiled at her indulgently. 'You're very romantic, aren't you, Ellen?'

'Yes. But it *is* romantic, when you look at it like that. Believe me, my mother is the least romantic person I have ever met, or so I thought. I'm beginning to think I don't know her at all. She left when she was young. Maybe the life she chose has hardened her. Certainly, the woman Dylan described didn't sound at all like the woman I know.'

'You're going to have to ask her all those questions.'

'I couldn't. I just couldn't,' she replied, shaking her head and turning away to look out of the window.

'Then you'll never know.'

'Perhaps some things are best left alone,' she said quietly. A sudden chill crawled over her skin. Conor was right, it was all much more complicated than she imagined.

Sensing her apprehension, Conor squeezed her hand. 'You're right, Ellen, it's better not to know.'

As they approached the house they saw another car parked in the driveway. Ellen didn't recognize it as belonging to her uncles. 'It could be Ronan,' she said.

Conor's jaw hardened. 'Then I won't linger,' he answered, pulling up beside it.

She bit her bottom lip. 'What shall I tell them?'

'That you spent the best part of the day in bed with me.' He grinned at her mischievously.

'You're so bad, Conor. If I tell them that they'll kill me.'

'You won't have to. They'll read it all over your face.'

'What's wrong with my face?' She ran her fingers over her skin. 'Have you given me a rash?'

'I'm not a horse!'

She laughed. 'No, but you're very bristly.'

'I'm talking of your glow. I'm afraid your face is a blatant display of your lustful behaviour.'

She slapped his hand playfully. 'Oh, you're teasing!'

'Only a little. Your reaction is priceless.'

'No rash, then?'

'None that I can see. But it *is* dark. So, what's your verdict? Beard or no beard?' he asked, obviously wanting to delay her departure for as long as possible.

'I like you with and without, actually. But if I had to choose, I'd say no beard. I see more of you without it. You're a handsome man. Why hide it?'

His teeth shone white as he smiled. 'So, I'll pick you up tomorrow morning.' He wound his hand around her neck and leaned forward to kiss her. His lips were soft and full, parted to kiss her fully. She closed her eyes to savour it, forgetting her anxiety about the lights from the house that beamed on them as if they were actors on a stage. When he pulled away he held her gaze for a long moment. Then he smiled incredulously, as if he, too, was astonished and grateful that they had found one another. 'Sleep well, Ellen.'

'I will. You've exhausted me.' She laughed shyly, unable to bear the intensity of his stare without blushing.

He lifted her chin and kissed her again. 'It's a bit late for bashfulness.'

'I know, you've stripped me of all modesty.'

'I'm so pleased. I'd hate to have missed a bit.'

'No, I think you just about covered everything.' They laughed together. He kissed her again and finally, with great force of will, Ellen stepped out of the car and watched him drive away.

As the tail lights disappeared into the darkness, she lifted her eyes to the sea beyond, where the ghostly silhouette of the lighthouse stood out against the night sky. The water glittered like fallen stars, tossed about by the waves, and a crescent moon shone brightly through a misty aura. She wondered whether the questions surrounding Caitlin's death would ever be answered, or whether Conor would simply erase the whole episode from his life and never speak of it. In his opinion, there was probably no mystery, just a tragic accident that the locals had whipped up into something more sinister for lack of anything else to gossip about. She knew for certain that she'd never be able to ask him about it. The darkness in his eyes assured her of that. She could imagine his temper when crossed. That face that so easily creased with mirth could just as quickly harden with fury, she had no doubt about that. However, her curiosity was as keen as ever. She hoped that in time he might confide in her.

She walked into the house to find Peg pacing the kitchen floor while Ronan and Oswald reasoned with her from the table. When she appeared in the doorway they all stared at her. She registered Peg's anguish immediately. Her face was pink and her eyes glistened with tears. 'What's happened?' Ellen asked, ignoring Mr Badger who padded over to sniff Magnum on her legs.

'Jack's gone,' said Oswald dolefully.

Ellen's looked at the jackdaw's chair in horror. 'Did he fly away?'

'We don't know what happened,' Ronan answered. 'He often flies off . . .'

'But he always comes back,' interjected Peg miserably. 'I can't understand it.'

'Might he have run into trouble with a bird of prey?' Ellen suggested, then wished she hadn't.

Peg paled. She dabbed her eyes. 'Jaysus, that's a brutal thought, Ellen.'

'I didn't mean to upset you.'

'I know, pet. We have to hope and pray that he comes back in the morning.'

'Has he ever spent the night away?'

'Not ever. I'm sick with worry. I don't think I'll sleep a wink tonight.'

Ellen noticed they were all drinking. She suspected Peg was gasping for a cigarette. Surely, in these circumstances, Oswald wouldn't mind if she lit up. Since meeting Conor, Ellen hadn't craved nicotine at all. She presumed that the constant rush of adrenalin masked her body's need for the drug.

'I suggest you go to bed, Mam,' said Ronan kindly. 'Do you want me to stay the night?'

'I have Ellen. I'll be all right. Don't worry.'

'And I'm next door should you need company,' Oswald added. 'As you know, I'm a terrible sleeper, so don't hesitate to come knocking. I'm always on for a midnight feast or a game of chess.'

'I don't suppose there's any point staying up. He's not coming home tonight. I hope he's found somewhere warm to roost.' Tears began to spill over onto her grey cheeks. She blotted her skin with the tissue. 'So silly to be sentimental about a bird.'

Oswald's face softened with compassion. 'No, Peg, it's not silly at all,' he said and his voice was so kind and gentle it sent a ripple across Ellen's skin. She thought he was going to add that her animals were like her children. The words hung in the air unspoken. But he did not. He didn't need to. They all felt it and Peg knew, for that was why she was crying.

'I lost my little girl, Ellen,' Peg said suddenly, and she stared at them all in surprise, as if the sentence had been spoken by someone else. Oswald and Ronan gazed at her, their jaws loose, not knowing how to respond. It was as if a great wall had at once collapsed after years of defending her against the onslaught of pain. She took a deep breath that sounded more like the howl of a wounded animal. 'Oh!' she wailed, her chin wobbling uncontrollably. 'Did I . . . did I . . . I don't know . . . my little girl . . . my little Ciara.' Ellen's hand shot to her mouth and her eyes welled with tears as she watched her aunt turn mad with grief.

In a moment, Oswald was wrapping his arms around her diminished frame, hugging her tightly to stop her shaking, reassuring her in his soothing voice. 'It's all right, old girl. You're going to be fine. This is good. All good. It's so much better out than in.'

Ronan got to his feet and hovered uncertainly. Ellen knew he wanted to comfort his mother but didn't know how. She felt just as powerless. For a moment they caught eyes. In that instant, Ellen found a bond with the one member of the family with whom she had previously felt no connection. She gave a small, sympathetic smile. His shoulders dropped and he sighed helplessly. 'There you go, Peg my dear, cry me a river and let your unhappiness be washed away,' said Oswald, as Peg's trembling subsided and her sobs grew quieter. Oswald was right, her grief was so much better out than in. Ronan smiled feebly at Ellen.

At last, Oswald helped her into a chair. She took a long swig of Jameson, neat, and wiped her eyes with shaky fingers. They all sat down and waited for her to speak. She didn't utter a word for what seemed like a long time, but when she did she let it all out, in a long, heartbreaking soliloquy.

They let her talk without interruption. Only Bertie's loud snoring from the stove disturbed the silence in the room. She spoke of the moment she realized Ciara had gone missing to the moment she was found, face down in the water. To speak about it was cathartic but desperately emotional. Peg tore the tissue to shreds, unaware of the nervous actions of her fingers, until Oswald put his hand on hers and she stopped, dropping her shoulders at once and taking a deep, cleansing breath.

'I pray for her every night,' she continued, calmer now. 'I light a candle and kneel by my bed and pray that the angels are looking after her. I pray that she's at peace. I pray too that she never leaves me, because I can't bear to be without her.' Her feverish eyes spilled over again. 'You're not mad, Oswald, but it's not leprechauns and fairies who blow out candles and move things.'

Oswald smiled tenderly. 'I know.'

'You know?'

'Of course I know, my dear Peg.'

She took a ragged breath. 'I want it to be her so badly my body aches with longing. Sometimes I think I'm going crazy and hearing things that aren't there.'

'She's still with you, Peg,' said Oswald, and the certainty in his voice was like a blanket to a woman stiff with cold.

'Do you think so, Oswald? Do you really?'

'I'm sure of it,' he replied, and the honesty in his face reassured her that he was.

Ellen decided now would be a good moment to confess about the candle. Peg was astonished. 'So, it's not just me, then?' She smiled weakly. 'I thought I was going crazy.'

'Do you think she's trying to tell you that she's still close?' Ellen asked.

'I don't know.' Peg looked to Oswald for an answer.

'Of course she is,' Oswald replied. 'And she won't leave you until you're ready to let her go.'

'How do you *know*?' Peg asked keenly.

'I've always known.'

'Always?'

'I've always had an overdeveloped sixth sense,' he said casually.

'Can you *see* things?'

'Oh, I'm sure I did as a child but I see nothing now. I sense things, though.' He smiled at her. 'Leprechauns and fairies.'

Peg smiled back. 'But they're not leprechauns and fairies, are they?'

He beamed at her affectionately, as if she were a child who had just unravelled a great mystery. 'No, old girl, they're not.'

She sighed and looked at Ronan, who was very quietly listening to his mother's every word. 'I'm glad you're here, Ronan. I should have talked to you boys about your sister. I should have shared her with you. After all, she belonged to you as well.'

He nodded, the muscles in his face taut with the effort of controlling his emotions. 'I think of her from time to time,' he said quietly. 'She was a happy little thing, wasn't she?'

'Aye, she was,' Peg agreed. 'She had the light and happy soul of an angel.'

They remained talking until the early hours of the morning, until Peg's eyelids began to droop with tiredness. Oswald and Ronan bade her good night, reassuring her that they'd both pray for Jack's safe return in the morning.

Ellen was about to take her aunt upstairs when Peg stopped in the doorway. She turned to her niece and grabbed her arm. 'Let's have a smoke before we turn in, shall we? Now the boys have gone.'

'You sure you're not too tired?'

'No, pet, I'm not too tired. I've been desperate for one all evening.'

'Then I'll keep you company,' Ellen replied, going back into the kitchen to find Peg's handbag. In the drama of Jack's disappearance and Peg's unexpected unburdening of her loss, they'd all forgotten to ask her where she had been. She was grateful for that.

'You know, I haven't smoked since meeting Conor,' said Ellen, sitting down and opening the packet.

'Then you shouldn't be smoking now, should you?' said Peg.

'One won't hurt.'

Peg took the packet away. 'No, Ellen, I'm not going to let you. You've been strong. I don't want to be the reason you break your resolve.'

'OK, you're right. I'll be good.'

'As for me . . .'

'Tonight, you deserve as many cigarettes as you like,' Ellen reassured her.

Peg put the cigarette between her lips and lit it. She inhaled deeply then blew the smoke out in a long, languorous breath, letting her shoulders drop with relief. 'I'm sorry I never told you about Ciara,' she said softly.

'That's OK. Alanna told me.'

'So, you see, that's why I don't go to the pub.'

'But surely people don't gossip about that any more?'

'I've been away for too long, you see. If I were to appear now they'd all start up again. I can't be doing with it. I had a fight with Father Michael after Ciara died. I saw her, my little girl, the night after she drowned. As clear as day, standing in my bedroom, smiling at me with this wise, knowing smile. I was a fool, I'm afraid. I told Father Michael and he said that it was my imagination. That in my grief I had imagined her. The silly man doesn't believe in that sort of thing. Pompous eejit! He made me doubt my own eyes. So, I stopped going to Mass. I stopped going to the pub. I withdrew. If I show up now, they'll all wonder why.' She shook her head. 'No, I can't be doing with all of that.'

Ellen watched her sudden defensiveness and wondered whether it wasn't gossip she was afraid of, but compassion.

Peg stubbed out her cigarette butt and smiled at her niece. 'It's nice to have a girl about the house again,' she said quietly. 'Even though you're a big girl, you're family. It's nice to have you here.'

Ellen put her hand on her arm. 'I'm glad, Aunt Peg. I like being here, too.'

'Shall we go to bed now?'

'I think we should.'

The older woman grinned. 'Don't think I haven't noticed the rosy glow in your cheeks.'

Ellen touched her face, startled. 'What glow?'

Her aunt shook her head. 'Really, child, you can't kid a kidder!'

Ellen laughed. 'Obviously not.'

'You had a nice afternoon, then, did you?'

She nodded. 'I did.'

'Good.' Peg got up stiffly. 'Off to bed now. Will you pray for Jack as well? The more prayers the better.'

'Of course I will.'

'Thank you, dear.'

Ellen followed her aunt upstairs. They parted on the landing. 'He'll come back, Aunt Peg,' Ellen said, but she didn't believe he would. Peg nodded and smiled sadly before closing her bedroom door behind her. Ellen imagined her kneeling in prayer beside the little votive candle, and wondered whether Ciara really was there, blowing the flame out in an effort to let her mother know that she was still close.

Chapter 22

Conor is in love and I cannot stand it. I watch him grow lighter and lighter and further and further away from me and there is nothing I can do about it. He is whistling as if he hasn't a care in the world, as if he didn't lose his beloved wife in a terrible fire five years ago. He has a bounce in his step and his lips are permanently curled at the corners as if he can barely contain his happiness. I feel my fury mount and build around me in a thick grey mist. There has got to be something I can do to focus his mind once again on his grief. It was better when he grew a beard and tore up and down the beach on his horse, cursing fate for having taken me from him, for leaving him alone and lost. It was better when he was miserable.

I resent Ellen for stepping into my place and letting him wrap his arms around her and make love to her as he once made love to me. The sweet nothings I mistook for lust I realize now are fuelled by love. I see it in the way he looks at her. It's all in his eyes and I cannot deny it any longer. He is growing to love her. If I had a throat I would choke on those words. So, I go to Peg's with the desire only to do Ellen harm. I don't know how, but if I can whisper into my son's ear in the middle of the night, perhaps I can whisper into hers.

It is dawn and a translucent veil of light hangs over the sea. The lighthouse looks as forlorn as an old shipwreck, abused and battered by the waves. I turn away from my memories, which are still painful, and find Peg standing in her overcoat, looking anxiously this way and that. I wonder what she is looking for. Her dog is at her heel, his ears pricked, ready to obey her order, but it never comes. She just stands, searching the skies for something. Then I realize she is looking for her bird. The bird I shooed away.

It is only when I see Ciara's familiar golden glow that I feel my spirit flood with shame. For beside her, bathed in her loving light, is the bird. Peg lets out a wail of joy as the bird flies towards her. She opens her arms and her face disappears into a big smile and tears of happiness spill onto her cheeks. 'Jack!' she cries, and above her the window opens wide and Ellen leans out sleepily. 'Oh, Ellen. He's come back. Our prayers have been answered. He's come back!'

Ciara watches with pleasure as the bird perches on her mother's shoulder. Peg hurries inside with her dog and closes the front door. Ellen withdraws and shuts the window. I imagine there will be much celebration in the kitchen this morning. I look at Ciara and I know that she can see my shame. But she smiles on me, too, with the same love with which she smiled on her mother. I don't understand. Perhaps she can even see the malice I harbour in my heart for Conor and Ellen. If she does, she doesn't show it. She just gazes at me with an all-knowing, all-understanding love, which makes my shame all the more intense.

And then I have an idea. If I can travel by thought, I wonder what would happen if I think myself in London, at Ellen's home, with Ellen's family? Can it really be that simple? I can't imagine why I haven't thought of it before. There's little I can do down here. But instinctively I feel there is a great deal I can do in London.

I have never been to that great city, but I will myself there, to Ellen's house, with the same focus of mind with which I think myself to Dublin. It is very easy and strangely natural, as if I have been travelling like this for all eternity. And here I am, in the hallway of an ostentatiously decorated town house, with a little rat-like dog yapping at me. He is small but ferocious and I see through his curled lip that his teeth are like needles. I fly at him with my arms, like I did with the bird, and he spins round and scurries away in fright, his claws making tapping noises on the marble floor.

'Waffle, stop that silly barking,' comes a very English voice from another room. 'Is there someone at the door?'

A young blonde hurries into the hall and looks through the peephole in the front door. 'Oh, really,' she says irritably, turning around. 'You're going mad, Waffle. There's no one there.' I follow the elegantly suited young woman through large double doors into an airy dining room, decorated with pretty wallpaper of birds and branches, and on into a lime-green study beyond. It is heavily upholstered with a green velvet sofa, high-backed armchair and a coffee table piled high with glossy Christie's catalogues.

'So, what was that all about, then?' the other woman asks. She is sitting at her desk, her shoulder-length dark hair neatly coiffed, in a navy-blue skirt and jacket, a silk scarf tied round her neck. I can see her blood-red nails and the gold and diamond bracelet dangling on her wrist. Then she turns and I realize that she is Madeline Byrne, Ellen's mother. The resemblance is undeniable, but only in her colouring and the shape of her jaw and mouth. Her eyes are different: they are blue like

Peg's, whereas Ellen's are brown. On closer inspection, I see that hers are red and anxious.

'I don't know,' says the girl, taking the seat next to her boss.

'He sounded jolly angry. Where's he gone now?'

'Shall I call him, Lady Trawton?'

'Yes, go and find him, Janey.' She sighs and shakes her head wearily. 'Ellen's disappearance is driving us all mad.'

Janey disappears into the hall, whistling for the dog. Madeline returns to her list. I look over her shoulder and see that she is planning a dinner party. But her pen doesn't touch the page. She is thinking and I imagine she is thinking about Ellen. Shortly, the girl comes back with the dog tucked under her arm. 'He was hiding in the conservatory,' she reports.

'Waffle, what were you doing in there?' Madeline asks, brightening. But the dog stares at me and growls. His mistress looks puzzled. 'Goodness, you silly dog. What's got into you today? Hmm?' I am bored of frightening animals, so I ignore him and after a while he calms down and allows Madeline to place him on her knee, like a furry napkin. 'Right, where were we?' she says, looking at her list again.

They are about to continue when the telephone rings. Madeline stares at it as if she is afraid it might jump up and bite her. Janey fidgets nervously, probably wishing she was anywhere but here. At last, Madeline lifts the receiver and puts it to her ear. 'Yes?' she says. 'Oh, hello, William.' Her shoulders drop with disappointment. She waves her manicured fingers at Janey, who leaves the room.

'Any news?'

'No, I haven't heard a word,' she tells him. 'Nothing.'

'It's ridiculous.' William sighs. 'How long do you think she's going to stay away?'

'I don't know. God knows what's got into her. One

moment she was at the Herringtons' cocktail party, having a perfectly nice time with her silly friend Emily, and the next I was reading the note she left in the hall. Your guess is as good as mine.' I am surprised to hear no trace of Ireland in her voice, just a sharp edge like a northerly wind.

'I think Emily knows and isn't telling us,' says William.

'Most likely. But I've tried to talk to her, lots of times, and she's not giving anything away. If Ellen had come to me and said she had pre-wedding nerves and needed to get away I would have been wholly supportive. I would have bought her a ticket to anywhere in the world. This running away business is absurd. Who does she think she is, worrying us all like this? It's terribly thoughtless.'

'I've sent her endless texts and emails. To be honest, Madeline, I'm now worried.'

'Of course you are, William. But she'll come back. I do think it's a case of pre-wedding nerves. You know, when she was a child she was frightfully rebellious. I did my best to knock it out of her and I thought I'd succeeded. I'm afraid it's coming out now. But she'll settle down once she's married.'

'If we ever get married,' he retorts petulantly.

'Of course you will, William. Don't worry, really. She'll be back soon, ashamed and repentant, and we shall all forgive her and forget about it.'

'She quit her job, that's not the action of someone planning to come back.'

'She wants to be a writer, or something like that. She's unfulfilled. Once she has a husband to look after and, god willing, children, she'll forget all about that nonsense. I promise you we'll soon be sitting around the dining-room table having a jolly good laugh about it.'

'I'm not sure *I'm* going to be laughing about it, Madeline.

It's the most selfish thing she's ever done, and totally out of character. We're talking about a girl who called me at least twice a day, every day. A girl who to all intents and purposes had moved into my apartment. To pack up and leave without a word is abhorrent.'

Madeline inhales impatiently. 'Well, what do you think inspired it, then?'

'I have no idea. I've been over the days before she ran off in great detail and I can find nothing to suggest that she wasn't entirely happy and excited about our engagement.'

'Then you have nothing to worry about.'

'Might she have run off with another man?' William's voice hardens. 'I could never forgive her that.'

'No, absolutely not,' Madeline replies quickly, horrified at the implication. 'She wouldn't do that to you, and besides, she loves you.'

'Then why isn't she returning my calls and reassuring me that she's OK? I'm losing patience.'

At this, Madeline stiffens, yet her voice assumes a wheedling tone. 'Oh, do try to be patient, William. We're all so looking forward to being one happy family. Ellen is, too. She's just a little scared. I do recall her being a bit on edge before she ran off. I imagine she's sorting her head out. Getting married is a very big step and she's always been wary of commitment. In fact, before meeting you she had never committed to anyone. You have tamed her and that's quite an achievement.'

'Well, it doesn't appear that I've done a very good job, does it?'

'I'll call Emily again and demand to know where she is. She's my daughter, after all, and I have a right to know. I will personally go and bring her back.'

'If you do, I'm coming with you,' says William, his voice

urgent now. 'We'll find her and talk sense into her. She's going to have a lot of explaining to do.'

'And I'm sure she'll have a perfectly sane explanation. You love her, don't you, William?'

'Of course I do, and I intend to marry her.'

'Good. This is nothing but a minor obstacle over which we shall all courageously jump. Leave it to me. I shall call Emily now.'

'I hope you have better luck with her than I did.'

'Of course I will. I won't take no for an answer.' And I'm sure that she won't.

'Thank you, Madeline,' he says.

'No, thank *you* for being so patient. You'll make a wonderful husband. She's very lucky to have you.'

When Madeline puts down the telephone she remains a moment lost in thought, rubbing the bridge of her nose with her thumb and forefinger, while Waffle remains inert on her knee in spite of my lingering presence. A moment later, Janey returns. 'Now, let's wrap this up. I want invitations sent out this afternoon. I'll discuss theme another time. I'm afraid I have to make another call before rushing off to my meeting. Let me know when the car's outside. Did you print out the minutes?'

'Yes, Lady Trawton, they're in your bag.'

'Good. When I'm gone will you take Waffle out for a walk?'

'Of course.' Janey calls the dog and walks briskly out of the room. Waffle takes one look at me and shoots after her as if his tail is on fire. Madeline dials the number – Emily's, I presume – but it goes straight onto the answer machine. With a frustrated huff, she hangs up. Again she remains at her desk, twiddling her pen in her fingers, deliberating what to do next. She looks at her watch, puts her pen down and gets up. I follow her up to her bedroom.

It is a light and airy room with big sash windows overlooking a leafy street of white stucco town houses. She stalks into the marble bathroom and begins to apply make-up. Then she stares at her reflection as if she is gazing upon a stranger. She remains there for a long time, just staring. I wonder what she is thinking. I would love to know. But I am unable to read people's minds. She has pretty blue eyes, pale as turquoise, and as I watch I see them darken and grow sad.

Suddenly, inspired by an idea, she hurries back into the bedroom and rummages in her bag for her telephone. She stands by the window and dials. When it goes onto answer machine she leaves a curt message: 'Emily, this is Madeline. It's been nearly two weeks now since Ellen ran off and I demand to know where she is. I am her mother and I will not take no for an answer. If you don't return my call I will simply have to come over personally and see you. I will be in a meeting until noon, but I will leave my telephone on vibrate so you can call me any time.'

She hangs up and throws the telephone into her handbag. Janey knocks on the bedroom door. 'Your car is here, Lady Trawton.'

'I'll be down in a minute.' She sits on the bed and heaves a sigh. She is clearly worried. There is a brittleness to her and yet, when she sits hunched, alone in her room, she is softer. It is as if here, in the privacy of her private quarters, she can be herself.

I notice framed photographs of her family. Her two blonde daughters on their wedding days, grandchildren, and Ellen with her fiancé, I presume, smiling as if she has found in him everything she ever wanted. I take a closer look. He is fair-haired and boyish, clear-eyed and pale-skinned, like a smooth young vegetable out of the very best nursery. It is no wonder that Ellen has fallen in love with Conor. She has exchanged a boy for a man; a man with a wealth of experience in his eyes. He is rugged and weathered, his face lined and his eyes dark and troubled. Not like this privileged youth whose shallow beauty betrays a lack of character and a lack of hunger. I can tell this William has no hunger for life.

Madeline looks right at me. For a moment, I am gripped with excitement, but it is short-lived, for she is looking *through* me, at the photograph of Ellen. She stands up and lifts the frame to stare into the face of the daughter she has lost. Her gaze softens and she frowns, questioning why with a barely discernible shaking of her head.

Aware that she has to leave for her meeting, she picks up her handbag from the bed and heads out of the door. I watch her go. I have no desire to follow her. I will whisper to her when she is sleeping. When her consciousness is open and her thoughts empty. When there is no resistance. I know the chances of her hearing me are slim, but I will not give up. It is the only way. Conor and Ellen have to be stopped and Madeline and William are the only two people who can make that happen.

So, I linger in the house, waiting for night. I have no wish to watch Conor and Ellen and their blossoming love, and I am ashamed to be seen by Ciara, for she is made of light and my world is growing increasingly dark. I am embarrassed to be dark. I know that it is not good – any fool knows the difference between a light spirit and a dark one. I have noticed recently that I am becoming a *heavy* spirit, as if I am made of dense fog that is weighing me down. I feel very earthbound.

Heaven feels so far away that I wonder whether I will ever find it, or whether I am to dwell here in this limbo for eternity, groping in the shadows. The answer is so simple and yet, distracted by my malevolent purpose, I am unable to see it.

Chapter 23

Ellen dressed hastily in a pair of jeans and sweater and ran down to the kitchen to find Jack returned to his perch and Peg filling the kettle at the tap. 'It's a miracle,' she said to her aunt, staring in amazement at the bird, who looked none the worse for a night in the cold.

Peg smiled, her eyes brimming with joy, and glanced out of the window. 'And would you look at that!' she said with a chuckle. 'We've got company!' With a rush of excitement Ellen joined her at the window, expecting to see Conor climbing out of his car. But instead of Conor's shiny Range Rover, she saw Johnny's rusty truck and Desmond's black Peugeot pulling up in front of the house, full of her uncles and cousins. Her heart froze in panic.

Conor was due to pick her up that morning. What if he arrived to find a kitchen full of Byrnes? What then? Would there be a terrible fight? Would Desmond shout at her? She had to call him at once and change the plan, but before she could reach the door, five burly men filled the hallway: Johnny, Joe, Ronan, Desmond and Craic. 'He's come back,' said Ellen, disguising her apprehension behind a triumphant smile.

'He has?' said Johnny, striding past her. 'Peg, is that right?'

'It's a miracle,' Peg replied. 'Come and have something to eat, all of you. Today, I'll make you the best breakfast you've ever had.'

'Jaysus, there he is!' said Desmond in astonishment. 'I thought he'd have come a cropper.'

'Me too,' Joe agreed, rubbing his hands together at the thought of breakfast. 'So, we've come to celebrate, then, Peggine. What'll you give us?'

'That's right, Joe. Sit yourself down and put in your order. Today, breakfast is on Aunt Peggine!'

'That's grand, Peg,' said Craic, placing a rough hand on her shoulder. 'I don't imagine you slept a wink last night.'

'Not much, but it doesn't matter. I'm happy now.'

'We came to help find him,' Craic added.

'I know you did. You're all very good to me.'

'I'm glad he's come back.' He looked at the jackdaw, now in the middle of the table, pecking at the birdseed Peg had put out for him. 'God's will,' he added gravely.

'God's will, for sure,' Peg agreed. She moved away to put the kettle on the stove. 'Ronan, be a good lad and go and tell Oswald. He'll want to know the good news.'

'When did he come back, Mam?' Ronan asked.

'Early this morning. He just came flying back. God knows where he went, but he doesn't look too bad for a night in the wild.'

'He looks just grand, Mam,' Ronan replied before leaving to find Oswald.

Johnny, Joe, Desmond and Craic sat around the kitchen table while Ellen helped Peg prepare breakfast. As Ellen laid out mugs and cutlery, Desmond asked her a favour.

'Alanna needs help in the shop, Ellen. Mary's let her down. She's still in Waterford so Alanna's all on her own in there. She thought perhaps, as you liked it, you might help her out. What'll you say? She'll pay you, of course.'

The thought of making some money really appealed to Ellen and she knew Conor would return to Dublin on Sunday. 'I'd love to,' she replied. 'What do you think, Peg?'

'I think it'll be just grand. You're not getting anything written at the moment, are you?'

Ellen went to the cupboard to take down some plates. 'No, not really,' she replied, not wishing to elaborate on *that* subject.

'Well, then, I think it's a grand idea and you'll make a bit of money, which is always nice,' Peg added.

'When would she like me to start?'

'Tomorrow?' said Desmond.

'Saturday?' Ellen hesitated.

'Or Monday, if that's better. We haven't given you much notice.'

'Monday would be better,' she said. 'If Alanna doesn't mind. I'm . . . I have things to do this weekend.' She took the plates over to the sideboard near the stove, where Peg was busy cracking eggs against the frying pan.

'The hens are laying like crazy at the moment,' said Peg. 'I don't know what's got into them. But it's good to use the eggs.' They crackled in the pan and the smell of frying bacon filled the room.

Ronan returned a short while later with Oswald, who glided into the room with his arms out. 'Let me see the miracle for myself!' he exclaimed. 'By Jove, it's true. That is indeed our dear Jack, returned to the bosom of his family. I am humbled.'

Peg grinned at him lovingly. 'Oh, really, Oswald, will you never quit messing with me!'

He put his arm around her shoulders and pulled her close. 'It's done with the greatest affection, I assure you,' he said in a quiet voice.

'Oh, I know that, Oswald, dear.' A faint blush seeped into her cheeks. 'Now, what'll you have for breakfast?'

'I've already eaten. But I won't say no to a cup of tea.'

Peg looked surprised. 'But you don't like tea!'

'Not if there's a glass of claret on offer. But it's too early for that, so a cup of tea will go down a treat. Now, let's take a closer look at our friend over here.' He walked to the table and peered at the bird. 'Hmmm, I think he's invigorated by his adventure. Look at him! I've never seen a more smug-looking bird!'

'You missed a great night in the pub last night,' said Joe to Ellen, as she placed a plate of eggs, bacon and sausages in front of him. 'Dylan played the accordion again. I don't know what's got into the man, but he was flying! Everyone was singing.'

'He's very gifted, isn't he?' Ellen replied proudly, feeling a sense of ownership. 'He's going to teach me to play the guitar.'

'Well, you two have hit it off, haven't you?' said Desmond.

Ellen shrugged. 'I like Dylan. He's a deep-thinker.'

Johnny laughed. 'That'll be when he's staring into a deep pint!' Desmond and Joe laughed with him.

'I haven't seen him drunk,' Ellen retorted defensively. 'In fact, every time I've seen him he's been totally sober.'

Craic nodded. 'That's true. I haven't seen him langered for a while.'

'Well, that's good, isn't it?' interjected Peg.

'He's making an effort to clean himself up,' said Ronan, biting into a piece of toast. 'I think that's because of you, Ellen.'

'Me?'

'Of course. He was a different man before you showed up.'

Desmond glanced at Johnny and both men looked a little uncomfortable.

Peg cut in, 'If Ellen is helping Dylan get over the past then that's a good thing, isn't it? Now, who would like another cup of tea?'

'Yes, please, Peg, my dear,' said Oswald jovially, holding out his mug. He smiled knowingly at Ellen. 'Dylan has found something in you that he lost a long time ago.' Desmond and Johnny caught eyes again and looked suddenly nervous.

'What's that then, Oswald?' asked Joe.

'A reason to live,' said Oswald wisely.

Ellen wasn't quite sure how she could possibly give Dylan a reason to live, other than by reminding him of the woman he loved. She shrugged and sipped her tea. 'I think music gives him a reason to live,' she said.

'Ellen's right,' Johnny agreed vigorously. 'If you'd heard him last night! Jaysus, he was singing his heart out!'

It wasn't long before they had scraped their plates clean and drained their mugs of tea. 'Well, we'd better be going,' said Johnny, pushing his chair out. 'I saw Mr Macausland's car parked outside his house yesterday, so we'd better look smart.'

'Is he chasing you, Ellen?' Joe asked.

Ellen's cheeks burned. 'I'm . . .'

'Ellen's not a fool!' Desmond interrupted in a voice that was more like a growl. 'She's been told.'

'Would you listen to you, Desmond Byrne!' said Peg, putting her hands on her sturdy hips. 'Ellen's big enough to make her own decisions and what's it got to do with you anyway?'

Desmond's face darkened. 'She's a Byrne,' he said.

'Half,' interjected Oswald. 'Only half.'

'I won't have one of ours mixing with that man.' He turned his dark eyes on Ellen.

'You don't want to wind up like Caitlin, now, do you?' Ronan cut in.

'Would you all move on now,' said Peg irritably. 'Let the poor man alone.'

'Don't go feeling sorry for him, Mam,' said Ronan firmly. His face was the colour of a beetroot. 'He's not the one who's six feet under.'

Peg rolled her eyes and went over to the table to stroke Jack. She wasn't going to give the subject any more of her time.

'He didn't put her there, Ronan, if that's what you're insinuating. I won't have you saying that.' Desmond's tone reminded Ronan that he was head of the family and was not to be contradicted.

'I agree with Desmond,' said Joe. 'He's no murderer.'

Desmond straightened and gave a brisk nod in Ellen's direction. 'Well, you just stay away from him, now. He's a man who gets everything he wants. He won't be getting one of us.'

'I think it's a bit late for that,' said Peg, turning to look out of the window. They all stopped talking to hear the sound of a car drawing up in front of the house.

'Ah,' said Oswald. 'Perfect timing!'

Ellen's heart began to thump very loudly in her chest. She put down her mug. 'He's not what you think, Desmond,' she said quietly. 'I respect your opinion, but I don't agree. He's my friend and I won't stop seeing him.' They watched her walk into the hall where she shrugged on her coat. A moment later they were crowded at the window, staring in amazement as she climbed into the waiting vehicle.

'Nothing good will come of this,' said Desmond ominously.

'I think you should keep an open mind,' Oswald advised.

'I found him charming in spite of myself,' said Peg.

Desmond rubbed his beard. 'It's his *charm* that I'm worried about,' he said. 'I hope she knows what she's doing.'

Ellen climbed into the Range Rover. 'Don't kiss me, Conor, we're being watched. Just drive.'

'That's asking a lot of a passionate man,' he replied with a grin, pulling out into the track.

His humour defused her nervousness and she laughed. 'Oh, God, I've just had a showdown with Desmond and I think I won.'

He took her hand across the gearstick and caressed her skin with his thumb. 'What did he say?'

'He doesn't want a Byrne mixing with *you*.'

Conor raised an eyebrow. 'That's rich!'

'Why?'

He didn't answer directly. 'I could object to a Macausland mixing with a Byrne.'

'Did my family do something wrong?'

He shook his head. 'Every human being is an island. I don't judge people by the actions of their family, but by *their* actions.' He sighed and glanced at her, his eyes a deep indigo. 'I like you, Ellen. I like you a lot. Possibly more than I have ever liked anyone. I don't care where you come from. You're an individual. Nothing else matters but *you*.'

She wanted to ask him again, but sensed he didn't want to talk about it. She squeezed his hand. 'It doesn't matter what Desmond thinks. I've always had a rebellious streak.' She grinned shyly. 'I like you too, Conor.'

It was later, when they lay naked beneath the sheets, that Conor suddenly decided to tell Ellen about Caitlin. She lay with her head on his chest while he played with her hair, warmed by the afterglow of their lovemaking.

'Ellen, there's something you need to know,' he began. Ellen remained as still as stone, her ear pressed to his chest, which vibrated with his deep and gravelly voice. His hand stopped playing with her hair and rested on her head. 'I didn't love my wife,' he said simply.

Those words were so shockingly honest and unexpected that she lifted herself onto her elbow and gazed down at him, incredulous. 'You didn't love Caitlin?'

He shook his head. 'I did at first, but not in the end.'

'What happened?'

'She drove me away.'

'How?'

He sighed as if it cost him a great deal to reveal the truth about his wife. 'She wasn't right in the head, Ellen. I didn't realize until I had married her that she had a problem. They probably have a name for it, I don't know, but she refused to seek help from anyone.'

'What sort of problem?'

'She had mood swings. Terrible mood swings. She was jealous to the point of obsession. One minute she was loving, the next she was violent, accusing me of all sorts of infidelities. She was unbalanced, desperately insecure and needy. That was what drove us apart.'

'But you loved her once?'

'I loved her in the beginning but she tested my love over and over until I had nothing more to give. She hated the city, so I spent most of the time in Dublin, and travelling, while she remained here at the castle. It was the best place for her. She didn't want to go anywhere. Unfamiliar places terrified her. She needed her things around her.'

Ellen kissed his temple. 'You poor man. How you must have suffered. Couldn't you get out of it?'

'Divorce was out of the question. I was terrified she'd do herself harm, and I felt responsible. She was the mother of my children and they loved her. I couldn't do it to them, however bad it got.' He looked at her guiltily. 'I didn't behave very well, Ellen. I lost my temper with her. I never hit her, but I wanted to. I hated the man I became when I was with her. She drove me to the point of madness.'

'The locals believe she was an angel.'

'Let them think that, if only for Finbar and Ida's sake. I don't want them ever to know that their mother was anything less than perfect.'

'She was very beautiful.'

'She was bewitching.'

'I have to confess that Johnny and Joe showed me the portrait of her in the castle.' For a moment, she thought she had angered him, for his jaw grew suddenly tense. He gazed up, examining her face as if deciding whether or not he could trust her. Then he sighed and averted his eyes. 'So, you can see why everyone fell in love with her, those who didn't know her. Those who did, understood what I had to live with.'

'Why didn't she get help?'

'She didn't think she had a problem.'

'I'm sure there's medication for that sort of thing. There's medication for everything.'

'Of course, but she'd never have taken it. She was like a child and the older she got the deeper she sank into her imagination. I couldn't trust her to be alone with the children so I sent my mother to help. But Caitlin hated to think that she was being spied on, and she knew my mother was immune to her charm, so she made her life so unpleasant that my poor mother lost heart and moved back to Dublin. So, I hired a nanny. Caitlin accepted her because she was dazzled by her. As long as she was adored she was fine.'

'So, when she died . . .' Ellen hesitated.

'When she died, it was a relief.' He sat up and put his head in his hands, rubbing his forehead. 'I was so ashamed, Ellen, that I could feel relief after such a tragedy. I hated myself. I wanted to feel bereft. I wanted to mourn her, but I couldn't. I loathed her. I hated her for her recklessness because she broke my children's hearts. I can never forgive her for that. She left them motherless.'

Ellen knelt beside him and wrapped her arms around him, desperate to absorb his pain so he didn't have to suffer any more. 'It's OK, Conor. I understand. You're only human. You did your best.'

'I hated her rowing out to the lighthouse. She did it to spite me. She wanted me to come and rescue her. It was another cry for attention, another trial to test my love. The number of times I had to take the boat out to get her is absurd. But on that particular night, she pushed me too far. Way too far. We had a massive row and she ran off to the lighthouse where she'd placed little candles all the way up the stairs.' He rubbed his brow as if trying to erase the image from his mind. 'She accused me of not loving her. She was right. I didn't love her any more. I wanted her out of my life. I never wanted to see her again. I wanted it to be over. And then it was. She must have caught her dress on one of the candles, for when she got to the top she was on fire. There was nothing I could do. By the time I reached her, she had thrown herself onto the rocks.'

'And you felt free,' Ellen said gently.

'Yes. I felt free, at last. I felt a mixture of horror and relief.'

He looked at her, appalled by his own admission. 'And they whisper that I'm a murderer.'

'They're ignorant.'

'I might as well have killed her.'

'But you didn't.'

He gazed at her sadly. 'I know I didn't, but I wished her dead.'

He put his arms around her and kissed her fiercely. 'You've made it all go away, Ellen,' he said, pulling back and sinking into her gaze. 'You've enabled me to move on. I didn't think I'd dare to love again. I don't know what it is about you, but I feel lighter when I'm with you.'

'But I have ...' she began, suddenly brave enough to tell him about her engagement. But before she could speak any further he was kissing her deeply and claiming her body once again.

Chapter 24

Conor and Ellen had the weekend to themselves, for Daphne was with the children in Dublin. They walked on the hills with Magnum, exhausted themselves making love, and watched movies well into the early hours of the morning. They were so content in each other's company that they required nothing more than the exceptional qualities they found in each other.

Ellen knew that things had gone too far now to tell Conor about William. He'd wonder why she hadn't told him before, when he had told her all about Caitlin. She'd just have to break off her engagement as soon as possible and hope that Conor never found out. She didn't feel it was fair, however, to tell her fiancé over the telephone. She'd have to return to London and do it properly, although she had no intention of leaving Ireland any time soon. She'd put it off as long as she dared. If she could put it off forever, she would. But postpone it as she might, she knew that at some point in the near future she'd have to go home and face not only William, but her mother, too, which was considerably more daunting. While she was with Conor in Connemara, she could forget they existed. After all, while she was in hiding, she was safely inaccessible. Conor would never know, and besides, what did it matter, because she didn't love William. He was irrelevant to the present moment, which she was giving to Conor with all her heart.

Peg was so pleased to have Jack back that she welcomed her niece's budding relationship with enthusiasm and delight. She had enough experience of life and death to know that nothing else mattered but love. In her opinion, Conor deserved to be happy, and she couldn't understand her brother's reservations. Desmond might be head of the family, but Ellen wasn't *his* daughter. He barely knew her. He had no right to tell her who she could date. But he was tribal and Ellen was blood and it didn't seem that anything could change his mind about the man many accused of having murdered his wife.

On Sunday morning, Conor and Ellen didn't go to Mass, but spent the morning in bed instead. The fact that their time together was running out only enhanced the sweetness of their lovemaking and made their feelings for each other all the more intense. On Sunday afternoon, Conor finally left for Dublin. He had work to do and was eager to throw himself into a new project. After five long, barren years, he felt himself again, fertile with ideas and brimming with the energy to bring them to fruition. He drove Ellen home in the early afternoon, cupping her face with his big hands and kissing her ardently. She savoured the smell of his skin and the taste of his lips and felt a sudden sense of loss when he drove off down the track. It was as if her whole world was contained in that car, and she wanted to cry with misery.

That night she finished *The Age of Innocence*, and allowed herself to cry. It was the most beautiful ending but so desperately sad. The parallel wasn't lost on her. Countess Olenska and Archer Newland were unable to be together because May, Archer's wife, was expecting a baby. Dylan and Madeline were also doomed because of a baby. That baby was Ellen. She considered it further. The dates suggested that Madeline got pregnant out of wedlock and had run off to England with Ellen's father, Anthony. But what if she had still loved Dylan? Hence, she christened her child Ellen, the secret name that meant something only to her and Dylan. Ellen tried to recall whether Dylan had looked surprised when she had introduced herself. She couldn't remember. Dylan had looked pretty strange altogether that first meeting. What if he had always known and it was that secret sign of enduring love that had fuelled his constant pining?

The question that bothered her more than any other, however, was whether her mother had ever loved her father. She thought of her father's kind face and constant patience and her heart reached out to him. Unlike her mother, he had never judged her and never made her feel inadequate when she hadn't met their high expectations. He had always smiled indulgently, as if he had found her antics amusing. She closed the book and hoped that perhaps her mother had loved both.

Ellen shared her thoughts with Conor when he called at midnight and he suggested she ask Dylan. After all, it seemed that Dylan had no reservations about talking to her about her mother. So, the following day, when she nipped out of Alanna's shop on her lunch break, she went straight to the Pot of Gold to find him. As she expected, he was at the bar in a black pea coat and woolly black beanie, chatting to Craic, a lime and soda in his hand. When he saw her, his face broadened into a wide smile and his big brown eyes lit up with pleasure.

'Ellen,' he said, putting a hand on her shoulder. 'I hear you're now a bona fide working member of the community.'

'I am,' she replied proudly.

'That'll mean you're staying, right?'

'I'm working on it,' she answered, wishing she could wave a wand and make her problem disappear so that she could stay in Ballymaldoon for ever.

'Good girl,' he said cheerfully. 'Fancy a drink?'

'I'd love one, thank you.'

'Are you on your lunch break?' Craic asked, taking down a glass.

'I made a sandwich at home. Do you mind if I eat it in here?'

'Of course not.'

'I'll join you,' said Dylan. 'I'll have a steak and kidney pie.' He grinned at her and rubbed his stomach. 'I'm a growing man.'

They sat at the table in the corner and Dylan took off his coat, hanging it over the back of the chair. When he pulled off his beanie, his black hair stood up in tufts. He didn't even bother to smooth it down. 'So, good first morning?' he asked.

'Slow,' she replied. 'I don't imagine Alanna sells much out of season.'

'It's full-on busy in the summer,' he assured her. 'Then the tourists fill the streets like ants and you can barely move.'

'Good for business, though.'

'Aye, it is, all right.'

She looked at his happy face and realized it would be unfair to ask him about her mother now. He might think she only sought him out to uncover the mystery of her mother's past, which wasn't true. She enjoyed his company. In fact, she enjoyed it so much she was loath to give him the impression that she wanted anything from him besides his friendship. 'Dylan, you know you said you'd teach me the guitar?'

'I did and I meant it. When do you want to start?'

'This evening?'

He grinned. 'Why don't you come to my house, then, and I'll put a spud in the oven.'

'Oh, you don't have to go to any trouble.'

He laughed. 'It's no trouble putting a spud in the oven! It's what I do when Martha's not there to cook for me.'

'Is she a good cook?' Ellen asked.

'A fine cook and more besides. She deserves better than me.'

'I think she's lucky to have you.'

'I don't think there are many who would agree with you, Ellen.'

'I'd like to meet her.'

'Well, you will if you stay in Ballymaldoon.'

'Doesn't she live with you?'

Dylan shook his head as if the idea was absurd. 'She's a good Catholic girl.'

'Gosh, it's full on, isn't it. This Catholic thing.'

'Religion is important. Nietzsche said, 'give me a why and I can survive any how'. Or something like that.'

'I don't suppose Nietzsche was Catholic.'

'No, he wasn't Catholic. In fact, he wasn't anything. He was a philosopher. But if he said that, he was very wise. Human beings need to know that their suffering has a purpose, otherwise it is rendered intolerable.'

'Are you a devout Catholic?'

'I like to go to Mass. I like the ceremony, probably because it's so familiar. My mam was very religious. When times are tough I find it comforting. I believe we're here to learn and evolve and one day, when we die, we go back to where we came from.'

Ellen remembered the deep feelings she had experienced

that first morning on the beach. 'I never really thought about it before I came here,' she told him. 'There's something in the stillness of the countryside that makes me question the point of it all.'

Dylan smiled knowingly. 'That's because you recognize in nature the still, eternal part of *you*.'

'Is that what it is? My soul?'

'Aye, that's what it is.'

'Doesn't sound very Catholic!'

'Religions are like clubs, Ellen. In order to be a member, you have to obey certain rules which have nothing to do with God and everything to do with human beings. It's the club mentality which sets religion against religion. Your club is *right,* which means everyone else is *wrong*. And who makes up the rules? Human beings. I don't agree with many of the rules. I'm not a rule-abiding man. But God is with me every day. I don't think Jesus meant to set people against each other, but to unite everyone in love. As usual the message got twisted to suit political ends. If he came down now, he'd feel more at home in a synagogue than a church; shoot me for saying it, but it's true.'

'Mum is religious. She goes to Mass every day,' said Ellen.

'As did her mother. Old Megan was a law-abiding woman.' Ellen could tell that Dylan didn't think much of her grand-mother.

'What was Megan like?'

'Tough as nails and as inflexible as iron.'

'Oh, she sounds delightful,' she chuckled.

'She was dogmatic in the worst kind of way. One of those religious people who puts dogma above common sense.'

'You're talking about you and my mother?'

He nodded. 'Aye, if it wasn't for old Megan things would

have been very different. At least, that's what I believe, although I'll never know for sure.'

'You're saying that if my grandmother hadn't been so religious, you and my mother might have had a future together?' She frowned. 'I don't understand.'

He gazed at her with eyes like wells, so deep she was unable to see the bottom. He put his rough hand on hers and sighed. 'If you don't tuck into your sandwich, you'll get hungry.' He leaned back as the waitress arrived with his lunch. 'That looks good.'

'I'll go and fetch you some mustard,' she said, walking away.

'What have you got in your sandwich?' He peered at it as she pulled it out of a brown paper bag.

'Chicken salad. Dylan, did you know I was called Ellen before you met me?'

He gave her a long, thoughtful stare, then he put down his knife and fork. 'I did, yes.'

'When did you know?'

She could tell from his expression that he wasn't comfortable divulging more information than he had perhaps intended. 'Your mother wrote me a letter after you were born.'

'Really? What did it say?'

'That she had called you Ellen.' He forked a pile of food into his mouth.

'That's all?' He nodded. 'There must have been something else.'

He thought for a while as he swallowed his mouthful. Then he took a swig of cordial. For a moment, he looked like a cornered rat with nowhere to run.

'I promise this will remain between us, Dylan. You can trust me.'

He gave her a wary look then lowered his voice. 'Your mother ran off with her English lord, pregnant with you. She wanted a different life. A life that I couldn't offer her. So she seized her opportunity and married a man she believed could give her what she wanted. But after you were born she realized there was more to life than material comforts. She asked me to come and get her.'

Ellen's heart stalled a moment before beating very fast. 'But you didn't.'

He shook his head. 'I did.'

'What happened?'

'I went to London. I stood outside her house. I watched her come out with her husband. It wasn't just her laugh that I didn't recognize, it was everything. She was like a different person.'

'What did you do?'

'I came home.'

'Did she know . . .?'

'She never knew.'

'So, she thought you'd ignored her letter.'

'Probably.'

'Oh, Dylan, that's awful.'

He patted her hand. 'It's all in the past.'

Suddenly Ellen's heart began to pound very fast. 'Dylan. Was I a mistake?' She noticed two weak splashes of red colour his cheeks. 'I mean, I know I was a mistake. Obviously. What I want to know is . . . I mean, I know I wasn't planned, and having a child out of wedlock is a terrible sin if you're a devout Catholic, but was I the reason you and Mum couldn't be together? If she hadn't got pregnant she might not have married my father. It might just have been a summer romance and nothing more. She might have married *you*.' At that,

Dylan hunched in discomfort, as if the missed opportunity still caused him pain. Ellen felt bad and was quick to put him at ease. 'She must have loved you very much to call me Ellen,' she added softly.

Then, quite unexpectedly, something prickly and uncomfortable sank into the pit of her stomach. She stared at Dylan as the two splashes of pink on his cheeks now deepened. She felt her own cheeks smart, too, and tried to ignore the sensation in her belly, or at least push aside the thought that had ignited the unwelcome emotion.

'Who knows, Ellen? Like I said, it's all in the past.' He obviously didn't want to talk about it any more.

'If I didn't know you personally, I'd turn your story into a novel,' she said gamely, longing to change the subject. Why, when only moments before it had inspired her deepest curiosity, did it now repel her?

Dylan recovered his composure a little and began to cut up his food. 'You can if you like. I've turned it into songs.'

'I'd like to hear them.'

'I'll play you one or two tonight if you're good.'

'We can sing in harmony,' she enthused.

'I think we're good at that,' he replied, grinning at her fondly, and Ellen felt the prickly feeling dislodge and eventually disappear.

Ellen returned to the shop after lunch. Alanna laughed when she told her that she'd had lunch with Dylan. 'It's a right romance,' she teased.

'Oh, really, Alanna, there's definitely no romance with Dylan!'

'Don't worry, I'm only messing with you. I know where your heart really lies.'

'I'm sure Desmond had a great deal to say about *that*.'

Alanna shrugged. 'Desmond has a lot to say about most things. Ignore him. It's none of his business anyway.'

'Conor's a good man,' said Ellen firmly. 'He's certainly not a murderer.'

'I'm sure you know what you're doing.'

'I do.'

'Good. Now, would you price up some stock for me? I had a delivery while you were out.'

'I'm happy to put my hand to anything.'

'That's the spirit.' Alanna pushed a box into the centre of the shop. 'You're doing me a big favour, Ellen. I don't know what I'd have done without you.'

'And you're doing *me* a favour. I can't sponge off Aunt Peg for ever. I'd like to contribute.'

'Oh, she's not minding about that.'

'I know, which makes me all the keener to pay her something.' She watched Alanna run a knife along the top of the box to open it. 'Oswald pays her in pictures when he can't pay the rent. I'd like to give her something, too.'

'You can share your royalties when you get your book published.'

Ellen thought of the blank page on her laptop. 'I'm not sure she'll live that long.' She laughed. 'I'm not sure *I'll* live that long.'

'Have you written anything yet?'

She smiled guiltily. 'Not a word.'

'Oh, well, I'm sure you'll get going soon.'

'I hope so.'

'If you wait for inspiration it might never come. Why don't you just start?' It sounded so simple. Alanna didn't realize how hard it was to 'just start'.

'You're right, Alanna. I'll do that. Now, what's in the box?'

*

That evening, Ellen left Oswald, Peg, Ronan and Joe playing a rubber of bridge in the sitting room and drove Peg's car to Dylan's. She had clear instructions to drive down to the quay where she'd see Dylan's pale-blue house sandwiched between a primrose-yellow house and an almond-pink one, a stone's throw from the Pot of Gold. Joe had quipped about Dylan being drunk so often that it was a miracle he hadn't wandered off the quay and drowned in the sea. But Ellen hadn't yet seen him drunk and rolled her eyes at Joe's teasing. She had grown fond of Dylan and no longer found her cousin's jokes about him amusing.

She drove into Ballymaldoon and parked the car on the quay in front of Dylan's pretty blue house. Little boats bobbed about on the sea, which glittered in the light of a crescent moon, and a black cat slunk along the side of the wall, his eyes shining through the darkness like yellow flames. She inhaled the refreshing scent of ozone and sighed with pleasure at the lapping sound of the sea and the sight of the navy sky, twinkling with the occasional star. She could just make out the lighthouse. It looked melancholy, like a night-watchman contemplating the long hours until dawn, or gazing out to sea, mulling over regrets. She couldn't imagine Caitlin jumping to her death and Conor watching her body breaking on the rocks beneath, for the beauty rendered it benign. Beauty rendered everything benign, even her own fears.

She didn't miss London. She didn't miss the noise of traffic and the orange glow of a city that was never dark. The quietness of Ballymaldoon appealed to her. She had never seen stars so bright or an ocean so vast. The fact that Conor was part of this romantic place made her love it all the more. She smiled as she thought of him. They had spoken at various times throughout the day. At one point, he'd called just to hear her voice, hanging up after less than a minute because he had to go into a meeting. Afterwards, she had held the telephone to her chest, as if his essence was somehow contained within it. When they weren't speaking, they were texting. Conor's texts were both erotic and affectionate and she couldn't wait for the weekend when they'd be together again.

With those happy thoughts she rang Dylan's bell. He opened the door almost immediately. A light-brown mongrel slipped through his legs and began to sniff her ankles excitedly. 'He can smell Mr Badger, I suspect,' said Dylan.

'I didn't know you had a dog.'

'Finch. He's a good boy. Martha and I fight over him and she usually wins.'

'But he lives with you.'

'He lives with both of us.'

'Sounds like the child of divorced parents.'

He chuckled. 'It does a bit, I suppose. He's a mongrel. He's happy wherever he is as long as he's fed and watered.' He stood aside. 'Let her pass, Finch. Come on in. I bought a Coke especially.'

'Thank you. How are the spuds?'

'Just grand,' he replied, following her inside.

Dylan's sitting room was very masculine, with a big, worn leather sofa and threadbare armchairs in rust-red and brown. A fire was crackling in the grate, filling the room with the smell of woodsmoke. An ashtray full of cigarette butts sat on one of the sofa tables and bookcases sagged beneath the weight of so many books. An upright piano stood against one wall with its lid up, the keys yellowed with age. Manuscripts and magazines lay strewn on every surface.

There was no order in the room at all and yet it had immense charm.

'So, this is where you create?' she said, noticing the guitar leaning against one of the armchairs.

'You can tell?' She glanced at him and saw that he was grinning. He scratched his bristly chin. 'I wonder what gives it away.'

'I think it's lovely. It's very *you*, Dylan. I bet poor Martha isn't allowed to touch anything.'

'You're not wrong, Ellen. Martha's barely allowed into the house at all. You're very privileged! Right, let me get you a drink and then we'll start playing. Are you hungry?'

'Not particularly.'

'Good. I'll give the spuds a little longer, then.' He left the room.

Ellen wandered around, looking at everything. She expected photographs of his beloved Maddie but there were none on display. She wondered whether he had hidden them somewhere, out of respect for Martha. She heard him humming in the kitchen and smiled to herself. She was pleased to be there and excited at the prospect of learning the guitar again, after a decade of not playing. Her mother had done everything in her power to prevent her singing in a band and yet here she was, about to jam with a real musician who just happened to be her mother's old flame. The irony of the situation made it all the more enthralling.

She wandered over to a chest of drawers placed beneath a window, and lifted a handwritten music score, entitled 'Connemara Sky'. Beneath the score was a heap of loose CDs, seemingly tossed into a careless pile. She picked one up. At first glance, she thought the photograph was of Al Pacino, but on closer inspection she saw that it was a younger Dylan. Peg

was right, he had been very handsome in a dark and brooding way.

She heard him returning and hastily replaced the manuscript.
She didn't want him to catch her snooping. He handed her the
glass of Coke. 'I've finished your iPod,' he said, picking up his
guitar. 'You've got a great playlist to write to. Don't let me
forget to give it to you, all right?'

'Will you give me some of your old albums to listen to as
well?'

For a moment, he looked a little shifty. 'I might have one
or two knocking around. I'm not sure,' he replied vaguely.

'But . . .' She was about to protest that she had just seen a
whole pile of various albums sitting on the chest of drawers,
but there was something in his demeanour which betrayed his
reluctance. The fact that he didn't want her to listen to his old
tracks made her all the more curious to hear them. 'If you
have any spare, I'd love to have one.'

'You'll have to brush off the cobwebs.'

'It wasn't that long ago!'

'Right, sit over here and let's begin. Play me the chord
of G.'

As she relearned the scale under Dylan's patient guidance, it
all came flooding back as it had in the chapel. The black
notes on the score he placed in front of her suddenly began
to make sense and her fingers felt the old, familiar patterns
she thought she'd forgotten. As she played a Beatles song,
Dylan sat at the piano and accompanied her by ear. Later, she
realized that he didn't really need to read music at all. Once
he'd heard a tune, he could play it beautifully on any instrument that took his fancy. Music was a language that he spoke
fluently, and after supper, when he sang her some of his own

songs, she realized that it was a means by which he was able to fully express himself.

They sang in natural harmony, their voices blending to create a rich and moving sound. And as they sang, they stared at each other in delight, both aware of the magic they engendered when their voices came together. Reluctant to stop, they followed one song with another, until they were composing together, their ideas bouncing off each other like a fast and furious ball game in which the players only just manage to keep up. Ellen felt her spirit inflate with happiness as it had done that morning on the beach when she had tossed her telephone into the sea. At last, she had found an outlet for her trapped and suffocated creativity.

It was late when Ellen got up to leave. If it hadn't been for the thought of her aunt listening out for the sound of her car, Ellen would have readily stayed until dawn. But it was after midnight and she knew that if she remained there any longer she'd give the town something else to gossip about. It was bad enough that she was seeing Conor; she didn't want to be accused of having a romance with Dylan as well!

Before she left, Dylan went upstairs to get her iPod. It didn't take her long to pinch a CD from the chest of drawers. She didn't feel too bad, because he had so many, and she translated his unwillingness as embarrassment at having composed so many songs about her mother. Perhaps they revealed more of his heart than he wanted to show her. Either way, she resolved to listen to the songs then return the CD without him ever knowing. As for the iPod, she wondered whether the music would imbue her with the same enthusiasm their jamming session had inspired tonight.

She returned to Peg's with a lightness in her heart. Her aunt did not come out of her room, but she sensed she was awake, like a mother listening out for her daughter. When at last she climbed into bed, she called Conor. 'Hello, my darling,' he said sleepily. 'Where have *you* been?'

Chapter 25

Lord Anthony Trawton is not as I expect. He is tall and thin, with greying fair hair and watery blue eyes, the colour of an English sky at dawn. He has a long, straight nose but his lips are thin and his chin recedes, which is not attractive, though I suppose he looks aristocratic, which is probably what attracted the young Maddie Byrne in the first place. He has a slight stoop and a gentle, almost apologetic, expression, and I wonder whether years of marriage to this ambitious, steely woman has somehow diminished him. He looks flattened, like a runner bean, while his wife is voluptuous and robust like a plum.

Lady Trawton is a striking woman. She has black shoulder-length hair, blow-dried into a shiny bouffant, and thick black lashes, which frame sly, feline eyes. Her skin is pale and her lips are scarlet but she is brittle and formidable and self-important. She has the manner of a woman who has always been beautiful. I know, because I was beautiful, too, and understood how to use it to my advantage.

Madeline is accustomed to being in control of her world. The house is lavishly decorated but as uncomfortable as a museum. Everything looks contrived, as if she has bought things to build an image but not a home. Those silk sofas are exquisite but too plump to sit on; the tables are arranged with magnificent objects but they tell you nothing about the woman who acquired them; even the vases of orchids look sterile, like those plastic-looking, tropical flowers in hotel lobbies I've seen in magazines. The rooms are expensive and grand but artificial, and I see that the only bookshelf is filled with glossy hardbacks on art which have clearly been ordered in bulk but never read. Conor and I chose everything with love, regardless of theme. We threw it all together over the years in a delicious salad of colours and textures and saw how harmoniously they fell into place, layer by layer. Our castle was truly our home because every object, every painting, every piece of furniture was chosen because we liked it, and every book was placed in the library because Conor had read it. But this house is as shallow as a pretty fountain and the water that runs through it is cold.

Lavinia and Leonora are tall and leggy with long blonde hair and their father's big blue eyes. They have an air of entitlement which money and privilege have given them. Confident, manicured and languid, they are women who do nothing but lunch in fine restaurants and waft around cocktail parties like fragrant lilies. Ellen might not have their stature, or their more classic beauty, but at least the girl has character. There is no doubting that. She has the spirit of an Irishwoman, all right. She has humour, wit and intelligence whereas these lovely creatures are as lifeless as shop dummies. It is hard to imagine that they are all from the same nest.

Ellen has sent them all into a froth of excitement over her disappearance. Madeline is not coping well, for she is a woman who is used to holding the puppet strings, but now the puppet has run off on her own, she doesn't know what to do with herself. She is restless and fretful and angry. Anthony is more phlegmatic; after all, he tells her, the girl has only been away a couple of weeks. He says she will come to her senses and return when she is ready, but Madeline senses the deeper issues that lie beneath, like entangled snakes in a pit that has always been hidden below the surface, growing fatter and more threatening on the food of Ellen's discontent.

So, Madeline is alone with her anxiety because her husband does not perceive the true nature of his daughter's running away. To him, she is simply taking a break from the stress of her impending wedding. But to Madeline, her daughter is repeating what *she* did some thirty-three years ago, and with her flight she is running her nails through the silt at the bottom of Madeline's orderly life, clouding the water with memories she would rather forget.

So, it is easy for me to whisper into her consciousness at night, because the seed of suspicion has already been planted by Madeline's own guilt. Ireland is on her mind, and when she is sleeping it is in her dreams, for she tosses and mumbles and I intuit that scenes from her past are now resurfacing and beginning to haunt her, like corpses resurrected in a graveyard. So, I haunt her yet more. I whisper the words that carry the most pain: Dylan, Ellen Olenska, Dylan, Ellen Olenska, over and over again. Remember, time is not an issue for me. I can remain at her ear for days and not grow weary or bored. And so I do, and drop by drop I water the seed and watch it grow, until I see the first green shoot of my labours.

'Ireland!' she gasps one morning, sitting up in bed and pushing her eyemask onto her forehead. 'Ireland!' She prods her husband, who lies sleeping beside her. It is dawn and the rumble of early traffic can be heard like the distant roar of the sea. 'Anthony, wake up. I know where she is.' She switches on the light at her bedside table.

Anthony rolls onto his back and opens his eyes with a groan. 'You know where she is?' he murmurs patiently, looking at his watch. 'How do you know?'

'I sense it. I can't think why I didn't think of it before.'

'Darling, why would she have gone to Ireland? She doesn't know anyone there.'

'Because it's the one place she knows I won't look for her.'

Anthony puts his hand on her arm. It is the first affectionate gesture I have seen him make. 'You're driving yourself mad with this, Madeline. You've got to stop worrying about her. She's not a child. She'll come back.'

'No, I'm sure I'm right.'

'Did you dream about Ireland?'

'Yes.' She gasps, as if he has just touched an open wound.

'Come on, let's have some breakfast.'

She climbs out of bed and hurries into the bathroom. 'I need confirmation. You know that silly Emily never called me back, so I'm going to go around and see her myself. The mountain will go to Muhammad.'

'If you like, darling,' he replies, wearily.

'Yes, I'm going to get it out of her one way or another. This is going to stop right now. I've had enough.' She stares at her face in the mirror, defeated a moment by the onslaught of age which is at its most aggressive in the mornings. 'How selfish of Ellen to put me through this! It's spoiling my beauty!'

That evening, I follow her to a white stucco building in Pimlico. It is dark and windy and the pavements glisten with rain. She sits in her chauffeur-driven Bentley, watching the window like a thief waiting to pounce. It is cold. The exhaust from the car disperses into the icy air like fog and there is a grey mist around the street lamps. I feel heavy and dark in my soul, as if the night is somehow penetrating my being and dragging me deeper into my limbo and further away from the light, which I know is out there somewhere, beyond my powers of perception now.

At last, a young woman in a belted coat and woollen hat appears out of the shadows and hurries up the steps to her front door. She fumbles in her bag for the key. Madeline does not wait for her to unlock the door and disappear inside. She is too shrewd for that. Instead, she climbs out before the chauffeur can open the door for her and in a moment she is right behind her.

'Emily!'

The girl turns, her face white beneath her black hat. 'Lady Trawton!' She has been taken by surprise. She looks as if she has just seen a ghost. I don't think she'd look any more frightened were *I* to materialize before her.

'As you didn't return my call, I decided to pay you a visit.'

'I . . .'

'Why don't we go inside? It's much too cold to be standing out here.'

Emily unlocks the door with trembling fingers and they both step into the hall. Her apartment is on the first floor and neither speaks as they climb the narrow staircase. Madeline looks around the small flat with detachment. She has no interest in it at all. I can tell you that it has infinitely more charm than No. 12 Eaton Court. Emily takes off her coat. She is wearing a fashionable skirt to the knee and fine leather boots. In the light of the apartment, I can see that she is a pretty young woman with light-brown hair, high cheekbones and deep-set brown eyes. She's too thin, which is the modern malaise, and if I were her mother I'd bake her a few more spuds to fatten her up. Madeline remains in the middle of the sitting room, without taking off her coat. She isn't intending to stay long. Just long enough to have her theory confirmed. I can tell that Emily doesn't stand a chance against Madeline Trawton. No one does.

'So, you know why I've come,' Madeline begins crisply.

Emily has stopped shaking. She wanders into the kitchen, which is attached to the sitting room, and takes a bottle of Chardonnay from the fridge. 'I don't know about you, Lady Trawton, but I need a glass of wine at the end of my day.'

'I know where she is, Emily.'

The girl pours the wine into a glass. She cannot drink it fast enough. No sooner has she put down the bottle than the glass is on her lips.

'She's in Ireland,' Madeline states, as if it is an immutable fact. 'Don't look so surprised. It was inevitable that I was going to find out eventually. I wasn't born yesterday.'

'Who told you?' Emily asks, without even trying to protest.

'I can't tell you, I'm afraid.'

Emily gulps her wine and swallows loudly.

'I want you to telephone her and tell her to come back.'

'I can't do that. I don't have her number.'

'You have her mobile telephone number, surely. She'll answer for *you*.'

'She threw it into the sea.'

Madeline is frustrated. 'What a silly thing to do. What's got into her?'

Emily looks anxious, then she blurts, 'She doesn't want to marry William.'

Madeline is shocked. 'Of course she does,' she snaps.

'No, she really doesn't.' Emily's shoulders drop in defeat, as if she is aware that she is betraying her friend and feels guilty.

'She's just got cold feet.'

'It's more than that. She doesn't love him.'

'She doesn't know what she wants.'

Emily drains her glass and refills it, then leans back against the counter. 'She told me she's fallen in love with Connemara and never wants to come back.'

Madeline's face swells, the colour of a pepper. Emily recovers, like an athlete who is back in the race after a brief stumble.

'What do you mean, she's fallen in love with Connemara? She's only been away a fortnight.'

Emily shrugs. 'I don't know. She told me a week ago. They're all singing "Danny Boy" in the pub, which is called the Pot of Gold.'

Madeline looks unsteady on her feet. Her voice grows quiet. 'And she said she never wants to come back?'

'Yes.'

'It's ridiculous.' But the venom has gone out of her tone. She sounds defeated.

'But true. I can assure you, wild horses wouldn't drag her up the aisle to marry William.'

'Oh, it won't take as much as that. Not after I've spoken to her. I'll go and bring her back myself.'

'What does it matter if she doesn't want to marry William? It's *her* life . . .'

For a moment, I see Madeline's carefully constructed facade crack slightly, as if she is a porcelain doll, breaking from the inside. She blanches. Her skin goes very white, against which her lips are as red as blood. She opens her mouth and lets out a little gasp. Her shoulders droop. I wonder whether Emily has noticed how this stiff, indomitable woman has suddenly taken on the demeanour of a lost child. She is trying to put her thoughts into words, but they aren't forming as they should. Emily takes another sip, seemingly oblivious to the pain which is so raw and desperate in the older woman's eyes. It is as if her tormented soul is crying out, but only I can hear it. Emily stands quite still, triumphant even, for she has shaken Ellen's mother to her core.

Without uttering another word, Madeline flees. She cannot explain to Emily what she feels. I don't think she can explain to anyone. But something has rattled her and it is momentous. She almost runs into the street. She tells her chauffeur to leave without her. She wants to walk home. There is no time for him to persuade her to get into the car, for she is already striding over the tarmac. It is a cold night and there is a gale, but Madeline doesn't care. I feel her need to be alone in the wind. The car drives off slowly, in case she changes her mind and waves for him to come back. But she doesn't, and eventually it disappears into the traffic.

Madeline begins to cry just as it starts to rain. She wanders slowly up the pavement, hands in pockets, shoulders hunched, her hair falling flat and wet about her face. Like a stricken animal in search of a private place to lie down and lick her wounds, she staggers off the main street, down dark alleys and narrow roads, until she finds a bench. She sits down on the watery seat and puts her head in her hands. Her sobbing shakes her whole body. I wonder what she is thinking. As I focus hard, I think I can tell.

I should feel compassion. But all I feel is a sense of triumph because now she will go to Ireland and bring Ellen back. She will take her daughter away from Conor and once again my husband will belong to me. I don't imagine the girl will fight her mother. I have seen Madeline at her most formidable and she is a force to be reckoned with. Ellen will marry William. He is the right man for her, after all. Ireland will be reduced to a bittersweet memory. Did she really think she would fit in there?

I watch Madeline grow soggier and soggier, until her sobbing dwindles to the occasional sniff and shudder. She remains there for a long time, in the drizzle, staring ahead as if her memories are being played out in front of her. She is lost in thought, far, far away, and I am trying to discern what she is seeing. But the strange thing is, as she sits there with her hair sodden and her make-up run, she looks like Ellen. Beneath the immaculate Lady Trawton is a young woman whose spirit is broken. I imagine this is what Ellen will look like when Conor turns away from her and she is plunged into the shadows along with all the other wrecks he has abandoned.

Strangely, I feel a sickness in my soul. It rises up from somewhere and fills me with sadness. I know it is compassion and I despise myself for my weakness. Compassion will not get me what I want. Compassion will lose me everything I treasure. I focus on my purpose and after a while I sense the familiar darkness surrounding me like a cloak as the compassion is forced away by my complete and utter loathing for Ellen.

Suddenly a Bentley turns the corner and the headlights shine on the bedraggled woman sitting alone on the bench. It pulls up beside her. Madeline snaps out of her trance and takes a deep breath. Her face registers her surprise as she recognizes the car. The door is flung open and Anthony steps out in a heavy coat, gloves and hat. He throws a blanket around her shoulders and helps her to her feet. She does not resist. I watch her climb into the car and think how much she looks like a child, being cared for by a patient, long-suffering father.

She rests her head against his shoulder as the chauffeur drives back to Eaton Court. No one speaks. For a while she was back in Ireland, sitting there on that bench, but now she has returned to the life she chose thirty-three years ago, in the arms of the man she preferred over Dylan. She has stared into the pit of her past, but I know it will only strengthen her resolve.

Chapter 26

Ellen now felt as if she had always lived in Ballymaldoon with Aunt Peg. Although she had only been there just over two weeks, the place felt like home. She had become a familiar face about town. The locals greeted her as she went to buy groceries for her aunt or sat in the Pot of Gold with Johnny and Joe, or Dylan. People no longer stared at her as if she were an alien, but accepted her as a Byrne. Her uncles had seen to that, forming a thick, protective wall around her, sending out a very clear message to the community that she was one of them.

She enjoyed helping Alanna in her shop. There weren't many customers, but friends and family stopped by from time to time for a 'chinwag' and she was never bored. Besides, she enjoyed Alanna's company. Her aunt was an uncomplicated woman with a dry sense of humour and a generous spirit, and was full of local gossip which she was only too ready to share. The two of them whiled away the hours chatting over endless cups of tea.

In the evenings, when she wasn't jamming with Dylan, she was playing chess with Oswald, or making up a four at the bridge table with Oswald, Peg and Joe. The days were punctuated with visits to the Pot of Gold, where she would always find her uncles and cousins and where Dylan would be wait-ing for her with a new idea for a song.

By Friday, her ache for Conor was almost unbearable. They spoke and texted but she missed his physical presence dread-fully. William and her mother had been relegated to the very back of her mind and she no longer worried about them. Conor filled every spare thought and he was so dominant there was little room for anyone else.

When he arrived on Friday afternoon, he picked her up at Peg's as before, but instead of driving her to Reedmace House, he stopped in front of the castle.

'What are we doing here?' she asked, excited at the prospect of being admitted into this inner sanctum she had assumed to be off limits.

'I brought Mam and the children down. But I thought, you're my girl and this is my house. There's little furniture but I could see no reason why we shouldn't use it.' He slipped his hand beneath her hair and wound it around her neck. 'And here we get total privacy.'

Ellen wanted to mention that she thought it was haunted, but kept quiet. He was gazing at her with smiling eyes and his mouth was grinning with the lascivious thoughts now career-ing through his mind, so she was soon distracted from the ghost of his wife. 'I want to sweep you upstairs and make love to you,' he said, leaning over to brush her lips with his. His kiss grew hot and passionate and for a while they forgot the castle and the bed that awaited them upstairs. Ellen closed her eyes, inhaled the familiar smell of him as if he were a drug and she a hopeless addict, and sank happily into the moment.

Reluctantly, he pulled away. 'Let's get out of here before I go too far and give Joe and Johnny a show they'll never forget!' Ellen laughed and climbed out of the car, following him at a run to the front door. He put the key in the lock and turned it. The big door opened easily and they stepped into the hall. Conor closed it behind them and bolted it from the inside. It was dim in the hall but the portrait of Caitlin seemed to catch the little light that came in through the windows and glistened eerily. Conor didn't dwell there, but took her by the hand and led her quickly up the wide staircase. Ellen wondered why he hadn't taken the picture down. If Caitlin had tormented him so much, why was she still hanging on the wall to torment him further?

Her thoughts were diverted by the charm of this beautiful old building. Although the furniture and other paintings had been taken away, the scarlet carpets were still covering the floors and the old cornicing and panelling were still as they were when the castle had been built half a millennium before. The building had beautiful bones, like a lovely woman who needs little adornment to enhance her natural splendour. Ellen could imagine how magnificent it must have been when it was a home.

Conor didn't linger but hurried down a long corridor, across a landing and down another red-carpeted corridor, until he opened a little wooden door at the end, so low that he had to stoop. On the other side was a steep and narrow staircase. The wooden steps were worn in the middle by centuries of treading feet.

'Where are you taking me?' she asked, enchanted by the eccentricity of the place.

'To the tower, where I'm going to keep you prisoner and do whatever depravity takes my fancy.'

'Lord, I can hardly wait!' She laughed, following him up the stairs. At the top a little landing was lit by a narrow, latticed window.

Conor opened another door. 'And here, my princess, is your prison.'

Ellen stepped into a round bedroom cluttered with Conor's things. There was a four-poster bed swathed with blue silk embroidered drapes, fringed in scarlet. Persian rugs covered the floorboards, a desk was piled with books and papers, an old wardrobe stood against the wall and she noticed it had been especially crafted to fit against the natural curve of the room. There were paintings on the walls, two windows, deep wooden-panelled window seats for reading in natural light and heavy silk curtains to keep out the cold. Next door was a pretty little bathroom. It was as if he had always lived up here, in this secret tower.

He pulled her into his arms. 'Do you like it?'

'I love it. How often do you come here?'

'Whenever I need to be alone.' He kissed her temple. 'You're the only woman I have ever invited up here. This is as far into my private world as you can possibly get. I want to share it with you.'

'Oh, Conor . . . I don't know what to say.'

'Then don't say anything.' He lifted her chin with a finger. 'Just let me enjoy you. I've been waiting all week for this.'

Making love in this isolated tower was more romantic than Reedmace House. Here, no one could find them. They were totally alone. It was as if she had crawled beneath his skin and burrowed into his soul. The vibrations were saturated with emotion; whether grief, fury, happiness or love, she imagined Conor had sought refuge here from every onslaught.

They took their time. There was no reason to rush. It was as if they were high up on a cloud where time could not reach them. They explored each other's bodies as if for the first time and savoured every intense moment of discovery.

The chemistry was so right that each touch seemed to unfold yet more layers of sensation and open more avenues of trust. When she looked into his eyes, Ellen saw no shadows, just the clear blue radiance of a summer sky.

Later, they lay talking. He told her how he had begun a new project to make a movie based on an adventure novel he had loved as a child. He was excited and fired up about it. She told him about Dylan and the music they were making together. 'You know, when we sing, something special happens with our voices.'

'Like Abba,' he teased, smiling at her fondly.

'Even more magical than that,' she replied. 'You know, he was apparently quite well known in his day.'

'I know. I probably even have one or two of his CDs.'

'Oh, I stole one. Well, technically, I stole it, but I like to think that I *borrowed* it.'

'Why didn't you just ask him to give it to you?'

'No, for some reason he didn't want me to have it. I asked and he pretended that he didn't have any. But I knew he did because I had come across a whole pile of them when I was looking around while he was in the kitchen.'

'So, what do you think of it?'

'I haven't listened to it yet.'

'Do you have it on you?'

'Yes, it's still in my handbag.'

'Let's put it on now, then.'

'All right. I bet it's good. He has a beautiful voice.'

Ellen found her handbag beneath the pile of clothes she had left on the floor, and pulled out the CD. She read the title. '*Voice of Silence*. It's going to be sad, I can tell.'

'Nothing wrong with that. He probably wrote the songs for your mother.'

'And she doesn't have a clue.' She sighed with impatience at the thought of her mother and handed him the CD.

He appraised her naked body. 'You're a fine figure of a woman, Ellen.'

'Thank you, Conor,' and she playfully wiggled her bottom as she walked back to the bed.

He put the CD in the machine then dived on top of her. 'Wiggling your bottom like that is a red rag to a bull.'

'So, you're a bull?' She gave a throaty laugh. 'Aren't you flattering yourself just a little?'

He silenced her with a kiss as the dulcet tones of the guitar resounded from the speakers. They lost themselves in each other for a while as Dylan sang of love and loss, but neither really concentrated on the words. The tunes were catchy and his voice deep and gritty, but they were too pre-occupied with each other to notice the theme that ran like a thread of pain through all the tracks. It wasn't until they lay entwined a while later, sated, that they paused to listen to the lyrics.

Conor's hand, which was stroking Ellen's hair, stopped. Ellen's body, which was limp and warm against his, stiffened and froze. Neither spoke. They just listened. The more Dylan sang, the more they became aware of the heart of his pain. At last Ellen sat up and stared at Conor. Her face was as white as the sheets. 'He's singing about me,' she said.

'I know,' he replied softly.

She put her hand to her mouth. 'I've had this weird feeling for a while now, but I couldn't put my finger on what it was. I should have guessed.'

'How could you have guessed?'

'But *you* did. I can tell by the way you're looking at me. You'd already worked it out, hadn't you?'

'Darling, why would your mother name you Ellen if you weren't Dylan's child?'

'Oh, God, I'm Dylan's child. I'm not Daddy's.' Her face crumpled into a frown. 'I don't want to belong to anyone else.' A wave of emotion rose up from her belly and exploded into a giant sob. 'I want to belong to Daddy, Conor!'

Conor sat up and put his arm around her. He kissed her head tenderly. 'I was wondering if you'd ever find out.'

'Would you have told me?'

'Of course not. Some things are better *not* known.'

'Well, the cat's out of the bag now, isn't it? I can't pretend I don't know. Nothing will ever be the same again.'

'What are you going to do?'

'I don't know. It's such a shock. I don't know *what* to do.' She sniffed and gave in to another wave of despair. 'I look nothing like my father, do I? I mean Anthony . . .'

Conor looked appalled. 'Ellen, he's your father, whether he made you or not,' he said firmly.

'I know. It just sounds odd now.'

'No, it doesn't. It's just biology. Your father's put in all the time, love and commitment.'

'Do you think Mum deceived Dad as well? Do you think he knows? I bet he doesn't. I mean, I've never ever picked up even a whiff of not being his. Never.' She shook her head. 'He can't know.'

'Your mother moved fast all right, if that's the case.'

'Why didn't she marry Dylan? If I was his child, why didn't she marry him?'

'You're going to have to ask her.'

'If you knew my mother, you'd know that *that's* impossible. I couldn't bring it up. She'd die.'

'She won't die, Ellen, and you'll learn the truth. I think you need to work on communication in your family.'

She turned to face him. 'She must have got pregnant with Dylan then passed it off as Dad's. That's why they married so quickly.'

'I wonder how Dylan knew you were his.'

'He received a letter from my mother after I was born, asking him to come and get her. I suppose she told him then.'

'What did he do?'

'He went, but when he saw her, she was so different from the girl he knew that he returned to Ireland.'

'And spent the next thirty-three years remembering her as she was.'

'Exactly.'

She stared at Conor, her eyes big and round and wet. 'Conor, tell me truthfully, do you see Dylan in my face?'

He studied her. 'Well, I suppose you have his colouring, and your eyes? They're his, all right.' He grinned kindly. 'But you're prettier.'

'God, what a mess!'

He kissed her again. 'Your mother did a very good job hiding it from you all these years. If you hadn't come to Ireland you might never have known.'

'That's why she never wanted me to come. Poor Dylan. He lost his child.'

Conor shook his head. 'It's bloody brutal. I'm a father and I can tell you, if my wife had run off with my baby I'd have ... I'd have gone crazy.'

'I think Dylan did go a bit crazy, from what I hear.'

'Well, he poured his heart out into his songs.'

'And they're beautiful.' She sighed sadly.

'Beautiful and about *you*, Ellen. I imagine he pined for you more than he pined for your mother.'

'No wonder I wanted to be in a band. It's in my DNA.' Her face livened. 'No wonder Mum tried to stop me. She stopped me doing anything that might lead people to suspect I didn't belong. She tried to make me like my sisters. Now I know why it never worked. I'm Ellen Murphy and Leonora and Lavinia are *not* my sisters. Deep down inside, I'm plain old Ellen Murphy!'

'I prefer Ellen Murphy to Ellen Trawton,' said Conor. 'Ridiculous name, if you ask me.'

She wrapped her arms around his neck and let him hold her tightly. 'Thank God for you, Conor.'

He pressed his lips onto the tender skin of her neck. 'Thank God for *you*, Ellen Murphy.'

Later, they dressed and descended the narrow staircase to the crimson-carpeted corridors. 'I don't want to leave you tonight, Ellen.' He stopped on the landing and took her hand. 'Are you going to be all right?'

'I want to go and see Dylan. Will you come with me?'

'Of course I will. Do you want to go *now*?'

'I don't think this can wait.'

'All right. Let's go.' He took her hand. 'We'll sort this out together.'

As the car motored up the drive, Ellen realized that Ireland had irrevocably changed her. There was no going back now. She had shed her skin like a snake and emerged a different person. She wasn't Ellen Trawton any more. It was as if London were a stage and Connemara her life. Reality had been here all along, lying in wait patiently and complacently, knowing that the profound currents of life would one day carry her home; and they had. Here she felt truly herself. There was nowhere else she'd rather be.

Conor took her hand and squeezed it. 'You're going to be all right, Ellen,' he said.

'Shouldn't I be wailing and gnashing my teeth? I feel strangely calm now.'

'You're in shock.'

'Perhaps. But on the other hand, Dylan has answered the most persistent question which has nagged me my whole life: Why do I feel different?'

'Ellen, you felt different because your mother tried to make you something you weren't. That way she emphasized your differences all the time. If she'd just let you be you, you would never have felt alien.'

'That's true. I had to work really hard to fit in. I always felt I was playing a part.'

'Maybe you're more Murphy than Byrne.'

'God, Conor, I'm one hundred per cent Irish.'

'That's fifty more than me.'

'I hope Dylan isn't cross that I stole the CD.'

'Are you crazy? You're his daughter.' He shook his head. 'He's waited over thirty years for this.'

Conor pulled up in the car park behind the Pot of Gold. It was only when Ellen climbed out and stood that she felt the trembling in her legs. Her heart began to thump clumsily against her ribs and emotion rose unexpectedly to the bottom of her throat, where it formed a tight ball. Conor took her hand. 'Are you sure you want to do this now?'

'Positive.'

'It's going to be busy in there.'

'I know. We'll just ask him to come outside, then I'll tell him.'

'Why don't I go and get him for you?'

'No, I want to come,' she insisted.

'All right,' he said, making for the door. 'Let's go and do this together.'

Conor pushed it open and they both entered. The pub was full of the usual people. If Ellen had stepped in alone no one would have paid her the least attention. But because she came in with Conor, a hush descended over the place and every eye in the room turned to watch them. Conor took control, ignoring the blatant curiosity as if he hadn't noticed. He scanned the faces for Dylan, finding him at the end of a table against the wall, beside Johnny and Joe. Without letting go of her hand, he led her through the crowd.

Dylan sat up expectantly. A shadow of concern darkened his face. For a moment, his eyes assumed the haunted look they had had the first time Ellen met him, and she felt her heart buckle with compassion. He stood up. She was only intending to ask him to step outside, but she felt herself carried on a wave of emotion and was unable to control herself. Here was the man who had given her life but never known her. How could her mother have done this to him? How could she have done it to *her*? Ellen fought back tears. She didn't want to break down in the pub, in front of all these people, but her whole chest was aching with the effort of restraining her feelings. 'Ellen?' Dylan enquired, gazing at her searchingly. He looked so worried that Ellen put her arms around him. 'Are you all right?' he asked.

'I *know*,' she whispered and held him tightly. It took a moment for her words to register. Then he relaxed and she felt his arms tighten around her, containing her trembling body.

'Oh, Ellen.' He groaned and his voice seemed to resonate from deep inside his chest.

'I stole one of your CDs, but I'm not sorry.' She pulled away and gazed at him as if for the first time. Conor was right, she had his eyes. 'I should have guessed, shouldn't I?'

Dylan stiffened as a murmur rippled around the pub. He turned to Conor. 'Let's go and have some tea. I'm starving, I could eat a horse.'

Joe was watching with interest. 'Jaysus, what's all this about? Am I missing something?' His father, whose face was long and serious, shot him a look that silenced him as surely as a slap. He said nothing but watched pensively as Conor, Dylan and Ellen stepped out into the night.

Chapter 27

Once outside, Conor took Ellen's hand. 'Do you want me to leave you and Dylan alone together? I don't want to impose.'

'No, I want you to come,' she replied. 'You don't mind, do you, Dylan?'

'Come on, then. I don't know about you, Conor, but I need a whiskey. I've got something soft for the little thief. You don't get your slippery fingers from me, Ellen.'

'I wanted to hear your songs,' she explained, following him down the road. Her hand still held Conor's tightly to steady her legs, which felt strangely dislocated from her body.

'Jaysus, what's your mother going to say about this?' Dylan groaned, thrusting his hands into his pockets.

'I won't tell her.'

'That's what you think, but everything comes to light one way or another.'

'I have a right to know who made me.'

'It's going to upset the apple cart,' Dylan warned.

Ellen was aware of one or two other revelations which were going to upset her mother's apple cart. 'I have so many questions,' she began.

'At least give the man a whiskey before you interrogate him,' said Conor.

'Wise words indeed,' Dylan replied, stopping at his front door.

'For a community that thrives on gossip, you sure know how to keep secrets,' said Ellen.

As they stepped inside, Finch jumped up at Conor, sniffing Magnum on his clothes and wagging his tail wildly. 'Down, boy!' Dylan commanded, taking off his coat and beanie and hanging them on the peg in the corridor. Conor took Ellen's coat and hung it up with his, then put his hand in the small of her back, accompanying her into the sitting room where Dylan was already pouring two large glasses of whiskey. He took a swig then handed the other tumbler to Conor.

'I'll go and fetch my Coke,' said Ellen, walking on into the kitchen. She heard the two men talking in the sitting room but not what they were saying. She opened the fridge. Besides bottles of soda and a few Cokes there was little in the way of food. She found a glass in the cupboard above the sideboard and opened her can. She looked about her and considered the man who had turned out to be her father. It was too momentous to digest. It made sense, certainly. It answered questions, too. But where did it leave her in a family where she had already felt out of place? Where did it leave her father? Nothing had changed except knowledge but somehow that knowledge changed everything. The past thirty-three years could not be altered or erased, and yet her perception of them had now shifted. She saw those years in a different light and therefore, in her mind, they *had* changed. The tingling in her body reflected her shock, but she wondered why she wasn't reacting in the normal way. Why she wasn't tearing out her hair, accusing her mother of deception and bewailing her life as a lie. She and Dylan had every reason to tear the place apart with fury.

When she went back into the sitting room, Dylan was sitting in the armchair, smoking a Rothmans, and Conor was on the sofa. Their glasses were already half empty. The golden liquid glistened in the yellow light of the lamps. Ellen took the space on the sofa between them and thought how extraordinary it was that these two men she had only recently met were now two of the most important in her life. A couple of weeks ago she hadn't known either of them and her life had been so much poorer.

Dylan smiled at her with affection, which Ellen now recognized as paternal. 'So, you know,' he said simply.

'I know,' she replied, suddenly feeling bashful. 'Your songs are very beautiful.'

'Thank you. I was inspired.'

'Surely, if you sang about the child you lost everyone who knew you and my mother must have known you fathered her child?'

'No one knew she was pregnant,' he said.

'Did *you* know?' Conor asked.

'Not at the time.' Dylan took another swig. His Adam's apple rose and fell sharply as he swallowed. 'It was in the letter.'

'The one Mum sent you after I was born?'

'That's right.'

'Do you still have it?' Conor asked.

Dylan nodded. 'I still have it. I'm a sentimental old fool. Ellen, bring me that cardboard box.' He pointed to the top of the tall bureau. 'You'll have to climb on the chair.' Ellen could just see the box peeping out from behind the decorative crest at the top of the piece of furniture.

'Let me,' said Conor, putting his glass on the coffee table. 'I'm tall.' Ellen watched him stand on the chair and reach up.

He lifted the box down and handed it to Dylan. Dylan settled it on his lap and lifted the lid. Ellen was curious to see what was inside.

Dylan rummaged about until he found the letter. He popped his cigarette between his lips and pulled the folded piece of paper out of the envelope. Ellen recognized her mother's pale-blue writing paper and the family crest engraved in gold on the flap. The letter itself was headed in the same gold with the address at Eaton Court. After looking at it for a moment, Dylan handed it to Ellen. She and Conor read it together.

My darling Dylan,

I don't know what to say except that I am sorry I left without saying goodbye. You must hate me for running away and I don't blame you. I hate myself for running away, too. I wish I could say that I had no choice, but we always have choices; I just made a bad decision, which I now bitterly regret. I hope when you read what I have to say you will understand. I hope you are sitting down.

I have a baby now. She's got your eyes, Dylan. I've called her Ellen, although Anthony wanted to call her Leonora or Lavinia after his mother and grandmother. These posh English families have a thing about names! But I fought for it and won.

Do you remember our last summer when I felt sick all the time and you composed that silly song 'Sick as a Dog' to make me feel better? It didn't take the sickness away but it made me laugh, all right!! Well, shortly after that I realized I must be pregnant. Anthony was hot on my tail. You were mad with jealousy, but I was flattered. I suppose I behaved badly, encouraging him as I did, without considering your feelings. I'm sorry, Dylan. I was selfish. I know that now. Anyhow, I was scared and didn't know what to do, so I told Peg. She was scared, too. You remember Emer Callaghan? We all wondered why she disappeared for such a long time and Johnny spread it around that she had gone to prison for shoplifting? Well, Peg told me that she had got pregnant and been sent to a convent. When she returned she wasn't broken because of prison, but because she had to give up her baby. I didn't want that to happen to me. As you know, Mam would never have allowed me to keep what she would have considered to be a bastard. I shudder to think what she would have done. Only God could separate me from my beautiful little girl. I am probably condemned to eternal hell for my sins, but it will be worth it. So, my only choice was to run away. You being as poor as a church mouse and Anthony being so rich, I chose to run off with him. I should have told you but I knew you'd try to stop me. I knew I'd let you.

Oh Dylan, I miss you every day of my life. I have everything I need, yet besides little Ellen, I have nothing I want. I dream of a life with you and wonder what it would be like to make a home together, far from Ballymaldoon and the Byrnes, where we could bring up our little girl. I miss Ireland. I miss my people. These Brits are as cold as fish. Anthony and I don't laugh like <u>we</u> used to. If I stay here much longer I think I'll forget how to laugh altogether!

So, I'm asking you to come and get me, Dylan. You loved me once and I'm praying you still do. I love you and always have. In fact, I love you more now because I know what torture it is to be without you.

Please take me home.

Yours forever, Ellen Olenska

'Does that answer your questions?' Dylan asked when Ellen had finished reading.

'Yes,' Ellen replied quietly. 'It doesn't sound like Mum at all.'

Conor noticed her flushed face and took her hand. 'Why didn't you bring her home?' he asked Dylan.

Dylan blew out a cloud of smoke. 'I had no money. What could I give her? What could I give *you*?' he said to Ellen.

'I don't think she cared about that,' Ellen argued.

'Not when she wrote the letter, perhaps, but I knew your mother.'

'Wharton's Ellen Olenska didn't care for money,' said Conor.

'This one did,' Dylan added. 'Listen, she was married. She was Lady Trawton. I thought about this long and hard. Anthony thought you were his. If I went bowling in there, claiming to be the father of his child, think of the scandal that would have caused. I couldn't do it to Maddie. She'd made her decision. I'm not a religious man but I wasn't ready to break up a family.'

'So, you walked away?' said Conor.

'I walked away. She never even knew I'd gone to see her.'

'And now, here I am,' said Ellen shyly.

Dylan smiled, incredulous. 'Here you are. Out of the blue.'

'Who else knows?' Conor asked.

'Your grandmother knew because Peg told her, which means Father Michael knows, because he knows everything.'

'Oh, Father Michael knows,' interrupted Ellen, recalling their conversation at Desmond and Alanna's house. 'When I sat next to him at lunch, he assumed I had already worked it out. He didn't mention me being your daughter, Dylan. I think he took it for granted that I already knew. Although one thing baffles me now. He suggested my mother had to forgive her mother. He gave me a very meaningful look when he said it. But what did she have to forgive *her* for?'

Dylan looked blank. 'I don't know.'

'You could ask Peg?' Conor suggested.

'Of course, Peg must know,' said Ellen.

'But you're here,' said Dylan, his big, sentimental eyes shining with emotion. 'I hoped we'd meet one day and here you are, in my sitting room. In my life. Who'd believe it?' His chin trembled and his mouth wobbled into a grin. 'One minute I had nothing but memories and now I have a daughter. A daughter who sings like an angel.'

A while later the food was ready and they sat down to eat at the small kitchen table. Dylan produced cold meat and cheese. He asked Conor about his new project and the two men discussed composers who might be suitable to write the film score. Ellen listened contentedly as they analysed the great writers and the movies they had written for. 'You know Elmer Bernstein wrote the soundtrack to the film of *The Age of Innocence*,' said Dylan.

'I recall it was nominated for an Academy Award for best original score,' Conor replied. 'But lost out to—'

'*Schindler's List*,' Dylan interjected. 'It was a great film and I rarely say that a film does justice to a novel.'

'You're right,' Conor agreed. 'It's one of my favourites. Ellen's never seen it.'

'But you read the book?' Dylan asked.

'I finished it,' she replied. 'It's got a sad ending,' she added to Conor. 'So, Ellen is an *un*lucky name.'

He squeezed her hand. 'Don't reduce yourself to a character in a novel.'

'Your name represents hope and love,' interjected Dylan. 'And what's luck if it didn't bring you to my door?'

'And to mine,' Conor agreed.

Dylan raised his whiskey glass. 'I'd like to make a toast.'

'Go on,' said Conor.

'To Ellen, for walking into my life like a spring breeze full of optimism. The future looks brighter because you're in it.' His eyes watered and he blinked self-consciously. 'I never thought I'd say that.'

Conor raised his glass, too. 'To Ellen.' His smile was full of gratitude. 'I couldn't agree more.'

It was after midnight when they parted. A light drizzle was carried inland off the sea and the sky was dark. Ellen embraced Dylan. They held each other tightly, silently affirming their determination not to allow any more years to come between them. Dylan stood in the doorway and watched them walk up the road, hand in hand, until they had disappeared round the corner. Then he went back inside and closed the door behind him.

Conor drove Ellen back to Peg's. 'Thank you for coming with me,' she said, as he pulled up in front of the house.

'I'm glad I came. You made Dylan a very happy man tonight. But how do *you* feel?'

'I'm fine. I should be devastated, but I'm not.'

'You're still in shock,' he said. 'Don't be surprised if it hits you like a truck in the morning.'

'I won't.'

'You call me if you're worried, won't you? I don't care what time of the night it is.'

She leaned over and wrapped her arms around him. 'Thank you.'

'And I'll come and pick you up tomorrow.' He nuzzled his face into her neck. 'I wish I could take you home with me now. I don't want to leave you to spend the night alone.'

'I'll be OK, I promise.'

'Come to Dublin,' he suggested suddenly.

'When?'

'Next week. I'll put you up in a grand hotel . . .'

'But I've committed to Alanna.'

'*Un*-commit.'

'I can't. It wouldn't be fair. I'll come to Dublin when the girl who works for her gets back.'

'Where has she gone?'

'I don't know. But she'll come back.'

'She'd better! Then I'll show you around my city.'

'I'm meant to be writing a book,' she protested, wanting to be persuaded.

He laughed at her fondly. 'You're my girl, which means you have to be where I am.'

'OK, I'll come to Dublin.' She smiled.

'That's a promise, all right?'

'It's a promise.'

He kissed her. 'Then I'll see you tomorrow.'

'Usual time?'

'Usual time. You're becoming a habit.'

She grinned at him broadly. 'Good. I hope you have an awfully addictive personality.'

He kissed her again. 'Oh, I do, and you have all the qualities to ensure I'm utterly dependent!'

She waved as Conor drove off, then hurried through the drizzle into the house. The light was on in the kitchen. She went to switch it off when a voice greeted her from the table. There, sitting on Jack's chair with a mug of tea, was Peg.

'Aunt Peg, I haven't kept you up, have I?' she asked, registering Peg's anxious face.

'Come and sit down, pet,' she said softly. Ellen wished she could go to bed. She knew she should discuss with Peg what she had learned, but she suddenly felt exhausted, as if the emotional wave had finally hit her. She did as her aunt requested, however. Peg sighed deeply and Ellen knew there was a serious purpose to her midnight vigil. 'Do you want a cup of tea?' Peg asked.

'No, thank you. It's a bit late for that,' Ellen replied, searching her aunt's weary eyes for a clue to her intention.

'I had Johnny over this evening. He said he'd seen you in the pub with Conor.'

'Yes, he came to find Dylan with me.' Ellen narrowed her eyes. 'If this is about Conor, I'm not going to skulk around like a teenager. I don't care what Desmond thinks . . .'

'No, it's not about Conor, Ellen, it's about Dylan.'

'Oh.' Ellen felt her pulse race.

Peg hesitated and looked pained. 'I wanted to check that you were all right.'

'I'm fine,' Ellen replied, but she knew her aunt was too perceptive to be fooled by that casual statement.

'It's just that Johnny said you were . . . a bit *strange*.'

'We went back to Dylan's for some tea.'

'I see.'

'Spuds. I don't think Dylan can cook anything else.'

'I think you're probably right. Martha's a fine cook, altogether. He should make an honest woman of her.' Peg looked at Ellen and frowned. 'I've been thinking about what you said, Ellen. That Maddie named you after Dylan's nickname for her.'

'Yes?' Ellen's tone was enquiring, but she knew what was coming.

'I think you know what I'm trying to say.'

'Dylan's my father,' Ellen stated simply and sat down.

Although Peg had already worked it out, Ellen's words hit her like a blow. She gasped and took a gulp of tea to play for time. Finally, she put down her mug. 'So, it's true. It had never occurred to me, not once. In all these years, I never considered it. Not until tonight. Johnny got me thinking.'

'Has it occurred to him, too?'

'Yes, we came to it at the same time. Or rather, he and Desmond already suspected, but it wasn't until tonight that their suspicions were confirmed. You see, you do have a look of him.'

'It makes sense, doesn't it?' Ellen said with a sigh. She felt wearier than ever.

'I don't suppose your father knows.'

'I'm not going to tell him. I just couldn't.' She bit her lip. The thought of hurting him gave her heart a painful tug. 'I love my Daddy.'

'I think that's probably wise. I imagine that is why Maddie never came back to Ireland. I've always wondered.'

'Why? Because she would have run off with Dylan?'

'Anything's possible. Our mother would turn in her grave if she knew. It was bad enough that Maddie got pregnant, but there was a little consolation in the fact that she married the child's father. It would have devastated Mam to know that Dylan was the father.'

'Aunt Peg, if Mum had told your mother she was pregnant, would she have sent her to a convent and given me away?'

Peg's face twisted with anguish. 'I'm afraid she might have, Ellen, dear. I'd like to say otherwise, but when it came to the moral path, any deviation was unacceptable to your grandmother. A child out of wedlock was a sin and a shame.

Maddie was right to run away.' Peg put her hand on Ellen's. 'She did it to keep you – I would have done the same. But I told Mam in the end because she couldn't understand why her favourite child had run away.'

'I'm sure she wasn't her *favourite* child,' said Ellen kindly.

'Oh, she was, and everyone knew it. She fell apart when Maddie left. I had to put her out of her misery. Of course, I only exchanged one type of misery for another. But once she knew, her heart hardened towards Maddie and we never mentioned her name in the house again. Mam went to the grave with a calcified heart, Ellen. She never forgave her.'

'It's very sad.'

'Aye, it's sad. I lost my little girl to the sea. That puts things into perspective. I could never get her back. But Maddie and Mam could have reconciled and they should have. You see, that is something I can't understand. It was as if Maddie had died. But Mam could have got her back if she had really wanted to. I can never get Ciara back, not with all the will in the world. Why wouldn't Mam have tried? Why did she bury her when she didn't have to?' Peg shook her head, disturbed by the resurgence of suppressed memories. 'God's way is love and Jesus taught us to forgive. But it's amazing how many Christians reject those two fundamental teachings . . . So, how did you discover that Dylan is your biological father?' she asked.

'I nicked one of his CDs and listened to his old songs. It was pretty obvious.'

'I'm so sorry. What a terrible shock.'

'I think I sensed it earlier, though. The moment I realized that Mum had given me the name Dylan used to call her. I was just too afraid to face the truth.' She laughed sadly. 'I tried to convince myself that she did it because she was still in love with him. And I did convince myself for a while, until the CD. Then I was forced to accept it.' She yawned and her eyes watered.

'You look as white as a sheet. I should let you go to bed. I just wanted to make sure that you're OK.'

'Thank you, Aunt Peg. But I don't know how I am, really,' Ellen said. 'I just feel numb.'

'Of course you do, pet. Come, let's tuck you up. You'll feel stronger in the morning.' Peg switched off the light and closed the kitchen door behind them. 'It's touching to think that Dylan sobered up for you, Ellen. He wants you to be proud of him.'

'He's a good man. I'm very fond of him.' She began to climb the stairs. 'It's strange how the knowledge that he's my father has bonded us suddenly. I mean, it's nothing but a thought. But that thought has changed the way I feel about him. It's changed the way I feel about Ballymaldoon.'

'In what way, pet?'

Ellen stood in her bedroom doorway. 'I want to stay,' she replied firmly.

'There's nothing to prevent you staying, if you want to.' Peg smiled. 'I'd like you to stay.'

'I have one or two things I need to sort out back in London.'

'Of course you do.'

'But I'd come back.'

'Yes.'

'That means I'll have to tell Mum where I am. I'm scared to tell her. Now I know the truth . . .'

'Don't think about that now, pet. It's late. Get some sleep. It'll all be so much clearer in the morning.'

So Ellen went to bed and laid her head on the pillow with a weary sigh. Dylan, her parents and Conor fought a moment for her attention, but finding no response they retreated, for Ellen was too tired even to dream.

Chapter 28

When Ellen awoke the following morning, it was still dark and the cockerel had yet to crow. She lay in the silence, bewildered by the strange chill in her heart and the loneliness that now engulfed her. Little by little the revelations of the evening before came back to her. She wasn't her father's daughter, she was Dylan's.

She sat up in panic and groped about in the darkness for the lamp. As soon as she found it, she switched it on and the room was flooded with light. She rubbed her eyes. Yesterday she had felt little emotion, but today she felt desolate. She stared into space and tried to find the root of her desolation. She considered it for a long time and at last came to the conclusion that, after having felt alienated from her family for most of her life, the fact that she *really* didn't belong now made her realize just how much she wanted to. It was ironic that all the while she had cursed her mother for trying to make her fit in, deep down inside she had actually longed to.

Her eyes filled with tears when she thought of her father and whether or not he knew the truth. He had never treated her any differently from Leonora and Lavinia. He hadn't given her more attention to compensate for the fact that she wasn't his — or less because his natural instinct was to favour his own.

He had been consistently fair, loving and sincere. The fact that she didn't look anything like him had never been an issue. Lots of children don't look like their parents. She had never questioned it, as children never do. It's grown-ups who comment on the mystifying distribution of genes, and they had always been very certain that she had inherited hers from her mother.

So, had her mother kept the secret from her husband as well as her daughter? If she had, how had she managed it? Ellen wasn't sure she'd have the courage to ask. Her mother's past had always been taboo. Well, now she understood why Ireland had been erased from the family history. Dylan was always here in Connemara as living proof of her lie. But now that Ellen knew, was it possible for *her* to conceal the truth?

She looked at her watch. It was 6 a.m. She didn't feel remotely sleepy. In fact, she felt agitated, as she used to feel at school the morning prior to an exam. It was dark outside, but she felt a yearning to be down on the beach. She knew she'd feel better there. So she dressed in jeans and a jersey and crept downstairs, careful not to go into the kitchen and wake Bertie. She didn't want to take him by surprise. She threw on a coat of Peg's, a woolly hat and rubber boots and set off down the hill at a brisk pace.

It was dreadfully cold. The air was damp with drizzle and an icy wind blew in off the sea. She thrust her hands deep into the pockets of Peg's coat and hunched her shoulders against the gale. She wondered what it must be like to be a sheep out here in the elements, night after night. She now knew why Peg counted them every morning – to see if any had blown away.

The sky was pale in the east where dawn was breaking weakly onto the wintry landscape. It gave her just enough light to see her way down the track and across the lane to the beach. She took pleasure in the roaring sound of the ocean and the blustering gusts of wind that thrashed the hills erratically. Somehow they soothed her soul and calmed her nerves, almost as if the tempest *outside* reduced the tempest *inside* on account of it being so much greater.

She walked along the sand to where the waves rushed up to flood her boots, and stood gazing into the blackness, as if at the threshold of a new existence. The view wasn't clear; she was uncertain about where she was going, but she knew that the change in the present would undoubtedly change her future, too: she just wasn't quite sure how.

She remained on the beach until the sun began to rise behind the hills and the lighthouse emerged out of the cloud, bringing thoughts of Conor in its silver lining. She watched it grow brighter, as if her future was being slowly revealed to her in symbols. In which case, Caitlin's tragic loss was her lucky gain. Her future was here with Conor.

The wind died down a little and day broke at last. She made her way up the beach, feeling a lot better. Her head was clearer and her heart less heavy. She decided to be positive; after all, not many girls could claim to have *two* fathers.

When she reached the house, Peg was in the field putting out extra feed for the ewes in preparation for the coming lambing season. 'You're up early, Ellen,' she said in surprise.

'I needed a walk.'

'You must be hungry, then. I don't suppose you dared go into the kitchen and wake Bertie.'

'Not after you told me how he mauled Oswald.'

'Come on, then. Let's have some breakfast.' She accompanied her niece inside. 'How are you feeling this morning?'

Ellen sighed. 'A bit uneasy about the whole thing, to be

honest. It's quite a lot to get my head around. But I'm feeling better having been down on the beach.'

'I bet you got blown away down there.'

'Very nearly.'

They took off their coats and hats and Peg put the kettle on the stove. Ellen was cold to the bone. She lay on Mr Badger's beanbag and put her hands in his fur to warm them.

'Don't be surprised if Johnny turns up this morning on his way to work,' said Peg, taking mugs down from the cupboard.

'I imagine most of Ballymaldoon knows that Dylan's my father now.'

Peg was quick to dispel her fears. 'Oh, Johnny won't have told a soul. Not about this.'

'I would have thought it irresistible.'

'Not when it involves shaming the family, Ellen,' Peg told her firmly. 'It was bad enough that Maddie ran away with her Englishman, but if she was pregnant with Dylan's child . . .' She sighed heavily. 'Jaysus, my mam would turn in her grave. Thank the Lord she didn't live to hear the truth. No, Johnny won't tell a soul, I can promise you that.' She glanced out of the window. 'But he'll be turning up, I guarantee it.'

They drank their tea and ate their porridge, their conversation repetitive as they asked the same questions over and over, which only Madeline could answer. A little while later, they heard the sound of a car drawing up outside the house.

'Told you,' said Peg, getting up to look out of the window. But she was surprised to see Conor's Range Rover on the gravel. 'It's your man,' she said, watching her niece's face light up. 'Why don't you ask him in for a cup of tea?'

Ellen hurried outside to meet him. She didn't climb into the car, but walked round to his window, where she leaned in to kiss him. He took in her wild hair and red cheeks and smiled at her appreciatively. 'Where have you been this morning?' he asked.

'Down on the beach.'

'Already?'

'I woke up feeling dreadful. The wind has blown my troubles away.'

He looked concerned. 'You should have called me.'

'It was still dark outside.'

'So? Magnum would have liked an early walk.'

'I'm with Peg. She knows about Dylan. We discussed it last night. Why don't you come in and have a cup of tea? She'd love you to.' He looked uneasy for a moment. 'The kitchen isn't full of Byrnes, I promise.'

But before he could answer, the sight of a gleaming black car motoring sedately up Peg's drive distracted them both.

'Who's that?' Conor asked.

'Well, it's not Johnny,' Ellen replied.

Peg, who had been at the window, now came outside. 'Would you look at that fine car! It must be lost. You're not expecting anyone, are you, Conor?'

'Not that I'm aware of,' Conor replied.

The car slowed down as it approached the house. They peered through the glass to see a driver at the wheel and a woman in the back seat in a thick coat, gloves and hat.

Ellen caught her breath and blanched. 'It's my mother,' she managed, before the driver got out and walked around to open the door for Lady Anthony Trawton.

Peg's hands dropped to her sides and she stared in astonishment and disbelief at the strange woman who now stood before her, beautiful but uncertain beneath her finery. For what seemed an interminable amount of time, no one said a word. They just gazed at each other warily, like cowboys in an old Western movie waiting for someone to draw a gun.

At last, Madeline broke the silence. 'Peg,' she said.

'Maddie?' Peg replied, searching the woman's face for the girl she used to know. 'Is that really you?'

'I've come for my daughter,' she told her steadily. She settled her chilly blue eyes on her child. 'Your note was unacceptable, Ellen. You will come home now and you will marry William and we will put this silly nonsense behind us.'

It was Conor's turn to look surprised. He turned to Ellen. 'You're getting married?'

'I was going to tell you—' she began.

'Of course she's getting married!' her mother interrupted. Her jaw stiffened and she turned her gaze onto the dashing man in the car. 'And you are?'

'Conor Macausland,' he replied coldly, but he didn't extend his hand or get out of the car.

By the look on her daughter's face, she instantly understood their relationship. 'She's engaged to William Sackville. Didn't she tell you?'

Conor's face flushed and hardened, and he closed his eyes a second, inhaling slowly through his nostrils.

'That's why I ran away,' said Ellen. 'Because I didn't want to marry him.'

When he opened his eyes, they were dark and unfamiliar. Ellen's heart plummeted.

'You should have told me,' he replied in a quiet voice.

'I was going to,' she replied.

He gripped the steering wheel. 'Were you?' He turned the key, and the roar of the engine made Ellen step back a pace. 'Look, I'm going to leave you women to it.'

'I was going to tell you, Conor, I promise,' she protested.

'When? Today? Tomorrow?' She didn't answer. Conor shook his head and his mouth twisted with disappointment. 'I trusted you, Ellen. I trusted you.'

She didn't know what to say. She had had countless opportunities to tell him and she had failed. She hadn't thought it would matter. She knew now that it mattered more than anything else.

'Conor, please don't drive off!' She choked, but he accelerated and the car sped down the drive and round the corner, taking her future with it.

Ellen rounded on her mother. 'How could you?' she shouted. 'I don't want to marry William. I don't love him. I love Conor. I ran away because I don't want the life you want for me.'

Peg saw what was coming and was quick to intervene. 'Let's go inside and talk calmly,' she urged.

But Madeline stood firm. 'Go and pack your things. I'll wait in the car,' she commanded.

'You think you can treat me like a child? You think I'm just going to go upstairs, pack my things and come home quietly? I'm thirty-three years old, for God's sake. I'll do what I please.'

'Ellen, be sensible. What's got into you?'

'Please come inside,' said Peg, more urgently this time. She glanced at the driver who was listening to every word, although he was pretending not to hear.

'No, Peg, I'm not staying,' Madeline replied loftily. 'I came to get Ellen. That's all.'

'Aren't you even going to say hello to Dylan?' Ellen challenged.

Peg stiffened. 'Jaysus, will you two listen to me. Come inside, right now!'

Madeline's mouth twitched at the mention of Dylan and she fidgeted her fingers in agitation. Reluctantly, she followed Peg and Ellen into the house.

Peg strode over to the Stanley to retrieve the kettle and set about making tea. Madeline stood awkwardly in the middle of the kitchen and removed only her hat and gloves. She looked around, taking in Peg's home with growing curiosity. Ellen wanted to jump into the car and drive after Conor, but she knew she had to resolve things with her mother before she could do anything else. She felt sick to her stomach. How had her mother found her?

'Now, let's all calm down,' said Peg, putting the kettle on the stove with trembling hands. 'Why don't you take your coat off, Maddie? You'll get very hot in here.'

Madeline dithered a moment, then slowly unbuttoned it. Beneath, she wore a grey silk blouse, grey flannel trousers and patent-leather court shoes; she looked as out of place in Peg's kitchen as a porcelain doll in a hayloft. Ellen sat on Jack's chair and when Bertie nuzzled her with his wet snout, she stroked his coarse hair fondly.

'I know about Dylan,' Ellen said softly.

This simple phrase floored her mother. She dropped her shoulders in defeat, as a cowboy drops his gun when he realizes his opponent is better armed than he is.

'I know why you called me Ellen,' she continued. She watched her mother take the chair at the other end of the table and sit down. 'He's my father, isn't he?' Madeline's eyes shifted to Peg, who paused her tea-making and looked at her sister fearfully. 'You can't hide the truth, Mum. I *know*.'

Madeline looked agonized. 'Yes,' she said at last. 'He's your biological father.'

Peg put down the kettle and held onto the sideboard for

balance. Although she already knew, to hear her sister confirm it knocked the wind out of her. 'Jaysus, Maddie,' she groaned.

When Madeline replied, her voice had lost its brittle tone. 'I'm sorry.'

'Does Daddy know?' Ellen asked. In the long moment before her mother answered, she wondered which she would prefer. She concluded that both 'yes' and 'no' were equally horrific.

Madeline looked down at her fingers and frowned. 'I don't know,' she replied.

Ellen's eyes filled with tears and she dropped her chin. Peg placed a mug of tea in front of her, then gave one to her sister and sat down between them. 'How did you find us?' Peg asked.

'I flew over yesterday and stayed in a hotel last night, psyching myself up. Then when I drove into Ballymaldoon I had to ask where you lived. A lady walking a dog gave me directions.' She swept her eyes around the room. 'You have a nice house, Peg.'

'Thank you. I like it.'

'Is Bill here?' she asked, referring to Peg's husband.

'Bill left a long time ago,' Peg replied tightly. 'We divorced.'

'I'm sorry to hear that. I remember your little boys, Declan and Dermot. They must be grown men now.'

'Oh, they are, and I'm a grandmother. You never met Ronan. He's my youngest, though he's a man now, too,' said Peg softly. There followed an awkward silence. They drank their tea. Mr Badger sighed heavily on his beanbag and closed his eyes. 'Does it look the same?' Peg asked.

'You mean Ballymaldoon? Yes, it looks the same.'

'Did you miss it, Maddie?'

Madeline took a sip of tea. Her lips quivered briefly. 'In the beginning, but I got used to being away.'

'You sound very English.'

'I suppose I do now.'

'You do. There's no trace of Ireland on you at all.'

Madeline's jaw stiffened and she grabbed hold of Peg with her steely gaze. 'I made a choice, Peg, and I had to live with it. That meant I had to give up my past and start again. I had no option but to erase Ireland from my life altogether.'

She looked at her daughter and her face softened. 'I couldn't tell Anthony that you weren't his. He wouldn't have married me and I couldn't afford *not* to marry him. He was my way out. My *only* way out.'

'Did you love him?' Ellen asked anxiously, hoping that, for her father's sake, she did.

'Not like I loved Dylan. But he was mad for me and he was my means of escape.'

'Why didn't you run off with Dylan? He'd have married you in a heartbeat.'

'And what would we have lived off? He had no money. I had no money. My mother would have disowned me. She was fervently religious and dogmatic. We'd have been destitute. That's not what I wanted for me and my child. Here was Anthony, a man of means, who could give me a secure future far away from Ballymaldoon. He knew I was pregnant and begged me to marry him. I'd have been crazy not to have taken him.'

'And what about Dylan?' Ellen asked. 'Where did that leave him? I was *his* child.'

Madeline laughed cynically. 'He was in no position to be a responsible father.'

'But you wrote to him and asked him to come and get you,' said Ellen.

Madeline was again taken aback by the amount that Ellen knew. She narrowed her eyes and lifted her chin. 'Yes, I had a brief moment of regret, but it passed.' She fiddled with the handle of her mug.

'Dylan went to get you.'

'No, he didn't. He's lying,' her mother retorted quickly. Her voice was hard with resentment.

'He's not lying. He went to get you after you sent him the letter telling him that he was a father. But when he saw where you lived and that you were happy, he knew he couldn't give you a life like that. He didn't want to break up your family, even though I belonged to him.'

'He told you that?' Madeline asked quietly.

'Yes, he did.'

'He came after all?'

'He did, Mum. He suffered for years, and you just tossed him aside.'

Madeline seemed to dismiss the information her daughter had just given her. 'What would you rather I'd done?' she snapped. 'Left your father and run off with Dylan? I gave you a good life, Ellen. You don't know how much it cost me, emotionally, to do that.'

'Why didn't you ever come back?' Peg at last found the courage to ask. 'You broke Mam's heart when you left.'

'Because you told her *why* I left!' Madeline retorted.

'How do you know I told her?' Peg flushed guiltily.

'I asked you to keep my secret but you went and told her.' Madeline sighed. 'I don't blame you. It wasn't fair of me to expect you to keep such a big secret, especially from our mother.'

'I had to tell her,' Peg explained. 'She was going crazy with grief. She died without ever having the opportunity to forgive you.'

Madeline's face grew taut with indignation. 'She didn't *want* to forgive me, Peg. Don't you think I tried to come home?'

'You did?' Peg frowned, bewildered.

'Of course I did. I wanted desperately to come home, but Mam wouldn't have me.'

'But you were married then. A respectable wife and mother. Why didn't she want you to come home?'

'Because I told her the truth.'

'You told her that Ellen was Dylan's?' Madeline nodded. Peg's eyes widened. 'She *knew* that Ellen was Dylan's?'

'And she told me never to set foot in Ballymaldoon again. She disowned me, Peg.' Madeline's eyes glistened with tears and her lips wobbled as she fought to control her emotions. 'I wanted to come home, but I couldn't. She wouldn't allow it.'

Peg's face sagged with sorrow. 'Oh, Maddie. I never knew. Here we all were, blaming you for staying away, without ever knowing that it wasn't your fault. Shame on us all!'

'How could you have known?'

'We should have known *you*. I'm sorry. Maddie, I'm so very sorry.'

For the first time since she had arrived, Madeline smiled. 'Thank you, Peg. You don't know how much that means to me.'

When Ellen heard the rumble of a car outside the window, her heart gave a leap. She hoped it might be Conor coming back to apologize. Mr Badger woke up and hurried to the door. Bertie grunted and trotted after him. Peg glanced anxiously at Madeline, who looked back at her, barely daring to breathe. They both expected their brothers.

None of them expected Dylan.

Chapter 29

My world has grown increasingly dark now. I dwell in a constant murkiness, although I know the skies are blue and the air is clear. I am heavy, too, as if I am made of cold mist, like the winter fogs that linger in the valleys and cannot lift. The pleasure I took in nature has been replaced by the perverse pleasure I derive from my unholy mission. I no longer notice the latticed burr oaks on the drive, the mirrored surface of the lake and the pretty yellow heather that grows on the hills, for I am aware only of my purpose and how pleasingly it is unfolding.

Conor now knows that Ellen is engaged to be married. It matters little that she does not want William and that she has no intention of walking up the aisle with him, because Conor knows she loves *him*; it matters only that she didn't *tell* him. It matters a great deal. In fact, trust is more important to Conor than anything else, and Ellen has let him down.

He doesn't drive back to Reedmace House because our children are there with Daphne. He would probably like to saddle his horse and ride out on the hills to vent his fury. Instead, he goes to the castle and stands before my portrait. I look down at him through the eyes of the painting and he stares up at me with loathing. I am not surprised by his expression, because love and hate are the opposite sides of the same coin. I let him down too, but now I am making it up to him.

He remains there for a long while, gazing at me, and he doesn't realize that I am here in his vision, if only he could see beyond the paint. Then he sits on the stairs and puts his head in his hands. I sit beside him. You see, I am with him always, and forever will be. He doesn't need anyone else but me.

While Conor is hurting on the steps of his castle, I am pulled back to Peg's house to watch the drama being played out in her kitchen. Dylan has come to see with his own eyes the woman he loved and lost. He stands in the doorway, hat in hand, his heavy coat making him look bigger than he really is. Madeline Trawton is so surprised to see him she doesn't know what to do. She is a hard-looking woman with big hair and lots of make-up, but as she pushes herself up and walks towards him I can see that her legs are trembling. Her blue eyes gaze into his soft, brown ones, and in them she undoubtedly recognizes the boy he once was.

'Maddie, it *is* you,' he whispers.

She is too astonished to speak. Her face softens as she contemplates his. 'You came for me,' she says, and I detect a hint of Ireland in the way she says 'for'.

'Ellen told you.'

'Yes.'

'Of course I came for you, Maddie.' He smiles sadly.

'I never knew.'

'No, you weren't meant to.'

'I thought you didn't want me. I thought you didn't want Ellen.'

His eyes settle on his daughter who is sitting on the chair with the bird. She is so still, it is almost as if she is a piece of furniture. 'Jaysus, Maddie, what did you think of me? I loved you then and I always will.'

She seems taken aback by this unexpected declaration of devotion. Dylan is gazing at her with his big, sentimental eyes and she doesn't know what to do with herself.

'How did you know I was here?'

'There's only one woman in a posh car who'd be asking the way to Peg's.' She frowns at him, confused. 'You asked my Martha for directions and she came back and told me.'

'Oh.' Madeline recalls the woman with the dog. 'Yes, I did.'

There's an awkward moment as they stare at each other across the vast distance that time has built up between them. They are so close but they might as well be oceans apart. Neither knows how to bridge the gap or how to erase the pain it has engendered. Perhaps it is too deeply entrenched in their hearts ever to be healed.

Dylan now steps into the gulf. He walks right through it with a determined and purposeful stride. She looks frightened, like a pampered poodle being set upon by a wild dog. But Dylan doesn't care. He is an instinctive, impulsive man. He fells the years with his unwavering commitment to the past and wraps his big arms around her. She stiffens, alarmed, but he only hugs her tighter. Ellen and Peg are both moved. If I didn't have such a hard heart I would be moved, too. But I am only interested in whether or not Ellen returns to London with her mother.

Madeline Trawton goes limp at last. She puts her arms around Dylan and embraces him back. Peg is quick to grab Ellen's attention and they leave the room together, hiding out in the sitting room where Ellen hasn't yet started to write her book. Once they are gone, Madeline begins to cry. She hugs him fiercely and he has no intention of releasing her. 'It's all right, Ellen Olenska, I'm here now,' he says, and I wonder whether he recognizes the girl beneath the woman she has become. I think her tears are the tears of Maddie Byrne. She is in Dylan's arms and Lady Anthony Trawton has vanished.

She pulls away and smiles at him shyly. Her mascara has run, leaving ugly black trails down her cheeks. 'You're still my Dylan, aren't you?' she says, and her voice is now soft with affection.

'I've always been your Dylan,' he replies, and those big brown eyes glitter with emotion.

'I wasn't going to come. I was scared. Ellen was an excuse. In my heart I wanted to revisit my past.'

'Ellen's a beautiful girl, just like her mam.'

Madeline's eyes fill with tears again. 'I'm so sorry, Dylan. I had delusions of grandeur. I wanted a better life than the one we could have had together.'

'Don't be hard on yourself . . .' he begins, but she cuts him off.

'No, I'm being honest, Dylan. Let me at least give you the truth. I knew you'd run away with me if I asked you to. So, I didn't give you the opportunity. I ran off with Anthony because I saw a better future.' Her lips quiver and her face floods with shame. 'But I realized soon after Ellen was born that I didn't fit into my new life. I pined for you and I pined for Ireland. I felt imprisoned in concrete and missed the hills and the sea. I regretted my decision and my lie ate away at me so that every time Anthony picked Ellen up and kissed her I resented him, because of my guilt. He wasn't Ellen's father but I couldn't tell him. It was too late. So, I wrote to you. I wanted you to come and get me. I wanted to start again. When you didn't come, I telephoned my mother and told her the truth.'

'Jaysus, Maddie. That was bold.'

'She disowned me, Dylan.'

'I bet she did.'

'So, I couldn't come home. Not ever.'

He takes her hands, for she now looks desperate. 'You thought we all deserted you. When that couldn't have been further from the truth.'

'So, I gave up and threw myself into my new life. I resolved never to speak of Ireland again. I tried to erase you from my memory. Then Ellen comes here and settles into my old life like a cuckoo – and she *can*, but I *can't*. She belongs here in Ballymaldoon like I once did. You can't imagine how much that hurts. Ellen has brought it all back.'

'And she's brought *you* back.'

'Yes, she has.'

'Which is a good thing.'

'I don't know.'

'Yes, it is,' he says firmly. 'You're both home now.'

They sit at the table and Madeline wipes her eyes with the handkerchief Dylan gives her, leaving black stains on the cotton. 'What'll you do about Ellen?' he asks gently. 'Wild horses won't get her down the aisle, you know.'

Madeline's shoulders sink in defeat. 'I know.'

'So, let her be. Why force her to be what she's not?' He grins. 'She's more like you than you realize.'

She pulls at the corner of the handkerchief. 'I was so worried that Anthony would guess that Ellen wasn't his, I tried to make her like him. But she broke out of the mould every time I made it, and I saw *you*, staring defiantly back at me with your big brown eyes, and they had the same wilfulness in them. And I felt guilty and afraid.'

'So, let her choose where she wants to be. Your mother was

wrong to judge you and she was wrong to stop you coming home. So, don't be like her.'

Madeline nods then sighs in resignation. 'What's this man like?'

'Conor Macausland? He's a good man.'

'I'm afraid I might have ruined it for her.'

'How?'

'He drove off in a fury when I told him that Ellen was engaged to a man in England. He accused her of lying to him.'

Dylan shakes his head. 'That's a shame.'

'What can I do?'

'Nothing. She must go and explain to him.'

'Do you think he'll forgive her?'

'He's a complicated man with a complicated history, Maddie. I don't know what he'll do. But Ellen needs to go and talk to him now.'

So, they go to the sitting room together, where Peg and Ellen are perched uneasily on chairs. They stand expectantly when Dylan and Madeline enter. 'Shall I make another pot of tea?' says Peg, who clearly finds comfort in the routine of tea-making.

Madeline looks different now. Her face is no longer hard. The black trails have dried on her skin and under her eyes. Her hair has fallen out of place and curled in the damp Irish air. She looks younger and fragile. 'Ellen, I think you should go and explain things to Conor,' she begins.

'I'm not coming home,' Ellen interrupts defensively.

'I know that and it's OK. I hope I haven't ruined it for you. Dylan says Conor's a good man.'

Ellen is surprised. She hadn't expected her mother to change her mind so easily. 'He *is* a good man,' she replies.

'Take my car, pet, and go and get him,' says Peg.

As Ellen makes for the door, Mr Badger begins to bark and wag his tail. 'Jaysus, Mary and holy St Joseph!' Peg exclaims. 'Can it get any more dramatic?' She opens the kitchen door and the dog bounds out to greet Desmond, Johnny, Craic and Ryan climbing out of their cars. Word has got around, as it always does in Ballymaldoon, and they have all come to see their sister.

Peg is so nervous she heads straight for the stove to wet the tea. As she takes the mugs down from the cupboard her hands are shaking again. Madeline and Dylan give each other a long, hard stare, and I think they both know that they are going to have to tell the boys the truth.

Ellen rushes past them and climbs into Peg's car. They are all parked closely together in front of Peg's house, but there is enough room for Ellen to drive out. She watches a moment as they enter the house. The scene reminds me of *Goldilocks and the Three Bears*. But there are four bears in this tale, and Goldilocks has come back.

Ellen finds Conor's car parked in front of the castle. She pulls up beside it and climbs out. Her face is pale against her dark hair and she looks terrified. As well she might. Conor has a vicious temper and nothing makes him more furious than lying. He trusted her and she abused his trust. I don't think he'll ever forgive her. In fact, I *know* he won't.

I watch her walk to the front door and try the latch. She finds it unlocked and opens it slowly, as if she is afraid of what she'll find inside. Conor is still on the stairs. He has been there for some time. When he sees her, he stands up. He puts his hands in his pockets and I am happy to see that he has surrounded himself with that familiar wall of defence I know so well. That impenetrable, invisible wall which is so good at keeping people out. Ellen finds herself on the other side, unable to reach him, and I feel her desperation. Conor is a stranger now, not the lover he once was. She has lost him, only she doesn't know it yet. There is still hope, she thinks. I could tell her that once up, it will take more than begging and explaining to bring that wall down.

'I didn't think it mattered,' she begins in a small voice. His cold eyes watch her impassively but he says nothing. So she rambles on, helplessly. 'I don't love him. That's why I fled. I came here to get away from him and my mother. I didn't want to break off the engagement by phone, and I didn't want to go back to London. So, I put my head in the sand and focused on you. William isn't important, Conor. You must understand that; *you* are.'

He takes a sharp breath through his nostrils. 'You should have told me, Ellen.'

'I know, I'm sorry.'

'I trusted you with everything. I let you in and what do I get in return? A slap in the face!'

'No! It's not like that at all. William no longer existed. In my mind I wasn't engaged any more. I fell in love with you and I let everything else go.'

'It's not kind to leave a man like that. You should have told him how you felt, not left him hanging on, waiting for you like an eejit. Poor sod! Did you ever think about him?'

'No, because I was thinking about *you*.'

'Well, you can go back now and tell him.'

'I will.'

'Unless you were just sitting on the fence, waiting to see if *we* were worth pursuing.'

'I always knew which side of the fence I wanted to be on.'

'Well, it doesn't matter any more. It's over between us, Ellen.'

She blanches the colour of a turnip. 'Don't say that, Conor!'

'I don't want to be with a woman I can't trust. I've been let down enough in my life to know the value of honesty.'

'I won't lie to you again.' She is clinging onto the shards of their splintered relationship like a shipwrecked sailor. 'Please, you have to forgive me.'

He gives a hollow laugh. 'Oh, Ellen. I thought you were different. I believed we were good for each other.' She begins to cry, but he remains hard-hearted, and I am willing him to stay strong and not to weaken. A woman's tears are powerful weapons and he must remain focused on what he *really* wants and not be swayed by them. I stare down from my portrait and he lifts his gaze and locks his eyes in mine. I see the resolve in them and I know that I have won.

He ushers her out and locks the door behind him. 'So, this is it?' she asks, astonished. 'You're going to drop me because I failed to tell you I was engaged? When I never intended to marry him!'

'No, because you're not the woman I thought you were.'

She struggles to speak through her tears. 'Then you're not the man I thought *you* were!' She climbs into her car and drives off without looking back. Conor remains there for a long while, watching her disappear into the distance. He stares down the avenue of trees as if he is half expecting her to come back. Finally, when she does not, he gets into his Range Rover and roars off in the other direction. I am triumphant. In spite of the fog closing in around me, I am victorious. Conor is mine again. This time I will guard him more closely.

In the heavy atmosphere of my darkening world, I find that I am not alone after all. I see faces at the windows of my castle and they are looking at *me*. Other unhappy spirits, stuck in their own murky limbos, stare out like prisoners behind bars.

I know now why I couldn't see them before: because I was made of a higher vibration. But now, I realize, I am one of them. I have sunk so low. I have fallen to their level. But I am not repentant. Blinded by the determination of my possessive heart, I am elated by the battle I have just won. I have protected my family from invasion, which is my duty as a wife and mother, so I am willing to sacrifice my soul. I am resigned to this low level of existence. Heaven is so far away now, I wouldn't find my way there even if I wanted to. But I do not. Here is where Conor is, where Ida and Finbar are. And as long as they are here, I will remain here also. And when they go, I hope that they will find a way to take me with them. I will not leave them. As long as I exist, I will not leave them.

Chapter 30

Ellen pulled up in a lay-by and sobbed onto the steering wheel. It was the same lay-by into which she had driven only a few weeks before, after she had met Conor for the first time. She could never have predicted then that she'd be here now, crying her heart out.

She should have told him about William. She knew that. And she should have been honest to William in her note, or to his face, which would have been kinder. She had messed up and she longed to turn the clock back and do it all again differently. Conor had been let down by his wife; now *she* had let him down – she wished to God she hadn't. She understood his fury, but she didn't understand his leaving. He had been so loving. How was it possible to switch his heart off so suddenly and so irrevocably? Was their relationship really worth so little to him that he could end it for one small misdemeanour?

She thought of her mother and Dylan at Peg's cottage with her uncles, and knew that she didn't want to go back there. So she drove further up the road and parked at the foot of the hill where Caitlin's little chapel stood above, overlooking the sea. She knew she'd find solace there.

She pulled her coat around her body and headed off up the path that cut through the heather and long grasses. The wind dried her tears and the beauty of the countryside filled the hollow sense of loss that ached inside her. She arrived at the gate and pushed it open. There on the left was Caitlin's grave with its marble headstone and habitual jar of red roses. The mystery of who was leaving flowers here distracted her a moment from her unhappiness, and she considered Caitlin and the secrets buried along with her. Perhaps the person leaving flowers was the reason Caitlin let Conor down. Maybe she had fallen in love with someone else and that was why they were fighting the night she died in the fire.

Ellen walked on up the path and pushed open the door of the chapel. It was cold and damp inside, but at least it was out of the wind. She wandered down the aisle and sat in the front pew, facing the altar. The place was dimly lit by windows clouded with mildew and the lack of light only added to her sense of desolation. She breathed in the musty air and wished she had a packet of cigarettes. If ever she needed a cigarette it was now. Her sorrow rose in a rush of self-pity and she began to cry again. Could she remain in Connemara without Conor? Was her family enough? Why did fate always give with one hand and take with the other? Why did there always have to be a negative to puncture every positive?

She remained in the chapel for a long time. The peace and silence enabled her to examine her predicament more calmly, and then, when her misery swelled to overwhelm her again, she remembered Dylan and the time they had sat here together, their voices echoing off the ancient stone walls, and she smiled through her tears.

When at last her stomach began to rumble with hunger she decided to go back to Peg's. She walked slowly down the hill. There was no hurry, no one to rush back for. It was still drizzling. Heavy grey clouds raced across the sky, chased inland by a cold, icy gale. She took solace from the magnificent view of the sea. The lighthouse stood defiant against the onslaught of wind and wave, like a knight in a white tunic refusing to surrender even though he is shot through with bullets and his ribs are laid bare. She stopped walking a moment and watched the white gulls wheeling above it like angels waiting to carry its spirit home. Yet there it stood, almost gritting its teeth with determination not to give in, clinging onto life with all its might. Suddenly she was struck by an idea for a song. *Oh, battle-weary lighthouse, still rising from the sea, don't you know it's over and the angels call to thee.* She stopped a moment and hummed it as a sliver of excitement slipped through the crack in her broken heart. She shook her head and put her hands on her hips. How ironic that she should get inspiration the very moment she decided to leave.

When she arrived at Peg's, Johnny's truck and Desmond's car were still parked alongside Dylan's and the driver of her mother's hire car was reading the papers in his shiny black motor. She drew up and took a deep breath for courage. She didn't feel like talking to anyone. Like a dog, she wanted to hide under her bed and lick her wounds. But as she stepped onto the gravel, Oswald came hurrying across from his house next door.

'Gracious, what's going on?' he asked, looking at all the cars in bewilderment.

'My mother's come back,' she told him.

'Good Lord. Is Peg all right?'

'Shocked, but all right.'

He took in her tear-stained face and sorrowful expression and smiled sympathetically. 'But you're not, are you, Ellen?'

'Not really.' She shrugged her shoulders helplessly. 'It's all gone horribly wrong, Oswald. I lied to everyone and I'm paying a dreadful price.'

'I'm sure you lied with good reason.'

'I thought so, but Conor doesn't want to see me any more.'

He glanced at Peg's kitchen door. 'Do you really want to go in there?'

'Not really.'

'Then come into my house and you can tell me all about it. I'm a wise old codger, you know, and I have more experience of love than you might imagine.'

She followed him into an immaculate sitting room. A fire was crackling in the grate and an easel was set up in front of the window, where he had laid out his paints and brushes neatly on a round wooden table.

'You're very tidy for an artist,' she commented, wandering over to see what he was painting. She caught her breath when her aunt stared out at her from the canvas. 'Good Lord, that's Peg.'

Oswald smiled secretively. 'Don't tell her. It's a gift.'

'She'll be astonished. It's really good. I mean, not that your other paintings aren't good, but this looks just like her.'

Oswald was not offended. He crossed the little hall and disappeared into the kitchen. Ellen stepped closer, taking in the modesty of Peg's smile and the warmth of her eyes, which contained both her sorrow and her joy. He had captured more than her appearance; he had painted her as he saw her when she looked at him, which was different from the way she looked at anyone else. Peg's spirit seemed to shine out from the paint and give her a gentle beauty that Ellen hadn't noticed before. She realized then that he must love her, and she smiled with the pleasure that thought gave her. She wondered whether, when he gave her the painting, Peg would realize, too.

A moment later, Oswald returned with two cups of coffee on a tray with a jug of milk and a bowl of sugar. 'Peg makes much too much tea,' he said, putting the tray down on the little table in front of the fire. 'You look like a coffee-drinker to me.'

'I haven't drunk coffee since I arrived. How lovely. I need warming up.'

'And cheering up,' he said. 'Now, what was your lie?'

She sat down and put a spoonful of sugar in her coffee. There was no point hiding anything any more. She wondered why she had bothered in the first place. 'I'm officially engaged to a man called William Sackville,' she told him.

'Ah, and how did Conor find out?'

'Mother told him.'

'And she'd like you to marry this William?'

'Yes, she thinks he'd be good for me because he's rich and grand, which, according to my mother, are the only important qualities in a man.'

'I see. So that's why you ran away?'

'At the time, I wasn't sure what I wanted. I just wanted to get away, from Mum and William and a future I don't want.'

'And Conor is cross that you never told him.'

'He says he can't trust me.'

'He'll get over it.'

Ellen shook her head sadly. 'No, I don't think he will.'

'He's just angry. Give him time.'

'I don't think he'll *ever* forgive me. You should have seen his face. It was as hard as stone. Unyielding. Horrible. Caitlin let him down in some way, and now I've let him down, too. I'm just as bad as she was and he ended up loathing her.'

'Is that right?'

'Yes, he can't bear her or the memory of her. Now he hates me, too.'

'But she's dead, my dear, and you're very much alive.'

'There's more. Dylan is my real father.'

Oswald nearly dropped his coffee cup. 'Good gracious! That's one I didn't see coming.' He put the cup on the table for safety.

'Neither did I, but there it is.' She shrugged. 'Pandora's box is well and truly open. That's what they're all discussing in the kitchen. Lots of lies, and now I'm just as bad as my mother.'

'You're going to have to tell me from the beginning, Ellen.' He took off his spectacles and pulled a handkerchief out of his breast pocket to clean them. 'And let *me* be the judge of whether you or your mother are bad!'

Ellen told him the whole story from the day her mother left Ireland to the moment she came back thirty-three years later. He listened quietly, taking it all in, his wise old eyes watching her with compassion. When she finished he put his spectacles back on. 'Where do you want to be, Ellen?' he asked gently.

'I wanted to be here. But I'm not sure I want to be here without Conor.'

'I see.' He looked like a doctor, taking in all the information before making a diagnosis. 'And what are you going to do about your father? Are you going to talk to him? You said your mother told you that she doesn't know whether or not he is aware of the truth.'

'I don't know what to do.' She looked at him helplessly. 'What *should* I do?'

He folded his hands in his lap. 'I'll give you my opinion, Ellen, but ultimately you must do what feels right for you.'

'OK.' She began to bite her thumbnail anxiously.

'I think you should talk to him. Otherwise, you will live a lie for the rest of your life and I think it's time for everyone to stop lying.' She nodded her agreement, although she dreaded the thought of having to confront her father and cause him unhappiness. 'And you should tell your William as soon as possible that the engagement is off, to his face, kindly but decisively.'

'And then?'

'You should come back.'

'But what about Conor?'

'Ah, only time will tell. But you fit in here, Ellen. You have a job in Alanna's shop, a room in Peg's house and a father who wants to get to know you. Ireland's in your blood, on both sides. It's no wonder that your heart has settled in here like a nesting sparrow.'

She drained her coffee and put the cup down on the table. 'I don't think I can,' she replied. 'I don't think I can bear it. Everything here reminds me of him. Every which way I look, he's there.'

'Then, if you're sure, we shall be very sorry to see you go,' he said sadly. 'Especially Peg – and I imagine Dylan. You will leave a very big tear in the fabric of our lives.'

'Oh, Oswald, don't say that.' Ellen began to cry again.

'It's true, isn't it?' He patted her hand affectionately. 'Haven't we decided not to lie any more?'

A little later, when Oswald and Ellen entered Peg's kitchen, they found the Byrne men squashed around the kitchen table with Madeline, Dylan and Peg. The atmosphere was heavy but it wasn't awkward. They were talking in low voices and there was a sense of unity about the group. They looked more like a band of thieves than a dislocated family coming together after over thirty years apart. For a moment, Ellen felt her resolve weaken. She thought of the formal kitchen back at Eaton Court and her heart sank. She had grown attached to Peg, Mr Badger and Bertie. She hadn't even met Reilly the squirrel who slept on in the laundry cupboard upstairs. She felt at home with her uncles now: they no longer alarmed her with their broad shoulders and dark faces. And she had found a kindred spirit in Dylan.

The room fell silent. Madeline looked at her daughter with concern. 'What did he say?' she asked.

'I'm coming home,' Ellen replied simply.

Peg was horrified. 'You're leaving?' she asked.

'But you've only just got here,' said Dylan. Ellen couldn't look at his face, and dropped her gaze to the floor. 'You're not going back to marry this man, are you?'

'Of course not.'

'But you'll come back, won't you?' said Peg.

'I don't know,' Ellen replied, swallowing back tears. Dylan's gaze was so intense it forced her to look at him. His face was grey and his large brown eyes full of sadness.

'You can't let Conor Macausland chase you out of Ireland, Ellen,' he said.

'I agree with Dylan,' said Johnny. 'He's a feckin' eejit.'

'Do you want us to go and talk to him?' Desmond asked, and Ellen was surprised at his unexpected offer of support.

'No,' she replied quickly. She didn't want her uncles muscling in and making everything worse. 'It's fine.'

'So, what'll you do now?' Peg asked her sister. 'You can't just turn around and leave the minute you arrive.'

'I was going to drop in and drop out very quickly,' Madeline replied sheepishly.

'But now?' Dylan asked.

'Well, I've got nothing to hide any more, so . . .'

'You'll stay the night, at least,' said Peg.

'I'll stay the night, at least,' she replied. Then, turning to her daughter, who still stood in the middle of the room with Oswald, she added, 'If that's OK with you, Ellen?'

Ellen nodded. 'As long as you want. You've got years to catch up on.'

'Then that's settled,' said Peg. 'At least we'll have you for another night, Ellen.' Ellen noticed her smile bravely at Oswald. She couldn't remain in that kitchen a moment longer, knowing that soon she was going to be leaving it, so she left them around the table and fled upstairs. She hoped that Conor might call, but when she switched on the telephone he had given her, she found he hadn't; nor had he texted. She threw herself onto her bed and lay staring miserably up at the ceiling.

She considered texting him, apologizing again, begging him to reconsider. But then the memory of his cold, uncaring face rose to remind her of his fury and she put the telephone down, knowing better than to anger him further. They had all warned her. They had all told her he was bad news. But every fibre of her body longed for him and she turned onto her side and hugged her pillow mournfully.

She must have drifted off to sleep, for when she opened her eyes her mother was sitting on the end of her bed. 'I didn't mean to wake you,' she said softly.

'It's OK,' Ellen replied, pushing herself up.

'I'm sure Conor will come round. You don't break up with someone for something so trivial.'

'You don't know Conor, Mum.'

'I've heard all about him.'

'Nothing good, then.'

'Actually, Dylan had nothing *but* good things to say. Darling, if he loves you, he'll come back.'

'I'm not sure he loves me enough. We haven't had time for that.'

Madeline smiled knowingly. 'Love doesn't need time, Ellen.'

'So, is it weird seeing Dylan again?' Ellen asked, changing the subject.

Madeline sighed. 'He hasn't changed at all. He's still the Dylan I knew and cared for.'

'We've been playing the guitar and singing together. He's incredibly talented.'

'Oh, I know.' She gazed at her daughter thoughtfully. 'You're so like him. Seeing you two together makes the resemblance all the more obvious.'

'Did Dad ever meet Dylan?'

'Yes, he did, but I don't think he'd remember. It was so long ago.'

'I'm going to tell him.'

Madeline's face hardened. 'You don't have to do that, Ellen.'

'I think we've all lied enough,' Ellen replied firmly.

'What's the point of making him unhappy?'

'I can promise you that by the time we leave Ballymaldoon, everyone will know that I'm Dylan's daughter. Have you forgotten what they're all like? Say, somehow, the gossip gets back to Dad? No, Mum. He has to hear it from you or me. And I think it's going to be me.'

'Don't rush into anything. Think very hard before you broach the subject. It all happened a long time ago.'

'It's still happening now, Mum. I'm proof of that. You can't bury *me* in the past.'

'Of course not, Ellen, but before you let the past poison the present, think about what it will do to him. Think about that. This isn't just about you, me and Dylan. Your father loves you.'

'And he deserves to know the truth,' Ellen added. Her mother's lips tightened and she lifted her chin. Ellen had seen a glimpse of the old Maddie Byrne, but Lady Anthony Trawton had been around for much longer. She was too old and set in her ways to become a girl again.

'I'll be very disappointed in you if you tell him,' she said, and her voice had found its hard outer casing again. 'Punish me for lying to you, for not telling you about Dylan and for giving you a life of privilege that you would never have had back here, but don't punish Anthony. He has only ever been a good father to you and a good husband to me. Now, we're going to have lunch in the pub. Craic wants to show it to me and I think I'd better meet the rest of my family. It will do you good to come with us. You can't lie around here all day, moping. That's not going to bring Conor back, is it?'

As much as Ellen didn't feel like seeing anyone, she had to admit that she found comfort in the family lunch at the Pot of Gold. Even Peg, who never set foot in the pub, was persuaded by Oswald to join them. Ellen was happy to see her aunt drop her shoulders in defeat at last, and take Oswald's arm. If she was worried about gossip she must have known that in her sister's company no one would notice *her*.

It wasn't long before word got around that Maddie Byrne had returned, and the place heaved with locals wanting to get a good look at the girl who had scandalized Ballymaldoon all those years ago when she had run off with her English aristocrat. It was the return of the Prodigal Daughter and she was treated like royalty, by family, friends and strangers who had only ever heard the story.

Madeline clearly relished the attention. As she drank wine and sank deeper into the bosom of her family, she seemed to soften a little. Her hair had grown tousled in the damp air. Her cheeks were flushed with emotion. Her smile was wide, and her body had lost its stiffness. Her laugh, usually so measured, was now husky and unrestrained. She looked younger. Ellen glimpsed Maddie Byrne before it all went wrong and life's disappointment hardened her. But she knew it would be short-lived. She wondered whether Dylan knew, too. The years in London had been too long and too determined to melt away so easily.

Ellen felt numb inside. The more she watched her family, Oswald and Dylan, the more it pained her to think of leaving them. But she found herself searching the faces for Conor, and every time the door opened her heart stopped for a brief, agonizing moment while she prayed it would be him stepping in with the wind. Of course, it never was. There was a strong chance it never would be. She knew then that she couldn't live like this. At least in London she wouldn't expect to see him around every corner. In London she had a better chance of forgetting. After all, her mother had managed it, hadn't she?

Chapter 31

Conor's misery is a sign of my success. I should be triumphant. But I am not. Something about his misery makes me uneasy; it is a different kind of unhappiness to the one that dogged him after my death. There was something dark and surly about him then, as if he was a man guilty of hiding a dreadful secret. There is nothing dark and secretive about him now. He is simply devastated and bewildered by his loss. He gave Ellen his love but more significantly, he gave her his trust, and she betrayed him. He is sick with grief. Before, I was jealous of his happiness; now I am jealous of his pain.

When Ellen leaves the castle, he watches her car until it has disappeared under the burr oaks. He remains standing there for a long while, as if he is expecting it to turn around and come back. But it doesn't. Ellen is gone and I hope she will now return to London and stay there. Time will heal his broken heart and he will come to realize that the love he feels for me is deeper than the superficial love he felt for Ellen. Women will come and go in his life like pretty lilies on a pond, but I am the current beneath, which is always constant.

He puts his hands on his hips and for a moment his face folds into a frown, as if he has suddenly thought of something which makes him furious. He turns and strides purposefully back to the castle door. Once inside, he stares up again at my portrait. I gaze down at him from the eyes in the paint and it is as if we are looking at each other as we once did in the flesh. I am sure he can see me. My heart jumps with excitement, for surely he would not be gazing at me like this if he could not intuit what is beyond the paint? His frown grows deeper, as if he is considering an impossible thing. But I am not impossible, my love. I am here in spirit, more real than I was in life. He shakes his head and contemplates my beautiful face. He gazes on my splendour and I know he is tormented by my death. But death is an illusion, Conor. I am here. If you close your eyes and trust your senses, you will feel me.

'Oh, Caitlin,' he groans. 'What have you done?' I am not sure what he means by this. I would like to believe that he is regretting our row at the lighthouse and my impulsive dash up the stairs and to my death. But there is something in his expression which tells me otherwise. He is angry with me. He is staring at me with eyes full of loathing. I am stunned and find myself reeling back out of the painting, into a darker limbo than the one I was in before. He shakes his head and smiles cynically. 'You are responsible for this,' he accuses, and I see his face grow hard with resentment. 'I should have known. You were jealous of me in life and now you're jealous of me in death. You have to let me go, Caitlin.' He pushes a hand through his hair and chuckles bitterly, dropping his gaze to the flagstones. He is aware that he is talking to himself and how crazy he must sound. But he doesn't sound crazy to me.

His words are like daggers that stab me in the heart and kill me all over again. Doesn't he know that everything I did was for love? If only I could explain that it was *he* who drove me to do what I did – that if I had been secure in his love I would not have pushed him so far and I would not have let him down. I would still be alive today and none of this would have happened.

He leaves me in the castle, but I am not alone. I turn and see the grey, unhappy creatures who were gazing down at me from the upstairs windows – and I realize that I am as grey and unhappy as they are. It dawns on me then that the universe really is made up of vibration: the faster the vibration, the lighter the entity. These poor souls are slow and heavy, as I am. I think of Ciara and her bright energy and wonder what I have to do to speed up my vibration so that I can reach her happy level of existence. I do not know. Perhaps I am destined to lurk at this level for all eternity. And I wonder what have I sacrificed heaven for? A husband who does not love me and children who barely know that I am here. I look around and sink still further at the thought of spending eternity with this sorry band of ghosts.

Conor returns to Reedmace House in a foul mood and snaps at Finbar when the boy asks him to play chess. 'We're leaving,' he growls, then shouts for his mother. Daphne is bewildered when she hears her son's unfamiliar tone, but she knows him as only a mother can. His face is grim, his eyes are raw and his heart is bleeding. She does not ask him what has happened because Conor will tell her when he feels ready and not a moment before. But she knows it is Ellen and her heart bleeds, too, because Ellen carried all her hopes and now she is gone.

They leave for Dublin by helicopter and I am so stunned and hurt by Conor's rejection that I remain in Connemara. I want to move on now. I want to leave my murky limbo, but it is too late. The light has gone and I am plunged into darkness. It is as if a heavy fog hangs over the land. I can barely see through it. I feel a yearning to be down on the beach.

Mustering up the little energy I have, I transport myself there. The atmosphere I generate makes it too dark to see the lighthouse, but I know it is there. I haunt this small slice of coast, floating up and down it like a leaf on the wind, sick in my soul. It seems as if everything is lost and I am in hell. Somehow I know that it is of my making, but I don't know how, and I don't have the tools to reverse it. I just know that my longing for light is stronger now than my longing for Conor and my children. I feel a terrible, searing homesickness in the heart of my soul: I want to go home.

And then I see two people walking along the beach. I don't know whether it is day or night because I am now in constant darkness. As they get closer I see that it is Peg and Madeline. What a strange pair they make. Peg is short and round, like a cabbage, and Madeline is tall and thin like a stick of celery. I am drawn out of myself and my misery as I watch them walk closer. They are talking, hands in the pockets of their coats, hats pulled low over their foreheads. They reach the waves and stop. There is silence but for the mournful cry of a gull wheeling overhead. They remain a moment, gazing out to sea. Then Peg sighs and slips her hand through her sister's arm. Madeline puts her hand over it and gives it a reassuring pat.

'It's OK, Peg,' she says gently. 'She's with the Lord.'

Peg's eyes fill with tears. 'I know, but I miss her.'

'Of course you do.'

'There's a hole in my heart that is never filled and a cold wind blows through it constantly.'

'Oh, Peg, to think I had no idea how you were suffering. We were always so close.'

'And I had no idea how *you* were suffering, Maddie. I thought you had everything you wanted. We should have kept in touch. We should have been there for one another.'

'We'll keep in touch now, though, won't we?'

'Aye, we will. I'm glad you came back.'

Madeline smiles sadly. 'Me too,' she replies.

'What about Dylan?' Peg asks.

'Dylan and I both know that what we shared belongs to a chapter that closed many years ago. We can't open the book and expect to take up from where we left off. Life doesn't work like that; there have been many pages since and we have both changed. But I'm glad we had the chance to talk. I love him, but I think I love the memory of him more.'

'And Dylan? How does he feel?'

'He's found a daughter, Peg,' she says solemnly.

'Ellen will come back, don't you think?' Peg is anxious now at the thought of losing her niece.

'I don't know. This Conor has hurt her badly and it's all my fault. I should have spoken to her in private. But I was so angry. I didn't think. I saw him and knew who he was and wanted him to go away and for things to return to the way they were.'

'She's a lovely girl, Maddie.'

'I know she is. But she's always been a difficult child.'

'Just like you.'

'I wasn't difficult!' Madeline protests, but she smiles because she knows that Peg is right.

'Oh, you were! Mam . . .' Peg hesitates, then she looks at her sister thoughtfully. 'Maddie, don't you think you should visit Mam's grave and pay your respects?'

'No,' Madeline replies quickly. 'I'm not ready for that.'

'But Jesus taught forgiveness.'

'I'm not ready to forgive. There's no point going through the motions if I don't feel it in my heart. I feel nothing but resentment, Peg. I can't help it.' I notice that every so often she gives a word an Irish lilt. The girl she once was is trying to break out of the woman she has become. But it is impossible; the outer casing has grown too hard. 'You, Peg, have to forgive *yourself*.'

'Oh, Maddie.' Peg gasps, and I see a wave of horror ripple over her. She recoils. 'I can never forgive myself,' she hisses, as if her self-loathing is a snake that has taken possession of her. It rears up its repulsive head and the sweet, loving Peg shrinks back in fear.

'Peg, it wasn't your fault. It was no one's fault. God wanted Ciara back. You cannot question His motives. You have to accept what He gives us.'

'But I can't!' she wails. 'If I had been more vigilant . . .'

'There are no ifs, only facts. It's over and you have to move on.'

At that moment I am blinded by a bright light. I know that the light is Ciara, even though I am not strong enough to look at it. The fog around me is immediately dissolved by this loving radiance and I watch Madeline wrap her arms around her sister and hug her fiercely. The light seems to penetrate Peg and she lets out a wail. It is as if all her grief is expelled in that dreadful howl. Then she falls silent. They remain locked together as the wind blows about them and the sea crashes onto the sand, like shipwrecked sailors who have survived a storm.

At last they unlock and Madeline takes Peg's hands. She gazes into her sister's red-rimmed eyes and smiles at her encouragingly. 'If you try to forgive yourself, Peg, I shall try to forgive Mam.'

Peg nods enthusiastically. 'That's a good deal,' she replies.

I know then that the light is love and that it is strong enough to slay the snake. I also know that I have little love in my heart which is not tarnished by jealousy. I realize then that

I *do* have the power to raise my vibration, after all, for the only thing capable of transmuting negativity is love.

'So, you'll come back then?' Peg asks.

'I will,' Madeline answers. 'I'll come back and perhaps feel strong enough to visit Mam's grave then.'

'I hope Ellen comes back, too,' says Peg.

They begin to walk up the beach, towards Peg's home.

'Ellen can do what she likes,' Madeline says evenly. 'Ironic to think that I spent all these years trying to hide Ireland from her, when she only went and found it all on her own.'

'All rivers run into the sea one way or another,' says Peg wisely.

'You're right about that. Perhaps it's destiny for her to wind up here. She will have what I was denied and I will try not to resent her for it.'

'And Dylan will be close to the daughter he wasn't able to watch grow up.'

'That too.'

'I'm sorry she came here and had her heart broken.'

'It will mend,' Madeline replies simply. 'Or at least she will learn to live with her loss and move on as I did.'

'Is she really so determined to talk to her father?'

Madeline looks pained. 'She is. I can't stop her.'

'That's not going to be an easy talk.'

'I've begged her not to. Now the past is going to rear its ugly head and bite me. I suppose I should have known. Everything comes out in the wash eventually.'

'I shall pray for you,' says Peg firmly.

'Thank you. Though I fear prayers will not be enough.'

They reach the house to find Ellen standing in the field with the donkey, gazing at the lighthouse. She joins them at the gate.

'What are you doing out here?' Madeline asks.

'I'm saying goodbye to the donkey,' says Ellen, and her breath rises into the soggy air. Her cheeks are gaunt and pale.

'Come in and have some breakfast,' Peg suggests.

'I will in a minute.'

'I'll make you porridge,' says Peg. 'I don't want you to fade away.'

'I don't care if I do,' Ellen replies sullenly, giving a little shrug. 'He's gone. He's not coming back to get me. It's over.'

'Oh, Ellen,' says Madeline and there is a warmth in her voice which takes her daughter by surprise. 'Come inside, you look freezing.'

'I'll join you in a minute,' Ellen repeats, averting her eyes because they are filling with tears. The two women head for the kitchen door, leaving Ellen in the field with the sheep, the llama and the donkey. It is a long while before she turns around and follows them into the house.

It is not long before Dylan, Johnny, Joe, Ryan, Desmond and Craic drive up to say goodbye. Oswald wanders over from his cottage and they all share one final pot of tea in Peg's warm kitchen. They all look gloomy and sad, but none more so than Dylan. The conversation is awkward. Joe makes a few bad jokes but they laugh just the same. They are all trying to be jolly when inside they feel as heavy as lead.

At last it is time. Madeline's taxi is waiting outside to take them to the airport. She embraces her brothers and Peg, hastily, so as not to crumble with emotion. She is English, after all, and the Irish passion is locked away with the Irish girl beneath the very effective steely veneer she has built around herself like a suit of armour. Then she hugs Dylan. He holds her close but even I can see that he finds the veneer impenetrable. He has seen glimpses of Maddie but he is resigned to the Englishwoman who has taken her place.

When he says goodbye to Ellen it is a different matter. I feel a strange pain in my chest as he takes her young hands in his old ones. I notice that his are trembling. He doesn't find the words, but gives her a CD, pressing it into her palm. She wraps her arms around him and lets out a muffled sob. They remain together and the pain in my chest grows stronger. And then I recognize it, this pain that weakens my jealousy and fills me with guilt. It is compassion.

Chapter 32

Ellen returned to London and to her old life with the weary acquiescence of a buccaneer whose adventure has ended in failure. She had only been away from London for a few weeks and it was still as she had left it; only *she* had changed. She no longer belonged. She felt like an outsider in a city she had previously felt she owned. In spite of breaking off her engagement with William, who didn't seem nearly as unhappy about it as she had feared, Ellen found her mother expected things to return to the way they were. But she hadn't liked the person she was then and she had no intention of slipping back into that skin ever again. Ireland had shifted something in her consciousness and it was irreversible.

After an awkward lunch with William, which had been more like ending a business contract than an engagement, she returned home. But it no longer felt like home. It was as if she had grown out of the room; even the bed felt too small. She lay down and listened to Dylan's CD, while the ache in her soul wracked her with homesickness for her new adopted land. When she heard the lyric to 'Ellen Across the Sea', she was no longer able to control her tears.

She had resolved that she wasn't going to lie any more. As much as her mother had tried to dissuade her, she knew that in order to live honestly she had to tell her father the truth about her birth. At first, her mother didn't believe she'd do it. She truly felt that once Ellen was back at home, life would return to normal and she would forget about Ireland. She called Emily and asked her to rally her friends and take her out, but Ireland was in Ellen's heart and in her tears, which spilled readily at the smallest provocation.

In spite of her efforts, Madeline could do nothing to stop her daughter from finding an opportune moment to be alone with her father in his study.

'Darling one,' he said, lowering *The Times* and smiling at her. 'What can I do for *you*?'

'I need to talk to you, Dad,' she said, closing the door behind her.

'Of course,' he replied, folding the newspaper and placing it on the corner of the club fender.

She sat down in the armchair opposite and laid her hands in her lap. He hadn't asked her how she was since she had split up with William and he hadn't asked her about Ireland, either. He had simply continued as if nothing had happened. As if she had been away with friends for a long weekend. She didn't know how to break it to him that she had dug up her mother's past and discovered that she was another man's child.

'So?' he asked, raising his eyebrows.

'I want to tell you about Ireland,' she began.

'Yes,' he replied, and she thought she detected a shadow of uneasiness pass across his face. 'How did it go?'

'I love it.'

'It is a very beautiful part of the world.'

'Mum never talked about it, so you can imagine how surprised I was to discover I had an aunt and four uncles.'

'I bet they were just as surprised to see you,' he said with a chuckle.

Ellen began to feel sick. 'I really felt at home there, Dad. I really felt I belonged.'

'It's in your genes.'

'Yes, the Irish in my genes is very strong.' She watched him, hoping for some reaction, but he looked at her with the same honest blue eyes and innocent face.

'I met your mother when I was staying at this rather magnificent old castle owned by a chap called Peter Martin.'

'I visited the castle,' Ellen told him. 'It's very romantic.'

'Is it still owned by the Martins?'

'No, they sold it and moved to Australia.'

'Good Lord, that's a long way to go. I often wondered what happened to them. I never saw them again after that summer.' He rubbed his chin thoughtfully. 'Peter's son, Lorcan, and I were friends at Eton and Oxford. He was a top man with a formidable forehand. I'll always remember that.'

'Did you ever meet a man called Dylan Murphy?' Ellen asked. She watched him closely for his reaction, but he shook his head and replied that he didn't think so. Ellen knew then that he couldn't possibly know about her mother's old lover, because her father simply wasn't capable of dissembling.

She stood up, suddenly agitated. 'Dad, I have something terrible to tell you, but I have to get it off my chest and I have to be truthful with you.' She felt a horrid sinking sensation in her stomach. She had now gone too far to turn back.

'Is it something about Ireland?' he asked, and when she looked at him, his blue eyes were strangely darker and deeper than before.

'Yes, it's something about Dylan.'

He nodded slowly, breathing in through dilated nostrils.

Then he rubbed his chin again, staring into space. 'Does this Dylan person have brown eyes?'

Ellen frowned. 'Yes, why do you ask?'

He looked at her steadily. 'What did Dylan tell you?' He was serious now.

Ellen's heart began to race. 'He didn't tell me anything,' she answered quickly. 'I found out on my own.' She was aware that her eyes were welling again with tears. 'Then things began to make more sense.'

'Sit down, Ellen,' he said calmly. She did as she was told and perched on the edge of the armchair.

'Mum begged me not to tell you, but I lost the man I love because I lied about my engagement. I don't want any more lies. I don't want any more secrets. And I can't live without you knowing what I know. Knowing that you *don't* know. And that you might find out, someone might tell you and then I'll have lied again, or withheld ...' She was rambling now, her nervous fingers fidgeting in sweaty palms.

'Ellen, I *know*,' he said gently.

Ellen stared at him in astonishment. 'You know? You know what?'

'I'm not your biological father. That *is* what you're trying to tell me, isn't it?'

The relief was overwhelming. 'How do you know?'

'My darling, do you really think I wouldn't notice that my daughter had brown eyes? Even with my limited knowledge of biology I know that it is impossible for two blue-eyed parents to have a brown-eyed child.'

'Is it? I didn't know.'

'And I spent all that money on your private education!' He smiled kindly. 'I imagine it must have been a terrible shock to find that out.'

'It was.'

'But it doesn't change anything, unless you want it to.'

'Doesn't it?'

'Why should it? The past is done and can't be *un*done. It is what it is. Finding out which sperm fertilized your egg doesn't change the fact that I have been your father for the last thirty-three years. It doesn't change the fact that I love you, Ellen. It doesn't change that at all.'

Ellen had never heard her father talk about love before. It moved her unexpectedly, to the point of making her chest and throat grow tight. He had always been uncomfortable discussing his feelings and Ellen had never probed. Now he was flinging open the emotional door and inviting her to step inside. It was unfamiliar territory for both of them. 'What did you think when I was born?' she asked in a small voice.

'That you were the loveliest little girl and I was very lucky to have you.'

'Really?'

'Of course. I loved your mother. It didn't matter that she was pregnant with another man's child because I wanted her at any cost. She was fleeing Ireland and I was happy to be her knight in shining armour and lower the drawbridge.'

'Didn't you think it odd when she called me Ellen?'

He chuckled at the memory. 'Well, it wasn't my choice, but she was determined. I thought it must be the name of her grandmother or some other relative.'

'It was Dylan's nickname for her. Ellen Olenska.'

'Ah, *The Age of Innocence*.' He acknowledged the information with a nod. 'Well, I suppose you were conceived in an age of innocence of sorts. Things got pretty complicated for her after that.'

'And she never told you?'

'No, she probably thought I wouldn't marry her if she told me the truth. I never discussed it with her because I didn't want to rock the boat. As far as I was aware, it was irrelevant.'

'Did you ever wonder who he was?'

'That didn't matter, either.'

'Mum thinks you don't know. She begged me not to tell you. I imagine she thinks it'll ruin your marriage.'

He smiled. 'Nothing will ruin our marriage, Ellen. Not then and not now. One has to be philosophical.'

'I always felt different, growing up,' she reflected. 'Now I know why.'

'You weren't different, Ellen. You were yourself. You're not simply a product of two people; you're an individual, unique soul, unlike anyone else. You've always been our daughter and a vital part of our family. You fit in irrespective of your differences, because you belong. Nothing can change that except your negative thoughts. If you go around thinking you don't fit in, you will eventually believe that you don't.' He grinned at her fondly. 'And it's your differences which make you compelling, Ellen. They make you special.'

'I never felt special.'

'Then that's our mistake, not yours.'

'I wish we had been able to discuss this before.'

'I don't think it would have been possible before. The timing is just right now. You had to go to Ireland in order to understand your mother's motives. She'd never have told you herself. I'm afraid this was the only way.'

'So, I suppose you're going to have to tell her that you knew all along,' she said, standing up.

'Yes, she might not be too pleased about that.'

'In which case, I'll make sure I'm out when you tell her.'

He stood up, too. 'Darling, you've been very brave.' He

pulled her into his arms and gave her a gentle squeeze. She
rested her head against his solid, reliable chest. 'I'd like you to
stay here at Eaton Court, but if you want to go back to
Ireland, I'll understand. Don't ever feel you're not free to do
exactly as you please.'

'Are you disappointed I'm not going to marry William?' she
asked.

'A little,' he replied and her heart stalled. 'I haven't seen such
a formidable forehand since I played with Lorcan Martin.'

'Oh, really.' She laughed and pulled away.

'No, I'm not disappointed. I'd have been much more
disappointed if you had accepted someone simply because you
thought it was expected of you.'

She looked at him steadily, pleased to see that his eyes were
light blue and full of amusement again. 'Thank you, Daddy,'
she said.

He kissed her forehead. 'You're my daughter, Ellen, and I'm
very proud of you.'

Chapter 33

In spite of her improved relationships with both parents, the following weeks dragged by for Ellen. She missed Ireland and Peg, and she missed Conor until it felt as if her pining had burned a hole through her heart. She knew now that he wasn't going to call her, but she couldn't bear to sever the final tie that made communication with him possible. She kept his telephone in her bag just in case. The constant disappointment of hearing nothing from him served to remind her of her stupidity and pull her deeper into her unhappiness.

Emily was a loyal and constant friend, but even she, after weeks of arranging dinners and cinema nights, lost patience. She suggested taking some of her holiday time early and flying off somewhere hot, but Ellen refused to go anywhere. She wanted to hide beneath the bedspread and never come out. Her mother told her to look for a job. There was nothing more corrosive to one's morale than sitting about doing nothing. 'What you need is a project,' she said briskly. 'At least do *something*. Why don't you come and help me with one of my charities? We're always looking for people to stuff envelopes.'

But her mother was right, she *did* need a project. With a racing heart, she pulled out her laptop and placed it on the desk in her bedroom. *Why don't you put on some music, light a*

*candle, inject a bit of atmosphere into the room, then empty your mind
and see what comes*, were Dylan's wise words. So she lit a candle
and played Dylan's playlist of songs on her iPod. The music was
stirring, her heart expanded with love and longing and her
fingers were a channel for her creativity to flow through her.

> Oh battle-weary lighthouse,
> Still rising from the sea,
> Don't you know it's over and the angels call to thee.
> It's time that you surrendered
> To the greater light,
> Rise up eternal being and put aside your fight . . .

She wrote pages and pages of songs, about Conor, about
Dylan and about the lighthouse, whose symbolism she didn't
quite understand. The words flooded her consciousness from
the still, eternal part of her she had discovered that first morning on the beach in Ballymaldoon, and spilled onto the screen.
Then she went out and bought a guitar and composed music
as Dylan had taught her to do. The songs she produced raised
her spirits and her sorrow found a vent. She now understood
why Dylan had poured his unhappiness into his songs, because
it made him feel better. Ellen's songs made her feel better, too,
and little by little the fog lifted off her future and she was able
to see it more clearly.

She realized that she was never going to be happy as long
as she stayed in London. She wasn't going to be happy without Conor and that was the truth. But she would rather pine
for him in Connemara than here in London, where she felt
isolated and disconnected. At least there she might bump into
him. In any case, she could work for Alanna, write her songs
and play them with Dylan. She'd help Peg with her shopping

and learn to look after all her animals. She would throw herself into her new life with vigour, because Connemara would be her home. The thought of going back filled her with energy and enthusiasm. She leaped off the bed and pulled her suitcase out from under it. For the first time in weeks she felt happy.

Chapter 34

Time moves slowly on. I don't know how many weeks go by but spring is here now. I see it blossoming in the apple trees outside Reedmace House in spite of the dense fog that follows me wherever I go. I imagine the sun is warm and the hills are bright with yellow and purple heather. I remember the troll's bridge and the lake, but I haven't the will to go and visit those places dear to me. I haunt the corridors of the castle with the other ghosts whose unhappiness chains them to this pitiful level of existence. It is not a place I would choose to be, but I feel powerless to raise myself up. My jealousy has robbed me of my freedom. It has taken everything. I am more alone than ever.

And then Conor comes back to Connemara. I am horrified by the state of him. He has not grown a beard or let his hair reach his shoulders like before, but his eyes are full of sorrow and his cheeks are hollow. I experience the same pain in my heart that I felt when Dylan and Ellen parted. My spirit swells with it, and I feel a warmth in me that I haven't felt in a long time. It grows stronger and more intense as I follow him into the castle and up the stairs to his tower.

This tower room was a storeroom when I was alive. Conor didn't need it then. When I died he made it his secret sanctuary. A refuge from the world where he could be completely alone. Now he seeks refuge from his pain, but he cannot drive it out because it is a thorn in his heart and only Ellen can remove it. He lies on his bed and pulls a pillow to his chest. I know he is not thinking about me. He's pining for Ellen, and for the first time since my death I want his happiness more than my own. I want it so badly; I'm willing to do *anything*.

This longing to take away his pain makes me feel strangely uplifted. I cannot extract the thorn and I cannot bring Ellen back, but still, the desire to do so fills me with joy. How odd it is to feel pleasure in this way. I have only ever thought of myself. My love was a selfish love and therefore not love at all, but neediness. I realize now that my whole life was driven by this desperate need – and my death a result of it. Oh, why didn't I know this before? Why now, when my existence has been reduced to this dark and stifling limbo? Did I really have to suffer so much to learn such a simple thing?

I long with every fibre of my soul to lift Conor out of his grief, even if it means losing myself in the process. If I could wave a magic wand and return Ellen to him, I would, even though I'd be forgotten and relegated to the shelf of unwanted memories. What would it matter? Conor doesn't want to remember me. After what I did, I am not surprised. How could I ever have believed that *that* brutal act would force his love? I should have been content with the love he gave me, but I wasn't. I wanted more and more and more and went to terrible lengths to get it. I never felt loved enough. But if I had only shown *him* love I would have felt loved in return, that's the irony of it. If I had only thought of what I could give and not of how much I could be given, I would have been happy. Why didn't I know that when I was alive? Why did I allow my jealousy to destroy my marriage? Why did I allow my jealousy to destroy *him*? I watch this strong and powerful man sob like a child on the bed and I realize it is because of me. I did this to him. I did it in life and I did it again in death. It is time I put it right. It is time I let him go.

But what can I do? There must be something. And as I think of all the things that might bring Ellen and Conor back together again, I notice my spirit growing a little lighter and the fog around me dispersing slightly. I feel more energetic and *alive*. With this new sense of selflessness I leave the castle and will myself to the beach where I seek inspiration from the sea. I could go to London and whisper into Ellen's ear. I could tell her Conor loves her and give her the idea to return to Ballymaldoon. I could find Ciara and ask her what to do. I could seek her help. I am sure I am not as powerless as I previously thought. I am power*ful*, if my actions are motivated by true love. I don't know why I know this. I just do.

It comes as a complete surprise, then, when I see Ellen on the beach with Peg and Mr Badger. They are walking up the sand, chatting, as if Ellen had never left. I wonder then whether I am not alone after all. Whether there is someone watching over me, guiding me from a higher level of existence? If there are lower levels, surely there must be higher ones too, where angels dwell. Levels that I can't see. With this thought I feel myself grow a little lighter, and, as a consequence, a little happier. I watch Ellen and know that there is something I can do to help. I just don't know what it is.

And so I follow her back to the house and I watch them drink tea and talk. I watch Oswald come over in the evening to play cards. I watch Dylan and Ellen strumming the guitar in the sitting room and singing in harmony. I watch Johnny and Joe turn up for breakfast. I watch Ellen working in Alanna's shop and having lunch with Dylan in the pub. I watch life go on, but with the sole purpose of somehow bringing these two distraught lovers together again. I know I can do it. I feel I'm being guided, with senses more alert and open because I am not consumed with thinking about myself any more. I know my opportunity will come and I anticipate it with joy.

I wait: after all, there is nothing else to do, and my waiting gives me pleasure. I notice the beauty of the countryside as the fog evaporates in the light of my love. I enjoy the longer days and the busy nesting of birds. I listen to their song and watch their flight. I notice the flutter of butterflies and the industrious little bees and my heart expands with the magnificence of God's earth.

And then it comes. I am so thrilled I can barely believe it. Ellen is alone one afternoon at the table in Peg's sitting room. Mr Badger is asleep on the rug in front of the fire which Peg has built because it has rained all day and it is damp and cold. Ellen has lit a scented candle and is playing Dylan's list of songs on her iPod. The room is infused with the sweet scent of fig and the stirring sounds of violins. Ellen is transported. Her mind is open and empty, and as fertile as the richest soil. It is easy for me to plant my seeds. She thinks she is going to write a song, but I intend to give her a story.

I drop my words into her mind and she channels them unwittingly onto the page. Her typing is fast and efficient, the flow of inspiration continuous and uninterrupted. It is easy and we are both quivering with exhilaration and surprise, too excited to question why or how.

October 8th 2007

It was not yet dark. A yellow glow smouldered behind the hills where the sun was setting, turning the sky a pale flamingo pink. The lighthouse was a black silhouette as we rowed out in the little boat that knew us both so well. It carried us over the waves with its usual determination, like a brave and loyal servant. I smiled at my lover encouragingly as he rowed. He was strong, with broad shoulders and a wide, muscular chest. He grinned back, his face full of adoration, and I felt my heart swell with pleasure. It was so pleasant to be loved with such abandon.

We had rowed out like this many times before, though I had done it more than he. The lighthouse was my secret place where only I ventured in my little boat, full of dreams. I liked to lie beneath the stars and imagine other worlds out there in the infinite space. I listened to the lapping of waves and the cries of gulls and took pleasure from the danger I was in, knowing the fury I would incite if I was caught. But tonight was different. I was not alone. I was with my lover and I had a plan. This time, if I was caught, it would be infinitely worse. I sensed that tonight something dramatic was going to happen. Tonight I would give him the opportunity to prove his love once and for all.

We reached the island and tied the boat to the rocks. The tide was out and the little pools were shallow and full of shrimps and crabs. It was a still night and the wind was a silken caress. He took my hand and we hurried up the grassy path to the lighthouse. Inside, the wooden stairs were lined with small candles. He lit them one by one and they glowed brightly through the dusk as the sun sank lower and the sky darkened above us. Up the stairs we climbed, through the avenue of little tea lights, until we reached the room at the top, which was round like a nest.

My room was as exquisite as Aladdin's cave. I had hung drapes on the walls in rich purples and greens, and the floor was covered with brightly coloured rugs and velvet cushions.

There was no electricity, for the lighthouse had not been used in years; the only light was given by the rows and rows of candles, in all shapes and sizes, which were placed around the room and filled the air with perfume.

We opened a bottle of wine and drank to our health and our future. We lost ourselves in each other. He whispered that he loved me, that he would die without me, that I was the very air he breathed. I told him I didn't believe him, so he kissed me even harder, trying to prove his devotion. I revelled in his valiant attempts to convince me that I held his heart in my hands. I basked in the warmth of his enthusiasm. 'I love you, I love you, I love you,' he murmured as he tried desperately to possess me body and soul. 'I love you, I love you, I love you,' he groaned. But I did not love him back. I could not, for there was only one man I loved and it was not he.

My lover heard the motor before I did. I was slowly coming down from the heady heights of his flattery, which had fulfilled me more than the physical pleasure of our lovemaking. He sat up in panic and lifted his nose, like a dog that senses danger on the wind.

'Can you hear that?' he asked and I listened. He was right. The sound of a motorboat rose above the sounds of the sea.

I sat up and feigned surprise. 'It's him,' I said, hurrying to my feet and searching for my clothes among the cushions.

'Jaysus! You've got to hide me!' he cried, pulling on his trousers.

'There is nowhere to hide,' I replied, and I watched his face contort with fear.

'What'll he do?'

'Leave it to me.'

'You said he was in Dublin!' he hissed.

'I thought he was,' I replied, buttoning up my dress. 'It might not be him,' I added. But I knew, because I had planned it just like this.

'It *is* him,' he replied and his big eyes gazed at me, full of dread. 'What'll you tell him?'

'That I love him.'

'That's not good enough!' he retorted. 'He won't believe you.' But it was the truth and the only truth. I had done this for him, for us. He would surely realize how much I needed him; that every time he left me I was at the mercy of predatory men who wanted me for themselves. He'd realize that he couldn't leave me. I needed him and I needed his love. If that didn't convince him of my need, nothing would.

'He'll believe me,' I told him. 'Trust me.'

I hurried down the stairs, past the burning candles, careful not to catch the hem of my dress in the flames. Outside, it was dark but for a sliver of moon peeping out of the cloud, which left a thin trail of mercury on the water. My husband was tethering his boat to the rocks. He lifted his eyes to the lighthouse and saw me standing in the doorway. I anticipated his fury and his fear, like a child anticipating the embrace of an anxious parent. He strode over the rocks and up the grassy path towards me. 'What's all this about?' he asked and his eyes weren't full of fury and fear, but of weariness and exasperation. I suddenly noticed how tired he looked and how unhappy.

'I thought you were in Dublin,' I answered.

'Where is he?' he demanded. There was nowhere to hide and my lover stepped out from behind me, sheepish and afraid.

My husband's face grew red with amazement. 'How could you, Caitlin? He's just a boy!'

'I'm a man,' said my lover bravely, pulling his shoulders back, but compared to Conor he was still a slender youth.

'Ronan Byrne. Have you no shame?'

'I love her,' Ronan declared.

'What would your mother say? Hasn't she been through enough already?'

'Don't bring Mam into this.'

'She's a good woman, Ronan. She doesn't deserve to have her heart broken all over again.' Ronan then stumbled, like a horse before a fence he suddenly realizes is too high to jump. 'Go on home,' said Conor wearily. 'I don't want Peg to ever learn about this, do you understand?' There was a warning tone to his voice which made my skin grow cold. 'I'll take Caitlin back in my boat.' Ronan didn't know what to do with himself. I could see him panicking, thinking of me and thinking of his mother. He remained trapped on the rocks like a terrified crab.

My anger boiled over in a volcano of jealousy. 'This is the problem. This is what it's all about. You don't care about me, Conor! You don't mind that I'm sleeping with another man. You don't love me any more. You wish I was dead!'

Conor's mouth twisted in anguish. 'Caitlin, I've had enough of your dramatics. You've pushed me over the edge now and you've only got yourself to blame.'

I began to sob. 'You don't love me,' I wailed.

'*I* love you,' Ronan cut in, emboldened by my tears. 'Come away with me, Caitlin.'

Conor interrupted impatiently. 'Don't be ridiculous, Ronan. Go on home to your mother and forget about it.'

'Caitlin loves me!' he protested fiercely.

'No, she doesn't,' Conor told him calmly. 'You're just a pawn in a bigger game.'

'That's not true. *You* don't love her,' Ronan accused, even more confident now. 'You don't care for her. You're never here. *I'm* here. *I* look after her. *I* give her what you can't.' He turned to me, his eyes burning with the spark of an idea. 'Run away with me, Caitlin. Right now. We don't ever have to come back.'

'I don't love you, Ronan,' I told him. 'I love Conor. I always have.'

But Ronan thought that I was lying to protect him. 'I understand,' he said quietly.

'No, I mean it, Ronan. I'm not just saying it. It's been fun, but I love Conor. I love him with all my heart and I will die loving him.'

Ronan's face crumpled like a little boy's as the sincerity of my words hit him like a punch in the stomach. 'It's not true, Caitlin. I don't believe you. You're just saying that to protect me.'

'I'm not,' I insisted. 'I'm sorry.'

'But we can be happy, far away from here, Caitlin. We can start again. I know we can. Let me show you how happy we can be.'

I smiled at him sadly. 'I'll never leave my home and my children, Ronan. Do as Conor says and go home.' Then I lowered my voice for only Ronan to hear. 'Please, my love, don't be a fool. Leave before he lays a hand on you.' He gave me a long, desperate stare, and then hurried past me, down the path to where we'd tied the boat to the rocks. I hoped he'd be safe, rowing out in the dark. I glanced up at the sky and saw the moon, now big and round like a crystal ball, and realized it would be sufficient to guide him back to shore.

'Come on, Caitlin,' said Conor, reaching for my hand.

'So you think this is a game?' I asked.

'You said yourself that you don't love him. You've been using him to get at me, but I'm unmoved, Caitlin. Unmoved.'

'He's been my lover for months,' I gloated provocatively. 'While you were in Dublin and America, I've been making love to Ronan. What does it matter if I don't love him, Conor? *He* loves *me*. You heard him! He loves me with all his heart.'

'What does it matter?' he repeated, horrified by my callous disregard for Ronan. 'Caitlin, have you lost your mind? He's a boy and you've destroyed him.'

'I wanted you to show me you care.'

'By provoking my jealousy?' He stared at me incredulously. 'You'd go that far to provoke me?'

'You don't understand me. After all these years, you don't know me at all.'

'No,' he said in a quiet voice. 'I don't think I do.'

At that point I could not contain my frustration a moment longer. 'What will it take for you to love me, Conor?' I cried in despair.

'I did love you, Caitlin, but you've drained me dry. I have nothing left to give.' He was shouting at me now, his voice strained with frustration. 'You need help, Caitlin. Professional help, because I don't know what else I can do. You're not in your right mind. I should have realized years ago instead of putting my head under the carpet and ignoring your cries for help. I've been callous. I'm sorry, darling. You don't need me but a good doctor who knows how to make you better.'

'You think I'm mad.'

'No! You're not mad, you're unbalanced. I know I can get help for you.'

'You don't want me any more! You want to claim I'm insane and have me put away.'

'I didn't say that.'

'You want me put away!'

'No.'

'You want me dead!' I whispered, shocked at the realization that he must surely want me out of the way.

'No, Caitlin, I didn't say that.' He reached for me, but I threw myself back. I suddenly felt the world spinning away from me. I felt detached, floating above the island and the lighthouse, miles away from reality. It was as if I knew I was on the brink of losing everything, but unable to stop myself.

'You want me dead!' I repeated and the calmness in my voice frightened me. 'When all I have given you is love.' I turned and fled up the stairs.

I glanced back to see that he was not following me. I wanted him to run after me and pull me into his arms and beg forgiveness. But he didn't. I was alone on the stairs. Alone as I felt I had been all through our marriage. I let out a desperate sob, turned back to the stairs and ran to the top. It wasn't until I reached the balcony which ran all the way around the lighthouse that I realized my dress had caught fire. It was consuming the fabric with such speed I had no time to rip it off. Before I knew what was happening I was burning. Crazed with terror, I had one final thought before I threw myself over the edge: *He'll realize he loves me when it is too late, and he'll regret it for the rest of his life.*

A moment later I was above myself, watching my body land and break on the rocks below. I saw Conor on the balcony, staring down in horror and disbelief. He *had* followed me, after all.

How clear everything is to me now. I had his love but I hadn't recognized it. How foolishly we behave when we know no better. Why does it take so much unhappiness to make us realize there is nothing of any value in our lives but love? That is all there is. It is all we take with us when we die. It is the only thing I will take with me when I move on. It is all that I am. I just never knew it.

Chapter 35

Ellen stopped typing. She stared at the screen in astonishment. The flow of inspiration had ceased to run through her. It had simply switched itself off like a light. She had nothing more to add. Not a word. The room felt strangely cold even though the fire crackled heartily in the grate. She rubbed her hands together. Her fingers were icy. She scrolled back to the beginning of the story and read it again, her heart pounding with excitement. These were definitely not her words. She simply couldn't have written this even if she had wanted to. They weren't her thoughts, either. When the names Ronan, Caitlin and Conor had dropped into the narration, she had been so stunned that she had almost ceased typing, but the story was being dictated with such force, she had had no choice but to keep going. Was it possible that Caitlin had somehow channelled her story through her? If so, why?

Without wasting another minute ruminating on things of which she knew nothing, she printed out the story and left the room. Peg was in the garden with Reilly, who had just come out of hibernation, trying to train him to use the new house Ronan had fashioned for him out of pine. Ellen hurried across the gravel to Oswald's house. He was in his sitting room, busily putting the finishing touches to his portrait of Peg.

'Oswald,' she hissed, falling into the room and closing the door behind her. 'I need you to read something for me urgently.'

Oswald looked at her over his spectacles. 'Ah, you've started, have you?'

'Not really. Just read this and tell me what you think.'

'But you wrote it?'

She handed it to him. 'Technically, yes. But otherwise, no.'

He frowned at her. 'Leprechauns,' he said with a knowing shake of his head. 'Typical.' He pushed his spectacles up his nose and sat down. It took him a short while to read it, but Ellen knew he understood when his hands began to tremble. When he had finished, he dropped the pages onto his lap. 'You do realize you have just been inspired?' He said the word 'inspired' with emphasis. 'And I'm not talking leprechauns.'

'If you mean that Caitlin has spoken through me, yes,' she replied excitedly. 'Is it possible that she's still here?'

'There's only one person who will know whether this account of her death is true,' said Oswald.

Ellen blanched. 'Conor and I don't speak any more, so how can I ask him?'

Oswald took off his glasses and crossed his legs. 'My dear girl, this is a clear message from the other side. Caitlin *wants* you to contact him.'

Ellen's eyes widened. 'Really?'

'But of course. Spirits don't go to all this trouble for nothing.'

'Why would she do that?'

'Because she wants to make it up to Conor, perhaps.' He waved the sheets of paper in the air. 'This is quite possibly the truth of what happened the night she died. I must say it makes sense. Dylan wasn't wrong when he said he saw someone rowing to shore in the middle of the night. Poor Ronan, he got a very rum deal. I think that's something we keep between ourselves, Ellen. Peg has had enough surprises recently.'

'Conor obviously never told anyone that Ronan had been there, not even the police.'

'If people knew that they'd agree that he's a better man than they think he is.'

Ellen flopped into the armchair, feeling suddenly drained. 'No wonder Ronan doesn't like speaking about her. He loved her.'

'And she used him most cruelly.'

'You know, Conor said she was unbalanced. I now know what he meant.'

'I imagine she's gained a bit of perspective where she is now.'

'I'm not psychic, so how did she know to use *me* as a channel?'

'Of course you're psychic. We all are,' Oswald said firmly. 'Most people dismiss it as coincidence or luck when strange things happen, and the more they deny a finer sense the less able they are to perceive with it.'

'If Caitlin can write through me, why doesn't Ciara write something for Peg?'

'That's a very good question. I'm afraid I don't know the answer. She's blown out candles, moved things, rattled things, goodness knows what else she's done which none of us have noticed. You have to remember that spirits are made of lighter vibrations so it's not easy to affect material things on our dense level of vibration. It must be frightfully frustrating if one's trying to let someone know one's still around.' He thought a moment, then added, 'I imagine the person down here has to be open and able to receive. Perhaps Peg, for whatever reason, has closed down that fine sense of hers. After the row with Father Michael, maybe she mistrusted what she had seen after Ciara died, and shut down. You must be very receptive to have received this information from Caitlin.'

'Unhappiness,' said Ellen with a bitter chuckle.

'And longing,' Oswald added kindly. 'You and Caitlin have that in common; a desperate longing for Conor.'

So, with Oswald's gentle persuasion, Ellen decided to pass Caitlin's message on to Conor. She missed him so much it was as if her heart wasn't an organ at all, but an open wound that failed to heal. She thought of him constantly, and in a strange way she derived comfort from all the things in Connemara that reminded her of him: the sea, the beach, the hills. They made her feel better, even though the memories they contained prodded and scratched the wound and occasionally caused it to bleed. Sending him Caitlin's message with a short message of her own would lose her nothing, because she had already lost everything.

She penned a simple note, deliberately keeping it brief: *Dear Conor, I sat down to write a song and this is what happened. I can't explain it, but I didn't write it. I simply took dictation. It's obviously for you. I'm here in Connemara, living with Aunt Peg. I hope you're happy. Ellen.*

She wanted to add how much she missed him and that she could barely live without him, but she restrained herself. There was nothing worse than a needy woman, begging to be taken back. She still had her dignity, if nothing else. She considered dropping the note through his letter box, but there was always a chance he might be at home and the thought of bumping into him filled her with mortification. So she gave it to Oswald, who was only too happy to act as postman. He disappeared in Peg's car, returning a little later to report that

Conor was in Dublin but the housekeeper had assured him she'd make sure he got it. Ellen resolved to think no more about it. He hadn't contacted her in weeks; there was little chance he would contact her now.

Life went back to normal. During the day she worked in the shop; lunches were either sandwiches, or eaten at the Pot of Gold with Dylan and her family. In the evenings, when Peg and Oswald played cards or chess, Ellen returned to the sitting room and wrote sad songs, which she would later sing with Dylan. Their voices blended beautifully, like sunshine and rain, creating a magnificent spectrum of colour.

Then one balmy summer's evening, after they had enjoyed a rare dinner in the garden, Oswald disappeared into his house and returned with the canvas, covered in a dust sheet. 'What have you got there, Oswald?' Peg asked, getting up to clear the plates.

'A present,' he said, smiling proudly.

'You've paid your rent,' she replied, confused.

'This isn't rent, Peg. This is different.' He leant it against the wall of the house. Ellen felt the air still around them as the expression on Oswald's face told Peg that this was no ordinary present. 'This is for *you*,' he said.

Peg's hand shot to her mouth and her eyes glistened. 'Oh,' she replied.

Slowly, he lifted the dust sheet to reveal the portrait. Peg's mouth fell open and she gasped. She gazed at her likeness and her blush deepened. 'But I'm not beautiful,' she said, blinking back tears.

'You are to me,' he replied softly.

'Oh, Oswald ... I never ...'

'Of course you never knew,' he said, smiling at her fondly.

'But you're the most beautiful woman in the world to me.' He walked over and took her hands. Ellen was rooted to the grass like a weed, wishing she was anywhere but here, intruding on their private moment. But they seemed not to notice in the sudden flowering of their affection for one another. 'I love you, Peg.'

'Do you really?' she asked, looking up at him beneath her frown.

'Really and truly, old girl. I have for a very long time.'

'I don't know what to say.'

'Then just say yes and make me the happiest man alive.'

Peg blinked but the tears broke through; she tried to speak but the words got stuck in her throat. So she simply nodded, smiled, then laughed with embarrassment. Oswald pulled her into his arms and squeezed her tightly. Ellen uprooted herself and tiptoed into the house. She went upstairs to her bedroom and retrieved from her bedside table the mobile telephone Conor had given her. A few minutes later she was heading down the path to the sea.

She stood on the sand, gazing across at the lighthouse, benign now in the soft evening light. She thought of Caitlin and her final moments and she thought of Conor, so deceived and unhappy. She watched the light fade and the first star twinkle above the lighthouse like a distant angel guiding the way home. She wondered about death and the purpose of life and knew that Caitlin was right. Love was all that matters. Without it our lives are pointless.

She held the telephone in her hand and remembered the time she had thrown her iPhone into the sea. That moment had changed her life so dramatically that it had now become a symbol of metamorphosis. Well, she needed to move on again, emotionally at least. Conor wasn't coming back. There was no use keeping a telephone that never rang and a hope that was never ignited. She didn't want to waste her life pining as Dylan had. She had to open her heart to the future: after all, her mother had moved on and found happiness with her father. So could she.

Ellen lifted her hand and pulled it back behind her ear. Just as she was about to throw the phone as far out to sea as she possibly could, it rang. She stumbled forward, grabbing it tightly as it was on the point of leaving her fingers. Stunned, she stared at it. The little window was lit up with his name.

'Hello,' she answered. There was a long pause. Even then she felt him down the line, his vibration breaking through the silence, ripping back the months.

'Ellen,' he said finally.

'Yes.' She barely dared breathe.

'I got your letter.'

'Oh, good.' She tried to sound casual. She told herself that this call meant nothing. He was simply calling about Caitlin's story.

'I'm not happy,' he said flatly.

'I'm sorry.' Guilt tugged at her heart like a leaden weight on the string of a helium balloon.

'Are *you* happy?'

She didn't know how to respond. He didn't want her; what did it matter to him if she was happy or not? 'I'm OK,' she replied. 'You know, life goes on.' Her voice trailed off. There was nothing else to add. She could feel her heart thumping against her ribcage, like the words that pounded against her restraint, desperate to break free and reach out to him with love and supplication. She bit her lip, determined not to cry.

'Where are you? It sounds windy.'

'On the beach.'

'What are you doing down there?'

'I like it here. It's a beautiful evening.'

'I read the story, Ellen.' He sounded very serious.

She suddenly wished she hadn't sent it. 'I'm sorry; perhaps I shouldn't have given it to you. It was intrusive and tactless.'

'Can you come to the castle?'

'Sure, when?'

'Now.'

'Now?'

'Unless you want to spend all night on the beach.'

She laughed in spite of herself. 'Well, I was going to go in at some point.'

'I want to show you something. It's important.'

'All right.'

His voice brightened. 'Great, I'll see you in a minute. I'll wait for you at the front.'

Ellen ran up the beach as fast as her trembling legs could carry her, desperately trying not to read too much into his desire to see her. She told herself that he was simply concerned about Caitlin's story. If he wanted her back he would have said so. He would have told her he missed her. He might have even apologized. But he hadn't. He'd simply said that he wasn't happy, but he could easily have been referring to the fact that she'd lied to him.

When she reached Peg's house, her aunt and Oswald were nowhere to be seen, so she wrote a short note telling them that she was going up to the castle to meet Conor, and left it on the kitchen table. The car was on the gravel. It was unlikely that Peg needed it but she didn't think they'd appreciate her shouting about the property to find out. She climbed in and turned the key with a shaking hand. A moment later she was driving up the lane towards Ballymaldoon Castle, her head engaged in a losing battle to control the optimistic swelling of her heart.

She drove beneath the trees whose sturdy branches were now adorned with waxy green leaves and roosting birds. The fields were wild with overgrown grasses, and beyond, the magnificent hills were silhouetted in the twilight. Ellen tried to convince herself that it didn't matter whether Conor loved her or not, because she was happy enough to live in this beautiful, untamed land. She needed nothing more than her family and Connemara, really, nothing at all.

As the castle came into view her pulse began to quicken. She noticed Conor's car and then she noticed him, standing with his hands in his pockets, wearing a blue shirt, jacket and jeans. His hair was longer now and his face darkened with an inch of stubble. He was thinner, too, and slightly hunched. Her nervousness vanished as she was blindsided by a wave of compassion.

She drew up beside his car and climbed out. He wandered over, his lips curling into a hesitant smile. He appraised her, but without his usual arrogance. 'You look great, Ellen,' he said.

'Thanks,' she replied. 'So do you.' Which wasn't entirely true. He'd lost his sheen, but his deep-blue eyes were still as startling as ever.

'So, you've moved here for good?'

'Yes, I'm happier here than in London.' She averted her gaze. The mention of London brought to mind her broken engagement and her lie. 'I feel at home with Aunt Peg.'

'What do you do with yourself?' he asked.

'I work in Alanna's shop. We have a laugh, the two of us. And I've started playing music with Dylan.'

'What happened to the novel?'

She shrugged. 'I'm a better songwriter, I guess.'

'I bet you and Dylan sing well together.' He shuffled from one foot to the other and Ellen thought how strange it was that once they were as close and comfortable as two dogs on a sofa. Now a cold wind whistled through the gulf that separated them. It was as wide as a canyon.

'How are the children?'

'They're just grand. Growing up fast, you know how it is. Ida asks after you.'

Ellen smiled. 'I'll paint her nails any time she wants.'

'Thank you. She'd love that.'

Again a heavy silence as they both struggled to navigate their way through the new formality of their relationship. 'Well, I said I have something to show you. I do. It's inside.'

'Great,' she replied, following him to the door.

She watched him open it and step inside. She remembered the time they had hurried in together and climbed the stairs to his secret haven in the tower. It was different now. They were strangers. Their brief romance was erased as if it had been embarrassing and wrong. Ellen swallowed hard as the realization that it was well and truly over struck her like a slap.

'I need your help to take down this picture,' he said.

'You're taking it down?'

'I want to show you something behind it.'

'Oh.'

'And I *need* to take it down,' he said meaningfully.

'OK.'

He stared at her a little longer than was natural and in that small moment she was sure she saw a glimmer of longing. He turned back to the picture and she was left wondering whether she had in fact seen it, or whether she had simply seen her own longing reflected back at her.

'Right, you take the left and I'll take the right and when I say lift, push it up, all right? Got it?'

Ellen put her hands on the frame and waited for his command. 'Got it,' she replied.

'Careful now, I don't want you hurting yourself.'

'I'm fine. It looks much heavier than it is.'

'Right, lift. That's grand, a little more. Done. Now gently bring it down. We'll lay it against the wall just here.'

They put the painting down and Ellen had a good look at it. Close up, it didn't appear so spooky. She wondered whether she had imagined Caitlin as a real person within it, or whether she really *had* possessed it. Now, leaning against the wall, it was just a painting. She glanced at the wall. There, built into the brick and plaster, was a safe. Conor was standing on a chair, unlocking it.

'Why did you leave the painting on the wall?' she asked, forgetting her awkwardness.

He opened the metal door and reached inside to withdraw a pile of books. He jumped down. 'I didn't know where else to put these,' he told her, showing her one of the fat, hard-backed exercise books.

'What is it?'

'One for every year of our marriage.'

'Diaries?'

'*Caitlin's* diaries.'

'Gosh, did she really write so many?'

'She wrote every single day of her life.'

'Have you read them all?'

He shook his head, horrified at the thought. 'Jaysus, no. Just a bit here and there. She sure rambles on.'

'So, you kept them here with her portrait? Why didn't you store them away somewhere else?'

'I don't know. I just couldn't. I felt so guilty. I'd driven her to her death. I couldn't pack her things away as if she meant nothing. I thought she deserved better. She was the mother of my children and I loved her once.' His face contorted with anguish. 'And then I got your letter. Come.' He went and sat down on the staircase. Ellen followed and sat beside him, so fascinated by the final episode in Caitlin's life that she didn't realize that slowly the wind was warming in the canyon between them. He opened the book to the last page.

'Read this. October 7th 2007.' Ellen leaned over and studied the entry. As she read the words her heart accelerated with excitement. It was written in exactly the same style as the account of Caitlin's death at the lighthouse. Her sentences were long and poetic, her imagery dreamy. She ended the entry with the words: *Tomorrow will decide everything. Tomorrow I shall test Conor's love. Tomorrow I shall know whether he cares. I hope to God that he does.*

When she finished reading it, Conor pulled from the inside pocket of his jacket the account that Ellen had typed. He held it against the back cover of the diary to compare. 'You see how it follows on?'

'I do. It's extraordinary.'

'She's still here, Ellen,' he said quietly.

'Why?'

'Because she wants me to know that she's OK. I think she wants me to know that she forgives me. I know it may sound strange, but I'm sure I've felt her many times over the last five years, especially in the children's bedroom. I don't know, perhaps I'm imagining things. But I promise you, there have been times I've woken in the night convinced that she's beside me, whispering in my ear.'

'Oswald thinks she's trying to give you a message.'

He looked at her intensely, eyes wide with honesty. 'Ellen, she wants me to move on now. Why else would she give you the story of her death to pass to me? I already know it. I was there. I think she did it . . .' He hesitated, bashful a moment, as if mistrusting his analysis. Then he dropped his eyes to the page. '*He'll realize he loves me when it is too late, and he'll regret it for the rest of his life.*' He looked at her again. 'I don't want to realize that I love you when it's too late, Ellen, and regret it for the rest of my life. If Caitlin taught me anything, she taught me that. I think she channelled her story through you because she wants us to be together.'

They stared at each other across the gulf. 'I missed you, Conor,' she whispered, her brown eyes glistening with tears. He needed no further encouragement. Taking her face in his hands, he pressed his lips to hers, bridging the canyon with a strong but tender kiss.

Chapter 36

'I've brought some great movies down from Dublin,' Conor says, pulling away and sinking happily into her adoring gaze. 'Fancy coming home to watch them?'

She smiles. 'I'd like that very much,' she replies, taking his hand and pressing it to her damp cheek.

'Do you want to call your aunt to let her know?'

'Oh, I think she's much too busy to worry about me,' she says with a knowing grin. 'After all, I'm not a child. I can do what I please.'

'Does that mean I'll wake up with you in the morning?' His smile is wide and mischievous, just like it used to be at the height of their romance.

'I think it does,' she answers.

'Then let's not waste another minute.' He gets up and pulls her to her feet.

'What do you want to do with the painting?'

'I'll hang it somewhere else so the children always remember their mother. But in its place I'll hang a new one. I think you'd look grand on canvas.'

She laughs off the idea as absurd. 'No, I think you should commission someone to paint the children. That way, you're honouring Caitlin. I couldn't replace her and I wouldn't want to.'

'All right, if you insist. But if I move back in, you'll come with me, right?' She inhales, trying to keep up with the sudden change of direction. 'You can plant your garden and watch things grow and you can play music with Dylan. You can choose your own study to write your lyrics in.'

'Are you suggesting we move in together?'

'I'm suggesting we spend the rest of our lives together.' He kisses her temple and leaves his face pressed against her hair. 'One thing I know for sure, the future is nothing without you, Ellen. I don't want to be without you ever again. Will you forgive me?'

'If you forgive me.'

He looks at her affectionately, drinking in her beauty and her sweetness like a man parched of love. 'There is nothing to forgive.'

And I am happy. I am filled with an effervescence I have never experienced before. It is light and bubbly as if made solely of joy. It lifts me up so that I am dizzy with this new sensation. Conor is happy and I have taken pleasure in his happiness, regardless of how it will affect me. How wonderful it is to be selfless, how blissful it is to bask in the elation of others. It has transformed me from a dark and miserable creature to a bright and buoyant soul. I wish I had known during my life what I know now. But I realize at this moment that our earthly sojourn is a learning experience and that we are always evolving, always moving towards a greater love. My life taught me much, and wherever I go now, I will take that knowledge with me in the form of a clearer, more loving vibration. I'm not sure how I know, I just do.

And as I rise above the lighthouse, I see that it is no more. The waves have swept in and washed it away. The ruins lie like bones on the seabed and I am free at last to move on. The light around me grows brighter and I see a wondrous sight. I gaze in amazement at the fine angelic beings who have always been with me, guiding me as they have done from the very beginning, with persistence and patience and love. I wasn't alone after all, I just didn't know it.

Out of the light, I recognize Ciara. She comes and takes my hand. 'You'll always be with them,' she says with the wisdom of a very old soul. 'But it's time now for you to come home.'

'I'm ready,' I reply, and I know for certain that I am. 'What's it like?' I ask.

She laughs and leads me towards a greater light. 'The same as when you left it.'

Chapter 37

'So, what do you think?' Daphne asked, standing back to admire the Darragh Kelly portrait of the children, which Joe and Johnny had just hung above the fireplace in the hall.

'It's grand,' said Conor, putting his arm around Ellen. 'It's a very good likeness, isn't it?'

'He's captured Ida's dreaminess beautifully,' Ellen replied.

'What does Magnum think?' Ida asked.

'He's wagging his tail so he must like it,' Finbar replied. Magnum was lying in front of the fire, weary after a long walk over the hills.

'It's a beautiful painting,' said Johnny, putting his hands on his hips. 'He's a fine painter, is Mr Kelly.'

Daphne smiled in agreement. 'Oh, he's very gifted. I'd love to paint like that, but I'm not good at people. I'm quite good at sketching dogs, though.'

'I know some birds who look like dogs: you could paint one of them if you like?' Joe quipped.

'Why don't you find yourself a nice bird?' Conor retorted. 'Preferably one who doesn't look like a dog!'

Joe shook his head and grinned raffishly. 'While there are flocks in the sky, why settle for one?'

'You will in the end, Joe,' said his father wisely. 'Everyone does in the end.'

'Have you hung the picture of Caitlin in the children's sitting room?' Ellen asked.

'Not yet,' Johnny replied. 'Come on, Joe. Let's finish up here. I'm ready for my tea. You going to come for a pint?' he asked Conor and Ellen.

'Not tonight. We've got a film to watch,' Conor replied, and smiled at Ellen. She frowned up at him quizzically.

'All right, fair play to you,' said Johnny.

'Can you give Dylan a message for me?' Ellen asked. 'Tell him I've written a happy song for a change.'

'Will you sing it for us in the pub?' Joe asked. 'I'm a bit bored of the old Irish ballads.'

'We might be persuaded,' said Ellen. 'As long as you don't make fun of us.'

'Now, why would I go and do a silly thing like that?'

'Because you're an eejit, Joe,' interjected his father, playfully. 'Come on, now. Let's finish up and go to the pub.' The two of them wandered off down the corridor.

'So, what's our movie?' Ellen asked when Daphne and the children had gone upstairs.

'*The Age of Innocence*. I promised you we'd watch it together but we never did.'

'With everything that's gone on, I totally forgot about it.'

'Well, tonight is our night.'

She grinned and added huskily, 'Every night is our night, Conor.'

He laughed. 'You know how to make a man feel good.'

'It feels good to be *here*,' she said seriously. 'I feel we both belong here now. Well, I feel *I* belong. Of course *you* always belonged.'

'No, with Caitlin, it never felt like home. It feels like home now.' He pulled her into his arms. 'You've made me a very happy man. I was a fool to . . .'

She placed a finger on his lips to silence him. 'No, don't say that. Let's not relive the past. The present is what's important, and the years ahead.'

He kissed her temple, then her cheekbone, tracing his nose down her cheek until his lips found hers. 'I love you more than yesterday,' he whispered.

'And I love you less than tomorrow,' she replied, closing her eyes and wrapping her arms tightly around him.

A little later, Ellen sat on Finbar's bed and read the children a story. It was called 'Stone Soup', about three Chinese monks who teach hostile neighbours in a mountain village a lesson in sharing through the simple task of making soup with a stone. She had brought it especially for the children and every time she read it, she thought of the Trawtons and the Byrnes and how they might come together one day over good food and wine.

'Ellen, do you think Mam is looking down on us from heaven?' Ida asked, as Ellen tucked her up in bed.

Ellen gazed into the child's enquiring eyes and smiled softly. 'Darling, I *know* she is.'

'How do you know?'

'I don't know, I just do.' She put a hand on her heart. 'Sometimes we feel things *here* which we can't explain. We just *know* things but we don't know how we know them. I'm certain that she is with you all the time, Ida. With you and Finbar and Daddy, too. I think we take our love with us when we die.'

Ida smiled, satisfied. 'Night, Ellen.'

Ellen kissed her forehead. 'Night, Ida.'

Just as she was leaving, Finbar called for her. She turned. 'What do you think she'd think of you living here with us?' he asked. It was a bold question and one that Ellen had been expecting for some time.

'I think she's happy that I'm looking after you, and wherever she is, she's looking after you too, only you can't see her.'

'Do you think she likes you?'

'I hope so. What do *you* think she thinks of me?' He didn't reply, but lay in bed thinking deeply.

'I think she likes you,' said Ida without hesitation.

Finbar remained silent beneath the covers. He was considering her question very carefully, trying to remember his mother. Then he rolled over and pulled his fluffy toy rabbit into his arms. 'I think she thinks you're all right,' he added and closed his eyes.

Ellen laughed. 'All right is good enough for me. Good night, Finbar. Night-night, Ida.'

The following afternoon, while Conor was on a conference call with Los Angeles, Ellen took Magnum for a walk. It was bitterly cold. The wind was laced with ice and snow lay thick and hard on the ground. Ellen loved the romance of the snow and the way it twinkled in the sunshine, although today the sun was snug beneath a duvet of cloud. She gazed about her at the bleak landscape and the grey sea and found a haunting beauty in its desolation.

She climbed the hills, warming up beneath her sheepskin coat, watching her breath mist on the frosty air. Magnum loped on ahead, following a trail of scent in the snow. Soon she reached the little chapel where Caitlin was buried. The church looked lost and lonely on the hill, as if it was staring out to sea, hopelessly searching the horizon for someone who was never coming home.

As she opened the wooden gate she saw to her left a grey figure hunched over Caitlin's grave. She looked closer and saw that he was replacing the dead rose with a fresh one.

'Ronan?' she called out. The man turned. To her surprise it wasn't Ronan beneath the brown hat, but Johnny. 'Johnny, what are *you* doing here?'

He stood up stiffly. 'I loved her, Ellen.' He shrugged and thrust his hands into his pockets.

'You too?'

He frowned. 'Oh, Ronan didn't love her. She broke him in two. He can barely hear her name mentioned without grimacing.'

'You know about Ronan and Caitlin?'

'Of course I do. I saw it all going on and I knew right from the start that it was going to end badly. Though I couldn't have predicted that it would end like it did.'

'You knew Ronan was on the island that night?' He nodded. 'How?'

'Dylan saw him rowing back to shore, but I found him sobbing on the road on my way home from Peg's. He told me everything. Poor lad, he was in a terrible state.'

'And you still love her?'

He looked at her steadily. 'I love her in spite of her faults, Ellen. She wasn't in her right mind. She was fragile and lost.' He turned his eyes to the sea. 'But now she's gone and the lighthouse is gone. Nothing left of either of them.'

'Does anyone else know about Ronan besides you and Dylan?'

'No, and I have no intention of telling anyone.' He glanced at her warily. 'And this will remain between us, all right?'

'Of course.'

'I just loved her from afar, Ellen.' He dropped his eyes to the grave. 'I know she's not in there. She's in heaven with the Lord, but I like to remember her.' He grinned sadly. 'I'm a ridiculous old romantic. That's all there is to it.'

'You're not ridiculous, Johnny. I think it's a lovely thing that you come here and remember her. I think this little place has got great charm. I mean, Dylan used to come here to compose love songs and I came here when Conor and I broke up; it made me feel better. Of course, the chapel was built by a sailor for his dead wife. It was built on love and it seems to have nurtured love in one way or another ever since.'

'You have a writer's imagination,' Johnny chuckled, scratching his beard.

'But it's true. The more I learn of life the more I realize that love is the only important thing in it.'

Johnny linked his arm through hers and they set off down the hill, followed by Magnum. 'You and Conor are right for each other,' he said. 'Like they say, the pot has rolled over and found its lid.'

'I'm very happy,' Ellen replied.

'He's a good man. Though if he gives you any trouble you know who to call.'

'I most certainly do.'

'You're not an island, Ellen. You're a Byrne.'

She laughed. 'And a Murphy.'

Johnny nodded. 'You can't do better than that combination. Fancy a quick drink to warm up?'

'Sure. I can see the alluring glow of the Pot of Gold from here. It's whispering to me.' She laughed and leaned into him affectionately.

'You see, you *are* all Byrne and Murphy.' He frowned a

moment then grinned at her broadly. 'No one appreciates that more than Dylan.'

'*Dear* Dylan,' she said fondly. 'Do you think he'll ever make an honest woman of Martha?'

'Dylan will never settle down. Not now. He's been too many years on his own.'

'Doesn't Martha long to get married?'

'I'd say she's past caring about marriage. She knows her man. She knows there's no taming him and I bet she's content with that.' He sniffed in the cold air. 'I wouldn't want to live with Dylan if I was a woman. It's living apart that keeps them together.'

'I think you're probably right.'

'Shall we go and find him?'

'I don't think we have to look too far, do you?' They both laughed.

'Not at this time of day,' said Johnny.

Magnum squeezed into the well of the passenger seat of Johnny's truck and the three of them made their way slowly around the icy lanes into town. The sun was setting behind the hills, saturating the snowy landscape with a soft pink hue. A spray of small birds took to the skies, silhouetted against the diminishing light like bullets, and to the left the capricious sea stretched out to the horizon. Beneath the waves, the lighthouse lay in eternal sleep. Silent, still and at peace.

They parked the car and wandered around to the Pot of Gold. Magnum followed dutifully behind. 'I'll call Conor and tell him to come and join us,' said Ellen, as Johnny opened the door. Yellow light spilled onto the pavement and the animated sound of voices wafted out into the damp air. Dylan's face lit up when he saw Ellen. He waved at her and she weaved through the crowd to join him. Tables were full of Byrnes, and in the far corner, Oswald and Peg were sitting with Ronan and an attractive young woman Ellen had never seen before. 'What'll you have?' Dylan asked. 'Your usual?'

'My usual,' she replied with a satisfied smile. The word 'usual' had a cosy ring to it; the same ring as 'belonging' and 'home'.

Epilogue

The morning of the wedding could not have been more beautiful. Spring breathed her warm breath onto the yellow and purple flowers that opened to attract the butterflies and bees playing about the heather. The sun shone warmly from a cloudless sky and greedy gulls circled the long tables piled high with the wedding feast in the castle gardens. A white-and-yellow tent had been put up on the front lawn, which Johnny and Joe had mown as immaculately as a cricket pitch, and the drive was an avenue of red tulips, yellow daffodils and sweet-smelling daphne odora. At the end, where the burr oaks gave way to the castle, the once forbidding stone walls looked radiant and welcoming in the cheerful morning light. The windows had been thrown wide open and pigeons cooed from the turrets as they watched the busy goings-on below. The shadow of sorrow had long gone, dispelled by the brilliance of love that now shone into every corner.

Ellen ran excitedly from the kitchens to the hall to the gardens in her curlers and dressing gown, checking that everything was as it should be on this very important day. The caterers were busy in the kitchen, cooking for the two hundred guests, and the florist, who had flown over from Dublin especially, had finished adorning the tent and was now decorating the donkey with yellow roses. Ronan had fashioned a little cart out of oak for the children to sit in, but whether the donkey would ever pull it was a question not even Peg was able to answer. It would all depend upon his mood on the day. He stood dozily, munching on the carrot the florist had given him, swishing his tail every now and then to brush away the odd fly. Ellen sighed with pleasure at the sight of such splendour and her eyes grew moist with happiness. To think that only a year ago she had believed she had lost Conor and Connemara for ever. She inhaled deeply, and silently thanked the God who had brought her this far and allowed her this much contentment. Dare she believe that He had given with *both* hands this time? She looked at her watch. It wouldn't be long before the guests started arriving and she had to be ready. Hastily she hurried back up the stairs, jumping two at a time.

Her bedroom was quiet and smelt of the bouquet of white roses and freesias Conor had given her at breakfast. She pulled a rose to her nose and savoured the sweet, powdery smell. She could hear Finbar and Ida down the corridor with Daphne. Their peals of laughter filled the castle with joy. She paused a moment and listened, her gaze lost in the half-distance, her hand resting gently on her belly.

Her dreaming was interrupted by the first cars motoring slowly through the tunnel of ancient oak trees and parking in the field in front of the castle. She peered out of the window from behind a curtain and watched as the wedding guests made their way across the garden to the tent. She turned to find Ida in the doorway, staring at her with wide eyes. 'Where's your dress?' the little girl asked.

'Do you want to help me put it on?' Ellen suggested, and the child's face lit up. 'You look beautiful, Ida. Daddy is going to be so proud of you when he sees you!' Ida squirmed with pleasure and looked down at the sparkly pink shoes Ellen had chosen for her in Dublin. 'Right, I'd better hurry up, hadn't I? I mustn't keep you and Finbar waiting. Will you help me take my curlers out?'

Conor greeted the guests enthusiastically, and Joe and three of his cousins acted as ushers, showing people to their chairs. It wasn't long before the tent was full to capacity with people clothed in their best Sunday suits and dresses. Small bouquets of yellow roses were arranged at the end of every row of chairs and larger arrangements spilled over vases to the left and right of the altar like elaborate waterfalls, saturating the air with the sweet scent of spring. The Byrnes took up the first eight rows on the right of the aisle. Peg's elder boys, Declan and Dermot, had come with their wives and children, and the sound of their chattering rose above the low murmur of anticipation. The English all sat together on the other side, conspicuous in their beautifully tailored morning coats.

Anthony and Madeline Trawton sat with Leonora, Lavinia and their aristocratic husbands. Leonora and Lavinia looked as out of place in their designer dresses and Philip Treacy fascinators as they felt. They were used to the formality of churches and found this rustic improvisation at once quaint and disconcerting. As they gazed about them, they discovered, to their added distress, not a single recognizable face. In London they knew everybody – and those they didn't know, weren't worth knowing. Their husbands whispered to each other behind their service sheets, loftily observing the provincial-looking locals who eyed them suspiciously and a little enviously, for they had an air of privilege about which *they* could only dream.

At last, the groom took his place at the end of the aisle in his perfectly pressed morning coat and shiny black shoes. He

chatted nervously to the priest who had come from a neigh-
bouring parish to wed them, occasionally glancing at his
pocket watch to check the time and looking back expectantly
for his bride.

A moment later, Ellen walked down the aisle with Finbar, Ida
and Conor. Ellen wore a pale-blue dress embroidered with little
yellow flowers and Ida's nails sparkled with pink glitter to match
her pink satin dress. Finbar held his father's hand and Conor
smiled down at him proudly, for he looked so handsome in his
long trousers and jacket. They grinned encouragingly at Oswald
and took their places in the front row. Oswald's heart began to
accelerate. He could sense his bride was about to appear and
fixed his eyes on the opening of the tent.

Suddenly it opened wide and Peg appeared with Ronan.
The congregation rose to its feet and turned to get its first
glimpse of the bride. She stood a little self-consciously in a
simple ivory dress that Ellen had helped her choose in Dublin.
It was adorned with mother-of-pearl beads and each one now
shone in the soft light of the tent. She took a deep breath,
overwhelmed by the sight of so many people and such beautiful flowers, and threaded her arm through her son's, looking
up at him for reassurance. He bent down and whispered
something in her ear, which made her cheeks flush with pleasure. Then she lifted her eyes and saw Oswald waiting for her
at the end of the avenue of yellow roses, his admiration so
clearly displayed in his wide and loving smile. She smiled back
hesitantly before taking the first step towards him and their
future.

As Peg and Ronan walked slowly down the aisle, Dylan
played a classical piano piece that Oswald had requested
especially for Peg. The tent fell silent as they listened with
admiration to Dylan's accomplished rendition and watched the

bride make her way towards the groom. Ronan gave his mother a kiss before handing her over to Oswald.

'Hello, old girl,' he whispered affectionately, and Peg beamed up at him, proud to be *his* girl and not at all worried about being old.

The service was unconventional. Peg hadn't wanted a religious service but she had very much wanted God to be present. They sang hymns, said prayers, Dermot and Desmond each gave a short reading and the priest gave an inspiring sermon. Finally, at the end of the service, Ronan stood in front of the congregation and unfolded a piece of paper with trembling hands. He turned to his mother and was about to speak, but seeing her there with Oswald, looking so happy, caused the words to catch in his throat. He swallowed hard and blinked back his emotion.

'I would like to read a blessing, one that you all know well, but to be honest it never really meant much to me until now.' He paused and took a deep breath to calm his nerves. Then he looked steadily at his mother and his eyes sought encouragement in hers. 'I know Ciara is with us. I know you know that too, Mam. She's with us every day, but never more so than today. It is love that binds us together and because of that, I know she will always be with us.' Peg wiped a tear from her cheek and held Oswald's hand tightly as Ronan read the famous Irish blessing:

> May the road rise to meet you,
> May the wind be always at your back.
> May the sun shine warm upon your face,
> The rains fall soft upon your fields.
> And until we meet again,
> May God hold you in the palm of his hand.

May God be with you and bless you;
May you see your children's children.
May you be poor in misfortune,
Rich in blessings,
May you know nothing but happiness
From this day forward.

May the road rise to meet you
May the wind be always at your back
May the warm rays of sun fall upon your home
And may the hand of a friend always be near.

May green be the grass you walk on,
May blue be the skies above you,
May pure be the joys that surround you,
May true be the hearts that love you.

Ronan's voice thinned on the last line but he managed the final words. As he returned to his seat, Dylan's piano-playing rose in a stirring crescendo.

Oswald took his wife's hand and pressed it to his lips. 'Did I tell you how beautiful you are?' he asked.

Peg's eyes sparkled with happiness. 'Oh, you old rogue,' she laughed. 'I'm too old for that sort of compliment.' But Oswald could see her face light up as she smiled through her tears. They turned to the congregation who, quite unexpectedly and with great vigour, erupted into loud applause. With a spring in their step and laughter in their faces, they walked back down the aisle, grinning broadly at friends and relations as they passed.

The congregation spilled out onto the lawn. The small children ran off to pat the donkey and ride in his little cart, supervised by their mothers. To their excitement, the donkey walked diligently around the lawn, following the carrots Ronan had placed on the grass to tempt him. The adults made for the food and wine. Ellen observed the English and the Irish with interest. At first, they remained in two separate parties: those in morning coats and those in suits, and neither dared penetrate the other. But then, as they drank champagne and ate from the sumptuous banquet laid out on the lawn, they slowly began to mingle. She was reminded of the story 'Stone Soup', which she read to the children at bedtime. Sharing brought them together. In this case it was the wedding feast and their mutual affection for Peg and Oswald.

Her gaze was drawn to Conor and Ronan, who were deep in conversation a little distance from the rest of the party, in the shade of a cedar tree. She took a gulp of elderflower cordial and watched them anxiously. Surely, on this special day, they could both find it in their hearts to forgive.

'What are you looking so anxious about, Ellen Olenska?' It was Dylan.

'Over there. Ronan and Conor.'

'We don't need to wonder what they're talking about.'

'Does it look friendly to you?' she asked anxiously.

'Not at the moment. They look like a pair of dogs standing their ground.'

'Surely, today of all days, they have to call a truce. Ronan can't still believe that Conor killed his wife!'

'Of course he doesn't and he never did. He was just so jealous that he had to think of a reason to hate him. In his heart he knows the truth.'

'That Caitlin never loved him?'

'Aye, a mighty hard truth to swallow. Come, leave them to it. They'll work it out eventually.'

'I do hope so.'

'Oswald has asked us to sing,' he told her.

She looked at him in panic. 'You and me?'

'Me and you.' He grinned mischievously. 'It's about time we sang to a live audience, don't you think? And we aren't half bad.' He put his arm around her waist and led her towards the tent.

Just as she was about to step inside, she glanced back to see Conor reach out and embrace Ronan, like a father embracing a son.

Inside, the tent was warm with body heat and fragrant from the flowers and perfume. The chairs had been placed around the edge and the middle was now left open for dancing. Oswald and Peg held court like a king and queen, surrounded by a crowd of happy courtiers. When they saw Ellen and Dylan, they called them over.

'Play us one of your songs,' said Oswald. 'We'd like to see what you've been doing these past months.'

'Do you have any happy ones?' Peg asked hopefully.

Dylan whispered to Ellen then sat at the piano and placed his fingers over the keys. 'Ready, Ellen?' he asked. She nodded, feeling her heart accelerate beneath the bodice of her dress. She silently prayed that she wouldn't let him down. The music started and Ellen took a deep breath. All eyes were upon her as she stood at the piano beside Dylan, and she was thankful that they couldn't see her legs trembling or the palms of her hands beginning to sweat with nerves. Dylan grinned up at her reassuringly and their voices broke into harmony, filling the air with its rich and magical tone. Peg looked astounded and Oswald bent down to whisper something, to which she nodded vigorously in response. Ellen began to enjoy herself. It wasn't so embarrassing once she got going. Her eyes swam over the heads of the crowd and settled on her mother. She noticed at once that she was holding her father's hand. She noticed, too, the proud and wistful look that made her eyes shine.

Drawn into the tent by the sound of music came Conor and Ronan and a few other guests who had remained on the lawn. A moment later the clapping began and then Oswald pulled Peg into the centre of the room and began to swing her around in a merry dance. She laughed and blushed and kicked her legs as the clapping grew louder. Dylan then played a song they all knew and everyone joined in. Conor grabbed Ellen's hand and led her into the throng of dancers. Even Leonora and Lavinia were being whirled about by their husbands, who had taken off their morning coats and now danced with their shirt tails hanging out of their trousers. Music united them all and no one enjoyed the dancing more than Oswald and Peg.

Conor pulled Ellen into his arms. 'You've given Peg a beautiful wedding,' he said, pressing his bristly cheek to hers.

'I couldn't have done it without you,' she replied.

She felt his skin grow hot against hers. 'How would you like a day like this for us?'

She lifted her chin and looked at him steadily. 'Are you asking me to marry you, Mr Macausland?'

'Yes, I am. I'm a traditional man at heart.'

A small smile crept across her face. 'Well, I think it would be *appropriate* if we did.'

The meaningful way in which she said 'appropriate' made him frown. 'What do you mean, Ellen?'

'Well, considering . . .' She grinned smugly and her eyes twinkled with maternal pride.

He stopped moving to the music and stared at her. 'You're not saying . . .?'

'I *am* saying.'

'Jaysus, are you really?' His smile widened with excitement. 'I hope you're not messing with me, Ellen Trawton.'

'I'm not messing with you, darling. You're going to be a father again.'

'Jaysus, Mary and holy St Joseph.' He laughed, wrapping his arms around her. 'Then we'd better do the right thing before your grandmother turns again in her grave.'

'She's turned so many times she must be quite dizzy by now!' Ellen smiled.

'When can we announce it?'

'Not yet. Not today. This is Aunt Peg's day.'

'Tomorrow, then?'

'Tomorrow.'

He pressed his lips to her temple. 'To think we have every tomorrow until the end of our days.'

'And if Caitlin has taught us anything, Conor, we have all the tomorrows afterwards as well.'

Acknowledgements

I really loved writing this book. The moment I set off on my fantasy to the west coast of Ireland, I was captivated by those wild and rugged hills, the ruined stone farmhouses inhabited only by the wind and sheep, and the cast of wonderful characters I met along the way. I fell in love with Ballymaldoon, and the hours spent in my imagination were immensely pleasurable. It didn't feel like work. But I did need help along the way, because I didn't want my characters to sound like they came from Chelsea! For that, I am indebted to my Irish friend, Jane Yarrow, who fell about laughing at some of things I made my characters say! Ah, we had *da craic*, all right! She is a great mimic and it wasn't long before the voices of Dylan, Conor and Peg were loud and clear in my head. They sprung to life and I'm certain that, when I next travel to Connemara, I will find them.

I'm fortunate that my agent, Sheila Crowley, is Irish. She has been a very good adviser, and one or two of the ideas she tossed my way have had a much greater impact on the book than she could ever have imagined. I'm enormously grateful to her for her expertise as an agent, but also for her inspiration and her friendship. I feel positive about the future and am very aware that I wouldn't be in such a fortunate position now if it wasn't for her. I'd also like to thank Katie McGowan and Rebecca Ritchie at Curtis Brown.

Simon & Schuster have thrust me onto the bestsellers list and I'm beyond grateful for that. They are a formidable team. Dynamic, enthusiastic, full of energy and ideas, but most importantly they understand my novels and how best to present them. The covers are stunning. They are beautiful windows through which my reader can leap into my imaginary world. All writers want their covers to accurately represent the book but it's amazing how many don't. Thank you Team S&S for *getting* me.

Therefore, it is with a rush of gratitude that I thank Suzanne Baboneau, my chief editor, Kerr MacRae, my Svengali, Clare Hey, who meticulously edited the book, line by line, and the fantastic band of hard-working professionals who lend their expertise to help produce and sell my books. They all do an incredible job. Thank you, James Horobin, Dawn Burnett, Maxine Hitchcock and Hannah Corbett.

On the other side of the Atlantic, Simon & Schuster US are an equally impressive team, bestriding a massive territory. When I go to New York, my editor Trish Todd is the only person capable of enticing me out of Saks! I look forward to our lunches with great enthusiasm and wish only that the Atlantic wasn't quite so big. She is a tremendous support and I feel very lucky to be in her care. I also thank my publisher Jonathan Karp, Kate Gales, Alicia Samuels, Andrea DeWerd and Molly Lindley.

As always, I would like to thank my mother for her editing. She gets the manuscript first and improves it enormously with her ruthless eye for ill-chosen words and bad grammar. But more than that, she is a great analyst of people and their relationships, and I think a little of that talent has rubbed off on me.

This novel has a strong spiritual angle, which is very much part of me and my experience. I thank my father for igniting my interest all those years ago and for keeping that flame alive during our long walks through the countryside and on the many chairlifts of Klosters. The last fifteen years have been a fascinating spiritual journey for me, thanks to my dear friend and sage, Susan Dabbs; but Daddy was my very first guru.

I thank my children, Lily and Sasha, for the gift of love, and my husband, Sebag, for his encouragement, ideas and advice. He is my champion and an inexhaustible source of joy. Because of him, I believe I'm the best I can be.

The Beekeeper's Daughter

Read on . . .
For an exclusive sneak peek of the
stunning new novel from Santa Montefiore,
out in hardback and ebook July 2014

Hardback ISBN: 978-1-47110-099-4
Ebook ISBN: 978-1-47110-102-1

**SIMON &
SCHUSTER**

London · New York · Sydney · Toronto · New Delhi

A CBS COMPANY

Chapter 1

Tekanasset Island, Massachusetts, 1973

Of all the weathered grey-shingled buildings on Tekanasset Island, Crab Cove golf club is one of the prettiest. Built in the late nineteenth century by a couple of friends from Boston who shared the sentiment that an island without a golf course is an island deficient in the only thing that truly matters, it dominates the western coastline with an uninterrupted view of the ocean. To the right, a candy-cane red-and-white lighthouse stands on a grassy hill, used more for birdwatchers nowadays than sailors lost at sea; and to the left, yellow beaches and grassy sand dunes undulate like waves, carrying on their crests thick clusters of wild rose. A softer variety of climbing rose adorns the walls of the clubhouse, and dusty pink hydrangeas are planted in a border that runs all the way around the periphery, blossoming into a profusion of fat, flowery balls. The effect is so charming that it is impossible not to be touched by it. And rising above it all, on the grey slate roof, the American flag flutters in the salty wind that sweeps in off the sea.

Reachable only by small plane or boat, the island of Tekanasset is cut off from the rest of the country, so that while the Industrial Revolution changed the face of America, it missed Tekanasset altogether, leaving the quaint, Quaker-inspired buildings and cobbled streets as they had always been, and allowing the island to settle into a sleepy, wistful rhythm where old-fashioned values blended harmoniously with the traditional architecture.

There are no unsightly road signs or traffic lights on Tekanasset, and the shops that thrive in the town are charming boutiques selling linen, gifts, pretty toiletries and locally crafted lightship baskets and scrimshaw. It is a nostalgic, romantic place, but not unsophisticated. Famous writers, actors and musicians from all over America escape the frenetic, polluted cities to breathe the fresh sea air and find inspiration in the beauty of the landscape, while wealthy businessmen leave the financial centres of the world to summer there with their families.

Crab Cove golf club is still the heart of the island, as it was always intended to be, but now it is no longer the hub of gossip that it was in the Sixties and Seventies, when society struggled to keep up with the changing times, and the old ways clashed with the new like waves against rock. Nowadays the young people who had fought so hard for change are old and less judgemental than their parents were, and conversation around the tables at teatime is more benign. But on this particular evening in July 1973, an incident which would not even merit comment today had whipped the ladies of Crab Cove golf club into a fever of excitement. They had barely glanced at their bridge cards before the subject which had been teetering on the end of their tongues toppled off into an outburst of indignation.

'Well, my dear, I think it's immoral and I'm ashamed on her behalf,' said Evelyn Durlacher in her low Boston drawl, pursing her scarlet lips in disapproval. Evelyn was the weathervane of polite society. Everything in her environs reflected her conservative values and high moral standards. From her immaculate cashmere twinsets and auburn coiffure to her beautifully decorated home and well-mannered children, nothing escaped her attention. And with the same scrupulous application, and a habitual lack of generosity, she passed judgement on those around her. 'In our day, if you wanted to be alone with a man you had to lose your chaperone. Now the young are out of control and no one seems to be keeping an eye.' She tapped her red talons on the table and glanced at her cards distractedly. 'Terrible hand. Sorry, Belle, I fear I'm going to let you down.'

Belle Bartlett studied her cards, which were no better. She took a long drag on her cigarette and shook her blonde curls dolefully. 'The youth of today,' she lamented. 'I wouldn't want to be young now. It was better back in the Forties and Fifties when everyone knew where they stood. Now the lines are all blurred and we have no choice but to adapt. I think they are simply lost and we mustn't judge them too harshly.'

'Belle, you always try to see the good in everybody. Surely even *you* must concede that Trixie Valentine has let herself down,' Evelyn insisted. 'The fact is, she has not behaved like a lady. Ladies don't go chasing boys around the country. They allow themselves to be chased. Really, it's very distasteful.'

'It's not only distasteful, Evelyn, it's imprudent,' Sally Pearson agreed, giving her lustrous waves of long brown hair a self-conscious toss. 'By throwing themselves at men they tarnish their reputations, which can never be restored.' She waved her cigarette between two manicured fingers and smiled smugly, remembering the exemplary young woman *she* had been. 'A man needs the chase and the woman needs to be a prize worth fighting for. Girls are far too easily won these days. In our day we saved ourselves for our wedding night.' She giggled and gave a little snort. 'And if we didn't, we sure as hell didn't let anyone know about it.'

'Poor Grace, to have a daughter shame her in this way is very unfortunate,' Belle added sympathetically. 'Horrible to think we're all picking at the pieces like vultures.'

'Well, what do you expect, girls?' interjected Blythe Westrup, patting her ebony up-do. 'She's British. They won the war but they lost their morals in the process. Goodness, the stories that came out of that time are shocking. Girls lost their heads . . .'

'And everything else,' Evelyn added dryly, arching an eyebrow.

'Oh, Evelyn!' Sally gasped and placed her cigarette holder between her lips to disguise her smile. She didn't want her friends to see her taking pleasure in the scandal.

'But do we really know she ran off with him?' Belle asked. 'I mean, it might just be malicious gossip. Trixie's a character but she's not bad. Everyone's much too quick to criticize her. If she wasn't so beautiful no one would even notice her.'

Evelyn glared at her fiercely, the rivalry in her eyes suddenly exposed. 'My dear, I heard it all from Lucy this morning,' she said firmly. 'Believe me, my daughter knows what she's talking about. She saw them all coming off a private boat at dawn, looking the worse for wear and very shifty. The boy is English, too, and he's . . .' She paused and drew her lips into a line so thin they almost disappeared. 'He's in a rock 'n' roll band.' She articulated the words with disdain as if they gave off a stench.

Belle laughed. 'Evelyn, rock 'n' roll is over. I believe he's more Bob Dylan than Elvis Presley.'

'Oh, so you know, do you?' Evelyn asked, put out. 'Why didn't you say?'

'The whole town is talking about them, Evelyn. They're handsome young British boys, and polite, too, I believe.' She smiled at the sour look on Evelyn's face. 'They're spending the summer here at Joe Hornby's place.'

'Old Joe Hornby? Really, you know how eccentric *he* is,' said Sally. 'He claims to be a great friend of Mick Jagger's, but have you ever seen *him* on the island?'

'Or anyone of any importance at all? He claims to know everybody. He's an old boaster, that's all,' said Blythe.

'Those boys are writing an album, apparently, and Joe's helping them,' Belle continued. 'He has a recording studio in his basement.'

'Joe hasn't produced anything in fifty years!' said Sally. 'He was a very mediocre musician in his day. Now he's simply past it. Anyway, who's bankrolling the project? Joe hasn't got the money, for sure.'

Belle shrugged. 'I don't know. But the word is, he's taking them on tour around the country in the fall.' She raised her eyebrows. 'That'll cost a small fortune, don't you think?'

Evelyn was determined to bring the subject back to the scandal. She glanced around the room cautiously and lowered her voice. 'Well, according to Lucy, Trixie Valentine and her friend Suzie Redford disappeared in a boat with the band on Friday evening and didn't come back until early this morning. Suzie told Lucy not to breathe a word to anybody. They clearly went behind their parents' backs. I can't say what they all got up to, but I don't think we have to stretch our imaginations too far to get close to the truth. You know how those sort of people live. It's disgusting!'

'Maybe Grace thought Trixie was at Suzie's!' Belle suggested. 'There must be an explanation.'

Sally cut in. 'I dare say, but that Suzie Redford can do whatever she likes. There are no boundaries in *that* family.'

'Well, I'm surprised,' said Belle quietly. 'Though I know

Grace has a difficult time with Trixie. But I really don't believe Trixie would have disappeared for three days without telling her mother. Besides, Freddie would never have allowed it.'

'Freddie's been away on business,' said Sally gleefully. 'While the cat's away . . .'

'It's all in the nurturing,' said Blythe. '*Cherchez la mère,*' she added darkly.

Belle stubbed out her cigarette. 'Isn't the saying *cherchez la femme?*'

'It amounts to the same thing, Belle,' Blythe retorted. 'You need look no further than the mother. Grace might be a paragon of virtue and I am the first to say she is the sweetest person alive. But she's much too lenient. Trixie needs a firm hand and Grace is weak.'

'Grace is indulgent because it took her years of heartache and miscarriage to conceive,' Belle reminded them. 'Trixie is the longed-for only child. It's no wonder she's a bit spoiled.'

'Grace buries her head in her gardens and tries not to think about it, I imagine,' said Sally. 'With a daughter like Trixie, wouldn't you?'

'Oh, she's a wonderful gardener,' Belle added emphatically. 'The gardens of Tekanasset were all very ordinary before she arrived from England and transformed them with her wonderful taste and expertise.'

Evelyn scowled irritably. 'No one is questioning her talent, Belle. It's her mothering which is open to debate. Now, come on, who dealt?'

'I did,' said Blythe. 'And I'm bidding one no trump.'

At that moment the four women were struck dumb by the appearance of Grace herself, followed by a large soufflé of a woman known to everyone as Big. Evelyn closed her mouth sharply. Big was the most respected and formidable woman on the island. Not only did she own the largest and oldest home, which had once belonged to the first settler back in 1668, but she was the only daughter of the wealthy oil baron Randall Wilson Jr., who died at the age of ninety-five leaving his entire fortune to her. It was said that she had never married because she could find no man qualified to match her in either wealth or spirit. Now that she was in her seventies, marriage was never mentioned or alluded to and Big showed no sign of regret. She treated her closest friends like family and took great pleasure, as her father had done before her, in sharing her wealth through the highly esteemed Randall Wilson Charitable Trust, or simply by writing cheques when she felt so inclined.

Grace Valentine looked as out of place in the clubhouse as a shire horse in a field of thoroughbreds. Her long mouse-brown hair was streaked with grey and pinned roughly onto the back of her head with a pencil, and her taupe cotton trousers and loose-fitting shirt were in sharp contrast to the starched perfection of the four bridge players. The only thing she seemed to have in common with them was the sparkle of diamonds in the form of a surprisingly exquisite bumblebee brooch pinned to her chest. Her nails were bitten down and the skin on her hands was rough from years of gardening. She wore no make-up and her fine English skin had suffered in the Tekanasset sun and sea winds. And yet her hazel eyes were full of softness and compassion and her face retained traces of her former beauty. When Grace Valentine smiled, few could resist the sweetness of it.

'Hello, Grace,' said Belle as the two women passed their table. 'Hello, Big.'

Grace smiled. 'Good game?' she asked.

'It's not looking good for me,' Belle replied. 'But I'm not very good at bridge.'

'Oh, really, Belle Bartlett, you're just fine,' chided Evelyn, tossing Grace a smile and scrutinizing her for signs of shame. 'She's just being modest.'

'Where would you like to sit, Grace?' Big asked, striding past the four women without so much as a nod. They shrank into their chairs guiltily. Big seemed to have an almost psychic sense when it came to unpleasantness, and she narrowed her eyes knowingly and struck the shiny wooden floorboards with her walking stick without any concern for the noise it made.

'Let's sit outside, if it's not too windy for you, Big,' Grace replied.

Big chuckled. 'Not at all. If there was a hurricane I'd be the last person standing.'

They walked through the double doors onto a wide veranda which overlooked the ocean. Small boats cut through the waves like swans and a pair of black dogs frolicked about the dunes while their master strolled slowly up the beach. The evening sun was low in the sky, turning the sand a pinkish hue, and an oystercatcher pecked at the remains of a fish with his bright-orange beak. Grace chose a table nearest the edge of the veranda, against the balustrade, and pulled out a wicker chair for Big. The old woman handed Grace her stick, then fell onto the cushion with a loud whoosh. A few wisps of grey hair fell away from her bun and flapped against the back of her neck like feathers. 'There, the hen is on her nest,' said Big with a satisfied sigh. She clicked her fingers and before Grace had even sat down she had ordered them both a cocktail. 'You need fortification, Grace,' she told her firmly. 'Never mind those hyenas. They're all so jealous of you, as well they might be: they have not an ounce of talent between them.'

'They're all right,' Grace replied. 'Believe me, I've encountered far worse.'

'I'm sure you have. British women make those four look positively tame.'

Grace laughed. 'Oh, I don't care what people say behind my back, as long as they're friendly to my face. The trouble with British women is they're much too outspoken, and I do hate confrontation.'

'I prefer the British way, if that's the case. If people have something to say, they should say it to your face and not behind your back. They should have the courage of their convictions or not speak out at all. Evelyn Durlacher is a terrible old wooden spoon and I'm quite prepared to tell her so. She should be ashamed of some of the trouble she's caused on this island with her stirring. It's as if she goes around looking for things to gossip about. The smugness of the woman is intolerable. She has placed herself so high on her pedestal, the fall will be devastating.'

The waiter placed their cocktails on the table with a china bowl of nuts. Big thrust her fat, bejewelled fingers into the bowl and grabbed a fistful of pistachios. Her face was deceptively gentle, with a wide forehead, full, smiling lips and spongy chins that gave her the look of a gentle grandmother, but her eyes were the colour of steel and could harden in a moment, turning the unlucky recipient of her displeasure into a pillar of salt. When she looked at Grace, however, she did so with surprising tenderness. 'So, what's Trixie up to, then? I imagine Evelyn has exaggerated the story for her own ends – anything to make her Lucy look good.' Big inhaled through her nostrils and the steel in her eyes briefly glinted. 'If she knew half of what her Lucy gets up to, she'd keep her mouth shut.'

Grace sighed. 'I'm afraid Evelyn's probably right. Trixie has fallen for a young man who plays in a band. I don't mind that, he's perfectly nice, I'm sure, but . . .'

'You haven't met him?'

'No.'

'Go on.'

'She told me she was going to stay the weekend in Cape Cod with her friend Suzie . . .'

Big raised her eyebrows cynically. 'Suzie Redford! That girl's trouble, and wherever there's trouble, *she's* in the middle of it.'

'I would honestly say they're as bad as each other.' Grace smiled indulgently. 'But they're having fun, Big, and Trixie's in love for the first time.'

Big looked at Grace's gentle face, her soft hazel eyes and soft windblown hair, and shook her head at the sheer *softness* of the woman. 'What am I going to do with you, Grace? You're much too kind-hearted. So, tell me, where did they *really* go?'

'With the band.'

'Where, with the band?'

'To a private concert they were giving in Cape Cod for a friend of Joe Hornby, who's in the industry.'

Big sipped her cocktail thoughtfully. 'But she was found out.'

'Yes, Lucy saw them all returning on a boat this morning and told her mother. Now, I imagine the whole island is talking about it. Trixie came clean before she went off to work. You know she's got a summer job at Captain Jack's. Anyway, I didn't have time to talk to her. In spite of her rebelliousness, Big, she's a good girl at heart. She confessed, at least.'

'Only because she was spotted by Lucy. I'm sure she wouldn't have told you if she thought she had got away with it. I'm afraid she's a disgrace, my dear, and you should ground her for the rest of the holidays. In my day I would have been beaten for less.'

'But it's not your day, Big, and it's not my day, either. Times are changing. Young people are freer than we ever were and perhaps it's a good thing. We can disapprove of the music they listen to and the inappropriate clothes they wear, but they're young and full of passion. They demonstrate against inequality and war – goodness, you only have to look at my poor Freddie with his one eye and that terrible scar down his face to know that there are no winners in war. They're brave and outspoken and I rather admire them for that.' She pressed her rough fingers against the bee brooch on her shirt. 'They're idealistic and foolish, perhaps, but they realize that love is the only thing that really matters.' She turned her hazel eyes to the sea and smiled pensively. 'I think I'd like to be young now with my whole life ahead of me.'

Big sipped her cocktail. 'Heavens, Grace, you baffle me sometimes. When everyone else is pulling in the reins, you're letting them out. Is that a British trait, I wonder? Or are you just contrary? Tell me, does Freddie know about Trixie's little adventure?'

The mention of her husband cast a shadow over Grace's face. 'I haven't told him yet,' she replied quietly.

'But you will?'

'I don't want to. He'll be furious. But I'll have to. Otherwise he'll hear it from someone else. Bill Durlacher teeing off at the fifth hole, most likely!' She laughed out of anxiety rather than merriment.

Big's large bosom expanded over the table at the thought of Bill Durlacher gossiping on the golf course. 'Bill's as bad as his wife,' she retorted. 'But you're right to tell Freddie. He won't want to be the last person on the island to know.'

'He'll be horrified, Big. He'll give her a lecture on discipline and probably put her under house arrest for the remainder of the summer. Then she'll spend all her time finding ways to see this boy behind our backs.' She chuckled. 'I know Trixie. She's got more of *me* in her than she knows.'

Big looked surprised. 'I can't imagine *you* breaking any rules, Grace.'

'Oh, I wasn't always so well-behaved.' She smiled wistfully at the memory of the girl she used to be. 'Once I was even quite rebellious. But that was a long time ago.' She turned her gaze to the sea again.

'What whipped you into shape?' Big asked.

'My conscience,' Grace replied with a frown.

'Then you would have done the right thing, for certain.'

'Yes, I suppose so.' Grace sighed heavily and there was a hint of defeat in it as well as regret.

'Do you want the advice of an old matron who's seen it all?' Big asked.

Grace drew her mind back to the present. 'Yes, please.'

Big wriggled in her chair like the nesting hen of her own description. 'You go home now and have stern words with Trixie. Tell her she's not to deceive you like that again. It's important that you know where she is and who she's with, for her safety as well as your peace of mind. You also tell her that she's not to leave the island again for the rest of the summer and it's non-negotiable. You have to make it very clear, Grace. Can you do that?'

'Yes, I can,' Grace replied half-heartedly.

'It's a matter of respect, Grace,' Big stated firmly. 'Really, my dear, you need to toughen up if you wish to assert any control over your child, before it's too late.' She took a moment to sip her cocktail, then resumed. 'When her father arrives, you tell him what happened but inform him that you've reprimanded her and that the business is done and dusted. Period. You think he'll drop it?'

'I don't know. He'll be very cross. You know how he likes everything to be in order.' She shrugged. 'I could play it down . . .'

'You mustn't lie to him, Grace. That's important. You two have to stick together. You're a soft-hearted woman and I know you want to support Trixie, but you chose your husband first and it's your duty as a wife to stand by his side on all matters.'

Grace looked beaten. 'Duty,' she muttered and Big detected a bitter edge to her voice. 'I do hate that word.'

'Duty is what makes us civilized, Grace. Doing the right thing and not always thinking of ourselves is vital if we don't want society to fall apart at the seams. The young have no sense of duty, and by the sound of things they don't have much respect, either. I fear the future is a place with no morals and a distorted sense of what's important. But I'm not here to preach to you. I'm here to support you.'

'Thank you, Big. Your support means a lot to me.'

'We've been friends for almost thirty years, Grace. That's a long time. Ever since you came to Tekanasset and turned my backyard into a beautiful paradise. Perhaps we bonded because you never knew your mother and I never had any children.' She smiled and took another handful of nuts. 'And everyone sucks up to me but you,' she said with a chuckle. 'You're a gentle creature but an honest one. I don't believe you'd ever agree with me just because I'm as rich as Croesus, as old as the Ark and as big as a whale.'

'Oh, really, Big!' Grace laughed incredulously. 'You might be as rich as Croesus but you're not as old as the Ark and you're certainly *not* a whale!'

'Bless you for lying. My dear, when it's a matter of age and size I give you my full permission to lie through your teeth.'

*

When Grace returned to her home on Sunset Slip the sun had turned the sea to gold. She wandered onto the veranda with her two retrievers and gazed out across the wild grasses to the beach and glittering water beyond. She soaked up the tranquil scene thirstily. The sound that soothed her more than anything else, however, was the low murmur of bees. It filled her heart with melancholy, and yet that wasn't an unpleasant feeling. In a strange way it gave her pleasure to remember the past, as if through the pain she remained in touch with the woman she had once been and left behind when she had set out for America all those years ago.

She went round to the three hives she kept along the side of the house, sheltered from the winds and sun by hemlock planted for the purpose, and lifted one of the lids for a routine check. She didn't mind getting stung occasionally. She wasn't afraid, either, but it caused her distress to think that, on stinging, the bee was sacrificing her own life to protect the hive.

Arthur Hamblin had taught his daughter everything he knew about bees, from their daily care to the tinctures of propolis he made to cure sore throats and other complaints. Beekeeping had been their shared love and tending the hives and extracting the honey had brought them close, compounded by the fact that they only had each other in the world. Grace remembered her father fondly every time she saw a bee. His kind face would surface in her mind with the gentle humming of the creatures he had so loved, and sometimes she could even hear his voice as if he were whispering into her ear: 'Don't forget to check that the bees are capping off honey in the lower supers.' Or: 'Can you see the bees guarding the entrance? There must be a threat. Wasps or robber bees perhaps. I wonder which it is.' Arthur Hamblin could talk about bees for hours and barely draw breath. Often he would talk *to* them, reciting his favourite poem, which Grace had heard so often she knew it by heart: *Marriage, birth or buryin', News across the seas, All you're sad or merry in, You must tell the bees.*

Now as Grace looked inside the hive, the bees were settling in for the night. The temperature had dropped and they were sleepy. She smiled fondly and allowed her memories to ebb and flow like a vast sea of images and emotions. Time with her bees was time to be herself again, and time to remember.

As she replaced the lid she sensed the familiar presence of someone standing close. She knew not to turn around, because the many times she had glanced behind her had revealed nothing but the wind and her own bewilderment. She knew to sense it and not to analyse it; after all, hers was an old house and Tekanasset was an island well known for ghosts. Even Big had stories to tell. The presence didn't frighten her; in fact, she felt strangely reassured, as if she had a secret friend no one else knew about. When she was younger she had confided in her mother, who she hoped was able to listen to her from Heaven. Nowadays, when she felt low or lonely, she'd come and talk to the bees and feel comforted by this ghost who gave out a loving energy and was perhaps as lonely as she was.

Recently she had begun to sink more often into her former life. It was as if with the passing of the years her regrets grew stronger and her attachment to her memories more desperate. For the last twenty-odd years she had thrown herself into motherhood, but Trixie was growing up and soon she would move away, and Grace would be left alone with Freddie and the fragile remains of their marriage.

'Hello, old friend,' she said and smiled at the absurdity of talking to someone she couldn't see.

FIND OUT
MORE ABOUT
SANTA MONTEFIORE

Santa Montefiore is the author of
twelve sweeping novels.

To find out more about her and
her writing, visit her website at

www.santamontefiore.com

Sign up for Santa's newsletter and keep
up to date with all her news.

Or connect with her on Facebook at

http://www.facebook.com/santa.montefiore

GROSVENOR HOUSE
A JW MARRIOTT HOTEL
LONDON

LITERATI

WIN A TWO NIGHT STAY IN AN EXECUTIVE SUITE

Grosvenor House, A JW Marriott Hotel is one of London's most historic hotels, centrally located in the heart of London in one of the capital's most desirable addresses; 'Park Lane'. Elegant and quintessentially British, Grosvenor House has been frequented by royalty and celebrities since opening in 1929.

Grosvenor House is delighted to offer one lucky couple the opportunity to win a two night stay, including breakfast, in an Executive Suite at Grosvenor House. Visit pages.simonandschuster.co.uk/competitions to enter.*

LITERATI events at GROSVENOR HOUSE

Taking the traditional book club a step further, Literati at Grosvenor House, A JW Marriott Hotel, is an elegant event that hosts authors to lead an intimate discussion of their latest book with hotel and external residents. Champagne and canapés are served, guests are encouraged to interact and ask questions and receive a signed hardback copy of the book.

Literati authors have included 'first lady' of broadcast journalism, Kate Adie, Lord Michael Dobbs of international bestseller, House of Cards, author and presenter Libby Purves, journalist and broadcaster Peter Snow, Royal Correspondent, Hugo Vickers and The Countess of Carnarvon of the 'Real' Downton Abbey, Highclere Castle.

* UK residents only. Subject to availability. Does not include UK Bank Holidays.

To hear about future Literati events, email literati@marriott.com or visit the website www.grosvenorhouseliterati.co.uk